DEAD MAN WALKING

Ian McMurdo
Ian McMurdo is now retired from a long career in the public education sector. He lives with his two dogs on the island of Arran, a few miles off Scotland's south-west coast.
This is Ian's sixth published book and his first foray into the world of fiction.

DEAD MAN WALKING

IAN MCMURDO

carn

© Ian McMurdo, 2022.
First Published in Great Britain, 2022.

ISBN - 978 1 911043 14 0

Published by Carn Publishing Ltd.,
Lochnoran House,
Auchinleck, Ayrshire, KA18 3JW.

www.carnpublishing.com

Printed by Imprint Digital,
Seychelles Farm, Upton Pyne, Exeter, Devon EX5 5HY.

Dedication

This book is dedicated to my late wife Nan, who passed away two years ago. She was my rock, my inspiration and my best friend, and I miss her more than any words could express.

1

The date was 17th August, the year 1973. A Friday, thank the Lord. For the entire 32-strong workforce, 'lousing' time on a Friday was the ultimate milestone. The elusive four-minute mile, the unassailable peak of Mount Everest, the final whistle in a bruising Scottish Cup Final after a dramatic last-gasp winning goal. A gruelling week that had seemed to drag on for ever was finally drawing to a welcome close. Fridays always felt like pulling your denims out of the washing machine and finding a crumpled fiver in one of the pockets.

There at Braddoch Brickworks, cast adrift in the middle of the sprawling moorland expanse of the same name, civilisation seemed about as distant as Saturn. Not even a decent splattering of larger lochs and smaller lochans populated by noisy flocks of indigenous grouse, curlews and waterhens could disguise the fact that the moor was desolation personified, a veritable wilderness by any other name.

Some days, the rain would batter down from clock-in time at seven in the morning till clock-out time at five in the afternoon, doing its utmost to accentuate the gloom. On others, a chill wind would accompany it, whistling through the willow bushes and loch-side reeds like some sinister ghostly spirit, turning sheets of rain to sleet or even snow.

For some reason, sunshine was a mere fleeting visitor to Braddoch Moor. It was almost as if it didn't belong there. However, today was one of those rarities, a beautiful sunny day, an absolute scorcher in fact. And the day was just about to get better. Completely unannounced, the brickworks' hooter burst into furious action, scattering a flock of moorland birds skywards and confirming that noon had arrived.

Young Ricky Anderson swept his dark, shoulder-length hair back from his sweaty forehead and flung his shovel into an old wheelbarrow, where it landed with a grating metallic clatter. It was 'piece-time' at last, the only thirty minutes in the entire day when the workers were permitted to down tools in exchange for a welcome break and some much-needed sustenance. Or as grumpy old foreman Jock Sanderson always called it, 'the three S's'. A seat, a sandwich and a shit.

Only a fortnight to go, Ricky sighed. He looked down at the palms of his hands. The skin was hard and filthy. By mid-September, it would once more be as soft and clean as a new-born baby's backside, courtesy of filthy boots and rusted tools having been replaced by brand-new biro pens and pristine notepads. For a young man whose closest daily companion these days was a clapped-out barrow, the irony was about as glaring as obscene graffiti on a church building.

Only three months back, Ricky had graduated from Glasgow University as a Bachelor of Science, and with First-Class Honours into the bargain. Not bad for a little nipper from a humble council housing scheme, he reflected, head nodding in wordless self-approval. Long, laborious twelve-hour-a-day shifts and five-day-weeks in the middle of a moorland wilderness might have seemed a never-ending exercise in mindless tedium for most of that time, but yet again it would prove to be a nice little summer earner. Certainly sufficient to bolster the kitty for the weekly groceries, occasional Indian curries and welcome pints of lager that would be required to sustain him through another tough academic session. Only two more weeks to go, Ricky-boy, he reminded himself in welcome corroboration, then I'll be out of this bloody place. Sadly, the others wouldn't be so fortunate, and Ricky knew it. This was their lot for the rest of their working lives, or at least until the stinking-rich Barnes-Dewar dynasty decided to pull the plug on this ailing industry and render the poor beggars redundant with little prospect of alternative employment.

The academic session that lay in wait for Ricky would be his fifth at the famous old university, the one which would see him attempt to convert his BSc Honours in Theoretical Physics into a PhD in Nuclear Physics. This was an area of science that had completely fascinated Ricky ever since the gut-wrenching drama over fourteen days in late-October of 1962 when he had been a highly impressionable ten-year-old. It was back then that he had clung onto every word and syllable uttered by countless TV and radio broadcasters the world over, as American President John F. Kennedy, Russia's Premier Nikita Kruschev and Cuba's firebrand revolutionary leader Fidel Castro had played out a deadly game of political brinkmanship with the world staring into the abyss of nuclear war, a seemingly inevitable Armageddon averted only in the very last minute of the eleventh hour.

Ever since that blistering fortnight, Ricky had been truly captivated by the phenomenon of energy. Several times in his secondary school's antiquated science laboratory, he had witnessed the sensational power of chemical reactions, thanks to the wanton bravado of his half-mad chemistry teacher, Dr McNulty, whose manic eyes and outrageous mop of frizzy hair always made him look as if he had been playing with live electric wires. In Dr McNulty's infamous chemistry lab, lids had been blasted off Tate & Lyle syrup tins injected with hydrogen gas, and wooden cupboard doors blown clean off their hinges by exploding chemicals of indeterminate identity, causing umpteen traumatised adolescents to run screaming out the door with perforated eardrums. Not only that, but as a child of the immediate post-World War II era, Ricky had often witnessed film footage demonstrating the enormous damage which could be caused by the detonation of a mere few pounds of Trinitrotoluene, or TNT to give it its Sunday name, a key component of the industrial and military explosive, dynamite.

What had really captured Ricky's imagination, though, was the almost unthinkable power, not of chemical reactions, but of their atomic counterparts. The nuclear fission bomb, 'Little Boy', which had destroyed the Japanese city of Hiroshima in August of 1945 had produced an astonishing yield of 14 kilotons, in other words an enormous blast equivalent to 14,000 tons of TNT, while its terrible sibling, 'Fat Man', which levelled Nagasaki two days later, had yielded 19 kilotons of destruction. Nowadays, the five so-called world 'superpowers' had developed and amassed literally thousands of thermonuclear fission-fusion bombs, each capable of delivering a yield of up to 25 megatons, or 25 million tons of TNT, any solitary one of which could completely obliterate a city the size of New York, Moscow or London.

However, it wasn't merely the unimaginably destructive power of nuclear bombs which fascinated Ricky. It was the almost limitless potential of his chosen discipline to supply the planet with affordable and sustainable energy, and also the vastly exciting prospect of man-made radioactive materials deployed within carefully-controlled clinical procedures to offer real hope of effective treatment and even complete cure for patients staring down the hopeless barrel of various cancer diagnoses. And if new energy sources and successful cancer treatments were ever to be realised, then Ricky Anderson was determined to be right there in the vanguard.

As Ricky emerged from his daydream, he gobbled what was left of his last cheese-and-tomato sandwich, stretched his legs and picked his trusty shovel back up from the wheelbarrow, ready to continue his shift as relief labourer. Silently, he thanked his lucky stars that his hard-grafting, brain-numbing moorland ordeal would soon be over, to be replaced by the hugely stimulating opportunity which awaited him in only a couple of weeks' time, and about which his muck-splattered workmates could only ever dream.

Ricky had been born Richard Thomas Anderson on 26 January 1952, in Ayrshire Central Maternity Hospital, located in the bustling Ayrshire seaside town of Irvine. For parents David and Janice Anderson, it had been the happiest day of their lives. The pair of them had now become three, and home for the Anderson family would be the little rural mining village of Glenside, situated on the outskirts of the much larger market town of Cumnock, and famed for its proud hard-grafting work ethic and strong self-supporting community spirit.

'Big Davie' Anderson, as he was much better known around those parts, was a time-served painter-and-decorator with the local authority, a quietly reserved but much respected man in both the workplace and the local community, while Janice Anderson, nee Robertson, had been a district nurse with the National Health Service ever since its inception back in 1947. If Davie was still as madly in love with Janice as on the evening he first stared into her hypnotic brown eyes at a 'record hop' in neighbouring Cumnock, then Janice simply worshipped the ground that Davie's size-tens walked upon. Both had a lot going for them. She was a gem of a lady, an absolute stunner to look at and the object of much male desire in Glenside and beyond. However, he was six-foot-three and built like a tank, and nobody in his right mind would ever have had the stupidity to try it on with Janice and incur Davie's wrath.

A handsome, robust and healthy child with real *joie de vivre* and an engaging sense of mischief, Ricky quickly became very popular with his peers, both in the school playground and in the much larger playground of community life, where his embryonic leadership qualities soon became evident. Alas, great tragedy was to hit the Anderson family only a few days after Ricky's fourteenth birthday. Davie was killed outright in a horrific road traffic accident when his motorcycle plunged into the back of a jack-knifed articulated lorry at over eighty-miles-per-hour and burst into flames, leaving Janice to pick up the pieces of her shattered life and see young Ricky through the remainder of adolescence into adulthood.

Sadly, Janice never did manage to recover, her happy and contented life slowly falling apart and spiralling into one of anxiety and depression. Meanwhile, Ricky soldiered on through his schooldays, his bright and enterprising young mind augmented by a very diligent attitude to work which some three years later would see him emerge as school dux in recognition of his stunning academic successes.

In all probability, and in other circumstances, Ricky might also have received the ultimate accolade of being appointed 'school captain', had those circumstances not been related to his occasional tendency to thrash the living daylights out of some school bully or other who needed to be taught a lesson. Ricky Anderson never started a fight in his life, but if someone started one with him, he would finish it, and finish it emphatically. And thus, Ricky soon unwittingly earned a reputation as a 'hard man', one he utterly detested but which inevitably got him into trouble from time to time with the school's Head Teacher, and on one occasion, with the long arm of the law.

The turning point for Ricky came one winter's afternoon in his fifth year at secondary school, when out of the blue his eyes suddenly met those of a beautiful young girl as they passed each other on the school stairwell. Totally smitten, he asked around and discovered that her name was Iona McNish, by which time she had done likewise and found out that his was Ricky Anderson. A blunt 'my pal fancies you' message to Iona from Ricky's next-door-neighbour and best friend, Andy Tennent, and the two of them would find themselves snogging each other's faces off later that same afternoon. Ricky and Iona were destined to be together from the very first moment they clapped eyes on each other, and together they would remain head-over-heels in love.

Happiness had returned at last to Ricky's life, after the desperate tragedy of losing his beloved dad at such a young age. For his mother, though, the pain and suffering continued, as indeed did the loneliness and pointlessness of day-to-day existence without her wonderful Big Davie. However, for Janice and her precious son Ricky, life was about to get a whole lot more interesting.

And a whole lot more dangerous.

2

If the first ear-splitting rendition of the brickworks' hooter had signalled the welcome relief of piece-time, then the second sounded to the workforce like a choir of angels.

For Ricky Anderson, the toot of the hooter heralded the end of another long and punishing shift. Time to pile into the back of Shug McMillan's battered-and-bruised Mark 1 Ford Transit pick-up truck before jumping out again at Cumnock's mercat cross and catching the bus home to Glenside, where his adorable mother would have a glorious cottage pie bubbling away in the oven for the apple of her eye. A hearty meal and a quick bath, and it would soon be time for another lip-smacking treat, this in the passionate clutches of the gorgeous Iona McNish.

When the big double-decker bus rounded the sharp bend at the top of Manse Brae just after six o'clock, another dreadfully dreich week had been scored off the list and another few quid were now safely tucked away in the kitty. Ricky rose wearily to his feet with a satisfied yawn and the bus conductress rang the little bell on the ceiling, prompting the driver to start going down through the gears before pulling into the designated bus stop at the foot of the hill.

Ricky jumped out with a respectful 'thanks mate' to the driver, then began strolling down the pavement between the two rows of modern local authority houses which faced each other on Dalblair Crescent, where once stood the much-loved old 'miners' rows'. Another bog-standard day, noteworthy for not a single jot, and that suited Ricky just fine, because in only a couple of weeks' time he would be back among his cherished cloud chambers and mass spectrometers in Glasgow University's much-lauded Physics Department, the spoils of his summer labours safely locked away in a Clydesdale Bank deposit account. Another day, another dollar.

Dalblair Crescent had finally lost the youthful appearance it once enjoyed back in the early 'sixties when the Scottish Special Housing Association had taken over the management of its 36 brand-new, semi-detached, two-storey houses on behalf of Southwest Scotland Council. More affectionately known to the good folks of the locale as the 'cooncil hooses', those were not to be confused with their more up-market counterparts on the west side of the village, the 'bought hooses', which as their name suggests were privately owned by the more upwardly mobile. The crescent began and ended at Manse Road, designed in a sweeping semi-circle, its pavement lined with alternating birch and ash trees which had begun their lives as innocent young saplings, but which had now grown almost to rooftop level, causing the crescent some particularly windy nights to take on a rather spooky appearance as their swaying branches and fluttering leaves swept back and forth across the yellow-orange neon lights like some sinister outdoor discotheque.

As Ricky began crossing the road in a bit of a daydream, his antennae suddenly sprang back into gear when out of the corner of his eye he noticed something rather strange. It was a very posh-looking white sports car, and it appeared to be parked right outside his own house. Not only did Ricky not know anybody who owned a classy car like that, he didn't even know anybody who knew anybody else who did. A strange sense of intrigue began to wash over him. By the time his industrial boots had whisked him to within a couple of blocks of his front gate, closer inspection revealed that the car was a Jaguar XJ-C. For a fleeting moment, Ricky half-closed his eyes and tried to imagine that the flashy wheels belonged to his own mother, and that any minute now the heavenly Janice Anderson would march confidently down the garden path dressed like a front-page *Vogue* magazine model before slipping elegantly into the driver's seat of the big white 'Jag'.

Alas, the image proved rather transient, Ricky's cold pragmatism soon getting the better of his wishful thinking. The blunt truth was that Janice was in a bit of a state these days, financially speaking and in many other ways too, the scant remuneration from her three-afternoons-a-week job as a relief receptionist in Cumnock's medical practice having proved no match for her much richer pickings in the good old days when she had performed the role of full-time senior district nurse with distinction.

Quite how Janice had managed to put Ricky through four years at university he had no earthly idea, and any time he had raised the matter she immediately slammed the lid on any discussion. Sure, Ricky was in receipt of the government's maximum student grant, and it was also the case that he traditionally put half of his wages from his labouring job into the family kitty from early June through till late August. But what about the other nine months while he was cooped up in the big smoke, bombarding unstable atoms with hostile neutrons? How the hell did his mum cope then?

No matter how she tried to dress it all up, the plain fact of the matter was that Janice Anderson was struggling, and struggling big-time. She had lost the only man she ever loved, she had lost her job and she had lost her way in life. And now, to make matters worse, she was in trouble financially. Or to use the local parlance, Janice Anderson was 'skint'. Just how skint, young Ricky had no idea. However, he was about to find out.

As he continued trudging along the pavement, he watched bemused as a middle-aged male figure emerged from the Anderson household, not running but looking in a bit of a hurry as he skipped down the steps and along the garden path before fumbling in his jacket pocket and shoving the key into the driver's door of the slick sports car. The man was about five-foot-ten and powerfully-built, distinctly sun-tanned with long oily black hair, and he was wearing a dark three-piece suit, its flared trousers flip-flopping over a pair of black shoes so ridiculously shiny that the early evening sunshine reflected off them like well-polished mirrors.

'Hiya pal, can I help you?' Ricky shouted.

Momentarily, the man stopped and turned, and their eyes met for a split second. He said nothing, slid into his car seat, booted the engine into action and sped away down the street like reigning Formula One world champion Niki Lauda, leaving a tiny puff of blueish exhaust fumes hanging in the Glenside air.

Ricky's pace increased steadily until he found himself running up the path to his own front door. It was locked. The door that was never locked.

'Mum,' he shouted through the letterbox. 'Are you okay?'

Nothing, not a sound.

'Mum, open the door. I haven't got my key. Open the door.'

Still nothing. Ricky ran down the driveway at the side of the house and through the rear garden gate. He tried the back door. Thankfully, it sprang open.

'Mum,' he shouted again, as he bolted through the kitchen and into the living room.

Janice Anderson was sitting motionless on the settee, just staring out of the window, her eyes bloodshot, tears dripping down her cheeks onto her light-blue polo-neck sweater. She looked absolutely shell-shocked.

Resisting the temptation to overreact, Ricky instead took a deep breath and sat down beside his mother, then wrapped his arm around her shoulder. The simmering rage would wait, the one that so often in the past had built up to a crescendo like steam in a pressure cooker until it had finally blown the lid all the way to hell.

Yes, the rage would wait, at least until he knew the full story. Then he would meet with the creep in the Jag.

3

Carol McCreadie stared at the big imposing door and took a long, deep breath.

She hated disturbing Councillor Monk during an important meeting, particularly one which at quarter-past-six on a Friday evening had already stolen a decent slice of the forthcoming weekend. She knocked twice and anxiously turned the handle. Five men dressed in dark suits lifted their heads in unison, but the short plump chap sitting in the big chair at the far end of the table did not.

'What is it, Carol?' he snapped.

She walked smartly across the big oak-panelled room and handed her boss a handwritten A5-sized memorandum, then waited nervously for his reaction. The Chairman of Southwest Scotland Council's Planning Committee read the note, rubbed his nose and eyeballed his five minions before gesticulating to them with a dismissive wave of his right hand.

'Meeting adjourned,' he said. 'Carol will be in touch with you about another date.'

A solitary hesitant voice piped up. It belonged to David McPherson, the council's Director of Planning.

'But Mister Chairman, we really need an urgent decision on how to deal with this Prestwick housing application.'

Monk gave his most senior officer the death stare.

'Are your bloody ears painted on, man?' he barked. 'I said, meeting over.'

The five suits hurriedly picked up their papers, stuffed them into their briefcases and made a beeline straight for the door. Carol waited like an obedient puppy. It was a good couple of minutes before Monk broke the heavy silence.

'Show him into my office.'

As the pleasant-faced secretary's high-heels clipped-clopped their way across the wooden floor, Monk read the note again.

'Councillor Monk, Mister Rafferty is downstairs at reception, and he insists on seeing you right away. He said that if you won't see him, he'll come up and take your door off its hinges. He looked very angry. Carol.'

The chairman threw his head back in dismay and sighed an exasperated sigh.

'The crazy bastard,' he muttered under his breath. 'He thinks he owns this place.'

Edwin Monk was one of the most powerful politicians in the whole of south-west Scotland, but right at that moment he had never felt so vulnerable. He rose from his chair and began shuffling his tubby frame out into the corridors of power, its century-old walls replete with grand framed portraits of provosts and other public dignitaries, past-and-present, and paintings of magnificent Ayrshire landscapes and seascapes. By the time he had reached his salubrious office facing the golden sands and gentle waves of the Firth of Clyde, Frank Rafferty was already sitting defiantly in the Chairman's high-backed leather chair.

'Close the door, Carol,' Monk commanded his personal secretary. 'And make sure we're not disturbed.'

Rafferty looked at Monk and grinned. It was a grin that carried with it a whole year's supply of menace.

'Take a seat, Edwin,' he said, gesticulating with a mock wave of his hand to confirm the role reversal.

Monk shook his head in resignation and planked his ample backside down on one of the wooden chairs which were normally reserved for his team of sycophantic gofers.

'Not here, Frank, not here,' he said. 'Walls have ears. You've already made your point with your grand entrance and we'll talk about it, but not here. Just say where and when.'

Rafferty leaned across the table and pointed a nicotine-stained finger straight into Monk's face.

'Last chance, Edwin. You've been pissing me about and you know it, so last chance. Sunday night, seven o'clock, my place. And bring that land survey report with you. You know, the one you keep telling me is too confidential to show to anyone.'

'Oh, come on Frank, you know I can't possibly divulge such politically sensitive information at this stage, not even to you.'

'The report, Edwin, I want the report.'

'But ...'

'But nothing, Edwin. I want the bloody report. And if you can't bring it with you, don't even bother to come. Instead, I'll come looking for you and this time I won't be alone. You'll have heard of my colleague, Robert McDaid, but I don't think you've had the pleasure yet, have you?'

Monk just dropped his head and nodded in resignation.

'Okay Frank, we'll do it your way. I'll see you on Sunday night.'

'And the survey report, Edwin?'

'Okay, Frank. Okay.'

Rafferty eased himself out of the chairman's luxurious chair and slapped Monk playfully on the shoulder.

'Seven o'clock sharp, Edwin. I'll have your favourite Columbian coffee percolating on the stove. Bring some nice biscuits, there's a good chap.'

And at that, he marched briskly out of Monk's office, his long dark oily hair and smug sun-tanned face as perfectly in synch as a slithering tongue from a reptile's mouth.

A cold shiver ran up Carol McCreadie's spine.

4

Ricky Anderson was in no mood to be patronised, not even by the woman who had brought him into this world 21 years ago.

'I'm going to sit here until you tell me, mum,' he said with unshakeable conviction. 'I'm going nowhere, even if it takes all night.'

His mother puffed her cheeks and stared out of the window. It was an unfocused stare. Seeing nothing, imagining everything. Even when upset, Janice Anderson's face still radiated a deep natural beauty, her dark and wavy shoulder-length hair tickling a light olive complexion brought alive by a pair of captivating brown eyes. She wiped away the latest stream of hot tears that were trickling down her cheeks onto her slender neck. The neck with the gradually reddening bruise.

'Can you make me a wee cup of tea first, Ricky?' a shaky voice pleaded. 'And get me a couple of painkillers too. They're on the window-sill beside my sunglasses.'

Ricky rose to his feet and made his way through to the kitchen, returning a few minutes later with a glass and two mugs. He sat the glass down on the coffee table, followed by the mug etched with a photograph of glamourous American actress, Lynda Carter, clad in a skimpy outfit which suggested that breasts had won the battle over brains.

'There you go, Wonder Woman,' he said.

Wiping the residual moisture away with the back of her hand, Janice just managed to reveal the faintest smile.

'Mum, I know you still miss my dad,' Ricky said. 'And I know it must be especially hard at times like this when the going gets tough.'

The steady stream of tears became a proper sob of anguish. Ricky got up, sat down beside her on the settee and gave her a big squeeze. She turned towards him and smiled one of the sorriest smiles he had ever had the misfortune to behold.

'Yes, I really do miss him, Ricky,' she said, 'So much that it actually hurts at times. And I would do anything to get my Big Davie back, anything at all. But do you know what? At least I've still got his big boy here to look after me.'

Silence reigned for the next few minutes, as mother and son sat there in a wordless trance, one eventually broken by the sudden rumble of local farmer Tam Hyslop's tractor lumbering past the window, leaving an unmistakeable agricultural stench in its wake.

'Another ton of shite for old Scobie, then?' said Ricky with an impudent grin. 'He's got so many weird-looking vegetables in that garden of his that he could feed the entire population of Ayrshire.'

'It's called dung, Ricky,' Janice retorted with an expression of mild shock, followed by a little giggle. 'Dung. And old Mister Scobie is a wonderful gardener. You need your mouth washed out with hot soapy water, my boy.'

Ricky could always make Janice laugh. Today, however, there wasn't an awful lot to laugh about, so he had done pretty well. She took a big deep breath.

'His name's Rafferty, Ricky. Frank Rafferty.'

Ricky rose from the archetypal seventies-style, apricot-coloured settee and relocated himself back down in the matching armchair directly facing his mother. He leant back and cradled his chin with his thumb and middle finger, his index finger pointing up over his cheek in what had now become the trademark Ricky Anderson 'deep concentration' pose. For a young man in the first flush of youth, he had an unnerving tendency at times to look rather Churchillian.

'Tell me about it, mum,' he said in a voice not much louder than a whisper. 'And in your own time but leave nothing out. I need to know the full story, so tell me everything.'

She did, and the essence of it was this.

Since having had to leave her full-time nursing job as a result of developing severe depression in the aftermath of husband Davie's tragic accident, Janice had begun to struggle financially. Yes, Davie had left her with a bundle of Premium Bonds as savings, but those only amounted to a few hundred quid in value. And yes, the work that her empathetic medical colleagues had offered her as a part-time receptionist in the surgery had helped to keep the wolf from the door, at least for a while. However, over the last couple of years, her savings had completely evaporated and the debts had begun to pile up.

Back in her secondary schooldays, one of her classmates was a boy called Frank Rafferty, who hailed from the nearby village of Mauchline. To say that Rafferty had difficulty in handling rejection would be putting it mildly. He had once tried to get his grubby hands on Nancy McDonald, one of Janice's closest school chums, and at first she had accepted his offer of a date, only to take cold feet at the last minute and give him a 'dizzy'. The very next evening, Rafferty had followed Nancy home through Cumnock's Woodroad Park, and he was in the process of trying to rape her when an elderly man appeared out of the mirk holding his little dog on a lead. When she screamed for help, the stranger ran towards them, at which point Rafferty punched him twice on the face and booted his dog in the stomach. The old man lost three teeth and his dog died of internal bleeding later that same evening. Nancy's irate parents reported the incident to the police, but although it was investigated, nothing ever stuck, presumably because the local chief inspector was none other than Rafferty's own uncle. Nancy had then lived in fear of Rafferty for the rest of her schooldays.

However, so too had Janice, because although he had never hurt or even threatened her, it was a well-known fact that he had the serious 'hots' for her, to the extent that he used to tell his subservient classmates that they should call her 'Janice Rafferty', so cock-sure was he of his eventual conquest. Several times he had asked her out on a date, but on each occasion she had spurned his advances, always taking care to do so as gently as possible to avert furious retribution. The long and short of it was that Janice had always considered Rafferty to be a bit of a creep, and a very dangerous creep at that.

Unknown to her husband Davie, Rafferty continued to try it on with Janice long after she got married, having propositioned her several times. She never once told him, though, for fear that her gentle giant might have half-killed him. However, she often wondered if it was more than coincidence that Rafferty still seemed to pop up in the locale every now and again, particularly since he was presently living in the swish up-market Ayrshire coastal town of Troon some twenty miles away, where he now ran his highly lucrative property development business. As for the business itself, it was one which had continually been mired in controversy, together with allegations of money-laundering and other such nefarious practices. Furthermore, Rafferty was also reputed to be an illicit money-lender, and both he and his notorious henchmen, who had since earned the dubious title of the 'Nutter Squad', had earned a fearsome reputation for their ruthless tactics in recovering their debts 'with interest'.

During one of Rafferty's unlikely impromptu appearances in Cumnock a couple of months back, he had cornered Janice in the car park of the local supermarket, Somerfield, and invited her out for a lavish dinner in Troon's classy Marine Hotel, no doubt with a deluxe bedroom booked for good measure. Janice had politely declined his latest nauseating offer, taking great care as usual to cause as little offence as possible and thereby minimising the likelihood of an unsavoury scene developing in a local public car park. However, when she got home that day, she discovered a small brown envelope sandwiched between the groceries in her shopping bag. Inside was a wad of five-pound-notes wrapped in an elastic band, and a business card with 'Rafferty Construction' inscribed in gold letters at the top, and 'Frank Rafferty, Managing Director' at the bottom. On the back was a brief hand-written note.

Mid-tale, Janice suddenly hesitated, before stretching over to lift her purse from her handbag. She steeled herself, opened the purse and took out the card, then handed it to Ricky. It read:

'For you, Janice. Buy yourself a new dress and we'll go out for a nice meal. Just say the time and the place. And there's a lot more where this came from. Yours always, Frank.'

Ricky grimaced, nostrils dilating in perfect synchronicity. His mother continued with her account of the sinister past events.

The wad of fivers turned out to be twenty in number, and in the early seventies a hundred quid was a lot of money, particularly for a widow with only a part-time job to support her and a young son studying at university. However, accepting charity was another matter entirely, especially from someone like Frank Rafferty. So, Janice had immediately grabbed her coat, stuffed the business card into her pocket and made her way up to the telephone box at the junction of Dalblair Crescent and Manse Road. She slid her 20p coin into the slot and dialled the number on the card, then immediately slammed the receiver back down again. She needed time to think about this. A hundred quid was an awful lot of money, and by God did she need it, charity or not.

It wasn't until the following morning that Janice had finally made up her mind. Frank Rafferty could shove his wad of fivers where the sun don't shine. She headed back up to the phone box, inhaled deeply and dialled the number. Rafferty answered on the second ring. On hearing her voice, he immediately launched into his trademark chat-up patter, which made Janice feel like puking onto the phone box floor. However, she managed to retain her composure sufficiently to inform Rafferty that while she appreciated his hundred-pound gift, she would be posting it back to him without delay. Unsurprisingly, he protested and asked her to reconsider things. What then took her completely by surprise, though, was his counter-offer, which was this. Don't think of the money as a gift, think of it as a loan which you can repay any time you choose.

In the event, Janice had found herself being forced into making a hasty decision, one she would live to regret, and big-time. She agreed to keep Rafferty's hundred quid for the time being and pay it back at a later date when she could afford it. The big problem was, of course, that Janice knew full well she would never be in a position to pay it back. In effect, she had entered into a verbal agreement which she could never honour, but her back was against the wall. Janice was broke, and here was a gift horse looking her in the mouth. Okay, the gift horse was Frank Rafferty, but he was absolutely loaded, so where was the risk? And more to the point, what was the alternative?

And so, Janice had reluctantly accepted Rafferty's money as a loan rather than a gift. At least, that was the way she saw it. About

21

a week later, a second brown envelope arrived, this one dropping through her letterbox along with the rest of the mail. Bearing a Troon postmark, it contained another wad of fivers, ten of them this time, and another nauseating note from Rafferty.

Again, Janice stopped mid-flow to delve into her purse, and handed the second note to Ricky, who proceeded to read it through gritted teeth.

'Hello again, Janice honey. Just add this to your loan. Fifty notes mean nothing to me, but I know you might find it handy. Yours always, Frank. P.S. You still haven't told me where or when?'

It all looked too good to be true. The pattern continued, a brown envelope arriving most weeks containing anything between twenty and fifty quid, always in fivers, accompanied by the usual sleazy note offering the world and all its riches to Janice, wrapped up in overtly suggestive demands, none of which had ever come to fruition. Until today, that was.

'And that's all I want to say, Ricky,' said Janice, by now visibly fatigued. 'I've told you as much as I can bring myself to tell you, and I'm sure you can work out the rest for yourself. You're a big boy now.'

'No chance, mum,' Ricky said. 'You've done really well so far, but I need to know the whole story. And that means everything.'

'No, Ricky, that's all I can....'

'Mum. Listen to me. I need to know what happened. To my own mother, and in our own house. The house that dad used to live in.'

Janice cradled her head in her hands. Ricky leaned forward and held them in his.

'Look at me, mum,' he said. 'Look at me, please.'

Janice raised her head. Her eyes were red and puffy, and the weal on her neck had progressed along the visible spectrum from red to purple.

'Mum, as you've just said, I'm not a wee boy anymore. I'm a grown man now. Please tell me what happened. I need to know and I can take it.'

Janice blew an exhausted sigh and nodded her head in resignation.

'Okay, Ricky ... I'll try. Just over an hour ago, I was doing the ironing and watching Blue Peter ... don't laugh, but I still like Blue Peter because it always reminds me of you sitting on my knee as a wee toddler....'

'Mum, come on. Just cut to the chase.'

'Okay, okay.'

Another deep breath. She closed her eyes and forced herself to press on.

'I heard a car pull up outside ... it was something about the noise its engine made ... and I saw this white car, one I had never seen before. Then the doorbell rang. I went to answer it, and it was him ... it was Frank ... Frank Rafferty. I nearly died with shock. Frank Rafferty at my own front door, my own home. Good God, I thought. The next thing I knew he was in my living room ... no, he asked me if I wasn't going to invite him in, and I must have said yes ... I think. Anyway, he was in my living room, all dressed up like a film star, and he sat down ... right there, where you're sitting now, Ricky.'

Ricky instinctively brushed the back of his hand along the seat, as if to wipe away the invisible contamination.

'And then?' he said.

'He started on about his letters, and about the money, and about me never getting back to him about our "date". I felt sick to my stomach. And that was when I asked him to leave.'

More tears, hands shaking like a hopeless drug addict gone cold turkey.

'He refused to leave, Ricky ... said something about ... you and I have a business deal to conclude, or something like that. Then he said I now owed him "a couple of grand". I asked him what that meant, and he said, "two thousand pounds, Janice". I started to panic and asked him why I owed him so much money. I told him that I thought the debt was less than three hundred pounds, and that he had agreed that I only needed to pay it back whenever I could. He laughed and said, "compound interest, Janice, compound interest" ... then he said ... he said ... "and I want it right now."'

'And then?' asked Ricky, intrigue rapidly escalating to deep concern.

Janice gulped, her hands still trembling.

'Mum?'

'This is very difficult for me, Ricky ...'

'Take your time, then.'

'Frank propositioned me, Ricky. He asked me to go ... to go upstairs with him. To go to bed with him, Ricky. To the bed that your dad used to sleep in.'

Ricky clenched his right fist but remained outwardly calm.

Inwardly, a surge of fury was fit to explode. His mother continued, staccato-style.

'I refused ... and told him that I wanted him to leave immediately. He flew into a rage. He ... he grabbed me ... grabbed me by the throat and pushed me ... pushed me onto the couch. I thought he was going to hurt me, Ricky ... like, you know, really hurt me in that kind of way? But he didn't. He just stood there above me, staring a horrible stare ... his eyes ... his eyes looked as if they were on fire.'

By now, Janice's whole frame was shaking as the graphic recollection of her ordeal came flooding back. She continued, her bottom lip pulsating.

'Then he seemed to change. It was weird, Ricky. One minute he was hovering over me like a ... like a monster ... with those horrible eyes. The next he was all suave and cool again. And he said ... "A week, Janice, one week. Either pay me my two grand or I'll be back ... and next week it'll be three grand." Then he said something like, "of course, we could just forget the whole thing if only you were nice to me every now and again. One week, sweetheart." He called me sweetheart, Ricky. Not even your dad ever called me sweetheart. It made me feel sick to my stomach.'

Janice closed her eyes and leaned back on the settee, physically and mentally washed out. Her final sentence came out like a drunken mumble.

'And then he just walked straight out the living room ... and straight out the door.'

For the next couple of minutes, mother and son just sat there in total silence, the former nursing her terror, the latter his wrath. It was Ricky who broke the wordless spell.

'It'll be fine, mum. It'll all be fine. Just leave this to me.'

Janice raised a hand in meek protest, but Ricky held up both of his in firm insistence.

'Just leave it all to me. I'm the man of the house now.'

'But ...'

'I'll sort it all out, mum. I'll sort it. I promise.'

The blue touch-paper had been lit. It was now time for the fireworks.

5

Frank Rafferty's home was a mansion by any other name.

Occupying a three-acre site in one of the most fashionable locations on the whole Ayrshire coastline, his sprawling eight-bedroom villa sat right on the sandy seafront, adjacent to the world-famous Royal Troon golf course. A recently converted, 'listed' Edwardian building accessed from the main road by a 200-yard-long driveway with neatly manicured lawns and an immaculate display of magnificent trees, bushes, shrubs and flowers on each side, any invited guests would definitely feel a sense of impending grandeur as they approached. At least, until they met the host.

Once there, Rafferty would be tripping over his own ego to impress them with his self-important 'royal tour' of the capacious two-storey building, crowing arrogantly about its many period features, including the exposed beams and fancy cornices which provided an authentic backdrop to the huge collection of expensive portraits and fancy mirrors that decorated most walls of its fifteen separate rooms, nooks and crannies. However, of all its multitudinous features, Rafferty's personal pride and joy was his enormous fitted kitchen with its vast array of built-in appliances and state-of-the-art accoutrements. The kitchen was also his wife Irene's favourite room in the entire house, which made it the only thing in their lives that they really agreed about.

As far as Rafferty was concerned, he considered himself to be the perfect example of a self-made man who had risen to the very top through a combination of sheer hard graft and serious risk-taking, a veritable role model to others of how to succeed in life. Never once had he even entertained the notion that breaking every legal and moral rule in the book, trampling over friend and foe alike and leaving a trail of heartbreak and destitution in his wake could possibly constitute anything other than astute business acumen. Everybody knew exactly what Frank Rafferty was, but nobody dared say it.

At least, nobody so far.

The doorbell chimed a haunting oriental tune and three massive Rottweilers shot to their feet, teeth bared and barking furiously. Genghis, Cassius and Zane had been chosen and named in Frank Rafferty's own image and beaten to a pulp as puppies until they eventually did his bidding for fear of their lives. Well, most of the

25

time. The bold Zane had once attacked Rafferty during one of his infamous temper tantrums, and bitten the top of his left index finger clean off, immediately after which he had called in Zander McGinn, one of his trusted henchmen, to hold the dog down while he wired its top and bottom jaws together and let the poor thing starve and thirst in agony for four whole days and nights. Frank Rafferty was a man who liked to be obeyed without question.

Irene Rafferty answered the door. She was dressed in a dark-brown, all-in-one trouser suit which drooped apologetically from her narrow shoulders like adult clothes on a starving child, her sad and baggy eyes screaming of long-gone carefree days now turned sour. Irene may have won the key to the seaside mansion, but she would not be winning any beauty contests.

A short, tubby figure stood on the doorstep. Two sets of anxious expressions met.

'Come in, Councillor Monk,' said Irene. 'I'll get him for you.'

'Thank you, Mrs Rafferty,' came the near-apologetic reply.

Frank Rafferty was lying stretched out on his favourite sofa when his wife entered the television room.

'What is it, Irene?' he asked, without even turning his head. 'I told you to knock before disturbing me, didn't I? And right in the middle of *Minder* as well. This had better be bloody good.'

'It's the councillor, Frank,' she answered. 'Councillor Monk.'

'Show him into the study,' he commanded. 'No, in fact, take him into the snooker room. And I'm going to let him stew in his own juice for a few minutes, so no tea or coffee. Comprendo?'

Frank and Irene Rafferty had been married for 23 years. They had got it on in the wake of Big Davie Anderson having tied the knot with the love of both his and Rafferty's life, that delectable little honey, Janice Robertson, who had spurned the latter's advances more times than he had had hot dinners. And more fool she, Rafferty had convinced himself, getting lumbered with a dimwit painter-and-decorator who had considerably more muscles than brains, rather than marrying a budding entrepreneur like himself.

The truth was that Rafferty had never forgiven Janice for having nothing to do with him, and he would simply have grabbed and ravished her in revenge some dark night, had it not been for the terrifying thought of what Big Davie might have done to him in return. Now, though, muscle-man was history, and all Janice had to protect her was that smart-arsed geek of a college boy who was away in the city most of the time anyway. So, someday soon she was about to find out what it was like to have a real man inside her. Just like all the other women whom Rafferty had lured into his bedroom, many of them scared witless, and most of whom the unfortunate Irene had known about but found herself powerless to complain, for fear of yet another merciless beating from her beloved husband.

'I'll take you along to the snooker room, Councillor Monk,' Irene said, desperate to offer him a refreshment but knowing full well the implications. 'In here, please, and make yourself comfortable. He might be a moment or two.'

It was a full fifteen minutes until Dennis Waterman had nailed his latest unfortunate victim in ITV's cult crime series, after which Rafferty wandered into his luxurious toilet for a leak. When he eventually strode nonchalantly into the dimly-lit, oak-panelled snooker room, Monk held out his hand in friendship. Rafferty completely blanked the gesture and brushed past him without even a glance in his direction, leaving the councillor standing there like a spurned extra in a cheap B-list movie.

'A wee game, Edwin?' he said, picking up his personalised snooker cue, the one with his name etched in gold on the name plate. 'One frame, you against me. You can have 40 of a start. I'll play you for a score. You know what a score is, Edwin? It's twenty quid, so your cue action had better be good.'

'I don't play snooker, Frank,' came the nervous reply. 'No use at sports at all, I'm afraid.'

'And not much better at politics either,' Rafferty teased. 'When you've got paid officials telling you what you can and can't do. Something I always wondered, Edwin? Are they in charge of you, or are you in charge of them?'

Rafferty smashed the white cue-ball into the triangular pack of reds with a mighty clatter, causing Monk to jump like a startled rabbit. He turned and gave the politician a steely glare.

'Show it to me, Edwin.'

Monk reached down and opened his briefcase, then pulled out a beige-coloured folder. He handed it to Rafferty, who placed his cue very gently on the snooker table then sat down on a green leather armchair which had been colour-coded to match the baize. He opened the folder, flicked through the eight-page report inside and tut-tutted.

'This is a photocopy, Edwin. Where's the original?'

'Frank, this is the best I can do. The original is in a locked filing cabinet in the Council Clerk's office, and there's just no way I can get my hands on it. I'm already taking a huge risk just asking for a photocopy, and an even bigger risk showing it to you before the Planning Committee has had the opportunity to consider it. You can do what you like to me, Frank. You and your ... your friends ... but I'm afraid this is the best I can do.'

Rafferty smiled. It was the smile of a monster. He got up, walked over to Monk and put his hand on his shoulder.

'You've done well, Edwin my old friend, very well indeed. Just leave the folder there on the snooker table and we'll say no more about it.'

Suddenly, Rafferty's face took on a puzzled expression.

'One other thing I meant to ask you, Edwin. You know that woman I spoke to you about? The one who was appealing against her Family Income Support application being refused? Her name's Anderson, Janice Anderson. What was the final decision of that other committee you chair?'

'You mean, the Appeals Panel? We rejected it, of course. Just as you told me to do.'

'Good man, Edwin, good man. I want to keep as much pressure as I can on that woman.'

'But I have to tell you, Frank, Mrs Anderson had a very strong case. What we did wasn't right, it just wasn't right at all. The poor woman has been to hell and back, and she really needs financial support.'

'But I'm sure that's not what the minutes of the meeting will say though, Edwin. Am I correct?'

Rafferty raised his dark bushy eyebrows in search of confirmation and Monk nodded. It was a nod steeped in shame-faced self-loathing. The gangster then marched the people's representative out of the snooker room, the former's arm around his puppet's shoulder.

'Oh, and Edwin,' grinned Rafferty, stuffing a brown envelope into Monk's jacket pocket. 'Here are your winnings. You know, for beating me at that game you don't play. Spend it wisely.'

Rafferty opened the big ornate front door. The three oversized Rottweilers bared their teeth and snarled at their guest. Looking anxiously around in all directions, Monk trotted towards his top-of-the-range BMW as fast as his little plump legs could carry him.

6

The bleak serenity of Braddoch Brickworks had always reminded Ricky Anderson of a post-apocalyptic scene in a cheap 1960s' horror movie. This place was dystopia with an Ayrshire accent.

Essentially a crude collection of old brick buildings so randomly scattered that they might have been dropped onto the remote moorland wilderness by an inebriated helicopter pilot, the Hanging Gardens of Babylon this was not. Unsurprisingly, the brickworks' inmates were a sombre lot, such was the desperate monotony of their hard-earned existence in a location so desolate that it would have made the middle of nowhere look like a Caribbean paradise.

Everything was tedium personified. The 'stackers' built up the grey clay walls inside the kilns, brick-by-brick. The 'firemen' fired the kilns into action one-by-one. The 'timmers' began the fearsome task of dismantling the slowly-cooling reddish-orange bricks, wearing rubber gloves to shield their hands from the searing heat and cloth masks to protect their lungs from the lethal dust, and all at only a few pence-per-hour more in deference to the more hazardous nature of their task. The conveyor belts then trundled the hot bricks to the waiting lorries, for onward transportation to God-knows-where. Everything was totally functional, but utterly brain-numbing. Indeed, the only reminder that a more vibrant world lay furth of Braddoch Moor was on the rare occasion of the telephone ringing in the manager's office.

Suddenly, the hooter signalled another piece-break. One more seat-sandwich-and-shit combo, thought Ricky Anderson, and one less day in this God-forsaken dump of a joint. Glory be.

In what had begun as a private conversation with his next-door neighbour and lifelong friend, Andy Tennent, a small audience was now gathering as Ricky told the sordid tale about the sinister stranger's intimidatory tactics against his defenceless and vulnerable mother. His monologue ended with a particularly chilling statement.

'I'm telling you, he's a dead man walking.'

'Come on, Ricky,' Andy protested. 'Do you really know anything about this guy? He sounds like bad news to me, a real nasty piece of work. And I'd be surprised if he wasn't surrounded by a team of heavyweights.'

The others nodded and muttered in accord.

'I can look after myself,' Ricky replied, steely eyed. 'I've never lost a fight in my life.'

'Aye, and that's what worries me, Ricky,' said Andy, shaking his head. 'I've seen you in action.'

'Dead man walking,' Ricky repeated.

The works' hooter blared out its resounding approval, and it was time again for the barrow-and-shovel routine.

'He's daft enough to take that guy on,' said Andy as the impromptu audience began to disperse. 'I've got a really bad feeling about this.'

The others just nodded in silence, as they watched Ricky lift his shovel above shoulder height before bringing it down with awesome force onto an unsuspecting red brick, converting it to smithereens.

It was never a good sign when Ricky Anderson's blood was up.

7

Iona McNish sat on the arm of the apricot-coloured settee, staring open-mouthed at her boyfriend who was pacing up and down the living room floor like a caged lion. She was agog with incredulity. Eventually, the words came out.

'You can't possibly be serious, Ricky. Tell me you're kidding? Please.'

'I've never been more serious in my life, Iona,' came the indignant reply. 'My mind's made up.'

'So, you're still determined to tackle that man on your own? What are you going to do to him? Beat him senseless with a baseball bat or something? Your mum has told you all about him. He's a gangster, Ricky. A gangster.'

'I can look after myself, Iona. Remember, this is the guy who marched straight into our house ... into this very room ... and grabbed my mum by the throat and threatened to harm her. I simply can't do nothing. I've got to get him off our case. I've got to stop him.'

'And do you think beating him to a pulp will stop him? Do you really believe that it would end there, that he'd just brush himself down, walk away quietly and leave Janice and you in peace? Get real, Ricky. His minders would be after you within the hour.'

'You're the only one who's talking about beating him up, Iona. Sure, I'd love to knock seven shades of shit out of the bastard, and believe me I'm capable of doing it, but I've thought about this and you're right. It would never end there, and a lot of people could get hurt, including mum ... and even you. No, there's another way to do this that doesn't involve any rough stuff. I've been doing my homework.'

'Never mind your homework, Ricky, this is a police matter. Go to the cops and leave them to deal with it.'

Ricky walked over to the settee and planked himself down on the seat beside his girlfriend, then grabbed her slender waist and hauled her down on top of him.

'I like you when you're angry, Iona McNish,' he whispered in her ear, before biting the lobe gently. 'You're like a wild lioness. It makes me want to tame you.'

'Tame me?' Iona gasped, feigning outrage. 'Nobody will ever tame me, Ricky Anderson.'

The couple sank into a long passionate kiss, which soon graduated into a few naughty fumbles. Suddenly, the front door opened. Iona giggled and Ricky cursed.

'Are you two lovebirds behaving yourselves? I'm home early.'

It was Janice Anderson back from her Monday coffee evening with her friends, or at least that's what Ricky had been told. The truth of the matter was that she had just returned from her fourth session with Caroline Morrison, a well-respected local trauma counsellor whose professional availability was like gold dust, but whom Janice had been able to access through the good offices of her colleagues in the medical centre. Rightly or wrongly, Janice had taken the decision to keep her therapy consultations secret from Ricky, to avoid causing him any further worry. She had, however, confided in Iona McNish, that darling little gem whom she trusted with her life. And, of course, with her son's life.

'Hi mum,' said Ricky, grimacing in frustration to his girlfriend as his mother hung her coat up the hall.

'Hi Janice,' said Iona, shooting to her feet and quickly fastening the top three buttons of her blouse with a silent giggle in Ricky's direction.

'Hope I'm not interrupting anything.' Janice joked with a twinkle in her eye, an expression rarely seen these days.

'No Janice,' replied Iona, 'Ricky was just telling me how he was going to take care of that man who paid you a visit. Weren't you, Ricky?'

The red-hot lovebirds exchanged red-hot glares.

'We've been over this about a dozen times, Ricky,' Janice sighed, as she slumped down rather theatrically in her favourite armchair.

'Just trying to protect you, mum,' Ricky remarked, shrugging his shoulders. 'That's all.'

'I know you are, Ricky,' she replied, 'But going after Frank would only make matters worse, and would almost certainly end with you getting hurt. I've been thinking about it a lot, and I've now made up my mind. I want to go to the police.'

Silence. Two sets of female eyes staring at the floor, one male set flitting from one to the other as the penny finally dropped.

'You two have been talking to each other, haven't you?'

Silence. Awkward glances between the two accused.

'I knew it,' Ricky snapped. 'I bloody knew it. And mum, stop calling that bastard "Frank". His name's Rafferty.'

'Language, Ricky,' Janice muttered, with only a modicum of conviction.

'Right,' Ricky said, sporting a familiar look of determination, one that often signalled an impending episode of truculence. 'I want both of you to hear me out. I've been thinking about this.'

Janice sighed again, threw her head against the back of the armchair and rolled her eyes. Iona sat back down on the settee beside her boyfriend.

'Right, here goes,' Ricky began. 'Something has got to be done to get Rafferty off your back, mum. Doing nothing is simply not an option. He'll come after you again and keep coming after you until he gets ... well ... until he gets what he wants. You'll be living in fear constantly. So, let's all agree that *something* has got to be done. Okay?'

Iona nodded. Janice said nothing.

'Mum, please?' Ricky pleaded.

'Yes, okay,' Janice agreed. 'Something needs to be done, because I can't just sit here waiting for Frank ... sorry, Rafferty ... to pop up at any hour of the day. But I've made up my mind, I want to report the matter to the police. He assaulted me in my own home, so they're bound to treat this very seriously.'

'No, they won't, mum,' Ricky replied, shaking his head in frustration. 'No, they won't.'

'Why not?' asked Janice, genuinely puzzled.

'Yes, why not?' asked Iona, similarly confused.

'I'll tell you why,' said Ricky. 'But you've got to keep it between the three of us. It's important that nobody else hears this.'

'Okay,' said Iona, nodding towards Janice who pulled an unimpressed expression before reluctantly nodding back.

'Right, I told you I've been doing my homework,' Ricky continued. 'The thing is that Rafferty has friends in high places, which makes him untouchable, or at least that's what he thinks. Two friends in particular.'

'Well?' said his mother, clearly becoming more irritated by the second. 'Are you going to tell us who they are, or not?'

'One of them is the Chief Superintendent of the Ayr branch of Southwest Scotland Police ... the big cheese ... whose name is Joe Fraser, and who just so happens to be Rafferty's full cousin. They call him "Smokin' Joe", after the world heavyweight boxing champion, Joe Frasier. And just like the boxer himself, Fraser is a proper street fighter who'll use every dirty trick in the book to go for anyone who takes him on. In other words, Chief Superintendent Fraser is one mean copper. And believe me, mum, if you grass Rafferty into the police, he'll run straight to his big cousin for protection. Your complaint will be brushed under the carpet and you'll be in a worse position than ever, with the cops as well as Rafferty on your case.'

Janice just shook her head and gave her son a look which tried to smack of rebuke but failed to conceal the concern that lay gnawing underneath. It was Iona who spoke next.

'So, who's his other pal, Ricky?'

'A guy called Edwin Monk, one of Ayrshire's most senior politicians. A councillor, and a very influential one at that. Chairman of Southwest Scotland Council's Planning Committee, and a member of the local Police Board as well, where he'll be rubbing shoulders on a regular basis with none other than Smokin' Joe himself. That's the long version. The short version is that going to the cops would be suicide.'

'So, what do you suggest, then?' Janice enquired, noticeably beginning to take her son's advice a bit more seriously.

'Well, that's what I've been thinking about, mum,' Ricky continued. 'Which takes me back to my homework. It seems to me that the key to solving this little problem of ours is Councillor Monk, or rather his relationship with this chancer, Frank Rafferty. Because ... and this is the really sensitive bit ... I've found out that Rafferty and Monk are as thick as thieves. Joined at the bloody hip.'

'How do you mean, Ricky?' enquired Iona, her soft brown eyes slowly filling with intrigue. 'Where are you going with this?'

'Think about it. Monk chairs the council's Planning Committee, which makes all the big decisions about planning applications for new housing developments and that sort of thing, and Rafferty is a property developer. And they're bosom buddies. All very neat and tidy, don't you think? Very cosy indeed, but maybe a wee bit too cosy. Have you been reading the controversy in the local newspapers over the past few weeks about this planned new development on the shorefront down at Sandbank?'

'Actually, yes I have,' Janice replied, perking up. 'Some new houses being built on the site of the old Sandbank Maternity Hospital that was closed a couple of years ago? What about it?'

'Well, guess who the developer is,' Ricky beamed, watching the change in his mother's facial expression.

'Not ... not Frank Rafferty?'

'Yes, mum, the very same. And the council is getting pelters from local residents for agreeing to a "change of use" application. Something about promises having been made to provide recreational facilities, rather than houses, on the seafront.'

'That's quite interesting, Ricky,' said Iona, 'but I don't see how this helps us?'

'Quite interesting? Well, let me make it even more interesting. The application was submitted by Rafferty himself, to allow him to build 136 new houses on the same site. The change of use was granted by the council's Planning Committee back in June, despite protests galore and a petition with over 2,000 signatures on it. The same Planning Committee which is chaired by none other than Councillor Edwin Monk. And rumours are doing the rounds that Monk has been receiving brown envelopes from Rafferty for services rendered. You've seen his brown envelopes yourself, haven't you, mum?'

Janice nodded, eyes widening.

'Was Councillor Monk not also the one who chaired that Appeals Panel meeting which refused my own application for Family Income Support?'

'Yes mum, I was just coming to that. And I'd wager my last penny that lover-boy Rafferty put him up to it, just to get back at you for not responding to his demands.'

Janice's mouth fell open. It was Iona who supplied the words.

'Now, that is very interesting. But you still need to explain how it helps us, Ricky?'

'Because if we can establish a direct connection between Monk and Rafferty, we can discredit both of them,' Ricky replied. 'And if we can prove that money has been changing hands, then the police would have no alternative but to take action. If it then went public, Smokin' Joe would have to completely disown his wee cousin. My guess is that he'd throw him to the wolves just to save his own skin.'

'Right then, Ricky,' Iona continued, 'But have you actually found any evidence of a definite connection between them? And I mean real evidence?'

'What?' asked Ricky. 'You mean, like Monk and his wife having spent three holidays in the past year at Rafferty's villa in France?'

8

The long sunlit nights of summer were becoming shorter and shorter, as another autumn season approached. Or as the natives of Ayrshire might have said, 'the nichts are fair drawin' in'.

Janice Anderson pecked her son gently on the cheek and opened the front door.

'I should be home by about half-ten, Ricky. Will you still be up?'

'Aye, mum,' came the dreamy reply. 'Probably.'

For once, Ricky was glad to have the house all to himself. Sure, with his mum out of the way for a few hours it would have been a wonderful opportunity to engage in ten rounds of wrestling with the gorgeous Iona McNish, but Ricky needed the time. Time to think. Time to plan. Time to devise his strategy and make the world a better place.

With Iona otherwise engaged in accompanying her mother on a trip to Kilmarnock Infirmary to visit an old ailing aunt and his own mother out with her neighbour-and-best friend Maggie Tennent at the local bingo hall, this was the perfect opportunity for a bit of deep lateral thinking and some serious scenario planning.

Over and above his academic achievements, Ricky had accomplished a great deal during his four years in Glasgow University's esteemed campus. Undoubtedly, his most impressive non-academic success had been his meteoric rise through the essentially hard-left medium of student politics, in which he had received the ultimate accolade some eighteen months ago when being elected as President of the Students' Union.

A working-class lad from a humble coalmining community, Ricky had been raised with a very clear set of values and a strict moral code, and he had learned life the hard way. Very few Glenside youngsters had ever got the chance to progress to university, and Ricky was acutely aware of the sacrifice that his widowed mother had made in giving him a career in academia. She would have done anything for her precious son. As for Ricky, he would have walked on hot coals to protect his wonderful mum. And if ever she needed his protection, it was right now.

One evening back in his 'fresher' days as a first-year student, Ricky and a couple of his mates had decided to tag along to a meeting of the university's Debating Society, which they had been told would be 'a right good laugh'. The subject of the debate was the contentious matter of immigration, a hot national talking-point which had been really stoked up in recent times by conservative MP Enoch Powell's controversial 'rivers of blood' speech opposing mass immigration, and rekindled more recently by a huge National Front rally in London pursuing the same agenda but with trademark hostility and violence thrown in for good measure. That evening, the debate had been a furious one, diametrically opposing views having been presented with great passion by both sides. The whole experience had electrified Ricky and immediately magnetised him towards the murky world of student politics, from which he would grow and finally emerge as *the great leader*.

Ricky Anderson was now a highly-skilled debater, adored by the working-class left-wing of the student masses and feared by the more privileged right-wing 'Hoorah Henrys'. Seldom, if ever, did Ricky lose a debate, his arguments always having been meticulously researched, carefully structured and delivered with calm authority and controlled passion. For Ricky, there was absolutely no conflict between his academic studies in nuclear physics and his political involvement. After all, had the great Danish physicist, Neils Bohr – one of the main fathers of atomic energy – not also been hugely influential in the pacifistic politics of the post-atomic bomb era? As far as Bohr had been concerned, the two disciplines were not mutually exclusive, they were inextricably linked. And if it was good enough for the great Neils Bohr, then it was good enough for Ricky Anderson.

Lying stretched out on the settee in his Glenside home that

evening, Ricky carefully pondered his options. The bottom line was that he simply had to find a way to get that chancer Rafferty off his mother's case. She was in debt to a seedy individual rumoured to be a serial extortionist, and one who had already displayed a *penchant* for violence.

This time, though, Rafferty's motivation was different. This time, it wasn't just the money he was after, it was something else entirely. This time, he had hatched the perfect plan. A plan to ensnare the love of his life, the girl whose charms he had coveted ever since his schoolboy days, the girl whom he had always loved and adored. This time, Rafferty wasn't really interested in the money. He was only using the money as a weapon finally to get his greasy paws on the woman of his dreams, the one who had spurned his lecherous advances on every single occasion. Now she would have to pay for her sins, if not in cash then as his ultimate conquest, willing or not.

This time, Frank Rafferty wasn't thinking with his brain. This time, he was thinking with his hormones. That was what now made him vulnerable.

Ricky had already developed his overarching strategy. It was pretty straightforward, really. Dig the dirt on bent councillor Edwin Monk, link him directly to crooked businessman Frank Rafferty, publicly expose and discredit both of them for the low-life creatures that they are, and leave the rest to the press and the cops. His strategy was fine. It was its implementation that would be the tricky bit.

Essentially, his *modus operandi* would be this. Go for Monk first, Ricky, but choose your moment carefully. A public meeting, one chaired by Monk himself. One that would be controversial and well attended. One to which the local press would turn out in force. Do your homework thoroughly and dig the dirt meticulously, then go straight for the jugular. And, of course, that was precisely where Ricky's own political grounding would come in very handy indeed.

Clearly there was still a good bit more meat to put on the bones, but that would come in due course. Ricky rubbed his eyes and switched on his TV set. *Top Gear* was about to start, presented by every married man's favourite bit of upper-class crumpet, the delectable Angela Rippon. However, the married men could keep Ms Rippon all to themselves, because Ricky had Iona.

And Iona was an angel.

9

As Janice Anderson sat staring out of the bus window, she prayed silently that Maggie Tennent wouldn't spill the beans and tell Ricky about her no-show tonight at the bingo hall. If she did, Janice would have a lot of explaining to do.

Some four miles and fifteen minutes later, the bus pulled into Cumnock's bustling Square. Janice jumped off, her heart going like the hammers of hell. Scanning around in all directions, she made her way past the magnificent blonde-sandstone church building which formed the salubrious centrepiece of the town square, and crossed the main thoroughfare, Glaisnock Street, towards the Royal Hotel, one of the town's oldest hostelries. She then marched briskly towards 'McCubbin's Corner' and stopped momentarily outside the tall building which housed the Craighead Inn, to survey the scene in forensic detail.

As it happened, she was right to do so, because there crossing the road was none other than Betty Ramsay, that poisonous old busybody who had more faces than the four-sided 'toon clock' perched high on the ornate tower of the old church. Anything that Betty couldn't find out from her serial gossiping sessions she would just have made up anyway, and the whole town knew it. Suitably alerted, Janice pulled up her coat collar and faced away until the danger had passed, then peeked around to check that the coast was clear before continuing on her way.

She turned left and began walking smartly up Townhead Street, another of the busy town's main roads. Staring straight ahead, she never once allowed her gaze to stray towards either of the two rows of old shops to her left or right, thereby minimising the chance of eye contact with any occasional passers-by. Her steps quickened as she passed her current place of employment, the local health centre. It was now quarter-to-eight on a Tuesday evening, but even in the unlikely event of one of her medical colleagues happening to make an impromptu exit from the prefabricated building, she just knew instinctively that tonight of all nights familiarity would not be her friend.

Looking up towards the car park adjacent to the old police station, Janice's heart skipped a beat when she saw the headlamps of a metallic-blue Mark 1V Ford Cortina flashing twice, then twice again. Her brisk walk progressed to an elegant canter, and in no time at all she had reached the parked car.

The male driver threw open the passenger's door. Janice slid into the front seat and pulled the door shut behind her. He leaned over towards her and kissed her gently on the lips. She threw her arms around his shoulders and kissed him back.

The Cortina then sped off into the distance.

10

It was mid-morning on 22 August, the second-last Wednesday before matriculation at Glasgow University, the big day when all the students from first-year freshers through to fifth-year postgraduates dutifully signed up for the next phase of their academic studies.

Ricky Anderson was free at last from his punishing chores at Braddoch Brickworks, a decent proportion of his hard-earned pickings now safely stashed away to help him through the coming year in the city's big smoke. For the past three months, Ricky's rusty old shovel had been energetically deployed in shovelling the rubbish from the brickworks' spent kilns. Now a somewhat more cerebral 'shovel' was ready to get to work on digging a different kind of dirt on the Chairman of Southwest Scotland Council's Planning Committee.

Ricky stood inside the big red telephone box at the top of Dalblair Crescent, listening to the autumnal rain battering down on its tiny window panes and wondering why all Ayrshire phone boxes seemed to smell the same, a curious amalgam of cigarette smoke and stale urine. How he longed for the day when his hard-pressed mother might be able to afford her own phone in her own home. It was a day which seemed a very long way off, thanks in large part to those two seedy low-lives, Rafferty and Monk, the former having saddled her with a huge and highly illicit burden of debt, and the latter having seen to it that her application for financial support was finally dead in the water.

For a mere nanosecond, Ricky found himself visualising the pristine telephone sets that would almost certainly be adorning the luxurious boudoirs of Rafferty's and Monk's grand residences, both furnished by their respective ill-gotten gains. Then he remembered something slightly more uplifting. The cells in Glasgow's HM Barlinnie Prison had none. And come hell or high water, the notorious 'Bar-L' was precisely where those two bad eggs would end up if he had anything to do with it.

Ricky took what was left of the change out of his pocket. It amounted to a couple of twenty-pence pieces. Heaven knows how many phone calls he had made since nine o'clock that morning, costing a whole fiver into the bargain, and he was now bursting for a leak, or as his dear departed dad used to say in deference to the old star of the silver-screen, 'a wee Lillian Gish'. Four times he had already vacated the phone box to allow others to use it, and now he only had one more call to make, thank the lord. It had been a highly productive morning so far, that was for sure. However, this was it. This was the big one.

Time was now of the essence. In the aftermath of Frank Rafferty's change of use application for the Sandbank housing development having been granted by Edwin Monk's Planning Committee, an open public consultation meeting had recently been arranged, as required by legislation, to discuss the construction firm's detailed proposals. The meeting had been scheduled for the Thursday evening of the following week, and due to the very high turnout expected and security concerns associated with what was feared might be a very hostile atmosphere, it had been deemed appropriate to stage it in the grand, capacious Council Chambers of the local authority's headquarters.

Such was the degree of contentiousness surrounding the developer's housebuilding proposals and the community fury that had followed the council's perceived lily-livered decision to approve the change of use application, that the local press would surely turn out in force. That morning, though, Ricky Anderson's mission was to make damned sure that they did. So far, he had managed to make personal telephone contact with the editors of all three local weekly newspapers, and then with their permission, with the reporters who would be covering the public meeting. All that was needed now was an opportunity to bend the ear of 'the main man'.

His name was Gerry McGhee.

McGhee was a freelance investigative journalist, one who had gained national recognition by writing regular hard-hitting columns in several national newspapers, including the *Glasgow Herald* and *The Scotsman*, both widely regarded as two of the most respected and balanced broadsheets in Scotland. He had also fronted a number of radio and television documentaries, normally investigating socially and politically controversial issues which were deemed to be in the public interest. In short, he was the archetypal champion of the underdog, and an absolute Rottweiler to boot. Ghengis, Cassius and Zane Rafferty would have run a mile from Gerry McGhee on a mission.

Ricky had already tried McGhee's number twice that morning, and twice he had received the same 'please leave a message and I'll get back to you' greeting, but since the Anderson family had no private telephone let alone any voicemail facility, he would simply have to keep trying. Thankfully, this time the celebrated reporter answered on the first ring.

'Gerry McGhee.'

Ricky took a deep breath before answering.

'Hello Mister McGhee, my name is Ricky Anderson and ...'

'Call me Gerry.'

'Okay ... Gerry. My name's Ricky Anderson and I've got a story which I think might interest you.'

'I'm listening.'

'Have you been following the controversy about the new housing development planned for Sandbank, near Troon? The one to be built on the site of the old maternity hospital?'

'Nope. Never heard of it, son, but go on.'

'Well, it's being built by a local construction company which is headed by a gangster.'

'You have evidence to prove that he's a gangster?'

'Well ... sort of.'

'"Sort of" doesn't wash, Ricky. What age are you, son?'

'Twenty-one, but I'm a grown-up twenty-one. Pubic hair and everything.'

A quiet snigger from McGhee. Ricky continued.

'There's more. You want to hear it or not?'

'Okay, but make it quick. I've got a lot more gangsters to catch.'

'The natives were up in arms when the local council passed the change of use application that will see it converted from a maternity hospital to a swanky private housing estate. And here's the thing. The Chairman of the Planning Committee that passed the application is in the gangster's pocket. And big time. Brown envelopes all over the place.'

'Same question. Do you have evidence? And I mean concrete evidence?'

'I'm working on it, and I'm confident that …'

'Without evidence, I'm just not interested. I've been led up more blind alleys than I've had loose women.'

'Hear me out, Gerry. What I do know for sure is that the councillor and his wife have spent three separate holidays in the businessman's villa in France in the past year.'

A moment's silence.

'Where can we meet, Ricky?'

'I don't have a car, but I could get the train. I'd prefer to meet you in your own office rather than here at home.'

'Where is home, Ricky?'

'A wee Ayrshire village called Glenside, just outside Cumnock.'

'Oh, I know the area well. Are Cumnock Juniors and Auchinleck Talbot still kicking the shit out of each other, then?'

'Aye, and always will be. I could meet you in Glasgow tomorrow about one o'clock. That any good?'

'Ideal. I'll buy you lunch. The Corn Exchange bar, straight across from Central Station. You know it?'

'Aye, I know it well. I'm a student at Glasgow Uni, so I know most of the city centre pubs.'

'A bloody student, I might have known. So, I'll be paying your way through Uni as well as paying for your lunch. See you at one. I'll be the ugly one with the fair hair and beard.'

'And I'll be the handsome one with the dark flowing locks.'

Gerry McGhee laughed heartily. This young whipper-snapper had already made a big impression on him. He had balls.

'One final question, Ricky. What's your motivation here? Good Samaritan helping the downtrodden and all that shite?'

'The businessman is called Frank Rafferty. He's also an illegal money lender with a passion for violence, and his latest victim is my own mother. One way or another, I'm going to stop him. The councillor is called Edwin Monk, and he's as bent as a nine-bob note. He's coming down too.'

'See you tomorrow, Ricky Anderson. And remember your table manners, son. This isn't the students' union beer bar.'

'I'll try. Fork in the right hand, if I remember correctly?'

'Something like that.'

'And one other thing. Don't call me son.'

'Okay, consider me suitably scolded.'

As Ricky marched briskly down Dalblair Crescent in the pouring

42

rain with a satisfied grin etched across his face, Gerry McGhee stubbed out his tenth fag of the morning into an empty teacup and began chuckling. The same thought occurred simultaneously to each of them.

This could get interesting. Very interesting indeed.

11

Ricky had only ten days left to get the rancid stench of newly-fired bricks out of his nostrils and recharge his batteries in preparation for another year's hard slog in Glasgow's University Avenue campus.

Ten days to get organised and mentally attuned for starting his PhD course in Nuclear Physics. And, of course, even fewer to do some serious homework on Frank Rafferty and Edwin Monk. Or Mutt and Jeff, as Ricky now called them, in deference to American cartoonist Bud Fisher's cutting caricatures of his famous pair of 'mismatched tinhorns'.

Ricky stepped off the Carlisle-to-Glasgow train onto Central Station's Platform 6 and made his way through the briefcase-and-rucksack-carrying throngs towards the station's grand entrance on Gordon Street. A long line of black taxi cabs crawled slowly forward as a steady flow of passengers shuffled towards the head of the queue, doubtless several minutes late for their next appointments, or God forbid, the big job interviews. A light autumnal shower rained down on Ricky's shoulder-length hair as he dived between a couple of cabs to cross the busy road.

Having been established away back in 1890, The Corn Exchange was one of Glasgow's oldest public houses, but it still retained huge popularity, not only with countless rail passengers who would often partake of a quick pint before jumping onto their train, but also attracting a regular customer base. Ricky pushed the door open and walked straight up to the bar, then ordered himself a pint of Tennent's lager. He looked around for the ugly one with the fair hair and beard, but managed to detect nobody of that unfortunate description among the twenty-odd patrons scattered around the various bar stools, tables and chairs, all of whom were sipping contentedly at their assorted beverages.

A slightly soggy copy of the *Evening Times* lay on the bar, its back page facing him. The sports headline read, 'Smith Bags a Brace as Gers Thrash Thistle', referring to one Gordon of that ilk scoring two goals in Glasgow Rangers' 4-0 demolition of city rivals Partick Thistle the night before. No sooner had he picked up the daily tabloid than a hand slapped him on the shoulder. A pair of piercing eyes met his own.

'You must be the handsome one with the dark flowing locks, then?'

'Aye, that's me,' Ricky replied, accepting Gerry McGhee's firm handshake. 'And I must compliment you on how well you fit your own description.'

Gerry McGhee laughed heartily.

'So, you're not only a clever young pup, but a cocky one as well? Away and sit yourself down at that wee table over by the window, while I order myself a pint. You want another one, son?'

'No thanks, I'm fine.'

McGhee walked over, placed his pint on the table and dumped a brown A4 folder down beside it, then took a Dictaphone out of his jacket pocket and sat it on top of the folder. A middle-aged, pot-bellied guy sitting at the next table glared at the journalist and blew a long plume of cigarette smoke straight towards him, before rising to his feet and heading for pastures new at the bar. His nostrils were so dilated in contempt that they could have accommodated his whisky and half-pint chaser with room to spare.

'What's his problem, then?' asked Ricky.

'It's a long story,' replied McGhee. 'Let's just say our paths crossed recently, and I won't be expecting a Christmas card from him. My newspaper columns don't miss and hit the wall.'

'So, I'm told,' said Ricky, with a glint of approval.

McGhee necked a big slug of beer and immediately got down to business.

'I'm going to tape this, Ricky, if that's okay with you? My handwriting's hellish. My editor says it looks like a hen scratching in the mud.'

'No problem, Gerry. I want everybody to hear about this.'

'Okay, then. Just tell me your story, warts and all, and we can grab some grub later.'

And so, the young physics student began recounting his tale to the most revered investigative journalist in the entire country. He had absolutely no idea how it would look in the press, or even if it would ever feature in the press for that matter, but one thing was for sure. If he wanted to nail Rafferty and Monk, he couldn't have a better ally than Gerry McGhee.

By the time Ricky had regaled him with all the sordid details, both pint glasses were empty and in need of replenishment. McGhee caught a passing barmaid's eye and asked for two more pints and two menus.

'Right then, Ricky,' he went on, looking a bit puzzled. 'Let me sum up the whole thing as I understand it. You've got yourself personally involved in this thing because this guy Rafferty has always had the hots for your own mother, who is now down on her luck financially. And she has got into even more bother by borrowing money from him, and he's now exploiting the situation to get her knickers off ... sorry, son.'

'No offence taken,' Ricky replied.

McGhee continued.

'Rafferty is a self-made man and a self-made crook into the bargain. He makes his money from two main sources, property development for which he crosses influential palms with silver, and money-lending which is a euphemism for extortion. He is also in league with this Edwin Monk guy, who is a corrupt local politician, and who is not only in Rafferty's pocket but almost certainly terrified of him as well. That about it, Ricky?'

Two more pints and two menus arrived. McGhee ploughed on, hands gesticulating, eyes skywards in deep concentration.

'Your mum is now in a very tricky situation. She has three options as I see it. Option one ... she coughs up the dough, which of course she can't do because she doesn't have it, and which was the reason she borrowed it in the first place. Option two ... she becomes Rafferty's wee bit on the side and he writes off the debt, which of course she won't do, because she's been going out of her way to avoid his tender charms ever since their schooldays. Option three ... she does nothing. And Ricky, I don't even want to think about how Rafferty would respond to option three, because this guy sounds like someone who will stop at nothing to get his own way. In other words, option three could get very ugly.'

'And then, of course, there's option four,' said Ricky, with a wry grin.

'And what exactly is option four, pray tell?' McGhee enquired, suitably intrigued.

The barmaid made her reappearance.

'Can I take your food order?'

45

'A few minutes, love,' said McGhee, with a dismissive wave of the hand. 'I'll give you a shout when we're ready.'

She walked away, rolling her eyes and muttering a quiet oath.

'Option four, Ricky?'

'You and I dig as much dirt as we can on Rafferty and especially Monk before next Thursday evening's public meeting in the Council Chambers. You make the bullets for me, Gerry, and I'll fire them. And straight between Monk's eyes. I'll link him directly to Rafferty and expose them both, with half of Ayrshire looking on. What's left of Monk's political career will be dead in the water, and Rafferty will run for cover. If we can also get the cops interested, the pair of them will have no option but to keep their heads down, which will get Rafferty off my mum's case. If the cops don't bite, you ... mister famous investigative journalist ... you then follow the whole thing up with a major expose, and with a bit of luck with one of your famous TV documentaries as well. Sound like a plan?'

McGhee took a sip from his second pint and scratched his ear.

'Tell you what I'll do, Ricky. I'll call in a few favours and get you as much stuff as I can on this chancer, Monk. I'll look into Rafferty's background as well. I'll get something to you by next Thursday morning latest. And I might just toddle along to the public meeting myself, armed with my trusty notepad. How does that sound?'

'Sounds fine to me, Gerry. I've got all the local weeklies lined up. And you'll follow everything up in the national press?'

McGhee chortled heartily. He caught the barmaid's attention once more.

'Fish 'n' chips, love. And he'll have the same.'

She turned and rolled her eyes again.

'Gerry?'

'Patience, lad. We'll see how Thursday goes and take it from there. How are you at public speaking anyway? You sure you won't shit your pants in front of all those angry people?'

'No chance. I've been president of the Students' Union for the past couple of years. I'm a natural.'

McGhee laughed out loud.

'Cocky young bastard. That's all we need, another left-wing commie in the making. I'll give you a rating for your performance.'

'Put me down for a ten.'

Another hearty laugh.

'Right, Ricky, here's your fish 'n' chips coming. And they're on a plate this time, not an old newspaper, so remember to use your cutlery. You're in the big city now, not the backwoods of deepest Ayrshire.'

'You start and I'll try to copy you.'

12

Charlie Reynolds blew a long impatient cloud of smoke up towards the fluorescent strip-light on the office ceiling. He leaned forward and stubbed out his fag-end in what remained of the cold tea lying in his Sherlock Holmes mug, the one his wife Donna had bought him twenty-two years ago in London's Oxford Street on their first ever holiday as man-and-wife.

He ripped out the sheet of paper that was curled around the mechanism of his well-worn Remington typewriter, crumpled it into a ball and chucked it into the wastepaper basket, where it immediately met the acquaintance of another half-dozen identical projectiles. For Detective Inspector Reynolds, this most certainly had not been a good day at the office. The door creaked open.

'Hey Charlie, you still here? Should you not be home sipping your Horlicks by now?'

The gruff voice belonged to his opposite number, DI Andy McTurk, who was already well into the shift that his younger colleague should have departed some two-and-a-half hours ago. 'Rockford and Columbo', the office girls called them, in deference to their respective likeness to the famous pair of American TV detectives played by the impossibly handsome James Garner and the diminutive scruff that was Peter Falk.

Reynolds's reply reeked of pure frustration.

'If I only got paid for chasing dead-ends, I'd be a bloody millionaire by now.'

'Go home, Charlie,' McTurk beseeched him, 'And pour yourself a big glass of whisky. Trust me, I've been at this game a good bit longer than you, and when your brain freezes, it freezes solid. It'll all come to you in the middle of the night, and out of nowhere. At least, that's how it works for me.'

'Okay, Inspector Columbo,' Reynolds sighed. 'You win, I'm beat.'

He pulled his feet off the desk, dragged himself up and grabbed his suit jacket from the back of his chair. DI Charlie Reynolds was renowned for being one of the sharpest-dressed guys on the force, but at quarter-to-eight on that autumn evening he looked like shit on a bad hair day.

'See you tomorrow, Andy. The middle of the night, you say?'

'Aye, the middle of the night. The missing piece of the jigsaw always comes to me in the middle of the night. And in a dream. Well, either the missing piece of the jigsaw ... or Joanna Lumley.'

Reynolds forced an exhausted laugh.

'See you in the morning, Andy.'

'No, you won't. I don't start till six at night, remember? I'll be in bed with Joanna till then.'

'Bet the poor wee lassie can't wait. I'm off, I'm knackered.'

Reynolds slipped out the back door of the Ayr police headquarters building and into the staff car park. A watery evening sun had just broken through some fast-moving clouds to shine directly onto the metallic-blue bodywork of his Mark IV Ford Cortina saloon car. Something caught his eye. It was a folded piece of paper pinned behind his windscreen wiper. Instinctively, he shot a quick look around in all directions.

Nobody. Nothing.

He lifted the washer blade and removed the offending article. Still surveying the scene in hopeful search of the shy messenger, he unlocked his car door, slumped into the driver's seat and unfolded the piece of paper. It was a note, hand-written in big bold capital letters.

ONE WORD OF ADVICE, LOVER BOY. YOU MIGHT WANT TO CHECK ON THE WELFARE OF YOUR WEE BIT ON THE SIDE. AND I WOULDN'T HANG ABOUT EITHER. HAVE A NICE EVENING.

Reynolds's eyes almost fell out of their sockets. He inhaled deeply, glanced at his wristwatch and booted the Cortina's two-litre engine into action. As his tyres screeched out of the car park, a couple of perplexed faces peered from the office windows to find out what all the fuss was about, but all they could see was the tell-tale signs of exhaust fumes and skid-marks.

It took him less than four minutes to hit the Holmston roundabout on the outskirts of Ayr, and only another twenty of the standard thirty-minute journey to his destination, raising umpteen pairs of eyebrows in the process as his car screamed through a succession of sleepy villages.

By the time he had reached Glenside, Reynolds was fully aware that he was now off-duty and well outside his allocated patch, but he couldn't have cared less. When he threw open his car door, the smell of burning rubber filled his nostrils. He bolted up the garden path and turned the handle on the front door. It refused to budge. He ran around the side of the house and tried the back door. Locked solid as well. By now on autopilot, he tensed every accessible muscle in his fifteen-stone frame and hit the door full-pelt with his shoulder. The lock burst immediately on impact. He ran through the kitchen and into the living room.

A highly-experienced and battle-hardened cop, Charlie Reynolds had witnessed many a gruesome crime scene in his time, but seldom one as graphically gut-wrenching as this. A woman's body lay prostrate on the floor, underneath the glass coffee table through which she had clearly been flung with considerable force. She was covered from head to toe in blood, much of which had already congealed a deep black-red. There were shards of glass everywhere, a number of which were embedded in her flesh, any visible bits of skin were punctuated with red weals and darkening bruises, and her face looked as if somebody had been using it as a punchbag.

Reynolds bent down, placed a couple of fingers on the lady's neck and checked her pulse. It was very weak, but at least she was still alive. He immediately radioed the emergency services for an ambulance and a police car, stating and repeating that this was now a matter of life and death.

He very carefully removed as much of the glass as he dared from the woman's head, face and torso. There were big dark bruises all over her legs, three of the fingers on her right hand had been forced back and fractured at right-angles away from her palm, and her head was visibly swollen. He stared in disbelief at her face, that beautiful face. Her nose had been broken, several front teeth were missing and the swelling and bruising were so extreme that her eyes were almost totally concealed from view. Whoever had done this had been someone who hurt people for a living. And someone who enjoyed it.

Reynolds knelt down on the floor beside the lady, cradled her in his arms and kissed her very gently on a pair of puffy lips that were bubbling with blood-soaked spittle. He whispered softly into her ear.

'It's all right Janice, I'm here with you now.'

13

Ricky kissed Iona goodnight and headed out the door of her parents'
Cumnock home. It was a much colder kiss than usual, and one
which got the response it deserved. When he reached the bus stop,
her words were still ringing in his ears, and in stereo.

'We've been going out together for five years now, Ricky, Don't
you think it's about time we started talking about ... well, you know
... about the future?'

'Soon, Iona,' he had retorted, far too quickly. 'But not now. It
just isn't the right time. I thought you understood that. It's not as if
it's the first time we've talked about it, is it?'

His business-like reply had clearly upset her, and Ricky hated
seeing Iona upset, especially when he had been the one to cause it.
However, he was convinced that now was not the time to even start
thinking about tying the knot. Sure, Iona was definitely the one, no
doubt about it, and wild horses would never tear him away from
her heavenly clutches. However, there was simply far too much
going on in his life at the moment. Firstly, he had to sort out this
Rafferty business and get his mum's life stabilised again. Secondly,
there was the small matter of a doctorate in Nuclear Physics to
negotiate. And thirdly, he had absolutely no money, at least none
that wouldn't be completely swallowed up by the extortionate cost
of living in Glasgow over the next few months.

Iona did understand, or at least so she had often tried her best to
convince him, but the truth of the matter was that she was so head-
over-heels in love with him that she couldn't even bear the thought
of another day on her own, let alone a whole academic session.
Moreover, the fear of her beloved Ricky falling into the arms of
some high-and-mighty intellectual beauty from university made her
feel physically sick to her stomach.

So, yes, the two childhood sweethearts were similarly smitten.
However, there was one essential difference. Ricky could separate
the practical from the emotional, but Iona could not. It would be a
sacrifice, he had told her, but even if it took another few months out
of their young lives, it would be one worth making. What neither
of them realised, though, was just how heavy that sacrifice would
soon turn out to be.

Ricky's journey home was an emotional blur, his innermost
feelings gyrating violently around his brain like a Christmas cake

mixture in an electric blender. However, the moment he stepped off the bus at the top of Dalblair Crescent, he could see immediately that something was very wrong and his trademark pragmatism kicked his emotions into touch. There were blue lights flashing further down the street and people scarpering around everywhere, some in police uniforms, some in medical tunics, others in everyday civvies. The big white ambulance was easy to distinguish, but why were the other emergency vehicles there as well? And more to the point, whose house had they converged upon? As Ricky's brisk march turned to a canter, he could make out two police cars? But were they outside old Mr Scobie's front door or his own? Please God, no, please not our house.

'Mum!' Ricky shouted, his canter now a lung-bursting sprint.

A burly police officer tried to grab him by the shoulders.

'Who are you, son, and what's your business here?'

'This is my house,' Ricky yelled, shoving the cop away. 'My house, so get your bloody hands off me.'

As he bolted up the garden path, another officer piped up.

'You can't go in there, son. Constable Cameron, stop him.'

When Ricky burst into the family living room, the sight that greeted him resembled a set from a Hammer horror movie. Two uniformed policemen stood there beside a tall distinguished-looking guy dressed in a dark pin-striped suit. All around lay a scene of devastation. It was as if a bomb had just been detonated. The coffee table which always had pride of place in the middle of the room was now a pitiful amalgam of splintered wood and shattered glass. Smoke billowed from the electronic innards of the television set which leaned unsteadily against the far wall, its legs buckled and broken. Shattered flower vases, china ornaments and other family keepsakes lay scattered across the floor. A framed family photograph of Davie, Janice and Ricky hung at a precarious angle from its picture-hook, its glass frame dissected by a long diagonal crack.

And then there was the blood. It was everywhere. In pools on the carpet and the linoleum, sprayed up the walls and soaked into the cloth fabric of the settee.

'Mum!' Ricky roared. 'Where's my mum?'

'She's in the ambulance, son,' the big fellow in the dark suit said. 'You must be Ricky. I'm Detective Inspector Reynolds.'

'What have you done with my mum?' Ricky demanded,

eyeballing him with deep suspicion and teetering on the brink of fury. 'Where is she?'

The plain-clothes officer immediately clocked the fire in Ricky's eyes, and took a couple of steps towards him, his left arm extended in a clear keep-the-head gesture. The rage in the youngster's cerebral pressure cooker suddenly went critical and the lid blew off. He clenched his right fist and with one mighty swing of the arm, caught Reynolds square on the jaw. As the detective careered backwards, a pair of bewildered eyes staring disbelievingly at his young long-haired assailant, the two uniformed officers rushed forward to grab Ricky and tried to wrestle him to the floor. They failed miserably. Ricky caught the first officer by his shirt collar and swung him around full circle then heaved him against the far wall, where the impact sent him crashing to his knees on the floor. The second officer afforded himself a momentary double-take before deciding that he had better show willing in the bright glare of a senior officer's presence, and he too lunged forward, only to receive a hefty kick in the groin for his trouble. As the two coppers struggled to get back to their feet and make another doomed attempt at apprehending their attacker, Reynolds had already got to his, however unsteadily.

'Leave him,' he shouted to his subordinates. 'Leave him be. I'll deal with this.'

Ricky continued standing there in the middle of the family living room with his fists clenched and eyes ablaze. Reynolds stood stalk still, both hands stretched out horizontally, appealing wordlessly for calm. He looked again at Ricky's eyes, a pair of well-stoked furnaces fed by pure oxygen. Instantly, he remembered the big film he had watched in Ayr Odeon at the weekend. It was called Straw Dogs, and it had starred Dustin Hoffman as an innocent man defending his home and family against those who would seek to destroy both. Right at that moment, Reynolds remembered how the film had ended, and he had no doubt that unless he now intervened very carefully, this incredible stand-off would end in exactly the same way. Hoffman had emerged victorious against all the odds, and this young Anderson lad would also take some stopping.

The detective put the back of his hand to his mouth and wiped a trickle blood away, then waggled his jaw from side-to-side to check that nothing was broken, other than his hard-earned dignity.

'Who taught you to punch like that?' Reynolds asked. 'Muhammed Ali?'

'My dad,' came the indignant reply.

'I want you to calm down, son ... and come with me,' Reynolds said, ushering Ricky towards the door with a wave of his hand. 'Please. I'm not telling you, I'm asking you.'

'And what if I don't?' Ricky growled.

'Then I'll stop asking you and start telling you,' Reynolds replied, his own eyes narrowing defiantly. 'And believe me son, you'll never get me with another cheap shot like that again. So, what's it to be?'

Ricky nodded and lowered his arms, then rubbed the knuckles of his right hand with the palm of his left. By the time they reached the ambulance, the back doors had just been slammed shut and the driver had already started the engine. Reynolds thumped the side of the vehicle twice with his fist. The driver wound down his window.

'Open up,' the detective commanded.

'Sir, I can't,' the ambulanceman objected. 'It's a blue-lights job.'

'Open the back doors,' Reynolds shouted. 'Just bloody do it. The boy and I are going to hospital with the patient.'

Inside, Janice Anderson was tucked up in a blanket on a stretcher, with only her face visible, assorted tubes and wires trailing from her motionless body to various mechanical contraptions which flickered and beep-beep-beeped continuously.

'I'm here, mum,' Ricky whispered into her ear, squeezing her hand. 'I'm here for you.'

Janice squeezed back. Ricky thought he detected the faintest smile, but her eyes were so badly swollen and bruised that he couldn't be sure. Fury still engulfed his soul.

'Just keep talking to her, son,' said the paramedic attending to her. 'But don't expect any response. She's in a really bad way.'

Ricky turned to Reynolds and stared him straight in the eye.

'I know who did this. It was a guy called Rafferty. Frank Rafferty. He's a businessman from Ayr. I just know it was him.'

'I know too, Ricky,' Reynolds replied, rubbing his chin. 'Your mum told me all about it, son.'

'When did she ... when did she tell you that?' Ricky enquired, his eyebrows furrowed in search of some kind of possible elucidation. 'You mean that you guys knew all along about this bastard, and you did nothing? You just let it happen?'

'No, Ricky, that wasn't it,' Reynolds went on. 'Your mum didn't report this to the police. She point-blank refused to report it. She told ... she told me.'

Ricky just looked at him, seriously perplexed. The detective took a sharp intake of breath before continuing.

'She told me … because your mum and I are … well, we're good friends. Very good friends, Ricky.'

'You mean … my mum and you …?'

'Yes, Ricky. That's exactly what I mean. And it's … well … it's a wee bit complicated.'

'Tell me. And right now.'

'I will tell you, Ricky. I will, but not in here. Walls have ears, you understand? Let's just concentrate on getting your mum into the safety of a hospital bed for now, where the medics can treat her injuries and nurse her back to health.'

'That thug Rafferty has got to be stopped.'

'Don't worry, son, we'll get him.'

'Not if I get him first. And don't call me son. Not ever. Only my dad got to call me son.'

Reynolds looked at Ricky and gave him a half-smile, half-grimace. This young lad sure had balls. However, he had something else too, something simmering away behind those big bright eyes of his. It was rage, pure unadulterated rage. He decided not to invite its re-release and instead to exercise discretion over valour.

'Yes, sir,' the detective said. 'Message received and understood.'

Ricky nodded his head. He was still in control of most of his mechanical functions, but his nostrils twitched to suggest that a much less controlled psychological process was gathering momentum and his eyes looked as if they might part company with their sockets. Like one of Ricky's beloved nuclear chain reactions, the rage was building towards criticality, only this time there were no cadmium rods on hand to control it.

God help anyone who now pushed the wrong button.

14

'Jesus Christ, Charlie, how the hell did you get mixed up in all of this?'

It was the exasperated voice of DI Andy McTurk, Charlie Reynolds's elder and opposite number. The two respected colleagues and close friends stood staring at each other in the kitchen of McTurk's two-up-and-two-down semi, a relatively humble abode for Ayr's predominantly swish suburb of Alloway.

'Smokin' Joe will have your guts for garters if he finds out. Think about it, man. One of his star detective inspectors has been found screwing the victim of a high-profile money launderer who just happens to be his own cousin. By next week you'll be walking the beat on Ayr High Street, sticking parking tickets on car windscreens. What an idiot, Charlie, what a bloody idiot. I thought you were smarter than that.'

'I didn't go out of my way looking for her, Andy. I just met her by chance one day and ... well ... you know.'

'No, Charlie, I don't bloody know. And it's none of my business either, but I'd sure as hell like to know. Have you told Donna yet?'

'Why the hell should I tell Donna? What's it got to do with her?'

'Because she's the mother of your children, Charlie, and you wouldn't want Alan and Jennifer finding out about this from the local weeklies, now would you?'

'It's got damn all to do with Donna. She was the one who left me, remember? And for that stuck-up ponce of a lawyer, McGoldrick. She's made her bed and she can bloody lie in it. I want nothing else to do with her. I'll speak to the kids when I see them next weekend. So, do me a favour, Andy. If you're not going to help, then spare me the sanctimonious lectures.'

Reynolds made for the door, but McTurk stopped him just in time by raising both hands in apology. At least, an apology of sorts.

'Okay, Charlie, okay. Let's calm down and take stock. How about a beer?'

'I don't want a bloody beer. I'm heading over to the hospital to see Janice. When she regains consciousness, I want to be the first one she talks to, not some overgrown schoolboy in a copper's uniform.'

McTurk's clumsy apology, already summarily rejected by Reynolds, didn't last long anyway. This verbal slog still had a long way to go.

'Charlie, you've got to get your arse out of there. You shouldn't have been anywhere near Glenside last night. It's away out of your jurisdiction. The Cumnock cops are dealing with it now, so you've got no further locus in the matter. Oh, and by the way, as the note on your windscreen correctly pointed out, she's just your "wee bit on the side". Remember that, Charlie. Arse out of there, and right now.'

'No, she's not, Andy.'

'No, she's not what?'

55

'No, she's not just my "wee bit on the side". She means a lot more to me than that. Janice is ... well ... a wee bit special.'

'Oh Christ, Charlie, no. Please tell me you're not in love with the wee lassie? Please.'

Silence reigned for a few moments, accompanied by blank stares. The tension in McTurk's kitchen was as thick as his old granny's homemade porridge. Finally, he spoke, only a bit more empathetically this time.

'What are you going to do, Charlie? You've got an awful lot to lose here, mate. Your career for starters, and maybe even your relationship with the kids.'

'I can't leave Janice like this, Andy. I just can't. She needs me. She's got a vicious gangster and his goons on her case. Janice needs my protection, and if it all comes out into the open ... well ... tough.'

'Leave it to the Cumnock cops, Charlie. It's not your problem.'

'It is now, Andy. I need to nail this guy. And I need your help. It's up to you. I'll understand if you want to have nothing more to do with it. Your decision, pal.'

Reynolds headed for the back door, and this time there was no stopping him.

'Of course, I'll help you,' said McTurk. 'But we'll need to watch each other's backs. This could turn nasty.'

'Thanks, Andy. That means a lot to me.'

Reynolds turned the door handle and faced McTurk, who tried to have the last word as usual.

'You're something else, Charlie, you really are. See you later, buddy.'

'Not if I see you first, you grumpy old bastard.'

15

For many years now, the resplendent old red-sandstone building that was Ayr County Hospital had claimed pride of place on the north side of Holmston Road, one of the main arterial routes leading into Ayr Railway Station and the seaside town's busy shopping thoroughfare.

It was a town immortalised in verse by Scotland's national bard, Robert Burns, one which extolled two of its all-embracing virtues:

'Auld Ayr wham ne'er a toun surpasses
For honest men an' bonnie lassies.'

The irony of the verse from the Burns' classic poem, Tam o' Shanter, which Ricky had learned to recite from beginning to end in his Higher English class at school, was certainly not lost on him that evening as he sat on a cold plastic chair beside his mother's bed in the hospital's intensive care unit.

Firstly, the Ayrshire county capital may well have been able to boast a respectable sufficiency of honest men, but Frank Rafferty sure as hell wasn't one of them. And secondly, the stunning features of the exceptionally bonnie lassie who was Janice Anderson had seen much better days, her body and face now having been mercilessly beaten to a pulp.

As Ricky held his mother's hand, he gawked in disbelief at the spaghetti-like conglomeration of wires and tubes which ran from assorted machines to various parts of her ailing body, and the once-beautiful but now battered face which he prayed silently would someday soon be miraculously restored to its former glories. The garish blue-white glare from the ward's fluorescent strip-lights had somehow managed to accentuate the horror of Janice's multiple injuries, but it was the clinical artificiality of the click-clicks and beep-beeps from the various life-support machines and the whoosh-whoosh of Janice's respirator that contrived to make Ricky feel so utterly helpless.

A deep voice broke the spell and made the normally placid university student jump with a start.

'Hi Ricky. How's she doing?'

Ricky turned in the direction of the voice. It belonged to the big cop, the one whose elegant pin-striped suit of the night before had now been replaced by a pair of light-blue denims and a black sweatshirt. The one whose ruggedly handsome face he had smashed with his own fist.

'I'm Charlie Reynolds. Remember?'

'Aye, I remember,' came the curt reply.

'What are the medics saying, Ricky? And don't worry, I won't call you "son" again. I wouldn't dare.'

'I spoke to the consultant about twenty minutes ago. My mum's still in a coma. She's had scans and X-rays and God knows how many tests. Too early to tell whether she'll ever wake up again, or if she's suffered irreparable brain damage. Or if she does wake up, whether she'll ever be able to walk or even talk. She's got a broken jaw, she's lost three teeth and the hospital dentist removed another three. Her right arm is broken, four of her fingers too, and she's in plaster up to the shoulder. She's got two broken ribs, and the surgeons have just removed her spleen. She lost four pints of blood, but they eventually managed to stop the internal bleeding, and she's now on umpteen drips and drugged to the eyeballs. Apart from that, she's absolutely brand-new.'

Charlie Reynolds closed his eyes and shook his head, before grabbing a chair and sitting himself down at the other side of Janice's hospital bed. He reached out to hold her hand, then saw the plaster. He leaned forward and kissed her gently on the cheek. Ricky visibly squirmed and turned away. Charlie looked straight at him and didn't flinch.

'How are you doing yourself, Ricky?'

'Me? Oh, I'm fine. But I'll be a lot better when I'm finished with that bastard, Rafferty. Or are you going to lecture me about leaving it all in the capable hands of your cop pals? If so, save your breath, because I wouldn't trust you guys with my granny's purse.'

Charlie Reynolds stifled a laugh. This lad of Janice's had all the guts and resilience of an alligator.

'No Ricky, I'm not going to lecture you, not at all, but I do think we need a wee chat about things. Don't you agree?'

Ricky just stared straight through the big policeman with a forensic gaze which had the immediate effect of unnerving him. There was something very different about this young man. He exuded a real presence, a strange aura. It was as if he knew exactly what Charlie was thinking.

The ward door opened with an eerie creak and in walked a small well-dressed, bespectacled gentleman with a stethoscope draped over his narrow shoulders. His sharp words smacked of authority and radiated a clear expectation that he would be obeyed without question.

'Right, I wish to examine my patient, so I need you both to leave at once.'

As they rose to their feet, the big cop piped up.

'Excuse me doctor, I'm Detective Inspector Reynolds of Southwest Scotland Police. As you can see, I'm off-duty at the moment, but I wondered if I could possibly ask you a couple of brief questions?'

The consultant was clearly irritated by such wanton non-compliance.

'Two police officers interviewed me this afternoon and I told them all I could. So, if you'll excuse me, I need to tend to my patient right away.'

'Two questions, doctor. Both very brief, but they're important.'

'Okay, if you must, but please be quick about it.'

'Mrs Anderson's son here told me that she has a broken jaw. Which jaw is it?'

'The right jaw.'

'And two broken ribs. Left or right side?'

'Right.'

'Thank you, doctor.'

Ricky gently squeezed his mother's hand once more and kissed her on the forehead, then followed the detective out of the room.

'Cup of tea, Ricky? We can go to the hospital canteen.'

'No thanks.'

'Can I buy you a pint in the Market Inn, then? It's just a couple of hundred yards along the road.'

'I know where it is.'

'One pint. Ten minutes of your time, that's all.'

'Ten minutes and I'm off. I want to get back to my mum's bedside as soon as possible.'

'Agreed.'

As the student and the off-duty detective began marching briskly along the neon-lit pavement of Holmston Road, it was the former who broke the uneasy silent tension that hung in the evening air like a cloud of leaked gamma radiation.

'Why did you ask the consultant which jaw was broken. And ribs too?'

'Because I wanted to know whether your mum's assailant was right-handed or left-handed. And since the breaks were to her right jaw and right ribs, then he must have been left-handed.'

Ricky shuddered at the horrific mental vision which assaulted his senses. The detective pushed open the pub door.

'Name your poison, Ricky.'

'Lager.'

Reynolds bought two pints of lager and carried them over to a table at the far side of the dartboard, where two scruffily-dressed, thirty-something guys were engaged in a heated arithmetical argument concerning which double the shorter one should be trying to hit.

'Cheers,' Reynolds said, raising his glass. 'And here's to your

59

mum's full recovery.'

Before Ricky could reciprocate, there came a roar from the taller guy at the dartboard, who had obviously just nicked the spoils. As his smug grin met his opponent's furious glare, his eyes drifted towards Reynolds.

'Bad smell in here tonight, Barney,' he said. 'Have you noticed?'

'Aye, Tam,' the other one replied. 'Smells like a pigsty, doesn't it? Must be a pig in here somewhere.'

Reynolds sat his pint down on the table, leaned back in his chair and smiled at them. It was a smile that radiated much more menace than nicety. The three-way staring match instantly reminded Ricky of a famous scene from his favourite western, *The Good, The Bad and The Ugly*, and no doubt about it, Reynolds had assumed the Clint Eastwood role. He could see the other two begin to crumble already.

'Listen, lads,' the detective said in a near whisper. 'I'm in here having a quiet pint with my friend and I really don't want to be disturbed. So, you've got two choices. Either you shift your arses over there to the other side of the bar and I'll leave you in peace, or you can pick a window because you'll be leaving. I'll count to three, and I won't be saying two-and-a-half.'

The two guys immediately collapsed under the big detective's unflinching glare. They exchanged a tell-tale glance and shuffled off with their tails wedged firmly between their legs, muttering inaudible expletives.

'So, what was all that about?' asked Ricky.

'Nothing really,' Reynolds replied. 'Just the perks of the job. Two ex-cons who always forget to send me a Christmas card. All mouth and no action. Housebreakers who would shit their pants if the family dog barked at them.'

Ricky was impressed but determined not to show it. He swiftly shifted the conversation back to his mother's predicament.

'So, now you know that the guy who beat up my mum is left-handed. Where does that leave us, then?'

'Frank Rafferty didn't do this himself. Rafferty is right-handed.'

'Well, if it wasn't Rafferty, then who was it?'

'My guess is that it was one of his heavies, a well-known hoodlum from Prestwick called Robert McDaid. McDaid is left-handed. His pet name is "Mad Rab" and he loves it. He also loves hurting people. He gets a kick out of it. Women are his speciality.'

Ricky closed his eyes as the vision returned, this time in glorious technicolour.

'How could anyone ever do anything like that?' he asked, staring at the wooden rafters on the pub ceiling. 'And especially to a woman?'

The off-duty detective smiled a mischievous little smile.

'That's a bit rich coming from you, isn't it? I'll cite this bruise on my jaw as evidence. My sources tell me that you've sorted a few out yourself in your time, Ricky.'

'Aye ... well, maybe so. But at least all of them were men. And they all had it coming.'

'I didn't have it coming, Ricky. I was just doing my job, that's all.'

'Aye well, maybe.'

'Was that an apology?'

'It's as near to an apology as you'll ever get.'

'I want you to leave this to us, Ricky. You can't get involved with Rafferty. He's bad news.'

'I could take him, no problem.'

'Well maybe you could, and maybe you couldn't. But you certainly couldn't take all of them. And even if you did take Rafferty, you'd then be a target as well as your mum. It would be one of those vendettas that would never end. It would just continue to escalate ... until ... well, let's not even go there.'

'No, not if I took Rafferty out. He would lose face and his puppets would lose respect for him. My dad taught me a very important lesson when I was a wee boy. If you're ever confronted by a gang, always go for the big guy. Take out the big guy and you take out the gang. It always worked for me. Go for the big guy, the bully. In this case, Rafferty himself.'

'I know what a great man your dad was, Ricky. Your mum has told me all about him. She misses him really badly.'

'So, what does she see in you, then? My dad was twice the man you'll ever be.'

'Maybe so, Ricky ... maybe so. But I've become very fond of your mum, very fond of her indeed. And it's now over eight years since your dad passed away, so don't you think she has the right to meet someone else ... to move on with her life?'

Ricky's laser gaze seared once more into the big cop's eyes.

'Are you married?'

'Yes, my wife's called Donna. We've got two children, Alan and Jennifer, both now left home. Alan's at college, Jennifer works as a sales rep for Marks and Spencer. Donna's left home too, Ricky. For a guy called Sandy McGoldrick. He's a good five years younger than me, he's absolutely loaded and he's a complete dick.'

Ricky stifled a giggle.

'So, what's the story with you and my mum, then? Wee bit on the side?'

The warmth on the detective's face disappeared like dishwater down a plughole.

'Right, Ricky. I've spent the last few minutes listening to your self-righteous remarks, but don't ever talk to me like that again. And while we're at it, don't ever speak so disrespectfully about your mum again, either. Got it?'

Ricky hadn't seen that one coming, and he immediately felt rather silly about the infantile remarks he had been spewing all over Reynolds.

'Sorry, I was out of order there.'

'Yes, you were, you certainly were.'

Ricky extended the hand of friendship and Reynolds accepted it. It was the latter who next spoke.

'You want to hear the story, then? Warts and all?'

Ricky nodded, more respectfully this time.

'I met your mum at a training course in Heathfield Hospital. It was a multi-disciplinary course on domestic abuse, and it was being run for teachers, social workers and medical staff. I was one of the speakers, since I've had a lot of training and involvement as a police officer in dealing with cases of domestic violence. We got talking over a cup of coffee and I asked her if she'd like to go out for a drink some evening.'

'Why?' asked Ricky, looking puzzled.

'Because I liked her,' Reynolds replied with an amused grin. 'She's a lovely person, and I don't know if you've noticed, Ricky, but she's not bad looking either. Good God, man, do I need to spell it out?'

'So why didn't she tell me herself, then?'

'She was going to tell you, Ricky, but she wanted to do it in her own time. She said that there was a lot going on in your life at the moment, and she didn't want to complicate things any further.'

'So, you've been going out with her, then? For how long? To

hotels and places like that? Or back to your place?'

'Nothing like that, Ricky. A drink in the Finlayson Arms in Coylton and then a meal in the Malin Court near Turnberry, that's about it. In fact, when I come to think about it, it's none of your bloody business. You've probably done a hell of a lot more with that wee lassie of yours, the one your mum seems to like so much. In fact, when she was washing your jeans the other day, a packet of condoms fell out of the pocket. Bet she didn't tell you that, did she?'

Ricky's mouth fell open.

'You're bloody joking, man?'

'Aye, of course I'm joking. But at least I now know that you and that wee lassie are doing the business, so don't lecture me about my morals.'

Seriously wrong-footed, Ricky just blew a big sigh of relief and smiled.

'You fairly got me there, detective.'

'Aye,' replied Reynolds. 'I'm the man. And don't you forget it.'

Gales of laughter. For Ricky Anderson and Charlie Reynolds, a friendship had just been born. And it was a friendship that would matter.

16

It was hardly shaping into a great day for young Ricky Anderson.

With a mere four days left to recover from his strenuous exertions at the brickworks and unwind before tackling the final lap of a highly challenging course of academic study at university, a really frenetic and potentially explosive next few hours lay ahead. The much-revered and now retired local bobby, Sergeant Malcolm Geddes, had once told a then-fourteen-year-old Ricky Anderson that he was 'a right tough wee bugger' after witnessing him thump the living daylights out of Glenside bully, David 'Dandy' McTear. Today of all days, though, that famed toughness would be put to the test like never before.

First, there was the relatively straightforward matter of shopping for the messages and getting the basic housework done while the lady of the house lay in a coma on a life support machine. Next, Ricky would need to catch a bus and head for Ayr, where he would join Gerry McGhee for a pint in Rabbie's Bar in Burns Statue Square, before meeting up with Iona and heading for Ayr County

Hospital to see his mum. Then, he would chaperone Iona back onto the bus to Cumnock and get himself a quiet corner in the bar of the Station Hotel, where he would grab some grub and prepare for the day's main event, the big public meeting in the Council Chambers. Thereafter, he would have a brief get-together with Gerry and the local journalists in the grand ornate foyer of County Buildings, to brief them on his plan of action. Finally, he would slip into the midst of the angry throngs and pick his moment to ambush Councillor Edwin Monk, and handcuff his questionable practices to his notorious accomplice, Frank Rafferty.

All that then remained for Ricky would be to watch the sparks fly and read the headlines in Friday morning's *Glasgow Herald* and the local weekly newspapers. Bring it on.

Gerry McGhee was already sitting at a table in the far corner of Rabbie's Bar, pint in hand, when Ricky walked in. The place was busy for a Thursday lunchtime, with the majority of its customers gathered around the bar area, necking their jugs of assorted draught beers and puffing on their fags as they noisily debated those twin evils, politics and football. The buxom lady behind the bar clocked Ricky immediately and gave him the 'come on' stare while she chomped on her chewing gum and poured her latest pint. He averted his eyes and bustled his way past the frenetic discourse to make his way towards McGhee.

'What are you after, then, Captain Marvel?' the investigative journalist enquired with a smile.

'Just a soft drink, Gerry,' Ricky replied. 'A coke will be fine.'

'A coke? And here was I thinking that you student types were all budding alcoholics?'

'Nah, you must be thinking about newspaper hacks. I've got a big day ahead of me.'

McGhee chortled, handed Ricky a beige folder and made his way to the bar.

'Have a wee look at that while you're salivating about your fizzy drink.'

McGhee returned with Ricky's coke and another pint of lager. He opened a packet of salt-and-vinegar crisps and spread them out on the table.

'Where the hell did you get all this stuff, Gerry?' Ricky enquired, nodding in bemusement at the contents of folder.

'I'm the man,' McGhee retorted with a smug smile.

'Not you as well?' Ricky remarked, recalling his conversation with Charlie Reynolds the previous night. 'Can I use it? All of it?'

'Well, yes ... and no.'

'Translate please, Gerry?'

'If you use it to accuse this guy Monk, his lawyers will come after you with all they've got. And if you can't substantiate whatever you accuse him of, which incidentally you can't, they'll have you for defamation.'

'And what is defamation when it's at home?'

'Defamation is the term used in the Scottish law courts for what would be known elsewhere as libel or slander. Broadly speaking, the delict of defamation occurs when one person makes a communication, written or verbal or otherwise, which contains a damaging and untrue imputation against the reputation of another person.'

'I thought you were a newshound, not a bloody lawyer?'

'I told you, son. I'm the man.'

'So, if I can't use this stuff because it will get me into trouble with the law, why show it to me at all?'

'Because you don't need to accuse. You just need to be smart. All you do is set some hares running and the rest will look after itself.'

'But how ... how do I do that without ...'

'Look Ricky, this public meeting tonight ... there will be dozens of people in that big hall, right?'

'Right. Maybe even a lot more than dozens, I'm hoping.'

'Right, then. You don't accuse Monk of anything. All you do is ask him a few questions. Start with some fairly innocent stuff, then crank up the pressure. Just let the audience draw their own conclusions. And don't worry about who said what, or Monk's people accusing you of accusing him, or any shite like that. I'll be recording the whole shooting match on my Dictaphone. Most of the other journalists will probably be doing the same. Ask questions, Ricky, but do not accuse!'

'Thanks for doing this for me, Gerry.'

'It's a pleasure. Those two low-lives deserve everything that's coming to them. Go get 'em, son!'

'And Gerry, one other thing.'

'What's that?'

'Don't call me son. Ever.'

'Okay, Captain Marvel.'

Ricky gulped back what was left of his coke, stood up and shook McGhee's hand.

'See you tonight, then?'

'Yip. I'll be the ugly one, remember?'

'How could I forget? I have nightmares thinking about you.'

17

By the time the double-decker bus had passed Ayr's celebrated Gaiety Theatre, Iona was already standing right at the door. Even after five years, she was still every bit as excited about seeing Ricky as she had been on the day they had first clapped eyes on each other on the school stairwell.

When she alighted at the Wellington Street bus depot, two male twenty-somethings waiting to board began giving her the lecherous once-over. Ricky stepped forward, took Iona's hand and gave her new admirers the death stare. Both pairs of eyes immediately began to search for something else to focus upon, anything at all. That trademark stare always seemed to have the effect of converting cocky bravado to shivering jelly.

Ten minutes later, Ricky and Iona were at Janice Anderson's bedside. The moment Iona saw Janice lying there beaten and bruised in her hospital bed, she was powerless to stop herself bursting into tears. Holding Janice's hand in her own, she leaned over and kissed her on the forehead.

'Oh, Janice,' she sobbed. 'How could anyone ever do this to you?'

And that was when Janice smiled. Iona didn't see it, but Ricky did.

'Mum?' he whispered. 'Mum, can you hear me?'

She smiled again, a very faint smile, but a smile nevertheless. Suddenly, Iona jumped.

'Ricky, she squeezed my hand.'

'Mum, it's me,' he whispered, leaning forward. 'It's Ricky. And Iona is here too. Can you hear me?'

Janice's lips began to twitch. She tried to speak, but no words came out. Ricky shot to his feet as a young nurse walked past.

'Nurse, can you get the doctor, please? And quickly?'

A couple of minutes later, Ricky and Iona had been ushered out of the ward and the curtains were being drawn all around Janice's bed to allow the duty registrar some privacy to examine her patient. As they sat hand-in-hand in silence on a couple of plastic chairs in the hospital corridor, their ten-minute wait felt like a life sentence in some God-forsaken foreign jail.

A pair of dainty feet began clip-clopping along the tiled floor, the metronomic sound becoming progressively louder as they approached. They belonged to a slim and pleasant-faced young lady whose auburn-coloured hair looked as if it had been piled up into its bun in far too much of hurry. She was smiling warmly.

'Hello. You must be Mr Anderson?'

'Yes?'

'I'm Doctor Galbraith and I have some good news for you. Your mother's condition has now resolved.'

'Resolved? Sorry ... what? What does that mean?'

'She's now out of her coma, Mr Anderson. She has regained consciousness. You can go back in and see her now, if you like.'

Ricky sprang to his feet. Iona did likewise and wrapped her arm around his waist.

'Just don't expect too much for the moment,' the young doctor counselled. 'She's been through an awful ordeal, and it will all take time.'

'Will she be okay, though, doctor? I mean, will she make a full recovery? Or any ... any permanent damage? Like, you know, brain damage ... that sort of thing?'

'Much too early to tell, but the signs are encouraging. She'll need a lot of rest and a great deal of support in her rehabilitation. Why don't you just go in and see her for yourself? I think you'll be pleasantly surprised.'

'Come on, Ricky,' said Iona, nudging him forward. 'It'll be all right.'

Janice's head was propped up on a pillow. She was smiling a forced smile. Both eyes were open, but they were little more than narrow slits camouflaged by heavily swollen sockets merging with black-and-blue cheeks. Her lips moved and a few laboured words escaped from bubbles of spittle.

'How's my big boy, then?' she mumbled. 'And how's my wee girl?'

Gentle hugs and tears of relief followed, as the process of recuperation finally got underway, the most important thing in Ricky's world right now. However, another process was about to spring into action as well, and it was so close that he could taste it. The process of settling the scores with perpetrator and puppet.

18

Ricky sat hunched over a cluttered table in Ayr's Station Hotel bar, right underneath the wall-mounted television set.

On the screen, glamorous presenter Viv Lumsden was busily waxing lyrical about the UK government's long-awaited Kilbrandon Report being almost ready for release, the one which many Scots hoped would signal the establishment of a directly-elected Scottish Assembly. However, the delectable Ms Lumsden's tidings of great promise simply wafted past young Ricky's ears, as he flicked through the pages of Gerry McGhee's dossier while making a few hasty scribbles on his notepad.

'Scampi-in-the-basket, sir?'

Ricky looked up, irritated by the unwelcome interruption. A plump, pleasant-faced young lady stood there brandishing his evening meal, and irritation quickly turned to anticipation. Ricky was famished, and the classic 1970s' pub-grub dish was just the ticket.

'Thanks,' he replied with a grateful smile, before eyeballing his scampi-and-chips with considerable fervour. 'Could I have some tomato sauce, please?'

'I'll see what I can do,' the waitress replied, fluttering her eyelids willingly.

Ricky giggled quietly as he began delving into his dinner. The waitress's welcoming smile could go and take a hike, Iona was safe enough. As he waded into his food, he kept fingering his way through the various documents, spreadsheets and newspaper clippings that McGhee had sourced for him. If the scampi-in-the-basket was proving to be a definite hit, then the journalist's veritable treasures were pure dynamite.

Half-an-hour later, Ricky paid his bill to the girl with the still-fluttering eyelids and gave her a generous 20-pence tip, considerably more than the standard ten-per-cent of the meal price, before setting off on foot for the moment of truth. The big public meeting.

The early-evening air was crisp and cool. Ricky decided to make his way down to the seafront venue via Ayr High Street. As he passed the Ayrshire and Galloway Hotel, he noticed that the normally bustling main drag ahead was eerily quiet. He stopped momentarily outside Hourston's, one of the town's longest-established clothes shops, to cast an envious eye over a black leather jacket that had been rather carelessly draped over a male mannequin whose plastic shoulders were much too flimsy to do it justice, and silently promised to treat himself to such classy attire the moment his first salary cheque arrived from his first paid job in a career which would be dedicated to propagating nuclear chain reactions for the good of humankind.

The first significant sign of life in the High Street came from the Tam o' Shanter pub on his right, where the jukebox was doing its best to drown out the rabble inside, but failing miserably on account of the latest patron's rather tame choice of music, young American crooner Donnie Osmond's canny rendition of 'Puppy Love'. Ricky's journey on foot then took him past Marks & Spencer, British Home Stores and Woolworth's, and along the Sandgate towards the seaside town's sprawling Low Green, beside which stood the grand old County Buildings themselves.

A shiver ran up his spine, not of fearful apprehension but of wicked excitement. The food was in the fridge, the housework done, his homework too, Janice and Iona were safe, and his belly was full of scampi and butterflies the size of sea-eagles. Soon, it would be showtime.

Bring it on.

19

By quarter-past-seven, Charlie Reynolds was back at Janice Anderson's hospital bedside, this time adorned again in his dark Ralph Slater suit. He sat down, took her good hand in his and kissed her softly on her lips.

'Does Ricky know, Charlie?' Janice whispered through laboured breath. 'About us, I mean?'

'Yes, he does, Janice,' the big cop said. 'I told him last night.'

Janice closed her eyes and sighed.

'Okay, then. How did he take it?'

'Badly at first. He hit me with a lot of stuff about his dad, then questioned my motives, but he eventually came around. I think Ricky and I are going to be all right, Janice. He's a feisty young lad. I wonder where he gets that from?'

'You don't really know me, Charlie. We've only just met each other.'

'I feel I've known you all my life.'

Janice's eyes glazed over. Charlie leaned over and held her as tightly as he dared.

'I'll be here for you,' he said, looking directly into her puffy eyes. 'I'll sort this all out, I promise you. And that young man of yours will be here for you too.'

'And Iona as well, Charlie. She's an angel.'

'I've never met Iona.'

'You will.'

Charlie sat stroking her hair like a toddler pampering a new puppy. Just at that, a nurse appeared on the scene, accompanied by two uniformed police officers, a sergeant and his duty constable. It was the nurse who spoke first.

'How are you feeling tonight, Mrs Anderson? Do you feel up to speaking to Sergeant Mackay and Constable Harris?'

'No, she doesn't, nurse,' replied the Detective Inspector. 'She's not well enough yet.'

'Hello sir,' the sergeant said, addressing Reynolds directly, if in a rather tentative fashion. 'I don't know if you remember me, but I was in your team during the murder investigation down in Girvan a few years ago. Sergeant Mackay?'

'Of course, I remember you. How are you doing, Jimmy? You look well.'

'Fine sir, fine, and so do you. As you'll be aware, the Cumnock police are now handling Mrs Anderson's case and Inspector Henderson has instructed us to get a statement from her as soon as she's well enough to give us one.'

'Well, she's not well enough yet, Jimmy, so just go back and tell Jock Henderson that he'll be the first to know when she is.'

'But sir, she looks as if she's well enough to speak to you. And more to the point, do you mind me asking why she's speaking to you at all? We're handling this now, not the Ayr branch.'

'I'm a friend of the family, that's why. Mrs Anderson and I have just been chatting. Chatting about the price of groceries these days.'

'Oh, come on, sir, we've got a job to do, and ...'

'Well, go and do it, Jimmy. But not here, not yet, she's not ready.'

'But sir ...'

'On your bike, sergeant. Discussion over.'

70

The two uniformed officers nodded politely, stuck their helmets back on their heads and marched sheepishly out of the ward. Janice Anderson smiled through the pain.

'So, you're a big bossy-boots, then, Inspector Reynolds?'

'Only when the occasion demands,' he replied.

'I'll look forward to occasions like that, then,' Janice teased.

Reynolds felt his blood stirring, but not in an unpleasant way. He hardly knew this woman. One drink in a local pub, one meal in a pleasant restaurant and a couple of nervous snogs in the front seat of a Ford Cortina, and that was about it. And yet, there was something really special happening here.

Charli Reynolds knew it. And so too did Janice Anderson.

20

Ricky Anderson thanked Gerry McGhee and the three local journalists who had come along to the public meeting, then made his way from the foyer of County Buildings up the grand spiral staircase to the first floor, where the Council Chambers lay in wait for the gathering throngs.

The others followed a discrete distance behind, to avoid displaying any overt semblance of cosy collaboration. In the murky world of journalism, forewarned was forearmed, and those guys had never been better briefed in their entire careers. Sparks would soon fly, and the assorted front pages had been well-and-truly held. For the enterprising hacks, two seedy characters were about to get their come-uppance at long last, and everyone wanted a front-row seat when the shit hit the fan.

As for McGhee himself, somewhat larger audiences beckoned for his latest good-over-evil project. His parting words to Ricky had really annoyed him, not so much for their sage advisory intention, but for their irksome repetition. Ever since their meeting in Rabbie's Bar earlier that same afternoon, the investigative journalist's central message had sounded like a stuck vinyl record.

'Now, remember, Ricky. Don't accuse, just ask questions.'

'Got it, Gerry, got it,' young Ricky had snapped at the foot of the staircase. 'I'm not bloody deaf.'

'Right then, go get 'em, son,' McGhee had responded mischievously, to wind him up him further and stoke up the fire already raging in his belly.

By 7.28 p.m., over a hundred local people had taken their seats in the public gallery of the Council Chambers, and they were still pouring in. Ricky remained standing, carefully surveying the scene to choose his best vantage point. Experience of student union politics had taught him that most effective 'agitators' tended to position themselves in the midst of the audience at a public meeting, rather than at the very back or very front, so he calmly wandered into the centre of the sixth row and sat himself down, *aide memoire* notes at the ready.

A few moments before the designated witching hour of half-past-seven, three individuals slunk their way rather self-consciously up the centre aisle and took their seats at the elevated top table. The silence in the hall was so deafening that Ricky could hear his own heartbeat.

It was the short, rotund, middle-aged chap with the ruddy complexion who rose to address his audience.

'Good evening, ladies and gentlemen, and thank you all for giving up your valuable time this evening to come along and hear the council's presentation on the Sandbank housing development.'

He waited for the customary round of polite applause. He could have waited till the cows came home. Anxiously, he pressed on.

'My name is Councillor Edwin Monk, and I am the Chairman of Southwest Scotland Council's Planning Committee. On my right here is David McPherson, our Director of Planning who will begin by giving you a brief presentation on the development proposal, while on my left is my secretary Carol McCreadie, who will be taking detailed notes of all the comments we receive tonight.'

Monk stopped again to await respectful applause. Instead, all he got was a stony silence, save for the shuffling of a few impatient feet. He cleared his throat, the one which Ricky and a fair proportion of the audience might happily have throttled. He then turned towards his right-hand man with a gesture of invitation.

'Mister McPherson.'

Clearly not looking forward to the evening's imminent exchanges, the Director of Planning rose to his feet rather apologetically. He was in his late 'forties, tall, slim and well-dressed in a brown three-piece suit with a matching shirt and 'kipper' tie, as was very much the fashion. When he spoke, his voice shook perceptibly, but his professionalism managed to let him force the words out.

'Good evening, ladies and gentlemen. I'm going to give you a short presentation on the proposed Sandbank housing development, which received outline approval from the council back in June of this year.'

With the high-tech media of laptops, Power Point and other assorted electronic aids still many years away from invention, McPherson wandered across to his overhead projector and placed his first plastic slide on the glass screen.

Suddenly, an impatient voice resounded from the back of the hall.

'Get on with it, man. We're here to ask questions, and you're here to answer them. We know fine well what your plans are, so the last thing we need is a bloody presentation.'

'Sir,' the Director protested, 'I understand that you might know about the general plan for Sandbank, but others present here tonight may not. And even for those of you who do, I just thought that a bit more meat on the bones might be helpful.'

'Well, you thought wrong,' the same guy continued, clearly very irritated. 'We've already had your letters and your leaflets stuffed through our letterboxes, so we're all well aware of what the developer intends to do. What we want to hear tonight is whether or not the Council is actually going to allow this abomination to happen. We were promised a recreational facility on the shorefront in Sandbank after the maternity hospital was shut, not 136 big fancy houses. So, we don't need your presentation, we need answers to our questions.'

Ricky chortled silently as a rumble of discontent slowly built up a head of steam. As he looked around a vast hall full of heads shaking and mouths tut-tutting, he spotted a familiar sight. There against the far wall sat a stocky-built, suntanned, middle-aged man with long oily hair. It was Frank Rafferty, no doubt about it, not only the would-be Sandbank property developer himself, but also the thug who had bullied and manhandled Ricky's own mother, then deployed one of his brain-dead neds to beat her half to death. When their eyes met, Ricky's blood began to boil. Rafferty was completely unprepared for the searing stare that radiated towards him, and quickly turned away to break eye contact.

It was Monk's next words which snapped Ricky from his trance, as the Chairman rose to his feet in support of his highest-paid minion.

'I hear what you are saying, sir. However, ladies and gentlemen,

73

can you please allow my Director to proceed with his presentation without any further interruptions? Once he has finished, we can then take all your questions and comments. Okay?'

'No, it's not okay,' another irate voice piped up, a young lady this time. 'The gentleman at the back has just told you. We don't need your presentation and we don't want it. We know what your plans are. What we want to know is if you, Councillor Monk, and your fellow councillors are really going to let this housing development proceed after all the promises you made. So, come on, we're all busy people, let's have answers to our questions.'

'Exactly,' shouted another woman in the second-front row. 'Open up the floor to our questions.'

That was followed by a gruff, 'Get on with it, Monk,' from an elderly gentleman near the rear of a gathering which by this time was beginning to get very restless.

'Okay, then,' said Monk, raising both hands in reluctant acceptance of his audience's demands. 'We'll do it your way. David, just sit back down, please.'

The Director of Planning shuffled back to the top table and slipped uneasily into his seat. Carol McCreadie, the Chairman's secretary, chewed her index finger nervously.

Monk stood up again.

'First question, then? And could I please ask you to raise your hand, rather than just shout out?'

There followed a series of searching questions from an animated audience, every one of which Monk batted towards his Director to provide a response. All were met with a hostile reaction. Three times Monk had to ask for 'a little bit of decorum, please', in a laughable attempt to retrieve some semblance of control over a meeting which was rapidly descending into complete farce.

Ricky smelt blood and decided that the time was now ripe to seize his opportunity. As the insults careered back and forth like battered tennis balls in a Wimbledon final, he calmly rose to his feet and just stood there, stalk-still. Monk spotted the fresh-faced young man immediately and latched onto him in forlorn hope that his comparative youth might somehow herald a less challenging question. More fool, he.

'Yes, son?' the chairman said, pointing his finger straight at him. 'Do you have a question?'

Monk's use of the word 'son' was hardly a good start. Ricky

grimaced, but managed to bite his lip. He continued standing without saying a single word, as the heads began to turn in his direction. Gradually, the widespread rumbles subsided until they receded into silence. With all eyes by now staring in intrigue at this rather dashing young man, he finally spoke in a soft voice.

'Good evening, Mister Chairman,' he said.

Looking around the room, he then addressed the whole gathering.

'And good evening, ladies and gentlemen. My name is Richard Anderson and I hope my contribution might prove helpful to you this evening.'

Ricky's eyes again met those of Rafferty, who took a sharp intake of breath as he clocked the connection. As cool as one of the seaside town's famed ice lollipops, Ricky continued.

'I have a number of questions for you, Mister Chairman. Let's start with an easy one, shall we? Could you please tell me the name of the developer for the Sandbank housing project?'

'The developer is Rafferty Construction,' the chairman replied with a smug grin. 'They won the contract, son, as I'm sure most people in here will already be aware.'

Murmurs of disquiet rumbled once more. Ricky soldiered on.

'Thank you, sir, and I'd be grateful if you don't call me son. I'm a 21-year-old man, and I find your use of the term both patronising and condescending. Can I ask you if Rafferty Construction has a representative present here tonight?'

Monk took a moment to consider where this line of questioning might be leading.

'Eh ... well, yes ... I think there might be a company representative here.'

'Excellent,' said Ricky. 'Could you please identify him, then, Mister Chairman? Or if you can't, perhaps he might identify himself? I'm sure your audience would like to know exactly who the developer is.'

A ripple of applause quickly built to a crescendo of approval. Monk froze, clearly unsure how next to proceed. He exchanged nervous whispers with McPherson before responding.

'I'm sorry, but the council's standing orders preclude anyone who is neither a council member nor a paid council official from participating in a formal council presentation without this first having been formally sanctioned by the council itself.'

Mutterings of deep irritation rumbled from the audience like fast-approaching thunder. Ricky raised both hands in a 180-degree sweep to appeal again for silence, got it instantly, then turned back to face Monk.

'Mister Chairman, I'm not asking the company's representative to make a formal presentation. I'm merely asking you to point him out, that's all. I'm sure everyone would just like to know what someone who wants to replace a maternity hospital with 136 big swanky houses actually looks like.'

Laughter rippled out from the audience. Monk directed a shaky finger in the general direction of Rafferty, who by this time was sitting with his arms folded in front of him so defensively that he might as well have been accused of shoplifting from Woolworths.

'I believe that the gentleman over there is the company's Managing Director. I believe that is Mister Frank Rafferty.'

Rafferty just sat there, his eyes ablaze, the fire directed at Monk, at Ricky and at everyone else in the room for that matter, particularly those dimwits who had just laughed at his expense. Did they not realise that they were in the presence of entrepreneurism at its finest?

'You believe, Mister Chairman?' Ricky continued. 'You believe that might be Mister Rafferty?'

'Yes, as far as I'm aware,' Monk muttered.

'As far as you're aware?' enquired Ricky. 'And as far as you're aware, Mister Chairman, did you and your wife spend a total of three separate holidays in the past year with Mister Rafferty and his wife in his villa in northern France?'

Communal gasps of incredulity from the public gallery. Heads spinning as disbelieving gazes shot from Monk to Rafferty and back again. Ricky ploughed on, intent on going for the jugular.

'Well, Mister Chairman? Did you, or did you not enjoy three foreign holidays with Mister Rafferty in France last year? As far as you're aware, that is?'

More laughter, only this time bordering on outrage, as Monk squirmed tight-lipped in the hot seat.

'I'll take that as a "yes", then?' Ricky continued. 'So, let me ask you this, Mister Chairman. Who paid for those three holidays? Bearing in mind, of course, that as an elected member your expenses are subject to public scrutiny?'

The gasps and mutterings increased in volume and intensity.

'This is outrageous,' Monk shouted above the rabble. 'You're out of order, young man, making accusations like that.'

'I haven't accused you of anything, Mister Chairman,' Ricky replied, displaying all the calmness of a wise old grandfather. 'I've just asked you two simple questions. And now, if you don't mind, I'd like some answers. As I'm sure your audience would as well.'

Monk just sat there grimacing amid the galloping hubble-bubble. As Ricky waited for order, the cacophony of chatter from a bemused audience receded once more to an intrigued hush. Monk spat out his next few words with venom.

'I would advise you to sit back down, young man,' he said. 'Before you say something you regret.'

'Life is too short for regrets, Mister Chairman,' Ricky replied, smiling. 'Perhaps it might help if I expanded on my questions. You will remember that there were two of them. First question. Did you, or did you not spend three separate holidays in the past year with Mister Rafferty in his property in northern France? Mister Rafferty, in your own words, being the Managing Director of the construction company which has been awarded the contract for building the Sandbank housing development approved by the council's Planning Committee, that committee serving under your chairmanship. Second question. Who paid the bill for those three holidays?'

Monk shot to his feet, shaking his head in exasperation. Eventually, words came stammering out.

'I refuse ... I refuse to answer such ... such ridiculous questions. Sit down, lad, or I'll have you evicted from the chambers.'

Cameras began flashing like strobe lights at a 'seventies-style disco, intermittently illuminating Monk's ever-reddening, sweat-covered face, in preparation of the stark photographs which would adorn the morning newspapers' front pages. By now, the audience was becoming decidedly hostile, demonstrated in spades by a succession of angry remarks.

'No, you won't, Monk. If he goes, we all go.'

'Answer the young man's questions, Councillor.'

'What do you have to say for yourself, Monk?'

'Do the honourable thing and resign, man. You're a bloody disgrace.'

As the exchanges became more and more aggressive, Ricky decided that the time was now perfect to put the boot in.

'Only another few questions, Mister Chairman, and then I'm done. Will you answer them?'

'Only if they're relevant.' Monk snapped back. 'Otherwise, no.'

'Oh, they're relevant all right, you have my assurance on that.'

'Try me, then.'

'Okay Mister Chairman, if you won't answer my first two questions, then how about a third one? The average salary for a male worker today in 1973 is slightly under £2,000 per annum. Other than your own councillor's allowance, you don't have a paid job or any other source of income, is that correct, Mister Chairman?'

'Absolutely irrelevant to the matter at hand, and absolutely none of your business.'

'Oh, I think the audience might not quite agree with you there, Mister Chairman. So, if you're not going to answer my third question, let me ask you a fourth one. When you bought your wife a brand-new MGB GT sports car in April of this year at a cost of £1,850 ... almost a full year's wages for the average Scottish worker and approximately six times your own councillor's allowance ... who signed the cheque? Was it Mister Rafferty?'

Howls of derision from the gallery. Monk lost the plot.

'That's a scurrilous accusation. You'll be hearing from my solicitor in the morning.'

'Mister Chairman, I haven't accused you of anything. I've just asked you four simple questions. And, might I add, not one of which you have even had the good grace to answer. So, now is your chance to set the record straight.'

'I've said all I'm going to say about those ... about those ... accusations ... those scurrilous accusations,' Monk stammered, beads of sweat trickling down a strained face, its hue rapidly progressing from deep-red to beetroot.

Smelling blood, Ricky proceeded to plunge the knife in still further.

'Okay then, Mister Chairman, let's leave the people here tonight to draw their own conclusions about the four questions I've asked and which you have completely refused to answer. I'll now ask you a fifth one. Do you, or do you not, have a number of other shared business interests with Mister Frank Rafferty? That's Mister Frank Rafferty, the Managing Director of Rafferty Construction?'

More gasps of disbelief. Monk retorted in fury.

'I completely refuse to answer that ... that ridiculous question.

My commercial interests have absolutely nothing whatsoever to do with the matter we're here to discuss tonight. In fact, they are none of your business, so mind yours, son.'

'Ah,' Ricky replied, his youthful voice still as calm and unflustered as a country millpond on a breathless summer's day. 'So, you don't think that your commercial relationship with Mister Rafferty ... the same Mister Rafferty who is the contractor for the Sandbank housing development which your committee approved under your own chairmanship, is any of my business, or that of the people here tonight? Is that correct, Mister Chairman?'

'I point-blank refuse to dignify that question with a response.'

'Okay, then, let's be a bit more specific. Question number six. Do you happen to have a financial interest in the new hotel which is currently being built by Rafferty Construction on the foreshore at Troon?'

'No comment.'

'Question number seven. Or the harbour development in Ayr town centre, also being built by Rafferty Construction?'

'No comment.'

'Question number eight. Mister Chairman. Is Rafferty Construction presently building you a holiday home on the seafront down the coast at Ballantrae? And question number nine, is Mister Rafferty picking up the tab?'

'That's an outrageous suggestion.'

'The same Mister Rafferty to whom the Planning Committee, under your chairmanship, awarded the contract for the Sandbank housing development which we're here tonight to discuss? It's not a "suggestion" at all, Mister Chairman, it's just a simple question.'

'This meeting is over,' Monk exclaimed, the veins on his neck sticking out like coils of ivy on an emaciated tree-trunk.

By now, the place was in near uproar. Ricky's work was done. He sat down, crossed his legs and let the restless natives take over where he had left off.

'Answer the lad's questions, Monk.'

'Hey Monk, you're nothing but a crook.'

'You're dead in the water, Monk. I've been a member of the Labour Party all my life, and I'll see to it personally that you're finished.'

'For God's sake go, Monk. Resign.'

And so it went on, until Monk and his two shell-shocked

colleagues had no alternative but to up sticks and head towards the door of the grand old County Chambers which had never before witnessed anything quite like it. As the beleaguered threesome tried to make their escape, umpteen members of a furious audience jostled them and pointed accusing fingers in their faces.

Meanwhile, over at the far wall, the sleazy-looking guy with the suntanned complexion and the greasy hair glowered at Ricky Anderson. Ricky glowered back and didn't flinch. All the former could see was the young whipper-snapper who was clearly intent on exposing his business empire. And all the latter could see was the monster who had half-killed his mother.

War had finally been declared. And like all wars, there would ultimately be a winner and a loser.

This would be a fight to the death.

21

Iona McNish stood on the northbound platform of Glenside railway station watching the image of the oncoming train expanding by the second as it chugged closer and closer. Her heart was as heavy as a cobbler's anvil.

Staring wordlessly into Ricky Anderson's azure-blue eyes, she felt her own well up in an impending flood of tears. With the trials and tribulations of a post-graduate doctorate looming for the man of her dreams, Iona knew that it could be a long time before she saw him again, a whole week perhaps or, God forbid, even two.

The train squealed to a halt and Ricky lugged his two laden holdalls onto the floor of the rear carriage, then immediately stepped back off again and grabbed Iona in a bear-hug. He kissed her on the tip of her nose and wiped some tears away from her eyes. She grabbed his hair and pulled him into a long passionate embrace. Words were superfluous.

The station guard blew his whistle, added an empathetic, 'Come on, son, we need to get going', and the young lovers were parted once more.

Ricky slumped down on the first seat he came to, heaving his bags onto the one opposite. He bit his lip and tried to swallow, but a lump formed in his throat. The train began easing its way out of the station, gathered speed and Iona's heavenly image receded to a mere speck in the evening gloom. Mercifully, Ricky was not to know that by the time she had reached her mother's waiting car, her heart was breaking. One day soon, they would be together for eternity. For now, though, the pain of parting was gloriously unbearable.

A few minutes later, Ricky's thoroughly pragmatic mind had all but kicked his soft, sentimental underbelly into the long grass. There were things to be done. As soon as he reached Glasgow's Central Station, he would take the pedestrian exit and walk the 400 yards or so down Union Street to St Enoch Square, where he would jump onto one of the city's subway trains and alight at Hillhead Station in the west-end of the city. From there, he would cross Byres Road and make his way to his rented three-bedroomed flat in Highburgh Road, right slap-bang in the epicentre of Glasgow's student quarter.

His two flatmates and kindred spirits, the incurable romantic and budding microbiologist, Robert 'Jack' Frost, and the football-mad chemical engineer, David 'Pele' Duncan, wouldn't be arriving until the following morning. So, once he had unpacked, Ricky would nip down to Tennent's Bar on Byres Road to anaesthetise the memory of that agonising farewell scene with Iona and the horror which Frank Rafferty had inflicted on his innocent mother. Yes, a couple of beers in Tennent's and a fish supper from Old Salty's sounded like a very good plan.

Some 25 minutes into his journey, the train's hydraulic brakes squealed again as it pulled into Kilmarnock railway station. Ricky leaned over, unzipped the side-pocket of his bulging holdall and took out his prized copy of last Friday morning's *Glasgow Herald*, the one he would keep for posterity. He drooled over the front-page headline for the umpteenth time.

AYRSHIRE COUNCILLOR and LEADING BUSINESSMAN
ACCUSED OF CRONYISM
MONK and RAFFERTY in the DOCK!

Gerry McGhee had certainly done the business on the 'Gruesome Twosome', as he referred to them, the ones Ricky preferred to call 'Mutt and Jeff'. His lead article, suitably augmented by similar assassination pieces in the three Ayrshire weeklies, had primarily garrotted Edwin Monk, but it had also flushed out the corrupt councillor's illicit relationship with Frank Rafferty and the property developer's highly questionable business ventures. With a fair wind, Monk's political career would soon be history, and his erstwhile associate would turn his back on him and run for cover, leaving him with no alternative but to give Ricky's abused mother peace at last.

That, at least, was the theory.

However, the consequential waves would ripple out a lot further, since Southwest Scotland Police would then be forced to investigate the pair's highly questionable business relationship and alleged nefarious practices. Head honcho, Smokin' Joe Fraser, might well be Rafferty's big cousin, but Fraser wasn't bloody stupid. You didn't get to the heady position of Chief Superintendent without making ruthless decisions and dumping a few losers in the process, and Frank Rafferty would be his latest expendable victim, flesh-and-blood or not. Moreover, one of his star detectives, DI Charlie Reynolds, knew the full story, warts and all. And Fraser knew that he knew it.

Ricky Anderson, aided and abetted by Gerry McGhee and a few other newspaper hacks, had played a blinder. Two criminals were going down and Ricky's mother would finally be left in peace. There was just one more thing that still needed to be done, and Ricky's temporary expatriation from the peaceful rurality of the Glenside countryside to the bustling anonymity of Glasgow's big smoke would provide him with the perfect cover to do it.

The thing that still needed to be done was for Ricky to pay Rafferty a little visit.

22

'Oh God, sir, where have you been?'

It was the voice of Ayr Police HQ's senior administrative officer, Cathy Cameron, concern and annoyance etched in equal measure across her attractive fifty-something face.

'I always like you best when you're angry, Cathy,' the Detective Inspector replied with a cheeky grin. 'You remind me of my mother when I had been a naughty wee boy.'

The office guru fought hard to conceal a smile. Charlie Reynolds always managed to make her laugh, the handsome big hunk of pure masculinity that he was. However, this was no laughing matter.

'You're still a naughty wee boy if you ask me, sir. I've had everybody tearing their hair out trying to track you down. The boss has been searching for you ever since he stormed in at half-eight this morning. And believe me, he doesn't look happy.'

'When did Smokin' Joe ever look happy?' replied Reynolds, eyebrows raised in quizzical fashion. 'He's turned into a right crabbit old git these days, if you ask me. Get me a coffee first, Cathy, there's a good girl.'

Her disapproving eyes met the mischievousness of his own.

'Please?' he said, smiling in familiar pleading fashion. 'Pretty please?'

Cathy just stared at him and shook her head in resignation.

'If he comes looking again, I'll tell him you've just arrived.'

'That's my girl, Cathy.'

There were times when she wished she was his girl. Many times. Charlie Reynolds's shift should have begun at eight-thirty, at least notionally. However, Chief Superintendent Joe Fraser would never have pulled Reynolds up for arriving late, never in a month of Sundays, and for two very good reasons. Firstly, DI Reynolds put in more hours than anyone else on the whole force, and Fraser knew it. And secondly, he was the best detective on his team, and every other division in the land would have done anything to prise him away from Fraser's clutches. Reynolds was a rising star, destined to make it to the very top of the tree. The only thing that could stop him was a complete catastrophe. The problem was, though, that he was now staring one straight in the face.

As Reynolds sipped his coffee, he began reflecting on the day's unfolding events. The fact that he had managed to inveigle himself into Janice Anderson's hospital ward at such an unearthly hour of the morning had been a bit of a triumph for him, and he was mightily chuffed that he had worked the oracle, even if it had required him chatting up the middle-aged ward sister. Janice's condition had improved markedly. Sure, her face still resembled a war zone and the bruising had now come out worse than ever, but the swelling was down considerably. At Janice's own request, the nurse had propped her up into a sitting position for Charlie's impromptu visit, which had clearly been an agonising procedure as her internal injuries, surgical wounds and splintered ribs would readily testify, but at least she could now hold a conversation with him. Well, some kind of conversation anyway, courtesy of the pain and discomfort caused by a pair of burst lips and seriously damaged gums where several shapely teeth once resided. However, the smile was back, and it once again melted Charlie's heart. That warm, honest and trusting little smile. And sexy, so unintentionally but undeniably sexy.

Charlie Reynolds had already been smitten by Janice's charms.

Little did he know that she felt the same way about him, and times ten. Had the nurse not reappeared to administer her morning cocktail of medicines, wild horses couldn't have hauled Charlie away from her side. And now here he was, back at his desk in Police HQ, still thinking about that captivating smile.

'Nice of you to give us the pleasure of your company, Inspector.'

Reynolds didn't even need to look up, but he did anyway. He could have picked that voice out from the middle of a hundred-thousand-strong crowd in Hampden Park, Scotland's national football stadium. Chief Superintendent Fraser stood there looking serene, all resplendent in his ornate uniform and associated regalia, but minus the decorated helmet which would be sitting centre-stage on his office desk as usual.

'So, you've found me out again, then, sir?' Reynolds quipped. 'Does that mean you're putting me on a lengthy suspension? I could do with a decent break.'

Fraser just frowned and brushed his fingers through his salt-and-pepper-tinted hair.

'My office now, Charlie, the wisecracks can wait. I need to speak to you urgently. Incidentally, how long have you been here?'

Reynolds showed him what was left of his coffee.

'Only about that long, sir.'

As the two senior officers marched out of the office, Reynolds gave Cathy a little knowing wink. She turned away, giggling.

'Shut the door and take a seat, Charlie,' said Fraser, pointing to one of the recliners sitting beside the coffee table, rather than as was customary for his other less esteemed minions who would invariably be ushered towards the more formal setting of the leather-backed chairs which adorned the big oval table in the adjoining conference room. Clearly, Fraser was about to embark on one of his infamous 'heart-to-heart chats', which was when he was always at his most dangerous.

'It's cards on the table time, I'm afraid,' he said, slumping down and staring straight at his prized charge.

'Mines or yours, boss?' Reynolds retorted, returning his gaze without blinking.

Fraser just blanked him.

'What were you doing at a crime scene in Glenside last Thursday evening, Charlie? That's way out of your jurisdiction.'

'I got a message telling me that a friend was in bother.'

'What kind of message and who was the friend?'

'A handwritten note pinned to my windscreen right here in the staff car park. The forensic lads are working on it.'

'And the friend?'

'You know fine well who she is, boss. Her name's Janice Anderson and she was beaten to a pulp. She's a widow, and I'm a poor guy whose wife left him for a complete dickhead, so it's no big deal.'

'No big deal, Charlie? One of my inspectors is screwing the victim of a serious assault carried out by someone we've had under close surveillance for the past three months, and you turn up at her house dressed in your Sunday best and still on duty, when you've got no bloody business being anywhere near the place. No big deal?'

'First of all, sir, I'm not screwing her, not that it's any of your business. And secondly, I was off-duty. My shift ended at six-thirty.'

'When did you leave the office, Charlie?'

'Ask Andy McTurk.'

'I'm asking you.'

'About five-to-eight, maybe slightly after.'

'Why were you in the office so late?'

'I'm a hard worker.'

'And how did you manage to get to Glenside by quarter-past-eight?'

'I'm a fast driver.'

'Last night, I got a call from Jock Henderson in the Cumnock office. His guys are handling Mrs Anderson's case, not us. Henderson is furious, Charlie.'

'Henderson is a prick, boss. He hates my guts and he'd do anything to cause trouble for me. Such lack of good taste, don't you think?'

'Charlie, for God's sake, man. Not only did you interfere in a case that had nothing to do with you, but you then held the victim in your arms and seriously compromised a crime scene. Your fingerprints were all over the bloody place.'

'And my fingerprints will be all over Frank Rafferty's neck when I catch up with him.'

'It wasn't Frank Rafferty who did this, Charlie. A left-hander did this. We've got Robert McDaid in for questioning.'

'So, who do you think gave the order, sir? Al Capone?'

'You're not listening, Charlie. Stay out of it.'

'I'll stay out of the formal investigation, but I'm involved with

Janice now. She needs my support and she'll get it.'

'Let the Cumnock cops deal with this. Understand?'

'Yes, boss, I do understand. And I will stay out of the formal investigation. But can I ask you for one small favour?'

'Try me.'

'Let Andy McTurk take over the investigation from Henderson.'

'Why?'

'Because Andy will get to the bottom of this in no time. Henderson couldn't win a game of Cluedo.'

'I'll think about it.'

'Well, think about this too, sir. McDaid may well have been the one who battered Janice, but Rafferty gave the order. And you don't want to be caught with your trousers at your ankles when your wee cousin goes down, do you sir?'

The Chief Superintendent sank back in his seat and blew a huge sigh.

'So, you know that Frank and I are family, then, do you?'

'Ayrshire is a small place, boss. The whole county knows. One way or another, Rafferty will get what's coming to him. And when he does, you need to be somewhere else.'

'Okay, okay, I'll phone Henderson and tell him that I'm putting Andy in charge. He won't like it, but he'll just have to lump it. By the way, did you hear about the big public meeting in the Council Chambers last week? It's been all over the papers. That young Anderson lad made quite a name for himself. Your girlfriend's son?'

'I told you, she's not my girlfriend … but yes.'

'Should I be worried about him, Charlie?'

'No, he's away back up to university. Let me worry about Ricky. You worry about getting your little cousin locked up and off the streets. He is one mean bastard, boss.'

'I know, Charlie, he always has been. And ever since he was running around in nappies.'

'I'm glad you're letting Andy deal with it, boss. He won't let you down.'

A long silence left Reynolds in no doubt that the meeting was over. He took his cue, nodded respectfully and rose to his feet. As befits a man in his exalted position, Smokin' Joe simply had to have the last word.

'And Charlie,' he said, as his detective inspector headed for the door. 'You are to have nothing more to do with this investigation.

Understand?'

'Yes, Sir,' Reynolds replied.

The last word still belonged to Fraser.

'And that's an order.'

23

Detective Inspector Andy McTurk stood at the corner of the bar in the Kirkton Inn, fidgeting with his biro pen.

A slave to punctuality, he stared at his watch for the umpteenth time and cursed under his breath. Unfortunately, his opposite number did not share the same obsession for good timekeeping. Moreover, it had been Charlie Reynolds's idea in the first place to meet in the splendid anonymity of the Ayrshire village of Dalrymple, and he was 25 minutes late already.

McTurk decided to head to the toilet for a leak, leaving his pint on the bar. When he returned, a tall well-groomed guy was standing there ordering his own. The middle-aged, bespectacled lady behind the bar eyed them both with intrigue. Gracie Lamont could have picked out a plain-clothes detective from outer space, and not just from his trademark snazzy haircut and confident gait either. No, it was the Ralph Slater suit that was the big giveaway. Whether made-to-measure or off-the-peg, a Slater suit draped over a tall, fit-looking guy was standard issue copper's uniform as far as Gracie was concerned. So, as sure as a Scotch pie needs brown sauce, Reynolds had been well and truly clocked. However, what about his short, scruffy mate? He was a different proposition altogether. Possibly a detective too, Gracie pondered, although he could also pass for an incognito informer about to trade vital information in exchange for a wad of tenners, couldn't he? No, Gracie just couldn't be sure, so there was only one thing for it. She would have to earwig into their conversation as usual.

'What kept you, Andy boy?' Reynolds quipped. 'I've been here for ages.'

'It's the earliest you've been late for a while, Charlie, I'll grant you that,' came the cutting reply. 'I don't know about you, but I've got other things to do.'

The two colleagues grabbed their pints and wandered over to a small table by the window. Gracie cursed under her breath.

McTurk took out his notebook.

'Right, enough of the idle banter, here goes ...'

'Before you start, Andy, how was Janice this morning when you spoke to her in hospital? I didn't get a chance to see her because I had to nip down to Stranraer to give my love to our esteemed gun-running nutter, Barney McTaggart. Got him as he stepped off the boat from Belfast.'

'I bet that went well?'

'As soon as he clocked me, he thought about making a run for it, but when I grabbed him by the nuts he decided otherwise. I had our new rookie with me, young Gordon. He did very well. Had the cuffs on big Barney in no time.'

'Aye, nice lad, young Gordon, but nobody's fool either. Right, let's get started. Mrs Anderson ... Janice. I'd be a wee bit worried about her staying on her own when she gets out, Charlie. We've got McDaid in the cells for now, but if he doesn't squawk, we'll need to let him go by tomorrow latest.'

'She won't be on her own. She'll be staying with me, either at her place in Glenside or at mine in Ayr. Right, give me the lowdown.'

'If Smokin' Joe knew I was doing this, he'd feed my favourite appendages to that big ugly German Shepherd of his.'

'Fraser wasn't born yesterday, Andy. He knows fine well that you'll tell me everything. We've done a deal. He takes Henderson and the Cumnock cops off the case, and you run with it. I take nothing to do with the formalities, and he takes nothing to do with his darling little cousin. Family or not, Fraser will throw Rafferty under a bus, because he knows he has it coming. Not only that, but Rafferty has now become a huge embarrassment to Fraser, and if he ever has any hope of becoming the next Chief Constable, he has to be seen to completely dissociate himself from the black sheep of the family.'

'Right, let's start with my interview with Janice Anderson. Nice wee lassie, Charlie. And by the way, I wouldn't climb over her in bed to get to you.'

'Get on with it, you old pervert.'

McTurk began flicking through his notes.

'The evening of Thursday the 23rd of August. Janice thinks it was about half-past-six. Knock at the door, she answers it. She remembers him as a big burly man with short-cropped hair and very tough-looking, with a purple scar from his lower lip right down underneath his chin. It's McDaid, Charlie, no doubt about it.'

'Half-past-six, Andy? You sure about that?'

'That's what she said.'

'So, that means she must have been lying there in that state for almost two hours before we got to her. McDaid must have duffed her up about six-thirty, driven down to our office in Ayr about seven o'clock and put the note on my windscreen, then buggered off for a few pints knowing that Janice would be lying there half-dead until I left the office and saw the note. The bastard, the complete and utter bastard. He could have killed her, Andy.'

'No, Charlie, McDaid is a pro. He knew exactly what he was doing. He's stupid, but not stupid enough to run the risk of facing a ten-stretch in the Bar-L for murder. All he wanted was to give her a right good pasting.'

'You mean, all Frank Rafferty wanted was for McDaid to give her a right good pasting?'

'I'll come to Rafferty in a minute. Back to Janice for now. She asks him what he wants, and he replies, "I want to come in for a wee chat". She says no, he grabs her by the throat, pushes her inside and slams the door shut behind him. She remembers a car sitting outside, engine still running, and what looks like a much younger guy at the wheel, fairish hair she thinks, but not sure. That Prestwick lad, I'm thinking ... Baxter, his name is ... Ralph Baxter, right wee ned he is too. Anyway, McDaid shoves her into the living room, she tries to scream but she can't because his hand is squeezing her throat. She flails out with her arms and legs. He punches her in the guts, then again and again. She can't breathe, she thinks she's going to die ... you all right with this, Charlie?'

'Hurry up.'

'He then thumps her several times on the face and body. And that's about it, that's all she can remember before she passes out. Other than a hazy memory of glass breaking all around her.'

Reynolds threw his head back and inhaled deeply. His policeman's instinct was to try to visualise the crime scene in as much detail as possible. However, his emotional reaction on this occasion was to blank the whole scenario from his mind. The thought of Janice suffering so badly at the hands of that mindless thug, McDaid, sickened him. And as for Rafferty having given the order, the whole thing was torturing his brain.

'So, you've still got Mad Rab in the cells, then?' Reynolds asked McTurk, quickly turning his attention away from the victim to the perpetrator.

'Aye,' McTurk replied, shrugging his shoulders. 'He's as cocky as ever, admitting nothing, denying everything. No witnesses and a rock-solid alibi from his latest floozie. She goes by the name of Brenda McLeish, a big overweight bleach-blonde horror show with a face like Frankenstein and teeth like a row of condemned houses. And that's not the worst part.'

'Tell me.'

'The whole crime scene was compromised the moment you broke in, Charlie. Your fingerprints were everywhere. The forensic boys have nothing to work with.'

'But you know he did it, Andy, and I know he did it. And there's more than one way to skin a cat.'

'Stay out of this, Charlie. You promised Smokin' Joe, and now I want you to promise me.'

'How can I, Andy? Just think how you would feel if it was one of yours who was lying there in that hospital bed.'

'Leave it to me, Charlie. If you pay McDaid a visit, you'll bugger the whole show. Do it, and no more secret meetings, no more info. Stay out of it. Promise me.'

'Okay, Andy, okay. It's your gig.'

McTurk looked straight at Reynolds, nodded in appreciation then looked down at the table.

'What is it, Andy?' Reynolds asked. 'What's up?'

McTurk hesitated before answering.

'Charlie ... it's about Rafferty.'

'What about him? Come on man. It's like drawing teeth.'

'He was seen in a restaurant in Normandy having a meal with his wife on the evening of Thursday the 23rd of August, the same night as Janice got duffed up.'

It took a few seconds for Reynolds to absorb and assimilate the information. McTurk immediately came to his assistance.

'Charlie, Frank Rafferty was on holiday in France on the evening that Janice Anderson was assaulted. He has the perfect alibi. He wasn't even around to give McDaid the order, or to learn of the outcome.'

'You sure? I mean absolutely sure?'

'Positive. The French cops have two reliable witnesses.'

'So, Andy, as far as you're concerned, Rafferty and McDaid have rock solid alibis?'

'Afraid so, buddy. They've both played a stormer.'

24

'Where are you off to at this time of day, then, young Richard?'

It was the cultured voice of Professor Jonathan Bernstein, the Nuclear Physics department's celebrated overlord, internationally renowned for his research in the field of experimental fast neutron reactors. With Russia's far-off puppet state of Kazakhstan now housing the world's first commercial prototype of its kind, Great Britain and the other leading global powers had found themselves lagging somewhat behind. 'The Prof' was now one of a select number of leading British academics who were determined to forge ahead and help their country to claim pole position in this exciting new field of efficient energy production, and Ricky Anderson was the protégé in whom he had placed so much faith.

Ricky stopped at the far end of the corridor, rucksack over his shoulder, and turned to face his esteemed mentor.

'I'm off to Ayr to visit my mum in hospital, Prof. Remember I asked you a couple of days ago if I could take the afternoon off?'

'Oh yes lad, so you did, so you did,' the tall elegantly dressed and moustachioed genius replied. 'How is it that I can recite four-page-long nuclear equations from memory, but ask me what day of the week it is and I wouldn't have a clue? I hope your mother is feeling a lot better now. It was a terrible thing that happened to her, you know. Dreadful, absolutely dreadful. You take as much time off as you need, Richard. You are a very diligent young man and I know you'll make up the time. Take care now, and much love to the dear lady. It would be a pleasure to meet her acquaintance someday soon.'

'Thanks Prof,' Ricky replied. 'I appreciate it. See you on Monday morning.'

He skipped down the big stairwell and exited the campus onto University Avenue, where a chill breeze and a few drops of rain served to remind him that late summer had now been superseded by early autumn. A brisk walk took him down Gibson Street and past its renowned array of top-class Indian restaurants, out of which the glorious aroma of assorted curries set his nostrils twitching. A left-turn then led him along the riverbank to Kelvinbridge underground station. There, he caught the next subway to St Enoch Square, from which a leisurely two-minute stroll took him into the concourse of Central Station, where the Glasgow-to-Ayr train would be arriving at precisely 1.15 p.m. to whisk him down to the seaside town and its alleged hordes of 'honest men and bonnie lasses'.

A couple of hours later, Ricky shuffled tentatively into Ayr County Hospital's intensive care ward. The sight that greeted him gladdened his heart. His mother was sitting upright with her head resting on a pillow, and she was sporting a big warm smile. Ricky walked over to her bedside, put his arms around her shoulders and kissed her gently on the cheek. Janice made a little 'ow' sound followed by a giggle, then kissed her son on the forehead.

'Sorry, mum,' he said, realising that his biceps were working more effectively than his brain. 'When I saw you sitting there smiling, I completely forgot how sore you must be.'

'I've been up for two hours today, Ricky,' she beamed through bruised lips and swollen gums. 'Sitting on that chair over there. I've even had a shower, would you believe? Although the nurse had to help me.'

'Aye, you're looking an awful lot better than when I last saw you,' Ricky said. 'Any word on when you're getting out?'

'I thought I might have got home today,' she replied, disappointment etched on her battered face. 'But the doctor said this morning that he wants to keep me in over the weekend for observation and to let the swelling and bruising go down. So, Monday, I'm hoping.'

'You can't stay on your own, mum,' Ricky said, giving her his best no-nonsense stare. 'I'll have a word with Prof Bernstein and ask for a couple of weeks off. The kind of research work I'm doing, I can crack on with a few things at home.'

Janice smiled and took Ricky's hand in her own. It was now or never.

'Sit down, Ricky,' she whispered. 'I've got something I want to tell you.'

His face fell, fearing the worst. She patted him on the back of the hand and went on.

'It's nothing bad, Ricky ... in fact it's something good. At least, for me it is. And I hope for you too, Ricky.'

'It's about Charlie, isn't it mum?'

Janice nodded and inhaled deeply before continuing.

'Ricky, I still miss your dad very badly and I always will. There will never be another man like him, and no-one will ever take his place. Not as my husband and not as your father.'

'I know, mum,' Ricky nodded. 'I also know it's been eight years … and that you could maybe do with a wee bit of company … especially now that I'm back at uni. I don't like the thought of you having another man, mum, but I do understand, I really do.'

Janice's eyes welled up, but she managed to sweep away the embryonic tears with the back of her hand.

'Charlie and I are just good friends, Ricky, that's all, I promise you. But he seems a really decent man. And he makes me feel … he makes me feel … safe. You make me feel safe too, Ricky, but you're 21 years old now, you'll be living in Glasgow for the next year at least, and then you and Iona will be tying the knot. Won't you?'

'Probably. If she says yes.'

'And who in their right mind wouldn't say yes to my big boy? The girl's head-over-heels in love with you, Ricky. And she's an absolute angel.'

Small talk wasn't exactly Ricky's bag, so he immediately refocused the discussion on his mother's predicament.

'Charlie and I went for a pint, mum.'

'I know. He told me. He also told me that you kind of scare him a wee bit.'

'Scare him? You must be joking. He's a copper and he's built like a tank.'

'He likes you, though, Ricky. But he knows he'll never replace your dad.'

'And he likes you too, mum. I could just tell. I think he wants to be more than a friend. A lot more than a friend, if you ask me.'

Janice felt her face and neck flushing.

'I knew it,' he laughed. 'You really fancy him. You can't fool me.'

'Stop it, Ricky,' she giggled. 'You're embarrassing me.'

Ricky returned the laugh, then immediately reverted to pragmatic mode, bringing a more serious tone back to the conversation.

'So, what's happening when you get out of here, then?' he asked. 'Will Charlie come and visit you?'

'I'm actually going to stay at his place for a wee while,' she replied, studying her son's facial expression and searching for any discomfiture in his body language. 'Just till I get better, Ricky.'

Ricky smiled and squeezed his mum's hand.

'I think that's a good idea mum, a very good idea indeed. Charlie seems a decent bloke.'

They resolved to meet at Charlie Reynolds's pad the following week, whenever Ricky could find a couple of hours to tear himself away from bombarding his innocent atoms with angry sub-atomic particles.

Sadly, it would be a meeting that would never take place.

25

Another day, another bus.

Iona McNish alighted from her latest double-decker contraption in Ayr's Wellington Street depot, situated just off the Sandgate. Her heart was all aflutter at the thought of seeing her beloved boyfriend again after an enforced separation of five whole days. The outfit she had chosen for the occasion was a pair of black knee-length boots over her favourite light-blue denim jeans, the dark-blue cashmere jumper that her dad had bought her for Christmas and a matching ankle-length coat. It was the third 'rigoot' she had tried on that afternoon, and she prayed silently that she had finally chosen correctly.

Iona looked all around, but the man of her dreams was nowhere to be seen. The embers of her fertile imagination slowly began to sizzle. Surely, he wasn't about to give her a 'dizzy', his very first in their five-year-long relationship? No, Ricky would never do that, never in a million years. He would just be a wee bit late, that was all, having spent more time than planned at his ailing mum's hospital bedside. But there again, what if he had met some gorgeous female Physics student who had swept him off his feet? She surveyed the scene again in an anxious 360-degree sweep, a familiar sickly feeling returning to the pit of her stomach.

No sign of him. Nothing. Just motor cars whizzing past on all four sides of the big square and people darting between them to get to the other side of the busy roads. And, of course, buses coming and going continuously, each bearing either the name of its planned destination or the words 'Ayr Wellington Street'. Yes, people, cars and buses galore, the occasional bicycle and big dog straining on its leash. However, no Ricky.

Suddenly, Iona's sight vanished, as a pair of rough hands enveloped her eyes. She spun around and found herself staring up into Ricky Anderson's smiling face. It was a smile of warmth underpinned by mischief. She tried to speak, but no words came out. Ricky grabbed Iona's hand and pulled her across the busy street and into a lane at the rear of a row of retail shops, where he pinned her against a roughcast wall. There between a pair of overflowing metal dustbins, the two lovebirds sank into a long passionate kiss.

Ricky pulled a small plastic poke out of his jacket pocket, fumbled for a few seconds and took Iona's left hand in his. He then dropped to his knees on the damp pavement, slipped the ring onto her wedding finger and uttered the words that for so long now she had longed to hear.

'Iona McNish, will you marry me?'

Iona immediately burst into tears.

Ricky dried her eyes with his forefinger and kissed her gently on the lips.

'Well?'

'Of course, I will, Ricky,' she sobbed. 'Of course, I will, you big idiot.'

After a long lingering kiss, they brushed themselves down and began walking in the general direction of the seaside, heads still spinning from the tumultuous event that had just changed their lives forever. A car horn peep-peeped in annoyance as they wandered mindlessly through the nose-to-tail traffic, still squeezing each other's hands as if one was trying to prevent the other from plummeting off the edge of a precipice. Before they knew it, they were standing outside the Pavilion Theatre on the edge of Ayr's vast Low Green, overlooking the town's three-mile-long sandy beach.

Another passionate kiss, another exchange of bewildered looks, then reality began to set in at last, as indeed did a few pangs of hunger. They decided to head for the Wellington Café, Ayr's famous long-standing eatery on the corner of Sandgate and Fort Street, where the whirlwind developments of the last half-hour would be brought back down to earth by a couple of traditional fish suppers, a few slices of bread-and-butter and a big pot of tea.

Some forty-five minutes later, Ricky was seeing Iona back onto the bus to Cumnock before sprinting the half-mile up the seaside town's High Street to the railway station to catch the train that would whisk him back to Glasgow, the young couple's respective moods now significantly bolstered by their glorious promises of betrothal. It would remain their little secret until the following weekend, when they would first meet with Janice, and immediately thereafter with Iona's parents, to tell them their wonderful news. However, in the midst of the drama now unfolding on an almost daily basis, a whole week seemed a very long time away.

Ricky reached the railway station just in the nick of time. Breathlessly, he handed the return portion of his ticket to the station guard, who grunted a 'Platform Two, son, and get a move on' command and opened the gate. No sooner had Ricky jumped into the rear carriage, than the guard blew his whistle and the train began rolling out of the station, *en route* to Glasgow's big smoke and the university's waiting ionisation chambers.

Looking around, he noticed a vacant window-seat further up the carriage, so he shuffled his way towards it and heaved his rucksack onto the luggage shelf above his head. The middle-aged bloke sitting straight across nodded politely and returned to bury his head in his tabloid newspaper, the hot-off-the-press latest edition of one of Ayrshire's three local weeklies, the *Ayrshire Herald*.

Ricky looked briefly at the back page that was facing him and noticed with only the slightest modicum of interest that the town's long-established senior football club, Ayr United, had just landed a plum tie in the Texaco Cup against English giants, Leicester City. Fascinating that this little piece of news would undoubtedly have been for the club's diehard fans, all Ricky could think about was the big headline that would presently be adorning the front page. He cursed himself that in all the day's excitement he had forgotten to buy a newspaper.

It wasn't until the train had pulled out of Kilwinning station, about half-way through the journey, that the quiet gentleman opposite folded his copy of the local rag and sat it on his knee, clearly preparing to take a nap.

'Would you mind if I had a wee look at your newspaper?' Ricky enquired.

'No problem, son,' the chap replied with a smile, and handed it over.

Ricky's eyeballs exploded from their sockets. The Herald's front-page headline read:

CRONYISM SCANDAL GATHERS PACE
MONK SUSPENDED, RAFFERTY IN HIDING

The weekly newspaper's lead story went on to report the sensational developments that had taken place since last Thursday's public meeting in the Council Chambers. Essentially, they were those.

Councillor Edwin Monk had resigned both from his position as Chairman of the council's Planning Committee and from the Labour Party whip. Furthermore, he was standing down from his role as a local councillor, a position he had held for the past seventeen years, and a by-election would soon take place in his constituency. 'Jumped Before He Was Pushed', the sub-heading implied. In other words, Monk's political career was now dead in the water.

Worse still for the long-time councillor, he had been questioned under caution by the police for allegedly accepting bribes from 'a well-known local businessman', in exchange for swaying committee decisions on planning applications in the businessman's favour. Moreover, 'local sources' had informed the *Herald* that Monk was now also under formal police investigation for alleged embezzlement from two charities in which he held the related positions of trustee and board member.

The same sources also claimed that in a characteristically narcissistic effort to protect his own interests and hopefully to persuade the courts to take pity on him and mitigate his sentence, Monk had blown the whistle on Rafferty's bribes and other financial inducements. As for Rafferty himself, he was understood to have flown the nest, quite possibly to his holiday pad in northern France, which had of course played host on several occasions to none other than Monk himself, and now both the Scottish and French police were hot on his trail.

Ricky put the newspaper back down on the seat beside its now-comatose owner and began reflecting. It had been a good day. First of all, his precious mother was on the mend and had met a guy whom she trusted and would take care of her while she recuperated, and who knew where that relationship might eventually lead? Secondly, at long last love had overcome pragmatism and Ricky and Iona were now engaged to be married. And finally, Ricky's masterplan was working out perfectly, because Monk's political career was in tatters and he would soon be in the dock to answer for his sins, and Rafferty was on the run from the law and therefore no longer a threat to his mum.

Yes, it had been a good day. A very good day indeed.

For Ricky, though, there was still one last thing to do. He had to get to Rafferty before the cops did. He had to look him square in the eye and register his displeasure over his treatment of Janice.

And register it firmly.

26

It was 8.30 p.m. on Friday the seventh of September, precisely one hour ahead of British time. The air was motionless and humid, and the thermometer on the west-facing wall of the old eighteenth-century French mansion house was still tickling the eighty-degrees-Fahrenheit mark.

Beads of sweat ran down Frank Rafferty's sun-wrinkled double-chin onto his camel-coloured silk shirt. Sweat from the relentless heat, sweat from the seething rage, sweat from his preoccupation with brutal retribution. As he necked another copious mouthful from his fourth dry martini and inhaled deeply on his Cuban cigar, he surveyed the scene, nostrils twitching in fury.

To his left, lay the sprawling half-acre of lush-green lawn which Marcel Lavigne kept manicured like a championship bowling green, the miserable old hook-nosed deadbeat that he was. Straight ahead, sat his ancient Baroque-style residence, facing the magnificent River Seine estuary in all its pomp. To his right, the Gallic sun's early-evening rays reflected like laser beams off the inviting azure-blue surface of the twenty-metres-by-ten swimming pool.

No bloody way was he about to lose all this, the empire he had built up from the toils of his honest labours, and especially not at the behest of some snotty-nosed little kid whose balls probably hadn't even dropped into place yet. The grand old building which had always been known locally as 'Beauvoir' may well have graced the vibrant seaport of Honfleur ever since the days of Napoleon III's Second Empire, but it now bore the name 'Chez Rafferty' in garish gold letters above the main entrance. And the frogs could like it or bloody-well lump it.

'Don't get mad, Frank,' he muttered contemptuously, blowing a thick cloud of cigar smoke up into the pristine French air. 'Get even.'

As Rafferty sat 'nursing his wrath to keep it warm', to borrow a few more words from Scottish bard, Robert Burns, his long-suffering wife's flip-flops began clip-clopping onto the terracotta tiles of the expansive patio.

'Dinner will be ready in ten minutes, Frank. It's your favourite,

Normandy pork with mustard sauce and apples.'

Rafferty pulled his sunglasses down from the bridge of his nose onto its tip and glowered straight at her.

'Not now, Irene,' he replied. 'I'm thinking.'

'Come on, Frank,' she said, 'you've been sitting out here for hours. You need to eat something, or that ulcer of yours will start playing up again. Just come in and ...'

'Are you bloody deaf, woman?' he snapped, eyes ablaze with exasperation. 'Just f—k off and give me peace. You don't tell me when I'm ready to eat, I tell you. Got it?'

Irene Rafferty immediately turned on her heels and high-tailed it back into the kitchen. Hands shaking, she poured herself a stiff vodka-and-tonic, and downed half of it in one despairing gulp. She was trapped, and she knew it. Trapped in a complete sham of a marriage. Trapped by a man who had become a monster, with his seedy business deals, his uncontrollable temper and his cheap-tart bits-on-the-side willingly dropping their knickers on command. Well, maybe now his luck was about to run out. Maybe now the great Frank Rafferty was finally about to meet his match. And when that glorious day arrived at last, he wouldn't see Irene for dust.

Having summarily dispatched his wife into the kitchen along with her Normandy pork, Rafferty was once more left to do what he did best. Seethe alone. He cursed when he remembered that young whipper-snapper slip of a lad making a complete fool of him in the Council Chambers, especially now that the local hacks had been having a field day plastering his name all over the front pages and seriously questioning his integrity. He fumed when he thought of that two-faced traitor, Edwin Monk, selling him out to the cops. And he raged when he realised the cataclysmic impact that this whole sorry mess was sure to have on his personal fortune, and God forbid, perhaps even his own liberty.

The very thought of life behind bars was anathema to Frank Rafferty. One thing was for sure, though. If he was going down, then he would not be going down alone. Edwin Monk would get what was coming to him. And come hell or high water, so too would that bastard son of Janice Anderson's.

As Frank Rafferty sat in the French sunshine scheming his revenge, little did he know that Ricky Anderson was presently stretched out on a settee in his Glasgow apartment doing exactly the same thing.

The immovable object was about to meet the irresistible force.

27

Charlie Reynolds was waiting at the front door of his three-bedroomed semi-detached villa in the Ayrshire seaside town of Prestwick when the ambulance pulled up. His ticker was going like the clappers.

He walked nervously down the garden path and opened the gate, just as the two ambulancemen began to likewise with the big vehicle's back doors.

'Are you the lady's husband, then?' the one with the standard 1970s moustache enquired.

The big copper heard a quiet giggle coming from inside the ambulance.

'No, he's not,' the soft female voice replied. 'He's my big brother.'

Reynolds chuckled quietly and stood waiting until the two guys slid the stretcher out into the fresh autumnal air. Janice Anderson's smile immediately melted his heart. He bent over and kissed her softly on the lips. She willingly kissed back.

'Quite fond of your big brother, then, Mrs Anderson?' the driver quipped, sporting a mischievous grin beneath his unruly mop of permed hair.

All four laughed as the paramedics set about wheeling the stretcher down the path. A couple of clouds parted momentarily, just long enough to allow a rather watery sun to reveal itself and illuminate Janice Anderson's face, accentuating the deep bruising which spoke a thousand words about her horrific ordeal at the hands of a vicious gangster. Not, though, sufficient to conceal the underlying beauty which once more held Charlie Reynolds captivated.

Janice's full recovery would be a long time coming, but for now she felt safe. Safe with the new man in her life. As for Reynolds himself, he was over the moon about the new woman in his, but consumed with anger about what those two thugs, Rafferty and McDaid, had done to an innocent young woman whose only sin was to have found herself down on her luck. He would deal with them in due course, and deal with them firmly. However, for the time being, the detective's priority was to nurse his patient back to health.

The two ambulancemen wheeled Janice inside and along the hallway, then slid her from the stretcher onto the double bed in the downstairs master bedroom, the one which had served as the Reynolds's matrimonial nest until the day when Donna had suddenly upped sticks and left home. However, be that as it may, it also happened to be the only ground-floor bedroom in the house, and with an *en-suite* bathroom to boot, it was precisely what the ailing Janice would require as she continued her recuperation.

The doorbell rang, the front door clicked open and a gruff voice shouted along the hallway. It belonged to Andy McTurk, Reynolds's opposite number and fellow DI.

'It's me, Charlie. Everyone decent?'

'Aye, Andy,' he shouted back. 'As decent as we'll ever be. Come in.'

Invitation or not, McTurk still gave a tentative knock on the bedroom door before entering. Reynolds met him with a firm handshake and an uncharacteristically affectionate man-hug.

'Thanks for coming, pal,' he said, before turning again to face the patient lying in the bed. 'Andy, you've already met Janice. Janice, Andy's my sparring partner at work. He's bloody useless, but he makes a grand cup of tea.'

'Don't listen to him, dear,' McTurk replied, with a playful wink. 'I'm his mentor, his spiritual leader if you like. Charlie couldn't tie his shoelaces without me. You don't know what you're letting yourself in for, darlin'.'

Janice giggled, then grimaced with the pain of broken ribs pressing on battered tissue.

'No, I don't, do I Charlie? For all I know, you could be a psychopathic monster. He's not, Andy, is he?'

'Well, now that you mention it, we've had our suspicions,' McTurk teased. 'But no proof as yet, at least none that would stick.'

Janice laughed again, recoiled again, and smiled at Reynolds, who held her gaze as if hypnotised. McTurk broke the deep, intense silence.

'Mind if I drag him away for a wee minute, Janice? Some boring business to discuss, you know?'

'Not at all,' she replied. 'It was nice of you to come over.'

Reynolds and McTurk walked back along the hall and into the kitchen, where the former switched on the kettle.

'She's a wee honey, Charlie,' McTurk said with a knowing look.

'An absolute gem. Now I understand.'

'She's going to stay here until she gets better,' Reynolds said solemnly.

'And then what?' McTurk enquired.

'We'll see, Andy,' Reynolds snapped, clearly irritated. 'We'll see.'

'I'm just wondering where all this is going,' McTurk continued, unabashed. 'That's all.'

'It's just not safe for her back in Glenside,' Reynolds replied, staring straight at his partner. 'Particularly with young Ricky back up at Uni in Glasgow. Jesus Christ, Andy, that bastard McDaid gave her some doing. Have you seen those bruises? You'd think she had been hit by a coal lorry.'

'The bruises will heal, Charlie. Sooner or later, they'll heel, and Janice's life will go on. And so will yours. But what then, Charlie? Have you thought about that? I mean, really thought about it?'

'All I can think about just now is getting Janice through this. And getting even with Rafferty and McDaid. This could get ugly, Andy.'

'That's exactly what I wanted to talk to you about. I've been doing some digging. But let me remind you of one thing first. You can't possibly get yourself directly involved in this anymore, Charlie. You're too hot. Leave this to me, to my own team. As far as you're concerned in this situation, you're not a copper, you're a civilian. You got that?'

'We'll see, Andy, we'll see.'

'We'll see, nothing, Charlie. I'm the investigating officer, remember? And it was you who suggested it to Smokin' Joe in the first place, remember that too. So, let me do my job. And if you do, I'll keep you fully in the loop. However, if you don't, all you'll learn is what you read in the papers. Understand?'

Reynolds heaved a sigh and nodded.

McTurk put his hand on Reynolds' shoulder.

'Right, go and make the tea, and I'll tell you what I know. Two sugars and one milk, as usual. And one of your mum's shortbread biscuits too.'

'Aye-Aye, captain, your wish is my command.'

While Reynolds dunked the teabags, McTurk began filling him in with the details of his investigation. The situation was very fluid. First of all, Mad Rab McDaid hadn't sung at all, not a single note, despite having been put under enormous pressure by McTurk and his squad. So, in the absence of any first-hand witnesses or other hard evidence which the local Procurator Fiscal would have insisted upon before even entertaining any criminal proceedings, the DI had found himself with no means of slapping McDaid with a charge that would stick, and therefore with no alternative but to release him from custody. Secondly, Edwin Monk had readily coughed up his guts to the cops, selling out Rafferty and agreeing to testify against him in court in exchange for a reduced sentence further down the line. Finally, Frank Rafferty had fled to France and holed up with his wife for a couple of days in his holiday villa in the harbour port town of Honfleur on the Normandy coast, but the local *gendarmerie* had screwed the show and allowed Rafferty to flee the nest before they could be bothered to move in and apprehend him.

The bottom line? Well, there was good news and bad. The good was that Monk's sleazy character had finally been fully exposed, his clandestine political career was in smithereens, and he would soon be doing time behind bars. The bad was that Rafferty was now on the loose, albeit with the French and Scottish cops hot on his heels, and sure to be a very angry man intent on revenge. McDaid and the rest of Rafferty's gang of goons would no doubt be waiting for instructions on how and when to enact that revenge, and since Monk was presently helping the cops with their enquiries and therefore untouchable, those instructions would be focused on one obvious target. Young Ricky Anderson.

Charlie Reynolds lit up a fag, handed it to McTurk, lit another for himself and shook his head.

'What are you saying, then, Andy?'

McTurk looked straight at Reynolds, stony-faced.

'What I'm saying is this, Charlie. Now that Janice is staying at your pad, I really don't think you need to worry about her for the time being. But if I was in your position, I'd be very concerned indeed about what might happen to her precious wee boy.'

'Jesus Christ,' said Reynolds.

'Aye,' McTurk replied. 'Ricky might need him.'

28

As a newly-qualified, post-graduate theoretical physicist pursuing a doctorate in a crucially important area of the development of the latest generation of 'Magnox' nuclear reactors, Ricky Anderson had fallen heir to a number of specific duties which, over and above his own pet research programme, he now had to perform for the university.

One of those duties entailed facilitating weekly discussion seminars for 'focus groups' of under-graduate students, to assist them in their studies through what were essentially question-and-answer sessions. Ricky hated the seminars with a vengeance. Statistical physics and quantum field theory had been coming out of his ears for four long years, and he had now had it with all the theoretical stuff. Over time, Ricky had developed into an eager and highly-skilled experimental physicist, and while he fully recognised the critically important role of the theory which spawned the practice and upon which the student seminars were focused, it no longer held the same fascination for him. Moreover, he almost puked every time he thought of that stuck-up, privately-educated fourth-year physics student who hailed from the posh suburbs of Edinburgh and went by the name of Miranda Fletcher-Greene, flashing her ample cleavage and fluttering her big bushy eyelids at him, a tiresomely sassy act which only served to remind him how much he was missing the delectable Iona McNish.

At 10.00 a.m. precisely, Ricky drew the Tuesday morning seminar to a welcome close and quickly ushered himself out the door before Ms Fletcher-Greene could slink her way towards him and stick her big tits in his face to ask her latest inane question.

When he got back to Professor Bernstein's office, a handwritten note was lying on his own workstation desk. It was from Moira Davidson, the Prof's personal secretary.

'Ricky, I'm away to a meeting with the boss. A gentleman called Gerry McGhee phoned you. He said you would know who he was and asked if you could call him urgently. See you when I get back. Moira.'

Ricky thought for a moment, then stuffed the note into the hip pocket of his denims and headed out the door. He made his way along the corridor and down the big stairwell out onto the campus grounds, then began walking down University Avenue until he reached the public telephone box at the junction of Byres Road. This was one phone call which he simply couldn't risk making from the hustle-and-bustle of a busy office. Walls had ears, ears could lead to wagging tongues, and wagging tongues could spell big trouble.

Ricky took out his pocket diary and looked up McGhee's number, then shoved a couple of coins into the slot and dialled.

Once more, the investigative journalist picked up on the first ring.

'Gerry McGhee.'

'Gerry, it's me, Ricky.'

'Ah, the Lone Ranger himself. How you doing, Kemosabe? I tried to call you at the uni, but the wee lassie said you were busy. She sounded very protective of you, Ricky. You shagging her, by any chance?'

Ricky stifled a laugh, before responding.

'Unfortunately not, Gerry, I wouldn't know where to find the time. What do you think I am, a newspaper hack?'

McGhee chortled.

'Right, Ricky my boy, enough of the idle banter. I've been doing some more digging. I bent the editor's ear and we're going to do an extensive feature in next week's *Herald*. Not sure about a telly documentary yet. Too early, methinks. Let's see how this sordid little tale unfolds.'

'So, what has your shovel turned up, then? Spill the beans.'

'Not over the phone, Ricky. How are you fixed this afternoon? Say about fourish?'

'I've got a meeting at three, one I simply can't miss. A bigwig academic from St Andrew's University is coming over. My boss, the Prof, wants me to give him the royal tour. I could meet you about five, or maybe just after?'

'Okay. Lauder's Bar on Sauchiehall Street. I'll be the ugly one, remember?'

'How could I forget?'

The morning came and went, as did the 'royal tour' of the department which the Prof insisted that Ricky should conduct personally, for reasons best known to himself. In the event, Professor Alan McDiarmid, himself a well-known authority in the Magnox field, had been so impressed with Bernstein's young protege that he had effectively offered him a job at St Andrew's University. Or, as the celebrated academic had put it, 'a hook to hang your coat on if you ever fancy a big gulp of North Sea air'.

Ricky looked at his watch. It was almost ten-to-five and he had agreed to meet Gerry McGhee at five o'clock, or as near as damn it. He could have walked down Gibson Street and Woodlands Road onto Sauchiehall Street, but Lauder's Bar was at the far end of Glasgow's most famous thoroughfare and the journey by Shanks's pony would have taken him the best part of half-an-hour. So, he figured that it would be quicker to walk back down University Avenue and catch the subway at Hillhead Station, jump off at Cowcaddens, then make his way down Cambridge Street to the pub.

It was 5.35 p.m. when Ricky breezed in and made his way straight up to the bar, where McGhee was sipping on a pint of lager and tackling the *Glasgow Herald's* daily crossword puzzle. The journalist turned and gave Ricky a disapproving stare.

'And what kind of time do you call this, my boy?' he enquired, feigning mild annoyance. 'So, you must be shagging the Professor's secretary after all?'

Ricky just blanked the rhetorical question and ordered a couple of pints from the plump barmaid with the red hair. He made his way over to a table at the window. McGhee downed what was left of his lager, grabbed his replacement, stuffed the newspaper under his oxter and trotted over to join him.

'Well?' the budding nuclear physicist enquired of the battle-weary investigative journalist. 'Pray tell.'

'My God, you're in a hurry tonight!' McGhee retorted. 'Is it past your bedtime?'

'I'm sorry Gerry,' he replied. 'Just desperate to collect more ammunition on the gruesome twosome, that's all.'

'Well,' said McGhee, pulling his reporter's notebook from his jacket pocket. 'I'll let you know what I know.'

'I'm listening.'

'First of all, there's not much more on your favourite politician, Edwin Monk, because he's lying low, awaiting his big day in court. His political career is completely shot, his constituents and the local community have disowned him, and even the good old Labour Party wants nothing more to do with him. In fact, some lovely person panned in his car windows with a crowbar a few nights back, so he's not exactly flavour of the month down there on the seashore. And as you already know, the police have charged him with perverting the course of justice and two counts of embezzlement. The word is that he'll go down for three to four years, but probably get out after two if he's a good boy.'

Ricky nodded, then raised his eyebrows expectantly.

'And Rafferty?'

'Ah ... Rafferty,' McGhee said, tilting his head back with an uncomfortable sigh. 'Well, that's a different story.'

'Tell me, Gerry.'

'I'm not sure if I really should, Ricky. And for your own good ... if you know what I mean?'

'No, I don't know what you mean, so tell me. I can handle Rafferty.'

'It's not what Rafferty might do to you that I'm worried about, Ricky. It's what you might do to Rafferty. My spies tell me that you've got form. Form in the sense of being able to look after yourself, I'm told.'

'Is that right, Gerry? Your spies seem to be well-informed. Well, I promise I'll be good. Now tell me.'

McGhee sighed again, rubbed his chin between his thumb and forefinger and took a big slug from his pint glass.

'Okay, you asked for it, so here goes. Rafferty and his wife were hanging out for a couple of days in their holiday pad in France, when he got word that the local *gendarmerie* was after him. He split as soon as he heard the news and a good couple of hours before the French cops got there, leaving the wife behind. The Ayr cops are furious that he's been allowed to flee the nest. Mrs Rafferty is now back home in Troon and pleading total ignorance of his whereabouts, and Her Majesty's finest have absolutely no bloody idea where he is. And that's about it, Ricky.'

Ricky eyeballed McGhee with his trademark hypnotic stare, the one which could often reduce others to jelly. The journalist stared back in silence, then broke eye contact and lit up a cigarette.

'Anybody ever tell you that you can look quite scary at times, Ricky?'

'Aye, a couple of people might have mentioned it. What are you not telling me, Gerry?'

McGhee leaned back and swept his bony fingers through his hair in preparation for coughing up the information that he knew could spell trouble, big trouble. He inhaled deeply on his fag, held the smoke in his lungs for a couple of seconds then blew a cloud of exhaust fumes skyward in resignation.

'Ricky, I know where Rafferty is.'

'What? Where ... where is he?'

'He's hiding out in his brother's caravan in Doonfoot. It's in the fancy part of Ayr.'

'Aye, I know where Doonfoot is. How sure are you that Rafferty's in Doonfoot?'

'My sources are very good.'

'Where exactly in Doonfoot?'

McGhee reached into his inside jacket pocket and took out a piece of paper. He unfolded it, laid it out on the table and brushed it flat with the palm of his hand. His diction was unusually hesitant, his voice almost apologetic.

'A map of Doonfoot, Ricky. "X" marks the spot. The caravan sits on a finger-shaped piece of land behind a row of trees. It belongs to his brother, Dan, who is also a partner in the business. It's anything but an equal partnership, though. Frank Rafferty is the big daddy who calls the shots, Dan Rafferty the wee boy who does his bidding. The word is that Dan hates his big brother's guts, but he's always been too scared of him to take him on.'

'And the cops don't know anything about Rafferty being in Doonfoot?'

'Not yet, but they soon will. They're dumb, but not as dumb as all that. I'd give them three or four days, a week at most. What are you going to do, Ricky?'

'I'm not sure yet. I need to think about it.'

McGhee began rummaging around in the pockets of his well-worn tweed jacket and produced a white A5-sized envelope. He glided it onto the table as deftly as a professional card-sharp would deal out his latest offering in a high-stakes poker game.

'Well, think about these too while you're at it.'

Ricky picked up the envelope, shoved his fingers inside and slid its contents out onto the table. Four photographs, all in black-and-white. Two of a couple standing in a passionate embrace on the steps of a caravan, and two more with clear closeups of their faces. Ricky felt his blood start to boil as he stared at his nemesis, the one who had hospitalised his defenceless mother. Involuntarily, he twitched his nostrils before responding to McGhee with consummate coolness.

'So, not only is Rafferty's wife lying through her teeth to the cops about not knowing where he is, but she's actually staying with him in his brother's caravan?'

McGhee raised his eyebrows rather mischievously, like a naughty adolescent schoolboy about to spill the beans on his classmate's romantic indiscretions.

'That's not Irene Rafferty, Ricky.'

'Who ... who is it, then?'

'That's for you and me to find out.'

The old-head investigative journalist and the budding nuclear physicist sat there in silence for a few moments, the former concealing his amusement at the latter's face contorting in confusion. It was McGhee who broke the spell, his reeking cigarette bouncing like a bandsman's drumstick as his lips moved.

'So, now you've got the gold dust you were looking for, Ricky my boy. The question is, what are you going to do with it?'

'I need to think about it, Gerry,' Ricky replied, still reeling from this latest twist in what was fast becoming one almighty conundrum.

'You certainly do,' McGhee opined. 'And think about it very, very carefully. But whatever you do, don't go near Rafferty. Set him up and watch the sparks fly, no problem. Grass him into the cops, fine and dandy. But don't go near him, Ricky. This guy is bad news.'

Ricky leaned back against the wall, took another sip of his lager and sat there eyeballing McGhee.

'I don't need you to tell me he's bad news, Gerry. I've seen my mum's face. Remember?'

'That's a nasty habit you've got there, young man' said McGhee. 'That creepy stare of yours.'

'Not as bad as the one you've got,' Ricky replied. 'The cancer sticks, I mean.'

'You've always got an answer,' McGhee laughed. 'Always a smart-arsed answer.'

Ricky grabbed the map, folded it up and stuffed it into the inside pocket of his bomber-jacket, then shoved the four photographs back into the envelope and did likewise. He held out his hand and shook McGhee's firmly.

'Thanks for all this, Gerry. For your information, for the map and the photos, for next week's article ... you know ... for everything. I really appreciate it.'

McGhee knocked back what was left of his second pint, grabbed his copy of the Glasgow Herald and stood up. He looked at Ricky the way a wise old dad would run the rule over his adolescent son.

'Think this whole thing through before you do anything, Ricky, and really carefully. But remember, whatever you decide to do, don't approach Rafferty. Just don't go near him, leave him to the cops. I don't want to be reading about you in our obituary column next week.'

Ricky rose to his feet, smiled a cheeky smile and gave McGhee a mock military-style salute. The salute was returned.

'You take care of yourself, Ricky Anderson,' the journalist said with the utmost sincerity. 'You're a fine young lad, and your dad would have been very proud of you.'

'Thanks, Gerry,' Ricky replied. 'That means a lot.'

'One final thing,' McGhee added.

'And what's that?' Ricky enquired.

'For Christ's sake, get yourself a haircut. You look like a big jessie.'

29

For the second day in a row, Ricky Anderson found himself standing on the gloomy subterranean platform of Hillhead subway station, having left the mellow autumnal sunshine upstairs on Glasgow's busting Byres Road, the social epicentre of the city's prized west end.

This was a designated 'research day' after all, one which rather cunningly he had informed his flatmates and university colleagues he would be spending in Glasgow's renowned Mitchell Library, one of the largest public libraries in Europe. With over one million reference books bending its shelves, and countless eager patrons tiptoeing around its corridors and strewn in cerebral silence around its assorted study tables, the wordless anonymity which this magnificent old building offered was all the cover that Ricky would need to vanish elsewhere undetected.

The perfect alibi, in other words. Especially if he swallowed his pride and wore the ridiculous hooded jacket that Iona had bought him for Christmas, the very latest fashion accessory which had its roots in the rapidly-emerging New York 'hip-hop' culture, inspired by the zany organisation Zulu Nation, and ostensibly designed to entice the disillusioned youth of the day away from gang life and drugs. However, clad in his grey-black 'hoodie' on that crisp September day, Ricky Anderson had zero interest in either gang life or drugs. His only focus lay in the fine art of retribution, which as far as Ricky was concerned was a euphemism for justice. Frank Rafferty had unleashed terrible violence on his defenceless mother, and now he had to answer for his sins. An eye for an eye. Or more appropriately, a tooth for a tooth, because let's face it, Janice had lost five of her own at the hands of that callous thug.

Yesterday's subway destination had been Cowcaddens station at the far end of Cambridge Street, but today's would be two stops further along the 'Outer Circle' line to St Enoch, the busiest on the entire underground network, situated slap-bang in the city centre adjacent to its main drag, Argyle Street. From there, a couple of flights of concrete stairs and a brisk walk would take him underneath the 'Heilanman's Umbrella', the huge railway bridge leading overhead from Central Station, Glasgow's busiest rail hub, and into the railway station itself.

Ricky's journey by subway and foot took him less than twenty minutes. Once at the station, he bought his ticket at a small kiosk near the entrance to Gordon Street, shoved it into the side-pocket of his hoodie and jostled his way through the milling crowds towards Platform 13, where the British Railways train was already waiting patiently to whisk its expectant patrons away from the big smoke to the seaside town of Ayr.

With a self-rebuking grimace, Ricky pulled the hood over his head and zipped the zipper right up to chin level, totally concealing his shoulder-length hair. He walked up to the last carriage, the one that would be first to arrive at Ayr station, and sat himself down on a front-facing seat next to a window. He had made this journey many times before, but this time was different. This time, he felt strangely ill at ease, the tiny butterflies which had started fluttering in the pit of his stomach a couple of hours ago having mutated to giant avian proportions.

The carriage was filling up rapidly, and the last thing Ricky needed right now was company. In uncharacteristically anti-social fashion, he dragged his backside from the window seat to its partner nearer the passageway and dumped his rucksack down on the one he had just vacated, in order to make it as awkward as possible for some unwanted guest to join him. When the station guard blew his whistle, a few tail-end stragglers scrambled into the carriage just in time, followed by one terribly obese forty-something chap dressed in a cheap-looking suit and lugging a bulging briefcase, who just managed to bustle his way inside before the doors pecked his ample posterior as they swished to the closed position. He trudged up the passageway, stopped momentarily to look at the vacant seat to Ricky's left, got the death stare instead and thought better of it, then shuffled onwards to dump himself down beside an elderly lady who appeared only marginally less welcoming.

111

The train began trundling out of Glasgow Central Station and in no time emerged from cover into bright daylight. When the sun's rays seared straight into Ricky's eyes, he cursed under his breath. Armed with all the technological know-how that would be required to blow up half the world and probably the other half too, he cursed that he still didn't have the smarts to choose the correct side of a train to sit on. Then, as quickly as it had arrived, the sun disappeared again under a heavy black cloud, and his pupils dilated in gratitude.

Ricky stared at the grey walls of the big ugly buildings that bordered the vast matrix of railway lines which radiated outwards from the station, criss-crossing like strands of leftover spaghetti in the aftermath of a hearty Italian meal. He knew that on the other side of those same walls lay the relative opulence of the Central Hotel, and the hustle-bustle of umpteen cavernous, open-plan offices. However, their bleak exterior and the first impressions they unwittingly conveyed to passengers travelling in the opposite direction into the city centre for the very first time were beyond dismal. How he wished, though, that he was now returning to the big smoke rather than leaving it, because that would mean that his work for the day was done. And, of course, the problem was that today's work would be dangerous. Very dangerous indeed.

Looking all around to make sure that the coast was clear from prying eyes, he then took Gerry McGhee's envelope out of his rucksack and spread the four photographs onto the small table in front of him. As the train gathered speed and shot past Crossmyloof ice rink, home of the Glasgow Dynamos ice hockey team, Ricky stared at each photograph in turn. He examined the couple's features and facial expressions with all the precision and intensity of a CT scan, the exciting prototype of which had just been invented the year before by engineer Godfrey Hounsfield and physicist Allan Cormack. Those worthy pioneers would go on to receive the coveted Nobel Peace Prize for their sterling efforts, but when Ricky Anderson eventually got his hands on Frank Rafferty, he sure as hell wouldn't be picking up the same award.

Ricky stared into Rafferty's eyes. There was evil in those eyes, no doubt about it, pure unadulterated evil. But there was something else too. Was it insecurity, or was it even fear? Ricky couldn't tell, but there was definitely something else, something other than the menace that was oozing out of those cold, inhuman eyes. He would find out, though. Once he eventually caught up with him and looked him in the eye he would know, because the bastard would turn to jelly. All the bad guys did.

As for the mysterious, middle-aged blonde woman in the photographs, almost certainly Rafferty's latest 'wee bit on the side', forensic examination would be superfluous, because her own body language was an open book. Her eyes radiated a strange amalgam of wild excitement and genuine fear. Ricky stared at her face again. Without question, a good-looking woman for her late-forties or early-fifties, but a lost soul whose eyes were bursting with arousal and yet screaming for help at the same time. Ricky surmised that she had probably fallen under bigwig Rafferty's spell and hadn't even noticed when her knickers had followed suit, by which time it was too late and she was hopelessly trapped in a hugely exciting but desperately pernicious relationship.

He slipped the photographs back into the envelope and replaced them with the map which McGhee had given him. Doonfoot, arguably the most salubrious of Ayr's leafy suburbs, that's where Dan Rafferty's static caravan enjoyed pride of place. Probably a rather comfy home-from-home from time-to-time for any number of Dan's assorted sparring partners, he had now offered it to his big brother as a temporary bolthole while the latter tried to secrete himself away from the Ayrshire cops. Meanwhile, good old Frankie-Boy was clearly making the most of the opportunity to screw the brains out of his latest conquest.

By the time Ricky had psychoanalysed the couple from their mugshots and deployed the map to work out the best route to Dan Rafferty's caravan, the train had already reached Prestwick railway station, adjacent to the international airport of the same name. After whizzing past a couple of sprawling golf courses and a succession of well-manicured back gardens, Prestwick had given way to Newton-upon-Ayr and then to Ayr itself, where he found himself alighting onto Platform 2 and marching briskly towards the seaside town's Burns Statue Square. A five-minute walk then took him to Wellington Street bus station, where only a few days ago he had pinned Iona against a brick wall and proposed marriage. Today's mission would be somewhat different.

Ricky made his way towards a waiting bus with the words 'Girvan via Doonfoot' emblazoned on its nameplate and stepped aboard, taking his seat rather inconspicuously towards the rear of the coach. It was a full ten minutes before the plump, pleasant-faced

113

bus conductress approached him, eyeing him suspiciously as he stared out from the subterfuge of his hooded jacket, and by which time the bus had almost reached his destination.

'A return to Earl's Way, please,' Ricky mumbled.

The conductress shoved a small cardboard ticket into the little machine dangling from her neck and gave the handle a quick turn. Immediately clocking that the young man hiding his youthful features under that sinister canopy was much more of a visitor to the plush suburb of Doonfoot than a resident, she thrust the ticket towards him with a brusque, 'twelve pence, son', before turning on her heels. As the bus passed the garden centre opposite the Balgarth Hotel, one of the most revered hostelries in a town blessed with more than its fair share, Ricky rose to his feet and pressed the little bell on the ceiling to alert the driver that he was now approaching his destination.

A couple of minutes later, he found himself striding briskly down the tree-lined pavement of the aptly-named Earl's Way, gawking in admiration at the swish residences which basked in the sunshine on either side of the road. From towering three-storey villas protected on all elevations by six-foot-high brick walls to sprawling bungalows circumscribed by gloriously manicured gardens bursting with autumnal bloom, this place really was the epitome of affluence. For one fleeting moment Ricky allowed his guard to drop, as he caught an ethereal vision of his own mother stepping outside to prune the roses in the magnificent front garden of the huge ranch-style bungalow he was now passing, before quickly reminding himself that hers was a modest two-up, two-down semi-detached council house in a humble coalmining village. One where people worked their fingers to the bone and walked the plank for each other. They, he assured himself, were the lucky ones, not those in the leafy suburbs, many of whom were probably 'all fur coat and nae knickers', as his dearly-departed old granny used to say.

One thing was for sure. No matter to which heady heights of academia he might eventually climb, Ricky Anderson would always have a healthy dose of inverted snobbery by his side.

Perpendicular to the foot of Earl's Way lay another long road, this adjacent to a stretch of gorse-covered scrubland which separated the residential area from the sandy beach and gently-lapping waters of the Firth of Clyde. As Ricky turned the corner, a silver Mercedes reversed out of its walled driveway and a middle-aged lady sporting the archetypal 'seventies-style blue-rinse hairdo eyed him with a disapproving stare. Overhead, a flock of noisy seagulls hovered in the sea breeze before diving down towards the gorse-clad *terra firma* in strange elliptical swoops, either absorbed in the developing dynamics, or more likely, in search of resident rodents about to draw their last.

After a brisk walk of only a couple of hundred yards at most, Ricky could just make out the small copse of trees behind which Dan Rafferty's caravan allegedly lay, at least according to Gerry McGhee's well-worn map. He continued his journey on foot until he had passed the trees where, as the old map had promised, a standard-issue, cream-coloured static caravan immediately revealed itself, lying recessed about thirty yards back off the main road, but connected to it by a rough and heavily potholed hardcore driveway.

Ricky inhaled deeply. The moment of truth was fast approaching.

The caravan itself wasn't nearly as big as he had imagined, nor indeed in as pristine a condition as might have been expected of a man in Dan Rafferty's exalted position on the Ayrshire social scene. Pretty disappointing really, although probably all that mattered to big brother Frank was the strength of the springs supporting the mattress on the double bed.

Checking to see that the coast was clear, Ricky strolled up and down the pavement opposite the caravan, in order to choose the location that would give him the best view of its front door. He then sat down on the concrete sea-wall and began mulling over his battle plan. After a few minutes of deep contemplation, he swung his legs over the wall and dropped down into the adjacent scrub. An easy scramble between some gorse bushes festooned with bright yellow flowers which camouflaged the jaggy thorns lurking underneath took him to a slightly elevated spot in a small sandy clearing surrounded by assorted foliage. A perfect vantage point, absolutely perfect. All that remained now was to wait for the gathering gloom of nightfall.

Then it would be showtime.

30

Janice Anderson was in no mood to be patronised, let alone mollycoddled. She was on a mission and the hounds of hell couldn't stop her now.

Her willing carer and prospective lover, Charlie Reynolds, meant well but he was beginning to push his luck. Sure, he had very caringly nursed her back to health from her near-vegetative state of only a few days back, as evidenced by the fact that she was now sitting fully clothed on his tan-leather settee instead of lying semi-comatose in an NHS hospital bed. However, Janice hadn't heard from her only child for several days now, not a cheep, and Charlie's valiant attempts to reassure her were beginning to grate.

'Nobody has a clue where he is, Charlie,' Janice repeated for the umpteenth time, pupils dilated in exasperation. 'Nobody. Not even Professor what's-his-bloody-name.'

'Bernstein,' the big cop replied, trying to conceal the faintest smile at Janice's previously unseen grit. 'Professor Bernstein.'

'Okay, Professor Bernstein, then. This isn't like my Ricky. It's just not like him at all. If Ricky was going away somewhere, he'd have told me.'

'It's his day off, Janice. A research day. He could be anywhere. Studying ... window shopping ... having a couple of pints in the city centre. Ricky's a very sensible young man. You need to trust him to do his own thing.'

'Right then, Charlie. You're the detective, so let's look at it your way, okay? I've phoned everybody I can think of. Nobody knows where he is. Not Iona, not Andy Tennent, not the professor, not his secretary, not his university chums, not his flatmates, nobody.'

'As I said, Janice, it's his day off.'

'Yes, Charlie, I heard you. Some of them even said he was supposed to be studying in the Mitchell Library. So, I phoned them too. And did he sign in at the library? No, he did not, not at any time. I then phoned his landlord, Mister Khan, who went and checked personally to see if he was back home in his flat, but he was nowhere to be seen.'

'Which only means that he decided to go somewhere else on his day off. Maybe he's sitting in the Odeon Cinema on Sauchiehall Street, watching ... I don't know ... one of those new movies like "The Exorcist". All the young kids are desperate to see it.'

'A movie, Charlie? No way would my Ricky be sitting in an old picture house on a sunny autumn afternoon, watching a movie. No way. Ricky has only two loves in his life, Iona McNish and Nuclear Physics. The first one's out, because I've spoken to Iona three times today and she doesn't have a clue where he is. And the second one's out too, because his colleagues in the Physics Department have no idea either.'

'Good God, Janice, have you now got that wee lassie into a stew as well as yourself?'

Janice glowered at Reynolds. Her eyes were on fire. It was the first time she had ever looked at him like that, and he sincerely hoped it would be the last.

'Jesus Christ, Janice,' he said, reeling from the shock. 'Now I see who that young kid gets his scary stare from. Can you give me one of your nice wee smiles again? Please?'

Janice stifled a little giggle. She knew she could sometimes freeze others to the spot with what her late husband, Davie, used to call her 'stare from hell', but Reynolds had been really good to her at a very difficult time and he didn't deserve that. Furthermore, the fact that he was a bit of a hunk hadn't exactly passed her by.

'I'm sorry, Charlie,' she whispered softly. 'Come here, you big dope.'

Reynolds didn't wait for a second invitation. He slipped nervously onto the couch beside Janice. She leaned forward and kissed him gently on the lips. He looked into her eyes, because he wanted to savour the moment. The anger was gone, and a different kind of fire radiated from those same eyes. How he yearned to pick her up and whisk her along the hallway into the master bedroom, but somehow his brain succeeded in putting the brakes on that which his galloping hormones struggled to comprehend, the sad fact that her battered body was still far from up to the fine art of horizontal gymnastics.

After a long, passionate embrace, it was Janice who broke the spell.

'What are you thinking, Detective Inspector?'

His reply startled her.

'I'm thinking I might be in love with you, Janice.'

She froze for a moment, before turning her back on him. Silence descended once more, deafening in its suddenness. For Reynolds, an awful ghastly silence. For her, one delivered from a divine power which she thought had long deserted her. Mere words seemed incapable of bringing it to an end, but Janice's tears eventually did. The more she sobbed, the tighter Charlie hugged her. Finally, the words came out.

'Charlie, my head's all over the place just now.'

117

'I know. I understand.'

'No, you don't. You really don't.'

'Try me.'

More silence, if one now laced with expectation that a great truth was about to be revealed. For Charlie Reynolds, it felt like one of those rare moments of unbearable tension when after weeks of stirring and digging, a hardened criminal was finally about to cough his guts up and spill the beans. Only this time, times ten.

'Charlie, a long time ago, I lost the only man I ever loved, and it broke my heart. Until I met you, I've never been with another man. And now that I have met you ....'

'What? What, Janice?'

'It scares me, Charlie.'

'What scares you?'

'The thought of getting close to another man ... and, well ... liking him ... liking him a lot. And then ...'

'And then, what?'

'And then ... and then ... he's taken away from me again. And then I get my heart broken again.'

'Come here,' Charlie whispered, gently turning her head to face him. Her eyes met his. He kissed her gently on the nose and wiped the tears from her cheeks with his forefinger.

'I'm going nowhere, Janice Anderson. Nowhere. You hear me? You'll need to kick me out first.'

'I might,' she giggled. 'You never know.'

Janice buried her head in Charlie's chest and lay there motionless.

'You make me feel safe, Charlie. And right now, I need to feel safe. I've been through quite a lot recently ... with all my financial worries ... and all this stuff with Frank Rafferty ... and now Ricky himself. I'm just not thinking very clearly, Charlie. And then you come along ... and, well ... sweep me off my feet.'

'Let's just take things slowly for now. You know, one step at a time and all that.'

'Okay ... but it might be easier said than done.'

'Let's just see what happens. Do you want to talk about Ricky? You know, tell me what's on your mind? Tell me exactly what you're worried about?'

Janice pulled her frame upright with a grimace of discomfort and leaned her head against the back of the settee. She steadied herself before continuing.

'Ricky was always a good boy, Charlie, never a minute's bother. But when Davie died, he kind of ... well, he went off the rails for a while. He got into a few scraps and ... well ...'

'And well, what?'

'He gave a few lads a hiding, Charlie, that's what. And I mean a real hiding. Soon, nobody would even dream about taking him on. He once leathered a pair of the school's so-called hard men in the playground after they had taunted him about his dad's motorbike accident ... so badly that it took four teachers to pull him off them, and after which both of the boys ended up in hospital. I got summoned to the headmaster's office that time, and the police were there too, but they never charged him or anything like that.'

'I know about that, Janice, I just didn't mention it.'

Janice turned and looked Charlie straight in the eye, astonished.

'How do you know ... and why didn't you say?'

'One of the officers involved in investigating the school incident was Andy McTurk, whom you met recently,' Charlie replied. 'He was a sergeant at the time ... in uniform, you know? I thought you recognised him the other day when he spoke to you. You did, didn't you?'

Janice blanked the observation, body-swerved the question and ploughed on.

'So, why didn't you tell me you knew about that incident?'

'Because it just didn't seem all that important, Janice. After all, it happened eight years ago. I did mention it to Ricky, though, the night we went for a pint in the Market Inn. Well ... obliquely, not directly.'

'Why did you mention it to him?'

'Because on the night of your assault when we were in the house and you were in the ambulance, Ricky hit me on the jaw. And I stayed hit. It was an absolute humdinger.'

'Oh my God, Charlie. You told me you got that bruise arresting a criminal. You should have said it was Ricky who did it.'

'What? Big tough cop trying to impress the new woman in his life gets gubbed by a young university student? I don't think so, Janice.'

'Okay, but why did you mention his earlier fights to him?'

'Good God, woman, it's twenty questions with you, isn't it?'

'Well?'

'I mentioned it because I wanted Ricky to know that I knew. I

119

suppose it was just my way of warning him off taking Rafferty into his own hands.'

'It won't work, Charlie. Ricky has never started a fight in his life, but he's fearless. Absolutely fearless. I think that's why he has … well, disappeared. Charlie, I think Ricky is going to go after Rafferty.'

Charlie Reynolds rubbed his nose for a moment, turned and kissed Janice gently on the lips, then rose from the settee.

'And where do you think you're going, then?' she asked, clearly non-plussed.

'Listen,' said Reynolds, 'I'm just going to nip into the office and have a wee word with Andy. The sooner we put tabs on this young superhero of yours, the better. We'll keep an eye on him until Rafferty eventually turns up, then we'll deal with it. We'll just watch him from a distance. He won't even know we're there. I'll be back in a couple of hours, okay?'

'Okay, but be careful. I could get used to you being around.'

'You'd better, because I'm going nowhere. Remember?'

31

Ricky Anderson sat on the raised banking concealed from view by a thorny circle of bramble and gorse bushes. He drained the last remaining drops from his can of coke and buried the empty container in the soft sand with the soles of his boots. Ricky hated litter-louts with a vengeance, but this was no time to be contemplating environmental matters.

Turning his watch towards what remained of a glorious autumn sunset, he noted that the time was now 8.20 p.m. and watched as the brilliant red-orange globe sank lower and lower towards the western horizon. For the merest moment, he allowed his mind to wander from the fearsome task that lay ahead back to his alter ego as a recently qualified scientist. Silently, he pondered the enormity of that same huge ball of fire which seemed to be about to extinguish itself a mere stone's throw away in the Firth of Clyde, but which he knew full well was raging continuously in flame almost 93 million miles away at an average surface temperature of over 5,000 degrees centigrade. Releasing its vast reserves of energy through the sinister process of nuclear fusion, he marvelled that our sun had been processing some six-hundred-million metric tons of hydrogen into helium every single second since our universe first exploded into being, and prayed wordlessly that it would continue to deliver the goods for a very long time to come. At least until he finally got the chance to get even with Rafferty.

As the heat of the day dissipated into the late evening air, Ricky felt the warm sand begin to cool beneath his rump. He stared mindlessly at the lights of the neighbouring houses springing to life one-by-one, slowly illuminating the planned evening activities of an unsuspecting Doonfoot community. He watched in detached indifference as a well-domesticated husband stood at his kitchen sink washing the grime from the dinner plates while his wife chatted on the telephone in front of her colour television, reflecting ruefully that it would be some time yet before his own mother would be fortunate enough to say farewell to her more modest black-and-white set.

A lazy evening slowly gave way to an even sleepier night, before the quiet ambience was suddenly split by the roar of a motorcycle screaming along the road adjacent to the sea wall. A horrific mental picture flashed through Ricky's mind. It was of his late father's final moments of life in a blazing inferno as his own motorbike thundered into the back of a jack-knifed articulated lorry. When would those gut-wrenching visions ever end? And what had a wonderful husband and dad ever done to deserve such a terrible fate?

A chill breeze suddenly whipped up some specks of sand to snap Ricky out of his vision from hell and remind him that autumn would shortly be passing the baton to winter. Something scurried around in the undergrowth, no doubt something small and furry. Instinctively, Ricky gritted his teeth and shivered. He hated rodents of all shapes and sizes, absolutely detested them, and the thought of a mouse running up inside the leg of his denims absolutely terrified him. A mindless gangster would be a piece of cake compared to a bloody fieldmouse.

By quarter-to-nine there was still no sign of life in Dan Rafferty's caravan, as it sat there protected by the small copse of trees that swayed contentedly in the evening breeze. The back door opened in one of the neighbouring houses, and the adjacent neon streetlight revealed a young couple emerging into semi-darkness. The lady locked up behind her, while her husband raised the up-and-over garage door. The sound of a car engine being cranked into action pierced the eerie stillness of the night, and a pair of headlights flashed straight into Ricky's eyes.

He hit the deck like a felled oak, certain that the couple must have spotted him standing there in the bushes like some kind of perverted voyeur. A few moments later, he watched in relief as the light-coloured car sped off into the distance, its occupants none the wiser that the vicinity of their home was being observed by a nuclear physicist who had serious retribution on his mind.

Pupils heavily retracted by the car's dazzling headlights, it was a good couple of minutes before they dilated sufficiently to allow Ricky's vision to re-adapt to the darkness of the night-time sky. When they did, he could immediately see that a solitary light had now appeared on the porch of the Rafferty caravan. His heart skipped a beat, and his breathing began to accelerate. He instinctively covered his head with his hood and pulled up the zip to fasten it securely under his chin.

It was time to boogie.

Very slowly and stealthily, he shuffled his way down through the bushes and swung his legs over the wall onto the pavement. Looking left and right like a toddler taking his first tentative steps across a busy road, he checked that nobody was watching and marched briskly over to the other side towards the wooded copse. Once there, he located a convenient gap in the trees which would perform the dual function of providing him with cover whilst giving him a relatively uninterrupted view of the caravan.

All that remained now was for Ricky to choose his moment. Over the past few days, he had run this scenario through his mind more times than he'd brushed his teeth, and he knew precisely what to do, down to the very last detail. Walk straight in, look Rafferty in the eye, confront him with the truth and ... well ... take things from there. And if that meant a bit of furniture rearrangement, then so be it. After all, the bastard had it coming.

With a bit of luck, Rafferty's latest belly-warmer wouldn't be on the premises, but if she was, she'd be so scared shitless that she would either freeze to the spot or bolt out the door. Either way would be fine with Ricky, because he just wanted Rafferty all to himself.

There was no turning back now. Ricky took another deep breath, checked in all directions for unwelcome passers-by and began tiptoeing in the direction of the caravan. No sooner had he left the relative security of the foliage than the front door of the caravan suddenly sprang open. Ricky quickly retraced his steps and dived for cover, hoping he hadn't been clocked.

From the dim light on the porch, he could just see the figure of a man making his exit, not running but not hanging about either. He was roughly five-ten in height, stocky-built and probably in his mid-forties, but apart from that it was almost impossible to establish any of the guy's other defining features. Ricky wondered if it was Frank Rafferty himself, but he simply couldn't be sure. If it was, though, where was he going in such a hurry? And if it wasn't, then who was it?

A car door clicked open, an engine fired up and a set of dipped headlights began snaking down the rough driveway towards the main road. The car then turned left and sped away in the opposite direction from the Earl's Way route that had led Ricky to the caravan earlier in the day. He strained his eyes to try to identify the make of the vehicle, but the surreal neon half-light made it impossible, other than to establish that it was dark in colour, and it certainly didn't look like a Jaguar. Almost certainly not Rafferty, then, Ricky surmised.

He pondered the situation for a moment, then made up his mind. He had to find out what was going on. After all, it was only a matter of time before the cops would eventually catch up with Rafferty, then his chance would be gone, so just standing there in the dark scratching his backside and dithering simply wasn't an option. Ricky had to get himself into that caravan and get in now. If Rafferty was there, then it would be Plan A as rehearsed *ad infinitum*. If he wasn't, then it would be Plan B, whatever that happened to be, because he sure as hell hadn't even thought of a Plan B.

Another big breath, another visual sweep for any nocturnal sightseers, another twinkle-toed advance towards the caravan and Ricky suddenly found himself standing at a set of three wooden steps, listening to the caravan door creaking as it swung backwards and forwards in the breeze. He grabbed the railing and climbed the steps one-by-one in slow-motion. Once on the top step, he leaned over as far as he dared and peered in through the porch door towards the living room, which was illuminated by one solitary table-lamp but almost totally concealed from the outside world by two sets of carelessly-drawn curtains.

Standing there straining his neck like a nosey cow peering over a country hedgerow, Ricky could just make out the outline of dark-haired man sitting casually on a built-in settee, facing away from him. He recognised him immediately. It was Frank Rafferty, no doubt about it. The dark shoulder-length hair and sallow complexion were the big giveaways. They somehow oozed of pretentiousness and deceit.

On seeing Rafferty sprawled out on the settee seemingly without a care in the world, an overwhelming feeling of rage overcame Ricky. He stormed in through the creaking door and slammed it shut behind him. He then filled his youthful lungs with an almighty inhalation of seaside air and bellowed so loudly that he was sure the whole street must have heard him.

'Rafferty! How would you like to dance with a man for a change?'

Nothing. Not a movement, not a word.

Ricky yelled again.

'Don't ignore me, you bastard!'

Still nothing, not a flicker.

Ricky bolted towards him, his left hand ready to grab Rafferty by the throat, his right fist clenched tight. Not yet, though, Ricky, he cautioned himself. First, he had to face Rafferty head-on. He had to look him squarely in the eye. He had to give him his death-stare and reduce him to jelly.

As Ricky turned to face his nemesis, his jaw almost hit the floor.

'Oh, God,' he gasped. 'Oh, my God. Oh, Jesus Christ almighty.'

And there before him sat Frank Rafferty, bolt upright, his light-blue shirt and tan-coloured trousers saturated in dark-red blood, his throat sliced open from one ear to the other.

32

Charlie Reynolds's last visit of the day was to a semi-detached council house at the top of Cumnock's Emrys Avenue, the street named after the late Emrys Hughes who served for many years as the area's Member of Parliament and whose father-in-law was none other than the legendary Keir Hardie, a founder member of the Labour Party and its very first parliamentary leader. Reynolds was off-duty and in his civvies.

When Doreen McNish opened the front door, she was sure that the big distinguished-looking guy who stood on her top step was yet another of those cocky door-to-door salesmen who always seemed to turn up at the most inconvenient time of day or night. For example, right in the middle of one of her favourite TV programmes, *Are You Being Served?*

'I'm sorry,' Doreen said, her demeanour polite yet firm. 'I don't know what you're selling, but we don't need any.'

'My apologies,' replied Reynolds with his best reassuring smile. 'I'm not a salesman, I'm a detective police officer.'

Doreen gave him the once-over and smiled back.

'Well, I'm no detective myself, but from where I'm standing you certainly don't look like one.'

Reynolds glanced down at his jumper-jeans-and-trainers combo and held up his hands in acknowledgement of her astute observation.

'You've certainly got me there, Mrs McNish. Yes, I'm off-duty at the moment as you can see, but honestly, I really am a police officer.'

'How do you know my name? And what is it you want?'

'I'm really sorry to disturb you, but I wonder if I might come in and explain. It's nothing to worry about, I promise.'

Just at that, a young lady appeared at the door. She was slim-built with dark wavy hair, a light-olive complexion and a pair of soft brown eyes that would have stopped King Kong dead in his tracks. Ricky had chosen well, Reynolds reflected, very well indeed.

'So, this must be Iona?'

Mother and daughter just stood there in silence, wondering what to make of it all. Was this guy really who he claimed to be, or just another chancer trying to get his foot in the door in a wily attempt to flog them his latest state-of-the-art washing machine? Reynolds clocked their suspicion. He addressed the younger of the two.

'Hi Iona, I'm Charlie,' he said. 'Charlie Reynolds. I'm looking after Janice, Ricky's mum. She's staying with me for a few days now that she's been discharged from hospital. I take it Ricky told you?'

'Oh ... oh, yes,' Iona exclaimed, the penny finally dropping. 'Yes, he did. Mum, are we just going to keep the poor man standing out there all night? Come in, please.'

A few minutes later, all three were sitting around the coffee table in the family living room, sipping at their cups of tea and tucking into Doreen McNish's home-made treacle scones, exchanging well-meaning pleasantries about Ricky's university exploits and his mother's continuing recovery. Soon, though, it was time for the big cop to get serious.

'Iona,' he said, studying her facial expression to gauge her

125

reaction to his opening salvo. 'Do you happen to know where Ricky is today?'

'No ... no, I don't,' she replied. 'I haven't spoken to him since Monday. He normally phones me every two or three days. Why? Why are you asking, officer?'

'Call me Charlie, will you please?'

'Okay then, Charlie, you're worrying me. Is Ricky ... is he okay?'

'As far as we know he's fine, Iona, and we have absolutely no reason to think otherwise. It's just that nobody seems to have seen him for a couple of days. His university colleagues, his mates, his landlord ... nobody.'

'But why are you even asking? What's the big problem? Wednesday is his study leave day, so he's probably been in the Mitchell Library, which is where he normally goes on a Wednesday. Or he might even have been at the shops, for all I know. He could be anywhere, really.'

'He hasn't set foot in the Mitchell, Iona. We've checked.'

'We? What do you mean we?'

'My colleague, Detective Inspector McTurk and me. We're keen to find out where he is, Iona.'

'But why ... why today of all days? I don't understand.'

Reynolds swept his fingers through his dark short-cropped hair and grimaced. He wasn't looking forward to his next offering.

'Has Ricky told you about what happened to Janice? I mean, about what really happened to her? And Iona, this is the important bit. About who he thinks harmed Janice?'

Iona shuffled nervously in her seat, trying to work out exactly where the off-duty detective's line of questioning was leading. It was her mother who spoke next.

'I think you should tell us both what this is all about. What exactly is going on here?'

'We're pretty sure we know who attacked Janice,' Reynolds replied. 'And we're equally sure about who gave the order.'

'A man called Frank Rafferty,' Iona interjected, looking first at Reynolds then turning to face her mother. 'Ricky told me, mum. And he's not a nice man.'

'Correct, Iona,' replied Reynolds. 'He's definitely not a nice man. And we're fairly certain that it was Rafferty who gave the order and arranged for one of his associates to attack Janice. And I know that Ricky knows, because he told me face-to-face. And that's what worries me, Iona. And it's worrying Janice too.'

'What ... what worries you?' Iona asked, becoming more and more agitated. 'I'm really confused here.'

'The gentleman in question ... Rafferty ... has gone into hiding and we, the police, are very keen to find out where he is, so that we can apprehend and question him.'

'So, what's that got to do with Ricky?'

'We're worried that Ricky might get to Rafferty first.'

'Oh my God. That ... that wouldn't be good.'

'No, it wouldn't, Iona. Ricky is very angry about what happened to his mum. And if he gets to Rafferty before we do, then ... well, you can fill in the blanks for yourself.'

Iona and her mother just sat staring at each other, lips uttering not a single word, eyes asking a thousand questions. Reynolds handed Iona a business card.

'Iona, I'm sure Ricky is fine. He's a big boy and he can look after himself. But if you can think of anything ... anything at all ... that might help us to track him down, please ring me on this number. If I'm not there, ask for DI Andy McTurk. You can trust Andy, and you can trust me. The minute Ricky calls you, please get him to call me. If he refuses, then you call me yourself. It's really important that Ricky lets us deal with Rafferty, instead of taking the law into his own hands.'

Iona brows began to furrow, confirming her escalating concern.

'What's the matter, Iona?' her mother enquired.

'He's been meeting some journalist chap,' she replied. 'Someone who writes in the daily papers and makes TV documentaries.'

'Do you have a name, Iona?' Reynolds asked.

'I think the name was McGhee,' came a hesitant reply. 'I can't be sure, but I think that was what Ricky said.'

'Not Gerry McGhee, by any chance?' asked Reynolds.

'Yes, that's the name,' she answered. 'Gerry McGhee. I'm sure of it. Do you know him?'

No,' replied Reynolds. 'Only by reputation. But you can be sure I soon will.'

33

Ricky Anderson stared open-mouthed at Frank Rafferty's blood-soaked corpse, near catatonic in shock. It was the distant rumble of a passing vehicle that snapped him out of it. His next words came out in a strangled whisper.

'Oh my God,' he wheezed. 'Oh ... my ... God.'

As Ricky stood rooted to the spot, his eyes darted around the caravan's living quarters like a feral cat casing a meadow for unsuspecting rodents, seeing everything, but unlike the cat, detecting nothing.

Inanimate objects abounded, all of them temporarily invisible to their beholder. A fitted dining table that seemed to be at loggerheads with its two foldaway chairs. A bulky television set hanging for dear life on four spindly legs. An enormous 'ghetto blaster' music system lying on the floor beside a pair of brown corduroy slippers. A vase of emaciated flowers begging for a drink on the window-sill. A bag of dirty golf clubs propped up against the far wall. A turquoise-blue hair drier lying on the wet kitchen drainboard just waiting for the opportunity to electrocute its next user. A pair of ladies' tights draped over the big chair that matched the settee where Frank Rafferty's inanimate body sat bolt upright like some ghoulish mannequin. Each item in plain sight in its own rightful place, but all splattered with the deep-red blood that had sprayed in every direction of the compass like a burst garden hosepipe the moment Rafferty's jugular vein had been severed.

To Ricky, the items possessed neither shape nor form. All he could see was the blood. Instinctively, he grabbed Rafferty's left wrist and felt for a pulse, the same way he had seen it done in *Marcus Welby MD*, his favourite American medical drama series. No pulse, not even the merest flicker. Of course, there's no pulse, he rebuked himself. I mean, come on Ricky, look at him. His head is hanging half-off and he's sitting there saturated in his own blood like something out of a horror movie. Ricky tried to swallow a nervous giggle, but it somehow managed to burst free as a hysterical laugh. This couldn't possibly be happening, it just couldn't.

In the subdued glow of the table lamp, something glistened on the floor, semi-concealed underneath the settee. Ricky bent down and picked it up. It was a kitchen knife. Not the kind of knife that his mum would ever have had in her own kitchen, but a proper knife, like something a real chef would use. It looked razor-sharp and it was thick with blood. Gloopy and semi-congealed blood. He stared at the blade for a few moments and could just make out his own distorted reflection between the bloodstains.

It was then that the pure folly of his actions hit him. He dropped the knife onto the floor as if it had suddenly become red-hot and kicked it back under the settee. This time, real words came out.

'Christ Almighty, Ricky, what are you doing, man? Get your arse out of here.'

Half-walking and half-staggering, he made a beeline for the caravan door and turned the handle. Looking around in the darkness of the night, he saw that the coast was clear. He leapt down the three wooden steps then bolted towards the welcome camouflage of the copse of trees. Another quick check in all directions followed by a gut-busting sprint across the road and Ricky was back among his favourite gorse bushes, from which he scrambled his way down onto the beach. In the darkness, the waves lapping on the sand just managed to make themselves heard above the heartbeat thumping in his ears. He took a few long, deep breaths, slowed his step to a canter and began making his way briskly along the shore in the direction of the town centre. With no moonlight to guide him, he would have to rely on the waves licking at his feet to keep him going in a straight line.

For the very first time in his purposeful young life, Ricky Anderson had absolutely no idea where he was headed, but one thing was for sure. He wouldn't stop till he got there.

34

An early morning shower began to bounce off the windscreen of the gold-coloured Hillman Avenger parked on Mitchell Street, the main northbound thoroughfare leading to Glasgow's busy city centre.

Its driver peered out at the magnificent Lighthouse building, designed by Charles Rennie Mackintosh, the city's favourite architectural son. These days, the famous old building played host to the *Glasgow Herald* newspaper, itself a world-renowned daily broadsheet founded away back in 1783, rendering it as old as the United States of America.

Detective Inspector Andy McTurk was in one of his foul moods that morning, having eventually given in to the ferret-like insistence of his opposite number, Charlie Reynolds, to allow him to tag along to his latest interview.

'If Smokin' Joe finds out about this, we'll both be cleaning the bloody lavvies come Monday. This is your first and last direct involvement in the formalities of the case, Charlie. And I mean it.'

'Aye, I know, Andy,' Reynolds replied, rolling his eyes. 'You've made your point a dozen times.'

'And a lot of bloody good it's done,' McTurk snapped back, determined to have the last word, whilst silently appreciating just how important the upcoming interview might ultimately prove to be to the security of the Anderson family, for whom his loyal sidekick had now clearly assumed the role of protector-in-chief. 'This one interview, Charlie, and that's it.'

Up on the third floor of the building, ace reporter Gerry McGhee lit up his tenth fag of the morning and inhaled deeply. The *Herald's* new whipper-snapper sub-editor, Dennis Grant, that super-ambitious young chancer whose pubic hair was probably still waiting to make its first appearance, was really doing Gerry's head in with his ridiculous deadlines. The exclusive which he had been burning the midnight oil to complete, the one on the crooked 'Mutt and Jeff' combo from down Ayr way, would be ready when it was ready and not before, and Dennis-the-Menace could go screw himself.

A gentle knock on the door disturbed McGhee's concentration for the third time in as many minutes. Margery Pettigrew certainly knew when to knock hard and when to knock gently. From the moment she had walked into the office and read the impatience in her boss's body language, she had clocked that this would definitely be a knock-gently morning.

'What is it this time, Margery?' McGhee enquired with an exasperated sigh, looking up over the rim of his glasses as she opened the door. 'I hope it's important. Please tell me the Russians have dropped a nuclear bomb on Hampden Park? God knows it could do with a facelift.'

'A couple of men here to see you, Gerry,' she replied, eyebrows raised as their gazes met, radiating her familiar be-on-your-guard expression. She then turned and chaperoned the pair of strangers through the door. 'They're police officers.'

McGhee looked up from his typewriter, tilted his head enquiringly, and stubbed out what was left of his cigarette into what was left of his tea.

'Good morning, gentlemen,' he said, rising to his feet and extending his hand in well-contrived deference. 'Please ... pull up a couple of chairs. How can I help you? And I really hope this won't take long, because I'm up against a pretty fierce deadline today.'

It was the older one who spoke first.

'So, you're the famous Gerry McGhee, then? I've read some of your newspaper articles and watched a couple of your television documentaries. You're very good.'

'Thank you,' McGhee replied with a forced smile, 'I am indeed. And who might you two fine gentlemen be, then?'

'I'm Detective Inspector McTurk,' the same officer replied, before gesturing towards his partner and adding, 'and this is Detective Inspector Reynolds. We're with Southwest Scotland Police, Ayr branch.'

It was the last two words that made McGhee catch his breath.

'Oh ... Ayr you say? So, pray tell, just what the devil brings both of you up from the sun-kissed sands to the grimy delights of our beloved big smoke?'

It was Reynolds who spoke this time. His tone was firm and sharp, in contrast to McTurk's, and clearly designed to stamp out the frivolousness in McGhee's own.

'A young man called Ricky Anderson,' he retorted, eyeballing the investigative journalist with intense concentration. 'Do you know him?'

A moment's uneasy silence.

'Ah ... I see,' McGhee replied, exuding a bit more outward calmness than he really felt in the pit of his stomach, the same feeling he always got when he instinctively knew that something wasn't quite right. 'Good cop, bad cop, is it?'

'Do you know him?' Reynolds repeated, his eyes fixed firmly on those of the journalist.

'Yes ... yes, I know him,' McGhee nodded. 'I've met him a couple of times recently. Nice lad, Ricky, but nobody's fool either. The boy will go far.'

'Tell us about your meetings,' Reynolds continued, without batting an eyelid. 'What were they about?'

McGhee reached over and opened the top drawer of his desk. He pulled out his trusty old reporters' notepad, closed the drawer and leant back in his chair.

'Are you sitting comfortably?' he asked his guests, mimicking the famous opening line from the cult children's TV series, *Watch with Mother*. 'Then I'll begin.'

He then proceeded to regale the two detectives with the full story,

131

blow by blow. They listened attentively, taking the occasional brief note but never once interrupting while the journalist was in full flow. When McGhee had finished his story, it was again Reynolds who spoke. Having forced the journalist down off his high horse and listened to him spilling the beans on his meetings with Ricky, Reynolds's tone was now much more conciliatory.

'He's gone missing, Mister McGhee,' the big cop said.

'Oh, Christ,' the normally cool and collected McGhee replied with a despairing shake of his head. 'I knew it. I bloody knew it.'

'You knew what?' McTurk enquired, leaning forward in his chair.

'I told Ricky to leave this to the cops,' McGhee continued, rubbing his chin and radiating rare agitation. 'I told him not to go near this Frank Rafferty guy. That he was bad news, really bad news. You know all about Rafferty, I presume?'

'Yes, we do,' Reynolds replied. 'But Ricky couldn't have approached Rafferty, because he has gone AWOL as well. Hiding out in northern France, we believe.'

McGhee shook his head.

'No, he's not.'

'No, he's not what?' Reynolds enquired, intrigued.

'No, he's not in France,' the journalist replied. 'Rafferty is in Ayr. He's holing out in his brother's caravan down in Doonfoot, the posh part of Ayr.'

The two detectives just stared at each other, their facial expressions a hybrid of disbelief and annoyance. An infamous hood on the run from both the French and Scottish police, and it takes a scruffy old newspaper hack to track him down. Bloody hell. Is this guy for real?

'Please tell me you didn't let Ricky know where Rafferty is hiding?' Reynolds continued, his eyes pleading. 'You didn't ... did you?'

Gerry McGhee's long silence made further elucidation unnecessary.

35

Never before had Ricky Anderson suffered such a night of fitful sleep.

The reason had nothing to do with his beloved mum having

upped sticks to move in with her new boyfriend in the coastal town of Prestwick. It had much more to do with the fact that a well-documented adversary of his was presently sitting in a dingy old caravan by the seaside with his throat sliced open. That, of course, and the sobering thought of his own fingerprints being all over the kitchen knife which had presumably done the slicing. Next, factor in the probability that Frank Rafferty's brutal murder had already been discovered, and it would only be a matter of time before the cops began battering Ricky's door down, either in Glasgow's Highburgh Road or right here in Glenside's Dalblair Crescent. And given time, both.

Having caught the last bus home from Ayr to Glenside the previous night, Ricky lay stretched out on his bed still clad in yesterday's denims and sweater, reflecting that his imminent prospects of peace and harmony now didn't look particularly encouraging. He began running the whole hellish scenario through his mind for the umpteenth time.

Yesterday had been his study leave day, the one he normally spent poring over piles of reference books in Glasgow's Mitchell Library. Only, he hadn't. Just another ordinary day at the end of which he would then have returned to his digs in the student heartland of the city's west end. Only, he didn't. And, of course, today was now the day when he was scheduled to meet Dr Bernard Blackshaw of British Nuclear Fuels Limited, to discuss the newly-formed national organisation's academic research requirements. Only, he wouldn't.

As far as Ricky's involvement in Rafferty's murder was concerned, motive and opportunity were certainly there in abundance, but now he himself had handed something else straight to the cops, and on a bloody plate. Clear forensic evidence. Right at that moment, his guilt looked absolutely nailed on. Once more, he ran his options through his head and once more he came to the same conclusion. There were only two such, and the trouble was that both had disaster written all over them.

Option One. Turn yourself into the police, Ricky, and spill your guts. They might believe you, especially with DI Charlie Reynolds fighting your corner. There again, with such an obvious motive and with your own fingerprints all over the murder weapon, they might not. So, can you really afford to take that chance, and leave both Janice and Iona to face the consequences of your folly and count the cost of what would certainly be a massive risk at best and an act of meek surrender at worst?

Option Two. Go on the run and fend for yourself, Ricky, while you gather enough evidence to prove your innocence. It might work. There again, it might not, particularly with the entire Southwest Scotland Police constabulary hot on your heels and chasing a fugitive who has now all but confessed his guilt by running to evade the law.

As Ricky squirmed restlessly on the duvet, attempting to weigh up the pros and cons of each option, one necessary and immediate course of action was becoming blindingly obvious. He had to get his backside out of there and fast. He had to buy himself more time. Time to think, time to make a firm decision, time to take the appropriate course of action. Any moment now, number 44 Dalblair Crescent would resemble a police convention as the boys-in-blue descended like flies on a dog turd.

Ricky shot to his feet, grabbed his rucksack and began packing. He would only need to stuff in a few essentials, enough for a few days at most. By then, he would surely have made up his mind. Stay or go? Stick or twist? Face the music or keep his own future in his own hands?

Ricky threw his rucksack over his shoulder and quickly made his way through to the living room. Taking one last look around, an ethereal vision suddenly blasted his senses with all the power of a force-ten gale. It was of a much younger version of himself sitting on the floor and playing with his toy cars, as his dad Davie and his mum Janice cuddled each other on the settee. At that precise moment, he would have done anything to resurrect that scene of contentment and joy. Anything at all.

He swallowed hard, wiped an unfamiliar tear from his eye and marched briskly out of his childhood home, perhaps never to return.

36

Janice Anderson fidgeted with her fingernails as she stared out of Charlie Reynolds's kitchen window onto the long, narrow back lawn that stretched beneath the jaggy hawthorn hedgerow towards the Ayr-to-Glasgow railway line.

Where are you, Ricky, she muttered under her breath? Where the hell are you?

The big problem was that she simply couldn't help reminding

herself of the number of times in years gone by that her precious young son would have gotten so wrapped up in his childhood adventures that he would forget to be home by the allotted time. However, she also remembered the innocent look on his little face when he eventually did, inevitably turning his mother's simmering rage into blessed relief. He'll be fine, Janice tried to convince herself. My Ricky always comes back to me.

Just for a fleeting moment, she found her attention drifting to another deeply emotive matter, as she contemplated the countless number of crisp spring mornings and lazy summer afternoons that the new man in her life must surely have spent over the years out there on that same lawn with the former love of his life, who had now seen fit to leave him destitute. Just how could Doreen Reynolds possibly have let Charlie go, she asked herself, that deeply sensitive and highly desirable big hunk, and for a boring little pen-pusher too? The poor woman really must have lost her marbles.

As Janice stood at the kitchen sink in one of her infamous daydreams, the sound of the doorbell immediately snapped her out of it. Instinctively, she spun around, only to be cruelly reminded of her recent ordeal by a sharp jab of pain shooting across her torso like a respectable electric current. With a long, slow intake of breath, she managed to regain her composure and made her way gingerly towards the front door. The bell rang again just as she was about to turn the handle.

'Iona,' she gasped, her eyes lighting up immediately. 'Are you a sight for sore eyes or what?'

After a big hug, Janice ushered Iona McNish into the living room, where the prospective in-laws sat themselves down on adjacent chairs. Iona's voice was noticeably tense and shaky.

'Have you heard from him yet?' she enquired, already knowing the answer that was coming. 'It's now well over a day since anyone last saw him. That's not like Ricky, it's just not like him at all. I'm worried, Janice.'

'I know,' Janice replied, sending out vibes that were considerably more positive than the ones she felt in her innards. 'But don't worry about him, Iona. Ricky could always look after himself. Mind you, he'll need to when I get my hands on him.'

'Charlie came to my door,' Iona said, looking straight into Janice's eyes for a reaction. 'You know, Charlie ... your new ... your new friend?'

'I know,' Janice smiled. 'It was my suggestion. I thought it would be sensible for both of you to have a wee chat. He's a good man, Iona, and he makes me feel safe.'

'Yes, and he's not the worst-looking guy I've ever seen either,' Iona quipped, with a twinkle in her eye.

'Can't say I've noticed,' Janice giggled, feeling her cheeks blush like a 14-year-old being asked out on her first date. 'Cup of tea, Iona?'

As the two ladies continued making small talk in the kitchen while waiting for the kettle to boil, they heard the front door click open and a pair of hefty footsteps began to clump along the hall. The moment Charlie Reynolds popped his head in to say hello, they both started giggling like naughty schoolgirls.

'What ... what have I done?' the big cop asked, perplexed.

'Nothing, Charlie,' Janice replied. 'Nothing at all. Iona and I were just talking about something when you walked in. You two have already met, haven't you?'

'Aye, we met yesterday,' he replied, pecking Janice gently on the cheek and still trying to work out the big joke.

Iona took the teapot over to the kitchen table, and the three of them sat down. It was Reynolds who brought the inevitable note of seriousness back to the occasion.

'My colleague Andy and I have been trying to retrace Ricky's steps, but so far no joy.'

'Oh, God,' Janice sighed, closing her eyes in obvious disappointment.

'Janice,' he replied calmly, 'We have absolutely no reason to believe that anything nasty has happened to him, none at all. I'm sure Ricky is fine, but for some reason he appears to be lying low for the moment. I'm picking up Andy in half an hour, and we'll be following up on a couple of things. Any ideas, ladies? Something we might not have thought of?'

It was Iona who piped up.

'Has anybody actually been to the house?'

'House?' asked Janice. 'His flat, you mean? We've checked with his landlord and his flatmates in Glasgow, if that's what you mean.'

'No, Janice, I mean your own house,' said Iona. 'In Glenside.'

A moment's silence.

'But why would Ricky go back home when he's supposed to be up in Glasgow studying?' Janice asked, eyebrows curled in confusion. 'It just doesn't make any sense.'

Reynolds stroked his chin, got up from the table, grabbed the telephone and began dialling.

'Hi Sandy, it's me,' he said. 'Can you come to my place as soon as possible? I need you to do something right away. Thanks, son, see you in five.'

As both women waited for an explanation, Charlie turned to face them.

'One of my team will be here very shortly. Sergeant Sandy Sutherland. He's a good guy. Janice, where's your house key?'

'In my handbag.'

'Good. Can you give it to Iona?'

'Of course, but ...'

'Iona, when Sandy arrives, would you mind going with him to Glenside, just to check if Ricky's there? You never know, he might be. And if he isn't, just have a good look around to see if there's any sign that he's been home recently?'

Iona stared at Janice, who just nodded.

'No, that's fine with me,' Iona replied.

Just at that, a car horn peeped, and outside sat a red Austin Allegro with its engine still running.

'That's Sandy now, Iona,' said Reynolds. 'Just dig around to see if there's anything that would suggest Ricky has been back home recently. Sandy will help you. Then come straight back here when you're both finished, okay? Janice, would you mind staying put and giving me a ring in the office when she gets back? If I'm out, they'll radio me.'

Two more silent nods. Reynolds again pecked Janice on the cheek and patted Iona on the shoulder.

'I'm now off to see Andy,' he said. 'We'll talk again when we've found out a bit more about Ricky's movements. And don't worry, we're on top of this.'

Reynolds walked Iona out of the door and up the garden path to their waiting cars, leaving Janice all alone once more with her thoughts.

Thoughts which were darkening by the minute.

37

Ricky boarded the 12.05 p.m. bus at foot of Manse Road, the

one that would whisk him to the nearby coalmining village of New Cumnock. Once there, he would catch his connection to Dalmellington, another of Ayrshire's numerous mining settlements, situated some twelve miles away on the edge of the vast Galloway Forest.

There was method in Ricky's madness and coolness in his preparation. Having emptied his bank account of the summer's hard-earned savings and filled his rucksack with sufficient provisions to sustain him for the next couple of days, he certainly wouldn't starve. Nor indeed would he succumb to the vagaries of the unpredictable Scottish weather, thanks to the 'ridge' tent he had collected hurriedly from the garden shed, the same one in which he and his late dad had previously spent many an enjoyable evening away back in the good old days of his early teenage years when worry and responsibility hadn't even been invented yet. Big Davie Anderson had taught young Ricky many an important life skill in the great outdoors, but now those skills were about to be put to the test for real.

Throughout his formative years, Ricky's upbringing had been one of strong infrastructure and comforting security, welcome gifts which had been so cruelly ripped away from him just after his fourteenth birthday by the devastating news of his father's horrific motorcycle accident, an event which shattered his entire universe. In the years that followed, infrastructure and security had only been fleeting visitors, rather than the omnipresent blessings they had once been. At least, until fate would introduce him to a beautiful young girl called Iona McNish who, quite remarkably, had rekindled his passion and lust for life within moments of their steamy introduction.

Today, though, those same blessings were about to recede again to infinitesimal proportions as Ricky took his next tentative steps into the dark abyss of uncertainty. Steps which he would happily have avoided like venereal disease, but which he knew he must now take if he had any chance at all of proving his innocence and nailing whoever was responsible for Frank Rafferty's grisly murder.

Admittedly, a couple of days back Ricky had deliberately set out to confront Rafferty, and quite possibly to take retribution into his own hands and mete out his own idea of justice to the heartless thug who had terrorised and half-killed his mother. However, he hadn't, and he certainly wasn't about to take the rap for someone else who had.

Today, there was only one thing for it. He simply had to go on the run and keep on running for as long as it might take for either the cops or Ricky himself to figure out what had really happened down there in that caravan by the sea. And, of course, why.

Ricky's next bus journey from Pathhead, on the northern extremity of New Cumnock, took him down along The Castle, the village's main drag, and up the Shilling Hill adjacent to its ancient watermill, then past the site of the old Knockshinnoch Castle Colliery, formerly the scene of one of the most tragic mining disasters in history. As the bus entered the small hamlet of Burnfoot, the conductress pinged the bell on the ceiling to alert the driver to draw into the next stop. Ricky watched detached as a dark-haired girl dressed in a white nurses' uniform walked past him towards the door and alighted, but not before turning around again to take a long, searching look at him.

Had his rustic charms worked the oracle yet again, Ricky wondered? There again, perhaps not, because there was something vaguely familiar about the girl's pleasantly plump face. The pieces of the jigsaw didn't immediately fall into place and he couldn't place her. The question was, though, had she just placed him?

A relatively relaxing thirty-minute, ten-mile moorland sojourn along the desolate, long-and-winding B741 brought Ricky to a bus stop at the western end of the village of Dalmellington opposite Doon Academy, the secondary school which served the teenagers of the extended rural locale. There he bade the driver a polite farewell and stepped off the bus, his hastily-assembled provisions stuffed into the bulging rucksack which he strapped over his right shoulder. For Ricky Anderson, his latest adventure in the great outdoors was about to begin. Only this time, it wouldn't be for frivolous entertainment. It would be for mortal survival.

A few spots of rain quickly progressed to a light drizzle. Ricky cursed and looked around to survey the scene and get his bearings. He pulled the hood of his zip-up jacket over his long hair and began marching briskly along the pavement until he reached a familiar road leading to his left. This, he recognised from a fond memory of an earlier excursion with his dad, was the opening to the one-mile-long driveway which would take him through the 3,000-acre Craigengillan Estate and up to the grand old seventeenth-century house of the same name. From the ancient stately home, a short stroll down a narrower footpath would then lead to a wooden road-bridge over the River Doon and herald a gloriously scenic walk up through the spectacular Ness Glen, a former aristocratic 'showplace' back in the Victorian era.

It was a full twenty minutes before Ricky reached the bridge, by which time the raindrops had been replaced by a seemingly never-ending swarm of midges that took great delight in escorting him up into the glen. As he skipped upstream from boulder to boulder alongside a succession of giant pools fed by cascading streams, he laughed at the recollection of his dad once stepping on a couple of old wooden planks which seemed to offer a secure crossing over a deep pool, only for one of them to crack under the substantial weight of his giant frame and plunge him waist-deep into the freezing waters of the River Doon. For the merest moment, laughter and tears battled for the upper hand, neither really emerging as the clear victor.

Ricky continued his steady climb up through the beautiful glen, marvelling at the ingenious pathway which had been hewn from granite rocks overlooked by 30-foot-high cliffs replete with nooks, crannies and hanging vegetation. He noticed that the current was becoming noticeably faster and louder by the minute, signalling that he was now approaching the waterfall which roared down from the man-made dam at the entrance to the vast Loch Doon. Soon the fast-flowing streams gave way to violent rapids, and gentle swishing to a thunderous roar, as the lofty dam came into view, sending its mighty torrent crashing onto the rocks below.

How ironic, Ricky contemplated, that he had somehow found himself at the upper-course birthplace of a young fledgling river, the very same one which had at its capacious estuary the scene of the ghastly murder from which he was now fleeing to prove his innocence. What he needed now was time to think, time to contemplate his strategy, time to rest his weary frame and re-invigorate his frazzled mind. First of all, though, he had to choose a basecamp. Somewhere he could pitch his ridge tent with at least some semblance of confidence. Somewhere he could get some peace. Peace to rest and peace to think.

Thankfully, Ricky had no trouble remembering the basic rules of tent assembly. Flat surface, good shelter, the back of the tent facing the prevailing wind and whatever unwelcome contents it might carry with it, and a nearby clean water supply. And, of course, in his rather unique circumstances, well away from any irritating busybodies who might want to start poking their big snouts into his affairs. After all, it would only be a matter of time before his own mugshot would be plastered all over the various broadsheets and tabloids. Today was Thursday and he'd give it until Saturday at the latest before the unscrupulous hacks began running the story. The vexed question of guilt or innocence would always be of secondary importance to the editors sprawled out on their leather recliners in their ivory towers. All that mattered was selling bloody newspapers.

With one notable exception, perhaps. But could even Gerry McGhee really be trusted once the sparks began to fly? The stark reality was that McGhee now remained one of Ricky's last remaining hopes of the truth eventually coming out. However, for that to happen, the journalist would have to go on digging, and the big question was this. Would he, or would he simply succumb to the demands of the cops when they came calling and threatened him to keep his big ugly nose out of their affairs? Either way, Ricky knew that he simply had to make contact again with the great man and take things from there.

Nothing ventured, nothing gained. Either die wondering or die trying.

38

The flashing lights descended on Doonfoot like a swarm of bluebottles drooling over a discarded fish supper, instantly turning the normally sleepy little suburb into a hive of frenetic activity.

Charlie Reynolds was not among the fifteen police officers, who in an impressive show of almost faultless synchronicity, began pouring out of their assorted vehicles. A blunt and completely unequivocal command from Chief Superintendent Joe Fraser had seen to that.

On DI Andy McTurk's signal, the dozen boys-in-blue and another two clad in smart suits converged stealthily in the direction of Dan Rafferty's static caravan. McTurk's raised right arm told them to stay put, while a brusque wave of his left gestured to his two suited wingmen to hit the door. A resounding crack and the unmistakeable sound of splintering glass signalled that they were in, at which point McTurk signalled to the cavalry to close in and encircle the caravan, making it impossible for any resourceful would-be escapee to slip from their clutches.

The sight that greeted the two detectives resembled something out of a B-list slasher movie. There, sitting bolt upright on the settee like an avid television addict, sat the ashen-faced, ghoulish corpse of a rotund middle-aged man, his entire torso saturated in an ocean of congealed black-red blood, which also caked the legs of his flared trousers and pooled on the carpet, welding his shoes to the floor like aspic. As a pair of well-fed rats scurried panic-stricken out of the door, the swarm of flies buzzing around the corpse's head and shoulders refused to do likewise, deciding instead to hang around for the continuing feast.

'Oh, Jesus Christ!' Detective Constable John Kerr exclaimed with a sickly gasp, before bolting into the toilet to puke his guts up.

'It's all right, John,' McTurk said calmly. 'Just take your time. You get used to it, son.'

'No, you don't, sir,' Detective Sergeant Eddie O'Brien muttered, shaking his head in resignation at the sight before him. 'You really don't.'

'No, I don't suppose you ever do, lads,' McTurk conceded. 'But it comes with the territory, so we just have to deal with it.'

There followed a moment's silence, a moment that seemed like an hour, as the three plain-clothes officers took time to gather their thoughts. It was the Detective Inspector himself who broke the troubled trance.

'Right, lads, don't touch anything, not a thing. Eddie, radio the station and tell them we've found a stiff down here in paradise. John, are you okay, son?'

'Aye, boss,' came the rookie detective's gargled response. 'I'm fine.'

'Right then, call the forensic boys and get them down here. And pronto. This stiff has been sitting here in all his glory for the best part of a day, and they need to get moving fast.'

'You see that, sir?' young Kerr added, bending down to get a closer look at a blood-stained kitchen knife poking out from underneath the settee.

'Leave it, John,' McTurk commanded. 'Don't even bag it. The forensic boys will deal with it.'

Turning to his second-in-command, O'Brien, he gave his final instructions.

'Eddie, I'm going outside to talk to the troops. I'll leave four

142

of them on watch until the coroner and the forensics arrive, just to protect the crime scene from any nosey neighbours. And when you're radioing the station, tell them that we know who the stiff is.'

'Do we, sir?' O'Brien asked, intrigued. 'Who is he?'

'He's a local businessman. Goes by the name of Frank Rafferty. And trust me, lads, now the shit will really hit the fan.'

39

The moment Charlie Reynolds turned the Yale key in his own front door, the aroma hit him. His gastric juices shot into overdrive.

When he walked into the kitchen, Janice Anderson was tending a large pan that sat on the electric hob. As she stirred its glorious contents with all the care and attention of a Swiss watchmaker mending a Rolex, Reynolds stopped in his tracks for a moment and took one long lustful look in her direction, whereupon a more primal stirring drew him towards her.

'What ya cookin', honey?' he whispered in her ear in his favourite Clint Eastwood accent, wrapping his arms around her waist while kissing her softly on the nape of her neck. 'It sure smells good ... but not as good as you.'

'We're not alone, Charlie,' Janice giggled, just managing to resist the temptation to spin around and snog the face off him. 'Iona's in the living room.'

'No, she's not,' Iona McNish laughed, immediately clocking her own clumsy intrusion and turning on her heels to retrace her steps in deep embarrassment. 'Sorry, folks.'

Reynolds immediately released Janice like a naughty ten-year-old schoolboy who had just been caught red-handed nicking a handful of sweeties from Woolworth's pick-n-mix counter.

'Iona,' he spluttered. 'It's okay, come back in. I was just ... I was just admiring Janice's cookery skills.'

'Oh, was that what you were doing?' Janice teased, refusing to let him off the hook.

Communal giggles provided Reynolds with a welcome escape route, preparing the ground that would allow his culinary appetite to regain the upper hand.

'Seriously Janice, what is that you're cooking?' he enquired, pupils wide with anticipation, nostrils likewise. 'It smells fantastic.'

'Hungarian goulash,' she replied, clearly feeling rather pleased with herself. 'It's a beef stew, slow cooked with onions and spices in a rich tomato sauce. I'm going to serve it with boiled rice and garlic bread. I think you'll like it.'

'It's one of Janice's signature dishes, Charlie,' Iona piped up for good measure. 'She's a wonderful cook, you know.'

Reynolds could scarcely believe his luck. Not only was the new love of his life an adorable little honey, but now he had discovered that she was a terrific cook as well. Right at that moment, he thought he had died and gone to heaven. At least, until he remembered that he had one very important question to ask.

'Iona, Sandy filled me in on your visit to Dalblair Crescent. Nothing, then? Not a trace?'

'Nothing, Charlie,' she replied, a downtrodden look returning. 'No sign at all of him having gone back home. Sandy was very thorough.'

Just at that, the doorbell rang. It was Iona who reacted first. She walked along the hall and opened the front door, and in walked Andy McTurk. He grunted a brusque, 'Thanks, darlin'', and marched along the hallway in the direction of the gastronomic delights that were filling the air.

'Hi Andy,' Reynolds nodded. 'Janice has been making Hungarian something-or-other. You want to try it? Janice, is there enough in the pot for a crabbit old copper with a face that could curdle milk?'

'Of course, there is,' Janice laughed, 'You're welcome to join us, Andy. Take a seat at the table. And it's Hungarian goulash, by the way.'

'Smells great, Janice,' McTurk replied, his forced smile failing miserably to disguise the concern etched on a rather lived-in face.

'What's up, old boy?' Reynolds asked, immediately clocking that something was seriously amiss. 'I'd recognise that look from outer space. What's wrong, buddy?'

'I think we should all sit down for a wee minute,' he sighed. 'There have been some developments. Some pretty major developments.'

Reynolds gestured to Janice and Iona to join Andy at the table, then sat down beside them. Silence reigned for a few moments, save for the sound of the beef stew bubbling on the hob.

McTurk seized the moment.

'It's not good news, folks.'

Very quickly, the appetites began to wane as the gurgling feast became a mass of culinary indifference.

'Let's hear it, Andy,' Reynolds said. 'The whole story, and no pussy-footing around. Janice and Iona are big girls now.'

'Okay, then, here goes,' McTurk responded, raising both hands in a resigned you-asked-for-it fashion. 'Frank Rafferty is dead.'

Gasps of shock came from both women, their hands covering their mouths in disbelief. Reynolds sat stalk still in his chair. It was only his lips that moved. They spat out four short words.

'Where? ... When? ... And how?'

'We hit Dan Rafferty's caravan at one o'clock this afternoon. And there was big brother Frank sitting on the couch with his throat cut. The place looked like a slaughterhouse, blood everywhere ... rats, bluebottles, you name it.'

Janice gasped and held her head in her hands, while Iona just sat there looking catatonic with shock. With McTurk now in full flow, Reynolds felt the need to put the brakes on.

'Okay, Andy, we get the picture. Yes, we need to hear the full story, but you could maybe spare us some of the gory details.'

'Sorry, folks,' McTurk mumbled in half-apology. 'I've probably been in this job far too long and I can get carried away with detail at times. Anyway, we found Rafferty sitting there. Dead as a dodo. Rigor mortis had already set in, and the lab boys have now said that the murder was probably committed between two and six hours earlier, putting his death sometime between seven and eleven o'clock this morning.'

'Murder weapon?' Reynolds asked, drawing an irritated stare from his colleague.

'I was coming to that, Charlie. The lads spotted a kitchen knife sticking out from under the couch. One of those really sharp jobs, covered in blood. We left it for the forensic boys to bag and analyse, which they have now done.'

'And?' Reynolds prompted.

'There's no easy way to say this, folks,' McTurk squirmed.

'So, just say it,' Janice pleaded, her eyes darting anxiously between McTurk and Reynolds. 'I need to know. Please.'

'Janice, I'm afraid your son's fingerprints were all over the knife handle,' McTurk said, conveying an uncharacteristic tone of empathy. 'And all over the door handle too.'

Janice and Iona exchanged wordless stares of pure shock. Reynolds's expression was more one of confusion.

'But how do you know they're Ricky's prints?' he asked his

145

partner. 'Has Ricky got previous form?'

'No, he hasn't,' McTurk replied, 'apart from one incident a few years back at secondary school when he gave a couple of young neds a right good doing in the playground, but the charges were later dropped. Charlie, the truth is that when you asked Sandy to go with Iona to Dalblair Crescent, I told him to take prints from some of Ricky's stuff. Just in case ... you know?'

Reynolds slumped back in his chair and blew a heavy sigh. Drama had just graduated to disaster.

'Anything else, Andy?' came the weary question. 'I mean, how much worse can this get?'

'Well, now that you mention it, a couple of things,' his partner retorted. 'First of all, we're a bit stumped about why a big powerful brute of a man like Rafferty was just sitting there as nice as ninepence while someone was slitting his throat with a kitchen knife. No sign of a struggle, none at all. My guess is that he was probably drugged beforehand, but the lab boys will tell us for sure.'

'And the second thing?' Reynolds enquired.

'There was another set of prints on the knife handle,' McTurk replied. 'A bit smudged, but still distinguishable, so we're now in the process of taking prints from others who might have had an axe to grind with Rafferty. And, believe me, the list reads like a phone book.'

'Who, for starters?' Reynolds persisted.

'Everybody and their granny,' McTurk replied. 'Rafferty has made more enemies than Adolf Hitler. Edwin Monk, Zander McGinn, Robert McDade and his other goons, previous business associates, Johnny Crawford, big Sam Templeton and the other broken-hearted husbands whose wives Rafferty had been bedding at some time or other. Further suggestions on a postcard, folks, we've got plenty of dusting powder left.'

Reynolds just shrugged his shoulders. McTurk was right. There was no point dressing up a disastrous situation in pretty clothes.

'Is that it, then?'

'Yip,' McTurk nodded, 'That's about it.'

Finally, Janice found her voice. It was trembling slightly, but still under control.

'So, where's ... where's my Ricky?'

McTurk hesitated before replying. He knew he had to choose his next words very carefully. They needed to carry a decent degree of sensitivity, but they also had to be sincere.

'We've got no idea at the moment,' he said. 'He has cleared his account with the Clydesdale Bank, so we've got to assume he's gone on the run. And I have to be honest with you, Janice. Ricky is now a prime murder suspect and we'll be going after him with everything we've got.'

'Ricky didn't do it, Andy,' she replied calmly, looking at Iona for support. 'Yes, he might well have gone after Frank. And yes, he might even have intended giving him a right good pasting. But there is no way that my Ricky could ever have done that to anyone. Never in a million years.'

Iona McNish said nothing. She just sat staring out of the window, frozen in dread.

McTurk pushed on.

'Janice, we have to find Ricky and question him. The longer he runs and tries to hide from us, the more and more his guilt will look nailed on. We've got to get to him before the situation becomes even worse.'

'Even worse?' Janice retorted, shaking her head in mock amusement. 'What could possibly be worse than ... than this?'

'Only one thing, Janice,' McTurk answered with the utmost sincerity. 'Rafferty's two thugs, McGinn and McDade. That pair getting to Ricky before we do would be worse. A lot worse'

Tears of pent-up distress suddenly brought Iona McNish's trance to an agonising end. Her life with Ricky had promised so much. Now, it lay in tatters.

40

Sleep hadn't come easily for Edwin Monk over the past few years, and for one very good reason. Guilt.

Guilt about his romantic indiscretions. Guilt about his seedy financial wheelings-and-dealings. Guilt about the people he had hurt or had allowed to be hurt. And all to feed his own insatiable desires for acceptance, power and wealth.

There were very few people whom Edwin Monk even liked, let alone loved, but the one he loathed most of all was himself. And it was this overwhelming feeling of ferocious self-loathing that had become one of the main reasons for a rapidly deteriorating sleep pattern which had more recently sunk to the depths of chronic insomnia.

However, now things were even more intolerable. Now there was the fear as well, an omnipresent fear for his own safety, for his own life. Back in the day – back in the good old days – Monk could have slept through a bombing raid in an earthquake. However, these days he was exhausted. Completely and utterly exhausted.

Right at that moment, how the fallen bigwig politician would have loved to turn the clock back. Indeed, right back to the sixth of May, 1962, the joyous day when he had married the delectable Christine McGuire, his childhood sweetheart, who after eight long years of courting had finally forgiven him for his clandestine capers with Barbara Campbell, Linda Fulton and the ever-willing Maggie McBride, to name the ones she knew about, and agreed to tie the knot.

Yes, sleep had come easily to Monk back then. Back in the good old days. However, that was before the politics. Before the bribes. Before the foreign junkets. And, of course, before FFR.

Frank F-----g Rafferty.

For Edwin Monk, life was now a living hell. Barred as a councillor and representative of the community he genuinely believed he had served with distinction for seventeen whole years. Kicked out of his beloved Labour Party. Charged with perverting the course of justice and two counts of embezzlement. Awaiting trial and facing anything up to five years in prison. And, of course, a prime target for Rafferty's brain-dead minders. Yes, life was now a living hell, a pure living hell.

The only remaining question was whether Rafferty would get to him first before the courts sentenced him to confinement in Glasgow's notorious Barlinnie Prison, aka 'The Bar-L', where the gangster's henchmen would eventually get him anyway for grassing their boss into the cops. Either way it was Hobson's Choice, simply a matter of time. Edwin Monk was a dead man walking. And he knew it.

He looked at his watch. A quarter-to-ten on a bleak autumn evening, and here he was walking all alone in the dark in the pissing rain. Walking to who-knows-where and God-knows-why. Any excuse just to get out of the house and away from the silent, subliminal but completely unmistakable disapproval of a long-suffering spouse who had been telling the whole world how she would stand by her man through thick and thin, but whom Monk himself just knew with innate certainty would rather be anywhere else on the planet.

It was the swish of wet tyres that snapped him out of his sombre daydream. That and the sight of a pair of brake-lights suddenly turning red, as the black Ford Corsair screeched to a halt. Monk caught his breath but could do nothing to prevent his heartbeat from going nuclear. The door on the passengers' side burst open.

'Get in, Monk,' a gruff voice bellowed.

Monk froze to the spot, unable to decide what to do next. If he did what he was told, he would be a helpless captive in the hands of some really nasty individuals. If he ran, they would catch him anyway and just drag him into the car. So, he froze there unable to move, the soles of his shoes welded in terror to the wet tarmac.

'I said, get in, Monk,' the voice repeated, only this time in a perceptively angrier tone. 'And I won't be asking you again.'

Monk just continued to stand stalk-still on the pavement, rooted to the spot. His heart was now fit to explode but his brain was miles behind. As the black-leather-jacketed brute of a man that was Robert McDade jumped out of the car, Monk sank to his knees and began sobbing like a baby. McDade grabbed him under the oxters and dragged him along the sodden pavement towards the Corsair, where another young muscular man opened the back door and pulled him in. Zander McGinn then slammed the door shut, climbed back into the front passenger's seat beside his blond-haired driver and the car screeched away.

With not another word being spoken, Monk stared through his tears in horror, as he and his sinister three-man entourage left the Whitletts roundabout and sped onto the A77 dual carriageway, convinced that the funereal-like black Corsair was about to take him on his final journey from his family home in the plush suburbs of Alloway to an agonising demise somewhere in the rural backwaters between Ayr and Kilmarnock.

Monk knew the score – the law of the jungle – and even if he did find his voice again, pleading his case would be an exercise in utter futility. Nobody grassed on Frank Rafferty and lived to tell the tale. Nobody, ever.

Eventually, his voice did return. It was warbled and trembling.

'Can I just ask … can I ask where you are taking me?'

Silence. Deathly silence.

'All I ask is …'

'Shut it, Monk,' snapped McDade, sitting to his side. 'You'll find out soon enough.'

Monk bowed his head and began sobbing again. Sobbing and shaking uncontrollably.

From the front passenger's seat, McGinn started laughing.

'Hey, Rab, what about this guy? What a right wee fanny.'

'And we haven't even started on him yet, Zander,' McDade chortled in response.

Monk, head still bowed and eyes firmly closed, clasped his hands tightly together and took several deep breaths. He now knew for sure who the two big brutes were. Mad Rab McDade and Zander McGinn, that's who they were, and their fearsome reputations had preceded them. He tried not to think of the terrible fate which awaited him but simply couldn't help himself. Whatever they were going to do to him, it was certain to be slow and horrific. He grimaced when he thought of the merciless beating that McDade might mete out in some abandoned warehouse. He shivered when he remembered being told of the time that McGinn had wired Rafferty's pet Rottweiler's jaws together and left the poor thing to starve and thirst, a punishment which would definitely fit his own crime of grassing to the cops. He squirmed in terror when he imagined the two heavies getting to work on his delicate parts with a pair of rusty pliers.

Eventually, he could take no more and let out a blood-curdling howl, at which point his burly back-seat companion drew his arm back and cracked him on the jaw with his elbow. A moment's searing pain immediately gave way to welcome unconsciousness.

When Monk woke up, he was all alone, chittering in a cold, dimly-lit garage of some description, tied to a wooden chair and surrounded by a collection of old cars and various items of heavy machinery. His vision was still blurred and his jaw really hurt. He could taste blood in his mouth, prompting further investigation by his tongue, which soon established the cause. Two teeth were missing, an incisor and a molar, both on the bottom row precisely where he had felt the elbow smash into his face before he had passed out.

Just as Monk's imagination began to take wings again, he heard heavy footsteps approaching, then the sound of a key being inserted into the lock of the garage door. While his pulse thundered in his ears, he watched as the handle turned and the door creaked open. No Rab McDade, nor indeed his similarly muscle-bound sidekick, McGinn. Only the stocky figure of a middle-aged man clad in an expensive-looking dark three-piece suit over which draped a long black overcoat.

At first, the man looked vaguely familiar to Monk. Not unlike Frank Rafferty, in fact. However, definitely not Frank Rafferty, whose evil face would forever be etched indelibly in Monk's mind. The voice sounded familiar too.

'Hello, Councillor Monk. We haven't had the pleasure, but I've heard so much about you that I feel I've known you all my life.'

'Who ... who are you?' Monk asked shakily, the blood still oozing from his mouth. 'And why am I here? I don't ... I don't understand.'

The man grabbed an old wooden chair, pulled it across the damp concrete floor and sat down facing his captive guest.

'My name is Dan Rafferty,' he said softly. 'And I thought we might have a little chat. My brother Frank is dead. Somebody cut his throat with a kitchen knife and watched while he bled to death.'

Monk let out a huge gasp and stared open-mouthed at his captor. By then, he was pretty much hyperventilating. When the words came out, he sounded as if he had just run the four-minute-mile.

'I don't ... I don't know ... anything ... anything about that. I promise.'

'I know you don't, Councillor Monk,' Dan Rafferty replied, taking a neatly-folded white handkerchief from the top pocket of his suit jacket and wiping some blood from Monk's bottom lip. 'I know you don't.'

'Well then ... what ... what has this got to do with me?' Monk beseeched him. 'What do you want from me?'

'Councillor Monk,' Rafferty replied, in a gentle voice. 'You now have two options open to you. Option one. You help us frame someone for Frank's murder.'

Monk threw his head back, totally bewildered. Every word and syllable sounded like an explosion in his ears.

'And ... and option two?'

'Ah ... option two?' Rafferty teased. 'Well, Councillor Monk, I'm afraid that option two isn't quite as attractive as option one. Essentially, it is this. If you don't cooperate, I ask my two associates to come in with their favourite toolbox and spend a couple of hours entertaining you, then feed what's left of you to my late brother's big dogs. They really have an insatiable appetite, you know.'

Shackled to his seat, Monk began to shiver violently. Suddenly, his bladder emptied, and a pool began to widen on the concrete floor. Rafferty tut-tutted and smiled.

'Oh dear, Councillor Monk, you should have asked to go to the toilet, shouldn't you? No need to worry, though, because my associates will be removing all your clothes very shortly.'

'Who ... who would I have to frame?' Monk stammered, swallowing hard to hold back the vomit that was threatening to make its grisly appearance.

'Someone you know, Councillor Monk,' Rafferty grinned. 'Someone you met at one of your big important meetings. I'm sure you'll remember him.'

'What ... what is his name?' Monk pleaded with his captor. 'Just tell me his name.'

'A young lad called Richard Anderson,' Rafferty replied. 'A young lad who has tried to bring down our business empire, the one I would have inherited on the occasion of my brother Frank's death. A young lad who has had it coming.'

41

An early morning downpour began battering off the canvas of the old ridge tent. Ricky Anderson awoke with a start.

His eight-hour sleep, an odd cocktail of restless exhaustion and weird dreams, had left him completely off-guard, and right at that moment an overwhelming feeling of vulnerability washed over his soul. As ethereal visions slowly gave way to harsh reality, the events of the past few days started flooding back. This wasn't just a bad nightmare. This was actually happening.

Sitting on the groundsheet in silent contemplation, he waited until the rain had slackened off, then poked his head out of the tent door which was flapping gently in the cool breeze. A watery sun gradually escaped the clutches of a few dark clouds and began bathing the whole place in a garishly bright light that assaulted his eyes. Looking around, he saw that his only neighbours were of the ovine variety, and that pleased him. The last thing Ricky needed right now was some unannounced bunch of inquisitive backpackers appearing out of the woods to stick their big noses into his affairs, so the splendid isolation was perfect. The sheep themselves seemed equally contented, as they munched mindlessly on the wild grass instead of paying Ricky even the slightest modicum of attention.

Scrambling out of the tent, he stretched his frame to full height, flexed his cramped muscles then surveyed the scene. Straight ahead, about fifty yards away and down a steepish slope, lay the great expanse of Loch Doon, its eerie dark depths overlain by oscillating surface waves, themselves peppered here and there by a few bobbing mallard ducks and waterhens. About a mile away to his left, he could just make out the huge concrete wall of the dam which separated millions of gallons of cool, clear water from the splendours of the magnificent Ness Glen, the length of which he had traversed only the night before. To his right, sat the ancient Loch Doon Castle and the south side of the mighty loch itself, protected by a vast backcloth of pine forests, through which he remembered from an earlier sojourn with his late dad wound the rough forest track that today would take him into the vast Galloway Forest and onward to a very uncertain future. However, with a bit of good fortune, his cross-country hike might throw any inquisitive pursuers off his trail.

Ricky wandered over to a tiny clump of trees and began picking up a few twigs and sticks, then returned suitably laden to his makeshift campsite. He arranged his pickings in a pyramidal shape the way his dad had taught him, smaller twigs at the bottom and bigger sticks on top. He then ripped out a couple of big handfuls of dead grass and stuffed it underneath the pile of wood. The first match sparked enthusiastically but then fizzled out in the pile of damp foliage. However, the second one caught immediately, and a few moments later the grass was crackling away nicely. He lay down on the ground and blew gently under the base of the pyramid to oxygenate it, and soon his morning fire was up and away. A few more of the larger sticks, and Ricky soon had himself a raging bonfire.

He took his 'tinny' out of his rucksack and walked over to a nearby hill stream which trickled its way down towards the loch, and filled up the metal container from the fastest-flowing part of the current he could find, thereby ensuring maximum filtration and minimum contamination. A few minutes later, he was sitting on a boulder beside his roaring campfire, tucking into the last remaining cheese sandwiches he had brought from home and sipping contentedly from his tinny of hot tea.

Time to hit the road, Ricky announced to a pair of sheep who were delving into a more botanical version of breakfast. Both stopped chomping and looked up at their latest visitor, clearly unimpressed, confirming that he was now very much alone with his thoughts as he faced the next and extremely precarious chapter of his young life. He rolled up his ridge tent, packed his stuff and shoved it into his rucksack, then stamped out the fire.

The big match beckoned. Ricky Anderson versus The Rest of the World.

By eleven-thirty, Ricky had covered the seven-mile trek to the ruins of Loch Doon Castle at the head of the loch of the same name, as it lay in the shelter of the 1,716-foot-high Craiglee Hill. For some reason, he remembered that the grand old fortress had originally been built on a small island in the loch and once had tenuous connections with none other than King Robert the Bruce himself, but was later moved closer to the shore when the dam was built and the water level raised, where its ruins still stood proudly to this day.

Having reached his latest milestone, Ricky unburdened himself of his weighty backpack, and sat down on the grass for a well-earned rest. Looking over the huge expanse of deep water, he allowed his mind to wander. His strategy was sound enough, a relatively a simple one which ought to buy him some more time to work out this whole conundrum and nail the real perpetrators of Frank Rafferty's gruesome demise. It would also give Charlie Reynolds a bit more leeway in doing what he needed to do to set the record straight, for as sure as night follows day, his new pal Charlie would be moving heaven and earth to fight Ricky's corner and prove his innocence. So too might the scruffy super-hack himself, Gerry McGhee. However, to reel both Charlie and Gerry in, he had to get a message to each of them, and soon. And, of course, he had to let Janice and Iona know that he was safe and sound, but in no mood to surrender and collapse willingly into the clutches of a police force he couldn't trust or a vicious gang consumed with mindless retribution. Sending those messages to Charlie and Gerry was absolutely vital. However, the problem was how to do it without giving the game away, or worse still, his whereabouts.

Ricky looked towards the far south-east end of the loch, where stood a small and very isolated cottage, probably now no longer functional and lying in ruins. He recalled that cottage from one memorable Sunday a few years back, when his dad had taken him on his first really serious hike across the forest track from the far side of Loch Doon to the magnificent Stinchar Falls, a few miles south of the Ayrshire village of Straiton. Later that same day, their next-door neighbour, Willie Tennent, had picked them up in his council van and driven the pair of weary explorers back to the big plate of steak pie and mashed potatoes that Janice had waiting for them all in Glenside. Happy days.

If Ricky could now relocate that same forest track, he might be able to retrace his own and his late father's footsteps and hit the main Ayr-to-Newton Stewart road by late afternoon, from which he could then hitch a lift south to the village of Glentrool. There on the banks of the beautiful Loch Trool, he could pitch his tent for the night in glorious anonymity, under cover of the swarm of backpacking ramblers who would doubtless have set up camp in preparation for the next morning's mountainous exertions on their ascent of The Merrick, which at 843 metres boasted southern mainland Scotland's highest peak.

Ricky rose to his feet, grabbed his backpack and set off in the general direction of the old track which led into the forests, egged on by the thought of a bit of time in the outback of rural Galloway, where people mind their own business.

Time to rest, time to think, and time to plan his next move.

42

Duty Sergeant Peter McLean was standing at reception when two pleasant-faced ladies walked rather apologetically through the front door of New Cumnock police station.

Leaning on the Formica top of the reception desk, he cast an inquisitive glance over the rim of his glasses and began his forensic assessment as prematurely as always. One in her mid-forties, the other an early twenty-something, McLean observed. Mother and daughter, almost certainly, and both looking a bit anxious and concerned. Another 'domestic', he postulated, drawing on many years' bitter experience in the force. What would it be this time, then? Probably, the erstwhile husband-cum-father staggering home drunk from the local Working Men's Club last night and panning in the telly and the living room window. McLean had seen it all so many times before. Another brain-numbing form to fill in, another radio call to the duty constables who would be galavanting around in their patrol car, another chin-wagging to the naughty culprit, and the whole bloody merry-go-round would go on and on *ad nauseam*.

'How can I help you, ladies?' McLean enquired.

'Show the policeman the newspaper, Isobel,' the older one said, exuding maternal authority.

'You've got it yourself, mum,' the younger one replied. 'It's in your bag.'

'Oh, so it is,' her mother replied, shaking her head in self-rebuke, before removing a crumpled copy of this week's hot-off-the-press edition of the *Ayrshire Herald* from her black leather handbag and spreading it out, front-page-up, on the reception desk.

Sergeant McLean looked at the local rag, then cast an enquiring glance first at mother then at daughter.

'So, what's this about, then?' he asked.

'She saw him yesterday,' the former announced, pointing to the black-and-white photograph adorning the front page. 'Didn't you, Isobel? Go on, tell the man.'

The sergeant's eyes lit up, as a routine morning suddenly promised to turn into a considerably more exciting afternoon.

'Would you mind coming through to the office, ladies?' he said in a tone which was intended to be a polite request, but which instead carried with it the air of a firmer instruction. He lifted the shelf at the end of the long desk and beckoned both women through, before poking his head around the corner to ask his colleague, a young constable called Norman Devlin, to assume temporary duties at reception.

'Make yourselves comfortable, ladies,' McLean continued, ushering them to take their seats at an old pine table in the cluttered back office of the police station. Turning to the office secretary in the adjacent room separated only by a glass partition, he knocked twice and signalled for her to come through. She complied immediately.

'Margaret,' he smiled, 'Could you bring us a pot of tea and a few biscuits, please?'

'Certainly, Sarge,' she nodded, turning on her heels to obey his command.

'Oh, and Margaret,' McLean added. 'Before you put the kettle on, could you phone the Ayr branch and tell them that we've possibly got an interesting new lead on the Doonfoot matter?'

'Will do, Sarge,' she nodded again.

McLean began by taking note of the ladies' personal details. He nodded in smug satisfaction when they confirmed his own astute observation that they were indeed a mother-and-daughter combo, the former calling herself Agnes McLatchie, a grand New Cumnock name if ever there was one, and the latter Isobel, the youngest of the McLatchie family's three girls. He then got straight down to business by asking Isobel to talk about her alleged sighting of the man in the *Herald* photograph. This she proceeded to do, hesitantly at first, but encouraged by the sergeant's gentle promptings and interspersed by her mother grating interjections.

Her story was a simple one. The previous day, Thursday the 13th of September, she had been returning home by bus from her duties as an NHS nurse at Ballochmyle Hospital, near the village of Mauchline, to her parents' council house in Burnfoot, a small but well-established hamlet located at the western end of the more populous village of New Cumnock. The time would have been about half-past-one in the afternoon, she estimated, but she couldn't be any more precise than that. Seated near the rear of the bus, Isobel had spent the last couple of miles of her journey looking at the young man sitting diagonally opposite her, a few rows down. She knew she had seen him before and she was fairly sure that he was Ricky Anderson, a former classmate at secondary school who had been very popular with his peers, the girls in particular. The problem was that the Ricky she remembered back in her schooldays had dark short-cropped hair, but the young man sitting in front of her on the bus that day was adorned by shoulder-length locks, albeit similarly dark in colour. The reason she had decided to turn around and take a good look at him when she was disembarking from the bus was to catch a glimpse of his eyes, because Ricky always had the most stunning eyes. And, of course, the moment she had gazed into them, she knew it was him.

'How sure are you it that was the young man in this photograph, Miss McLatchie?' Sergeant McLean asked.

'One hundred percent certain,' Isobel replied. 'Without a shadow of a doubt, it was Ricky Anderson on that bus.'

By the time the tea and biscuits had arrived, the formalities of the interview were more or less over, leaving McLean with the relatively simple task of dotting the 'i's and crossing the 't's in his handwritten notes. He then thanked the McLatchies, junior and senior, for their welcome assistance, saw them to the door and immediately called Ayr police station himself to track down Detective Inspector

McTurk, whom everybody in the general area of Cumnock knew to their considerable amusement had taken over the investigation from that seriously overrated local tosspot, Jock Henderson.

Surprisingly, though, McTurk was uncontactable, and wouldn't be available for some time. Whatever he was up to, thought Peter McLean, it must be very important, because this was the most exciting day in his own entire career.

43

Edwin Monk's house was considerably more salubrious than might have been expected for a local politician living on a councillor's modest allowance and with no other legitimate means of financial support.

After all, a luxury detached five-bedroomed villa situated on a sprawling two-acre site in the centre of the much-sought-after suburb of Alloway really was the dream home for most of Ayr's upwardly mobile elite. There again, not everything in which Edwin Monk had got himself involved over his two decades in public service could have been described as legitimate, far less squeaky-clean.

Detective Inspector Andy McTurk rang the doorbell in anticipation. That of driving another nail into the coffin of one of the worst kinds of villain, a devious cheat who would have shopped his own granny to make his latest illicit buck. Instead of the bog standard 'ding-dong', though, the bell proceeded to play a little tune, one which McTurk quickly recognised as the chorus in old crooner Frank Sinatra's classic, 'I Did It My Way'.

'Aye,' he muttered to his junior partner, Detective Sergeant Sandy Sutherland, 'you did it your way, Monk. And now you're about to pay the bloody price.'

The door opened and a wiry-framed, middle-aged woman peeked out, staring rather suspiciously at the two officers. Her wrinkled face was plastered with makeup, her sagging eyelids caked with mascara and her thin lips painted a deep blood-red with shiny lipstick. As she stood there in a bright-orange, two-piece designer trouser suit that would have looked much more at home on a teenager straight out of high school, McTurk formed his customary first impression. Mutton dressed as lamb. And well-matured mutton at that.

'Yes?' the lady enquired, with a heavy hint of apprehension.

'Mrs Monk, I presume?' McTurk ventured. 'I am Detective Inspector McTurk and this is Detective Sergeant Sutherland. Southwest Scotland Police, Ayr branch. Is your husband at home? We'd like to speak to him.'

'Well, yes … yes, he is,' she replied, eyes darting furiously from one officer to the other and back again. 'But he's … he's resting. He's been through an awful lot recently, you know.'

'Can we come in, Mrs Monk?' McTurk ploughed on. 'This shouldn't take long.'

She sighed heavily and ushered the two policemen into the hall. Her hands were trembling, and quite noticeably. This sure is one nervous lady, McTurk surmised in an instant.

'He's in here,' she said, opening the second door on the right. 'He likes to spend time in his study. He says it helps him to unwind.'

Edwin Monk was drawing on his umpteenth cigarette of the morning when the detectives walked in. A big pall of smoke did its best to disguise the prominent black-and-blue weald on his left cheek but failed miserably. The place looked like a foggy day in Leith docks.

On seeing the two detectives, Monk immediately clocked his big opportunity, the one where he could enact the frame-up that the Rafferty clan had insisted upon. He had always been a master of deception, and now the curtain had been raised for his long-awaited Oscar-winning performance.

'Who … who … what do you …?' he stammered, knowing fine well who his visitors were and why they were here.

'Hello *Mister* Monk,' McTurk smiled, cleverly emphasising the 'mister' to underline the now-historical nature of his previous title, 'Councillor'. 'Southwest Scotland Police, Ayr branch. I'm D.I. McTurk and this is my colleague, D.S. Sutherland. Can we sit down?'

'Oh God,' Monk gasped, radiating panic as he stubbed out his fag in an overflowing ashtray. As both detectives took their seats, he leaned back in his leather swivel-chair and covered both eyes with the palms of his hands. 'Please, please, can you just leave me alone? I've told you people everything I know.'

'We would like to sir, but I'm afraid there's been a further development,' Sutherland interjected. 'We just want to ask you a few more questions, that's all.'

Monk stared at the ceiling. He looked like a ghost, a petrified ghost searching for the peace and sanctity that he just knew would be impossibly elusive.

'You were interviewed recently by our colleagues about your relationship with a certain Mr Rafferty,' McTurk continued. 'Mr Frank Rafferty, now deceased.'

'I know … and I know Frank is dead,' Monk replied, shaking his head and still staring into space. 'I gave the police a full statement when they spoke to me at the time. I told them everything I know. Absolutely everything. And I know nothing about Frank's death. You have to believe me.'

'Are you sure you've told us everything, sir?' Sutherland waded in, squinting his eyes accusingly at the disgraced former champion of the people.

'What are you suggesting, officer?' Monk asked, turning to face his youthful accuser and feigning false offence. 'Are you suggesting that I'm lying?'

'Perish the very thought, sir,' Sutherland continued, making it subliminally clear that this was exactly what he was suggesting. 'I'm just asking if you really have told us everything. Let me help to refresh your memory. Do you happen to know a young man called Richard Anderson?'

Monk froze. The young detective pressed on.

'I believe he made quite an impression on you during one of your big important meetings in the Council Chambers last month. It was all over the newspapers. I'm sure you remember that meeting, don't you?'

Monk paused, then nodded.

'Well, sir,' Sutherland continued. 'I'm afraid that Mister Anderson has now gone missing, and we were wondering if you could tell us anything that might help us with our enquiries? About his whereabouts, I mean?'

Monk's heartbeat began racing up through the gears. This was the moment he had been waiting for, the one he had been yearning, yet at the same time dreading. He knew he now had two diametrically opposite courses of action open to him. Either spill the beans to the cops about his seizure by Dan Rafferty's thugs and invite certain violent retribution, or set young Anderson up as instructed by Rafferty and get the goons off his back for good. In an instant, he made his choice. It was based on one overriding criterion. His indescribable terror at the hands of Rafferty's madmen.

'Okay,' he replied, gulping in preparation for spewing out the biggest lie of his life. 'What do you want to know?'

McTurk took over the reins from his junior colleague.

'The full story this time, and no more time wasting. And if it incriminates Rafferty's people, we might look at giving you and your family some police protection. Might, that is, depending on how well you cooperate with us. It's completely up to you.'

'It won't incriminate them at all,' Monk mumbled, his mind finally made up. 'It might incriminate the Anderson boy, though.'

McTurk and Sutherland exchanged perplexed glances, both somewhat wrong-footed. The latter flicked over another page in his notebook and continued scribbling.

'We're listening,' said McTurk, eyeballing him with contempt disguised as intrigue. 'The full story, Mr Monk. And this time, no bullshit.'

And thus, the fallen politician began spewing out his carefully rehearsed litany of lies. The truth didn't matter a jot to him, nor indeed did the thought of an innocent young man going down for something he hadn't done. All that mattered to Edwin Monk was self-preservation, and to hell with the consequences for others. It was a *raison d'etre* that had served him well all his life, and he sure as hell wasn't about to change it now.

Monk began by assuring McTurk and Sutherland that he had only ever met Ricky Anderson's acquaintance on one previous occasion, and that was on the evening of Thursday, the 30th of August at the public meeting in the Council Chambers, one which had been so well documented and publicly reported that the two detectives agreed they needed no further elucidation. Thereafter, Monk informed them, there had been no further contact between Anderson and himself. Well, at least not until last night, that was. A quarter-to-ten last night, to be precise.

As both plain-clothes officers listened intently, Monk went on to spin his web of fabrication by informing them that he had been out walking alone near his Alloway home, when completely out of the blue he was approached from behind by a young man with shoulder-length hair. At first, he hadn't recognised the person, but as he drew closer he soon realised that it was the same youngster who had set out to disrupt the public meeting at the end of August, a lad whom he now knew was called Richard Anderson.

Monk told the detectives that he had immediately felt threatened and asked Anderson what he wanted, to which he replied, 'I want you to pay for my mother's suffering'. The young lad, showing enormous physical strength, then grabbed Monk around the neck, pushed his arm up his back and frogmarched him across the road and behind a row of rhododendron bushes. The next thing he knew, Anderson had landed an almighty blow with his right fist straight onto Monk's left jaw, at which point he fell to the ground and passed out. When he regained consciousness a few seconds later, blood was pouring out of his mouth and two of his teeth were missing, one of which was lying on the wet grass beside him.

Anderson then told Monk to get up and face him 'like a man', but he simply couldn't move because of the shock. So, Anderson physically hauled him back up onto his feet, and staring Monk eyeball-to-eyeball, gave him what was essentially an ultimatum. It was that he must now pay for his sins or suffer the consequences. Anderson's demands were that he should set up a 'standing order' to his mother's bank account, for the sum of fifty pounds per month. The young man, whose eyes in the neon-lit semi-darkness looked ablaze with fury, then stuffed a note containing the transaction details into Monk's coat pocket.

As the two detectives listened to Monk's surprisingly detailed account of last evening's traumatic events, they watched intrigued as the once influential politician's trembling performance finally gave way to floods of tears.

McTurk continued, unmoved.

'Do you still have that note?'

'No,' Monk replied, far too quickly. 'It must have fallen out of my coat pocket when I ran home.'

'What a pity,' McTurk said. 'And how convenient. Did Mister Anderson threaten you, Mister Monk? I mean about the consequences of you not coming up with the money? Did he say specifically what would happen if you didn't pay up?'

'Yes ... yes,' Monk blubbered through his crocodile tears. 'He told me he'd kill me.'

'Can you remember what he said?' McTurk pressed him. 'His exact words, I mean?'

Monk fished a paper tissue from his trouser pocket, wiped his eyes and blew his nose, then sucked in a huge gulp of the nicotine-enriched air.

'Yes ... yes ... I'll never forget them,' he blubbered. 'He said ...

he said that Frank Rafferty was now "dead meat" and that he ...
Anderson ... had cut his throat open. And he said ... he said ... "and
that's exactly what will happen to you if you don't stump up".'

The two detectives gave each other a quizzical look. This guy
Monk was either telling the truth or he was a bloody good liar.
Either way, the need to track down young Ricky Anderson had just
escalated from high priority to critical.

44

It was 3.35 p.m. when Ricky Anderson eventually emerged from
the rough forest track onto the undulating rural road which runs
between the villages of Straiton, on the north edge of the capacious
Galloway Forest, and Glentrool, some twenty miles to the south in
its very midst.

Ricky had just trekked all the way from the head of Loch Doon
through the northernmost slice of the forest. His route had taken
him past the man-made dam of Loch Riecawr, lying resplendent
in the shadow of the 2,520-foot-high Shalloch-on-Minnoch, one
of Scotland's numerous 'Corbett' mountains, perched imperiously
on the border between Ayrshire and Kirkcudbrightshire. He had
then headed westwards across the inhospitable moorland to Loch
Bradan, yet another of the various reservoir dams in this essentially
wild and remote part of the country's sprawling south-west. A final
strenuous hike had then taken him onto the rather desolate hill
road, from which his plan was to try to hitch a lift from a rare
passing vehicle.

Ricky's intended destination for the night was Glentrool, a
relatively remote but picturesque little village resting on the shores
of Loch Trool, and one from which over the years many throngs
of eager hillwalkers had made their way up the demanding slopes
of The Merrick. Glentrool village had always been a haven for
hillwalkers and backpackers alike. As such, Ricky knew that where
there were hillwalkers and backpackers, invariably there would
be campers too, complete with their tents of all shapes and sizes.
And, of course, where there were assorted tents, his own modest
ridge could lose itself among them, camouflaged from prying eyes,
predators and would-be glory-hunters.

How Ricky needed a decent meal and a good night's sleep. His
gastric juices and overworked psyche purred at the prospect. All he

needed now was a lift, any lift at all. Even a lumbering old tractor would do. Anything to rest his weary legs and get him to that campsite. His strategy was sound, his progress thus far had been excellent, and with a fair wind the cops would already be off his trail and floundering to the north, south and east of Dalmellington, rather than through its heavily forested west. Or at least, so he thought. What he hadn't factored into the equation was a former classmate-turned-NHS nurse spilling the beans to the local constabulary.

The first two vehicles that rumbled past him were heading northwards in the direction of Ayr, the seaside town which he had left in a hurry just over a day ago upon discovering Frank Rafferty's near-decapitated corpse, and the very last place on planet earth that he wanted to be right now. As his aching feet continued to propel him in the opposite direction, his antennae suddenly perked up at the sound of a car engine humming some way behind him. Turning around and thumbing enthusiastically, he watched crestfallen as a dark-blue Ford Escort trundled past, its snotty-nosed female driver snubbing him with a disapproving stare. He cursed and plodded on for another half-mile or so, before reluctantly giving in. He needed to rest his weary backside for a few minutes, so he threw off his backpack and slumped down on the grass verge like a vanquished boxer taking the compulsory eight-count.

No sooner had he done so, than a familiar sound began tickling his eardrums. It was that of a Commer lorry, the distinctive whine of its engine unmistakable to Ricky from his earlier student days when he had once plied his trade in the summer months delivering wooden crates of lemonade from the Commers which stocked up on a daily basis from Currie's soft drinks factory in the Ayrshire village of Auchinleck. Suddenly energised with anticipation, he shot to his feet and stood there as the whine got louder and louder, and the lorry closer and closer. A few moments later, Ricky found himself scrambling up into the cab of the big lorry, as its burly bearded driver pulled away from the roadside with his latest cargo of felled pine trunks.

He turned out to be a man of few words, which suited Ricky just fine. After a courteous exchange of pleasantries, he began drifting helplessly towards the sanctuary of sound sleep. A nanosecond later, he was well and truly comatose, dreaming fitfully about everything from Iona's beautiful brown eyes, to Frank Rafferty's butchered throat, to armies of uniformed policemen rampaging over the moors in hot pursuit while Ricky tried desperately to escape their clutches, his feet hopelessly anchored in the glue-like marshes.

'Will this do you here, son?'

Ricky jumped with a start as his trance was cruelly ended by a strange, gruff voice. He opened his eyes and stared at the bearded driver in confusion, before the reality of the situation came flooding back in technicolour.

'Aye ... aye, thanks mate,' he mumbled, while pulling himself upright and looking out the window of the cab to get his bearings. 'Where are we?'

'Glentrool,' the driver answered. 'That's where you said you were headed, remember? Mind you, son, this place is the middle of nowhere. There's not much here other than country bumpkins and midges. I'm going to Newton Stewart, if you fancy it. At least we've got a couple of pubs there.'

'No, here's fine,' Ricky replied, still in a half-daze. 'Thanks for the lift, pal.'

Still a bit bleary-eyed, he extricated himself from the cab, pulled his backpack over his shoulders and stood there surveying the scene while the big Commer gathered speed and disappeared around the bend at the other side of the village. If this was the middle of nowhere, then it sure was a much more eye-pleasing middle of nowhere than the other he had vacated only a couple of weeks back, the one that went by the name of Braddoch Brickworks. Two rows of towering pine trees lined the narrow tarmac road that ran all the way through the quiet little village, those providing suitable camouflage to an endearing assortment of quaint little houses, the occasional parked car spoiling its near-linear geometry. The only thing that was missing from this sleepy little place was people.

A couple of hundred yards ahead on the other side of the road sat a small convenience store, the single-storey building only distinguishable from its other similarly constructed neighbours by a gently swaying Fine Fare sign hanging from a free-standing metal tripod anchored to the narrow pavement. Ricky made a beeline straight for the shop, hood draped self-protectively over his head, and stomach rumbling in anticipation of some much-needed sustenance. Once there, he pushed the door open, prompting a bell to ring far too loudly above his head, and confirming what he had already surmised. This joint sure wasn't Marks and Spencer during the Friday rush hour.

A few moments later, a young lady appeared from the back-shop. She looked to be in her late teens, with a pleasantly rotund face, semi-concealed by a trendy strawberry-blonde hairstyle complete with 'Cilla Black' fringe, and a figure which was considerably more Mama Cass than Twiggy.

'Can I help you?' she beamed, demonstrating a level of enthusiasm disproportionate to the task in hand. 'There's a basket on the floor over there at the door. Just help yourself. My name's Molly, by the way.'

'Hello, Molly,' Ricky smiled from underneath the hood that was trying its best to conceal his long dark hair, but not quite succeeding. 'I'll just have a wee look around, if that's okay?'

'Of course,' Molly replied, smiling warmly. 'Just let me know if you need any help.'

He picked up a basket and began collecting a rather odd conglomeration of items, its variety diverse enough to make Molly giggle in amusement, but not sufficiently strange to raise her suspicions that some total weirdo might just have strolled into town. Among Ricky's shopping were four pork sausages, half-a-pound of Ayrshire bacon, half-a-dozen of the local farmer's free-range eggs, a loaf of bread, four cans of Skol lager, a pair of scissors, an Ordnance Survey map and a beige-coloured golf cap.

'Quite a shopping you've got there,' Molly grinned, clearly hoping for an explanation of Ricky's purchases, and preferably one that might give her some sort of clue about his reason for being in Glentrool in the first place. And, of course, about his eligibility.

'Aye,' Ricky replied. 'Don't know whether I'm coming or going these days. All I know is that I'll need the beer to wash down the sausages.'

Molly laughed. Ricky immediately took his cue and moved into information-seeking mode.

'I understand there's a campsite somewhere in the village? I'm going to climb The Merrick in the morning.'

'Yes, there is. When you leave the shop, just turn right and walk up the road until you see a rough track on your left, with a signpost for Bruce's Stone. The track will take you past a few houses and straight to the campsite. You can't miss it, but it'll be quite busy at this time of year.

'Thanks, Molly,' Ricky replied, and headed for the door.

'Maybe see you again tomorrow?' she called after him. 'You

didn't tell me your name?'

'No, I didn't, did I?' Ricky smiled.

The campsite was perfect, absolutely perfect. A small field adjacent to the vast watery expanse of Loch Trool, with a toilet-cum-shower block on site, the whole facility bounded on three sides by tall trees punctuated with smaller bushes and shrubs of all descriptions and on the fourth by a steep hillside which marked the way for the ascent of The Merrick. In other words, a base with plenty of natural cover and floral camouflage, but also blessed with a quick egress route for good measure. And tents galore, eleven of them to be precise, ranging from the large-and-exquisite to the tiny-and-humble. Ricky's mid-sized ridge tent would be suitably anonymous among that lot, he nodded contentedly to himself.

He chose a quiet spot at the back of the field underneath a large beech tree and adjacent to the wooden signpost which heralded the start of the hill-path that could, if required, double as an escape route, should any unwelcome pursuers happen to creep along in the dead of night. He pitched his tent, unpacked the essentials and headed over to the toilet block, plastic poke in hand containing the necessary accoutrements, and locked himself into a cubicle.

Taking out his newly-purchased scissors, he then proceeded to lob off his long dark locks, those which Iona had often said made him look 'a bit like Jim Morrison, only better looking', referring to the much-revered lead singer of her favourite rock band, The Doors, who had died in an Amsterdam bathtub almost exactly two years earlier. Once he had finished off his own merciless haircut, a shorn and stubble-chinned Ricky wondered if Iona would ever look at him longingly again. If he ever saw her again, that was.

He headed back over to base camp, grabbed his tiny portable gas cooker and frying pan, and immediately set about cooking the most enormous fry-up of his life. By the time he had eaten his fill and washed the whole lot down with a couple of beers, only two of slices of bacon and three eggs had managed to cling onto survival. Ricky lay back on the grass with his head resting on his rolled-up sleeping bag and knew for sure that it would soon be early dark.

'Hi mate, how are you doing?' a male voice enquired, its lilt more east coast of Scotland than west.

Ricky looked up from his hazy daydream. A young couple of around his own age stood over him, he with a friendly smile on his heavily acned face, she with a slightly more cautious expression under a rather unruly mop of red hair.

'We're in the next tent over there,' the guy continued. 'We just wondered if you fancied a beer?'

Ricky's sharp intuition kicked in fast. The very last thing he needed right now was company. He was exhausted from his two-day ordeal and from his recent taxing hike across the rigours of the vast Galloway Forest, and his stomach was full at last. He was now bushed, totally and utterly exhausted, and all he wanted was a bit of peace and quiet, and a really good night's sleep. Moreover, with Her Majesty's finest undoubtedly hot on his trail, familiarity was now his arch enemy.

'Sorry, mate, but I'm knackered,' Ricky apologised, pulling himself up onto his feet. 'I've walked about twenty miles today and I can hardly keep my eyes open.'

'No problem,' the guy replied, extending a bony hand which complemented his tall and lanky frame. 'I'm Mick, by the way, and this is Maureen.'

'Hi Mick … Hi Maureen,' Ricky responded with a forced smile, shaking the hand of each. 'I'm … I'm Jim.'

If the late, lamented Jim Morrison was good enough for Iona, then he'll be good enough for me in my hour of need, Ricky figured. Some brief social discourse followed, after which Ricky repeated his excuses and bade his new chums goodnight, deeply conscious of the fact that two complete strangers could now easily identify him when the cops came calling armed with their mugshots and 'photofit' sketches. In fact, make that three when they dropped in to ask young Molly in the local shop. And four, if they ever caught up with the bearded driver of the Commer lorry.

Yes, anonymity was beginning to prove rather elusive for young Ricky. He refined his strategy in an instant. Tomorrow morning, he would rise very early and move on. To where, he had no real idea, but he knew without a shadow of a doubt that he simply had to keep moving. Moving until he found a way to make contact with the two most important people in his life, his mum and Iona. And, of course, with the only two others who could help him unlock the great mystery of who had committed Frank Rafferty's murder, Charlie Reynolds and Gerry McGhee.

However, Ricky knew he had one major trump card. If only he could manage to find a way of getting a message to Charlie in particular, he could tell him something that the cops would never have found out on their own when they hit that caravan, something that he had actually witnessed himself. The night that Frank Rafferty had his throat cut, Ricky had seen another man hurrying out of the caravan. The cops almost certainly had not. And if he ever saw the guy again, he was sure he would recognise him.

It was a trump card that might yet double as a get-out-of-jail card.

45

'Bloody hell, Sandy, it would freeze the balls off a brass monkey in this place. If this is autumn, what the hell is it like up here in the wintertime?'

'They breed us hardy in New Cumnock, boss,' DS Sandy Sutherland replied with an amused grin. 'Not like you soft Ayr boys, with all your sandcastles and sunshine.'

DI Andy McTurk just frowned and turned up the collar on his raincoat. He checked the door number at the Burnfoot address which the local police station had given him, and rang the doorbell. A powerfully-built, middle-aged man opened the door and eyeballed them both with deep suspicion.

'Aye? Can I help you?' he enquired, his voice radiating more irritation than invitation.

'Good afternoon, sir,' the older one replied. 'I'm Detective Inspector McTurk and this is my colleague, Detective Sergeant Sutherland, Southwest Scotland Police.'

'And what do you want?' came the gruff retort.

'We'd like to speak to your daughter, Isobel. We understand she's expecting us. Sergeant McLean of New Cumnock police station gave us your address. Isobel has already been very helpful to us with our enquiries into an important matter and we'd like to ask her a few more questions. Can we come in?'

'Aye, okay ... I suppose so,' local coalminer Barney McLatchie muttered. 'She's through there in the kitchen making the dinner. I hope you'll not be long, because I need to get fed before I leave for my shift at the pit.'

'We'll be as quick as we can,' said McTurk. 'We appreciate you're a very busy man.'

A plump-faced young lady poked her head around the kitchen door as the man of the house ushered the two detectives into the living room. The room was small but immaculately tidy, and the black-and-white television set was up at full-blast.

'You must be Isobel, then?' McTurk enquired with a friendly smile, extending his right hand which the youngster accepted with a cautious shake.

'Aye, that's me,' she replied, before turning to face her father. 'Dad ... dad ... for God's sake ... would you turn the telly down? We can hardly hear a thing in here.'

'Not before this last race is bye,' snapped her old man, as he slumped back down in his favourite armchair to watch Newmarket's 4.05 p.m. sprint handicap. 'Away and make your visitors a cup of tea in the kitchen and give me peace to watch it.'

McTurk and Sutherland exchanged knowing glances and made their way towards the lip-smacking aroma of pots bubbling on the kitchen stove, at which stood another chubby lady, this one in her late-forties or early-fifties.

'Smells good,' McTurk remarked with an approving nod.

'Mince and tatties,' young Isobel replied. 'My dad's favourite. He says it puts a good lining on his belly when he's down the pit. My mum taught me everything I know about cooking, didn't you mum?'

Agnes McLatchie shrugged her shoulders rather self-deprecatingly.

'Take a seat here at the kitchen table,' the matriarch said to the two police officers, whilst gesturing to her daughter to join them. 'What is it you want to know? Isobel told the sergeant everything yesterday.'

McTurk nodded politely and turned to face her daughter, who was picking her fingernails anxiously.

'How sure are you that the young man you saw on the bus two days ago was Richard Anderson?' he asked, flicking through the pages of his well-worn notebook.

Isobel McLatchie looked lost for words.

'Well ... tell the man, Isobel,' her mother urged.

'I'm sure it was him,' she said. 'Absolutely sure.'

'There's no need to be worried, Isobel,' DS Sutherland interjected with a reassuring smile. 'You've done nothing wrong. In fact, you've been a great help to us so far. We just need to gather as much information as we can about the man you saw on the bus. What he looked like, how he behaved and so on. Any little details that might

170

help us further in our enquiries, that's all.'

McTurk gave his junior charge a sarcastic glance. Smart-arse, he muttered under his breath, secretly wishing that he possessed young Sutherland's charm with the ladies. Undaunted, the boss ploughed on.

'Just take your time and tell us everything you remember, Isobel. Every little detail will help, no matter how small.'

'Well ...,' she continued. 'I was up the back of the bus, and he ... Ricky ... was about six or seven rows down on the other side.'

'Which side of the bus were you sitting on?' McTurk asked.

'On the left,' she replied.

'So, he was on your right-hand-side and you saw the left side of his face?'

'I suppose so.'

'Can you describe his appearance?'

'Well, the Ricky Anderson I remember had short dark hair, but the one I saw on the bus that day had long dark hair, down to about his shoulders. Mind you, it must be a good four or five years ago since I last saw him.'

'So, what makes you so sure that it was Ricky Anderson?'

'It was him, no doubt about it.'

'What was he wearing, Isobel? Can you remember? Think hard.'

'He was wearing a pair of light-blue jeans ... and a pair of boots ... black, I think ... no, brown, definitely brown ... not flashy cowboy boots or anything like that, but sturdy ... like walking boots.'

'And a jacket, or coat? After all, summer's now gone.'

'He had an anorak on ... no, not an anorak, a kind of bomber jacket thing ... that's right, I remember now, a bomber jacket ... and it had a hood ... black, I think. Or black and grey, maybe.'

'What makes you think it had a hood, Isobel? It's a bit odd for you to remember something like that, is it not?'

'Because after I turned around to look at him when I was getting off the bus, he pulled it over his head. Like ... like, you know, like he was trying to hide his face.'

'Okay, Isobel, that's really helpful. Anything else?'

'There was a big bag lying on the seat beside him ... it had straps on it, like one of those bags you pull over your shoulders.'

'A rucksack, you mean? The kind of bag that hillwalkers might carry?'

'Yes … yes, that kind of thing. It looked a pretty heavy big bag. Lots of stuff in it, you know? I remember wondering where he might be going with all that stuff.'

McTurk leaned back on the kitchen chair and stroked his chin. It was Sutherland who asked the question that was already forming on the DI's lips.

'Isobel, what makes you so sure that it was Richard Anderson … Ricky? You seem so certain.'

'His eyes,' she replied instantly. 'Ricky always had the most beautiful eyes.'

Agnes McLatchie stared straight at her daughter and noticed her face starting to flush. Young Isobel continued, looking a bit embarrassed.

'All the girls at school fancied Ricky. They always said he had … sorry, mum … he had "come to bed" eyes.'

Turning to his boss, Sutherland smiled and said, 'Bet they never said that about you at school, sir.'

The two ladies stifled a giggle. McTurk gave Sutherland the evil eye and turned again to face the young nurse.

'Anything else you can tell us about the man you saw, Isobel? Anything unusual? Anything else he was carrying … other than his backpack I mean?'

'He had a book on his knee. No, it wasn't a book, it was a map. One of those big maps that fold up like a book. Like the ones we used in my Geography class at school.'

'An Ordnance Survey map?'

'Yes … yes, that's what it was, an ordinance survey map. And I remember the title as clear as day. It said, "Glentrool, Loch Trool and The Merrick".'

'How did you manage to remember that, Isobel? It's a very specific bit of detail, if you don't mind me saying so.'

'Because that's where Uncle John and Aunt Betty took us for a picnic a few years ago, wasn't it mum? Remember dad and Uncle John climbed that big mountain? And Aunt Betty and you and me went for a sail on a wee boat?'

Agnes McLatchie's eyes lit up.

'Aye, I remember it well. It was a smashing day. Apart from the midges, though. We all got eaten alive that day.'

'Well, thanks for everything, Isobel,' McTurk said, rising to his feet. 'You've been a great help. We'll be in touch if we need to speak to you again.'

The DI clocked a sudden change in the young lady's body language. She looked troubled.

'What's the matter, Isobel?' he asked. 'Something bothering you?'

'The Ricky Anderson I remember wouldn't harm a fly,' she replied. 'He was a really quiet boy who just got on with things. All the lassies were daft about him, but he was already spoken for.'

'Did you ever hear of him getting mixed up in any trouble at school?' Sutherland interjected. 'Fights, that sort of thing?'

'Yes,' replied Isobel. 'I remember one story going around about him giving a couple of yobs a right good hammering, but they were horrible boys and they got exactly what they deserved. Ricky could never have done anything like what's been in the papers, though. You know ... that stuff in the caravan.'

The two officers nodded politely and made their way back into the living room en route to the front door.

'Did your horse win, sir?' asked Sutherland.

'Did it hell,' Barney McLatchie grunted. 'Beat in a photo finish, story of my life.'

'Never mind, sir,' McTurk remarked, bidding the family goodbye. 'Your daughter's mince and tatties smell wonderful.'

Within the hour, a massive police search had been launched, with orders to comb its way from New Cumnock in a southerly direction all the way down to the Solway coast and south-west through the Galloway forest.

The epicentre of the search would be the village of Glentrool, towards which the force's Rapid Response Team was already winging its way.

Ricky Anderson sure hadn't banked on that little development.

46

'See you tomorrow, Isobel,' Sister Karen Mitchell said with a warm smile. 'You did really well today, especially the way you dealt with that awful drunk man at reception. Here's hoping tomorrow will be a wee bit less dramatic.'

'Thanks, Sister,' staff nurse Isobel McLatchie replied, before pushing open the big swing-doors that led from Ward 6A out into the cool late-evening breeze.

A sensitive young lady afflicted by much more self-doubt than either her engaging personality or professional talents really merited, Isobel always responded eagerly to praise. She felt like she was walking on air.

Yes indeed, it had certainly been a dramatic day, even by Ballochmyle's standards. The old NHS hospital, a tired collection of antiquated traditional and prefabricated buildings situated in the shelter of the woods between the Ayrshire villages of Catrine and Mauchline, had seen it all before, but if truth be told, the dilapidated place had now had its day.

Isobel had earned her corn today, that was for sure. Working an eight-hour shift which had soon extended to twelve due to staff absence, and with an emergency Caesarean section and two serious car-crash casualties thrown in for good measure, the time had really flown in. Yes, she could have done without that horrible little ned with the Mohican hairdo staggering into reception pissed out of his brains and looking for a fight with the charming Doctor Singh, who had earlier refused to prescribe him with barbiturates for his 'nerves', but she had dealt with the situation as calmly and professionally as usual. And very importantly, Sister Mitchell had been really impressed.

All that remained now was for her to catch the last bus home to Burnfoot on the westerly fringe of New Cumnock, where a hearty meal would be waiting, followed soon afterwards by sound sleep, then she would be suitably refreshed and raring to go again in the morning. Happy days. Even happier days, though, if only she could get herself a man, something about which her overbearing mother was often much too prone to remind her.

As Isobel began skipping along the well-worn tarmac pavement in the direction of the bus-stop which stood on the main road just outside the hospital complex, she realised that she was all alone. Of course, she was. After all, her shift had been extended well past the customary clocking-off time. And if there was one thing that Isobel McLatchie hated, it was being all alone. Especially all alone in the dark.

The wind fairly whistled through the row of huge beech trees that lined the hospital's main access-egress route, scattering its autumnal leaves in a ghostly cloud illuminated by yellow-orange neon lights. Isobel shivered at the eeriness that seemed to descend over her like a shroud, and began to quicken her step. Something

174

stirred in the rhododendron bushes to her left, probably something small and furry, and her brisk walk quickly became a canter.

Only fifty yards to go and she would soon be in the security of the bus shelter on a main road which was always busy with traffic, even at this God-forsaken time of night. Only thirty yards, almost there. Twenty. Ten.

A puff of smoke rose through the near-golden glow which emanated from the streetlight adjacent to the exit gate. Isobel strained her eyes to try to locate the locus of the smoker. As her rapid footsteps drew her closer still, she could just make out the figure of a man standing a few yards back from the wooden 'Welcome to Ballochmyle Hospital' sign. A big man. In fact, a very big man. Still wondering whether his presence might enhance her personal safety or threaten it, she slowed back down to a calm stroll.

'Hiya,' Isobel said as she drew level with the man, hoping for an equally sociable response.

None was forthcoming. Only another puff of smoke from the red glow at the end of an invisible cigarette. Her heartbeat accelerated and her mouth began to feel as desiccated as if she had just necked a whole packet of crisps in one go. She focused on the bus shelter across the road and marched straight ahead, arms pumping furiously.

The big guy moved quickly, far more quickly than his oversized frame ought to have allowed. He shoved the palm of his left hand over Isobel's mouth and his right around her neck, causing her to drop her handbag at her feet. She tried to scream, but nothing came out. She tried to breathe, but the pressure on her throat made inhalation impossible. The neon lights flickered and began to fade.

The next thing Isobel knew, she was lying on her back on the damp grass behind the bushes with this enormous brute of a man on top of her, his left hand still covering her mouth. However, at least now she could breathe, if only through her nostrils, because his right hand was no longer squeezing on her windpipe. Instead, it was brandishing a knife. A long, pointed knife that glistened like a warlord's sabre in the macabre glow of artificial light.

Again, she tried to scream. Her assailant put paid to that by keeping her mouth covered with his sweaty palm. He smiled at her and increased the pressure. She could now taste her own blood, as sharp incisors bit into soft gums. Finally, the man spoke, but in a voice that barely made itself heard above the wind whistling through the foliage.

'Now, then, Miss Isobel McLatchie,' he whispered, as his victim squirmed in vain under the sheer dead-weight of his colossal frame. 'I'm going to take my hand away from your mouth. If you scream, I'll slice your throat open and you'll drown in your own blood right here on the grass. If you stay quiet, you will live, and we can have a nice wee chat. Your decision, sweetheart. Nod, or shake your head. Live, or die. It's up to you.'

As Isobel lay there completely traumatised, clarity of thought was a forlorn hope. However, mortal survival was not. Somehow, she managed to summon up the presence of mind to nod her head. The big guy pressed the blade of the knife against the flesh of her throat, just enough to make the slightest nick and draw blood, then slowly began to slide his sweaty hand away from her mouth. His eyes looked on fire, although whether with primal desire or evil rage Isobel simply could not tell. She said nothing, terror having taken total control.

'Right, Isobel,' he said, staring into her eyes with a menace the likes of which she had never before had the misfortune to witness. 'I want you to listen carefully. Very, very carefully. You understand, sweetheart?'

Words still failing her, Isobel just nodded again.

'Two coppers came to your house yesterday, didn't they?'

Another nod, tears streaming down her cheeks as the horror of her situation began to come into very sharp focus.

'And they asked you a number of questions about a young man called Ricky Anderson. You saw him on the bus a couple of days ago, didn't you?'

Isobel nodded again, bewildered and terrified. What was all this about, and who was this horrible big man pinning her to the ground and holding a knife at her throat? And how could he possibly have known that I spoke to the police yesterday about Ricky?

'I just want to know one thing, sweetheart. And if you tell me, I'll let you go. But if you don't, you'll die. You understand?'

Another wordless nod.

'Okay, here comes my question. Are you ready, Isobel? And do you understand what is going to happen if you don't tell me the truth?'

Finally, she spoke. By now she was sobbing hysterically.

'Yes … yes, I understand. I just want to go home … please.'

'I know that, Isobel. So, all you've got to do is answer one little question. My question is … where was Ricky going that day on the bus?'

'What? What do you mean?'

'Where was he going, Isobel? Where was he headed? Now think hard, because your life depends on it.'

'He was going to … to Glentrool, I think … camping or something.'

'You sure about that, Isobel?' the big guy glowered, increasing the knife's pressure underneath her chin. 'Like … one hundred percent sure?'

'Yes … yes, I'm sure … he was going to Glentrool … he had a map … he had a map … that's all I know. I promise. Please let me go … please.'

'Did you tell the cops that he was going to Glentrool, Isobel?'

'Yes … yes, I think so … yes, I did.'

'Okay, sweetheart, you've done really well. I'm going to leave you now, but I want you to do something for me. I want you to stay very still and count to one-hundred before you get up. If you don't, or if you scream, I'll come back and cut your throat. You understand?'

Isobel closed her eyes and nodded.

Her attacker pulled the knife away, shoved it into his inside jacket pocket, then placed both hands on the grass and pushed himself up onto his knees. Isobel inhaled a huge gulp of air as her ribcage expanded in relief.

'Oh, and one more thing, Isobel,' he said, rising to his feet. 'Tell anyone about this … especially the cops … and I'll be back. Only next time, we won't be having this pleasant little chat. And I might make sweet love to you first before I cut your throat. Comprendo?'

And at that, the huge giant of a man shuffled out of the bushes and disappeared into the dead of night.

Isobel McLatchie just lay there trembling, licked her parched lips with her dry tongue and began whispering through the tears.

'One … two … three … four …'

47

Charlie Reynolds could scarcely believe his luck.

As he lay stretched out in bed, a shaft of early morning sunlight managed to sneak its way through a crack in the vertical blinds, illuminating the dark curls of hair that tickled the nape of Janice Anderson's neck. He remained motionless for a few minutes, watching her chest rise and fall as she slept. Soon, the temptation became too much. He wrapped his right arm around her shoulder and pulled her gently towards him.

Janice opened her eyes and stretched her frame as much as she dared, to avoid incurring the wrath of three broken ribs pressing against badly bruised flesh. Reynolds kissed her softly on the lips. She smiled that same irresistible smile.

'Good morning, handsome,' she mumbled, just stifling a yawn. 'What's on your mind?'

'What do you think?' he smiled back. 'But I'm not sure if you're up to it yet.'

'I'll be the judge of that,' she whispered into his ear.

The two lovebirds sank into a deep, passionate embrace. Breakfast could wait. The telephone rang. Of course it did.

'Just ignore it, Charlie,' Janice giggled. 'They'll call back.'

They did indeed. Whoever was trying to get through was in no mood to wait in line. Reynolds just instinctively knew that something wasn't quite right.

'I have to take this, Janice,' he said, releasing her from his clutches with a hefty sigh of frustration. 'It might be important.'

'I know,' Janice replied, rolling her eyes. 'I suppose I'll just have to get used to this, won't I?'

Reynolds swung his legs out of bed, and answered the second call with a brusque 'hello' that carried with it more irritation than a power cut in the middle of the Scottish Cup Final. However, it was nothing compared to that in the voice on the other end.

'My office, Charlie. Now.'

Reynolds grabbed his wristwatch from the bedside table. It registered 7.25 a.m. More to the point, 7.25 a.m. on a Saturday morning, the first Saturday he had had off for six weeks.

'And a very good morning to you too, Sir,' he said through gritted teeth. 'What's the big rush? It's my day off and I need my beauty sleep.'

'Half-an-hour, Charlie,' the voice snapped. 'You and your bloody sparring partner.'

Then the line went dead.

Reynolds rubbed his eyes and tried to gather his thoughts. A few moments ago, he had been about to make love to the delectable new woman in his life, and for the very first time. Now he had been summoned to appear before the Big Cheese, and for a right good ball-bashing by the sound of it. But for what? He dropped the phone on its cradle, picked it up again and dialled.

'What's wrong, Charlie?' Janice asked, concern beginning to get the upper hand over tiredness.

Reynolds turned and put his forefinger to his lips, clearly indicating that something was awry. The ringing in his earpiece soon brought a click, at which point a grumpy voice confirmed that another copper's free weekend had already been ruined.

'Hi Andy,' Reynolds said. 'Sorry to drag you away from Joanna Lumley, old boy, but I've just had Smokin' Joe on the phone. Apparently, I've to get my arse into his office in the next half-hour.'

'Mines too,' came McTurk's deadpan reply.

'Aye, I thought so. Any idea what we've done?'

'Nope.'

'Me neither. Suppose we'll just have to wait and find out. See you in a bit.'

'Suggest we both get there pronto.'

'Aye, you're probably right. I'm really looking forward to this.'

'Me too. It promises to be a gas.'

Reynolds sat back down on the bed, leaned over and kissed Janice again. It was a kiss that radiated apology over passion.

'Are you going to tell me what's wrong, Charlie?' she asked, not at all sure that she really wanted to hear the answer anyway. 'Is it about my Ricky?'

'No, no,' he replied, 'At least I don't think so. Fraser wants Andy and me in his office right away. Sounds like he's going to give us a right good kicking.'

'What have you done?' she enquired.

'I have absolutely no idea, Janice, not a Scooby Doo. But he sounds really pissed off, even by Smokin' Joe's own standards.'

Reynolds took a quick shower, dressed and hotfooted his way out the door with an apologetic wave of his hand.

'See you in a wee while,' he smiled. 'And don't bother getting dressed.'

'Your word is my command,' she teased.

Reynolds slid into his car and made straight for police headquarters. By the time he had pulled into the car park, Andy

179

McTurk was already standing outside the main door, trademark fag in mouth.

'Any ideas yet?' Reynolds asked.

His partner gave a quizzical shake of the head.

When they reached the office door, it was the Chief Superintendent himself who met them. He was wearing a face like thunder.

'In there,' he commanded, pointing towards the big conference table in his private office.

Shit and double shit, thought Reynolds. No cosy heart-to-heart chats around the coffee table this morning, so it must be serious. Fraser, impeccably dressed as always in his full police regalia, planted his ample backside down on the high-backed, leather-clad chair at the top of the table and signalled to his two senior officers to flank him on either side. Christ, it really is serious, he realised, knowing that McTurk would be in telepathic accord as always.

'Just a couple of very simple questions for each of you,' the Chief Super began, eyeballing his charges with simmering fury. 'Let's start with you, Charlie, shall we?'

'Fine with me, Sir,' Reynolds replied, as inscrutably as ever.

'Did I, or did I not, instruct you to stay completely out of this Frank Rafferty business?'

'Yes ... yes you did, Sir.'

'And did you then ask me to let Andy take charge of the investigation?'

'Yes, I did, Sir.'

Fraser smiled sarcastically, then turned to face McTurk.

'Your turn now, Andy. When I put you in charge of this case - and at Charlie's own request, as he has admitted - did I, or did I not, instruct you to keep him completely out of it?'

McTurk lowered his head and squirmed uncomfortably in his chair as the dawning realisation hit him. So, this is what it's all about, then.

'Well,' Fraser continued. 'Cat got your tongue?'

'Yes, you did, Sir.'

Fraser smacked his lips in smug self-satisfaction, leaned backed in his chair and began swivelling his gaze between one officer and the other. A few seconds of awkward silence, then he continued.

'Right, then. Would either of you like to say anything? Anything at all?'

McTurk made to speak, but Reynolds immediately cut him off

by raising his hand.

'My fault, Sir,' he piped up. 'All my fault. Andy told me at least three times that I had to keep out of it, and I didn't. I'll take the rap for that, nothing to do with Andy.'

'Jesus Christ almighty!' shouted Fraser, his face reddening in rage. 'Two of my most senior officers and you're both behaving like school kids. If one of you put your arse in the fireplace, so would the other one.'

Two heads nodding sheepishly. The top dog ploughed on, a big man in a big hurry.

'Charlie, you are far too closely involved in this already, through your ... your relationship ... with that Anderson woman from Glenside, who just so happens to be one of Frank's latest victims. It's the clearest conflict of interest I've seen in years. Are you really too dumb to see that, man?'

'No, Sir,' he replied, head bowed.

Fraser smelled blood. Whether he intended to spill it or not, time would tell.

'And as for you, Andy ... well, where do I bloody start? Let's start with deliberately disobeying an order, shall we?'

Another few moments of awful silence, two sets of eyes staring at the laminated floor, another glaring at the ornate ceiling. Finally, it was McTurk who broke the spell.

'Can I say something, Sir?' he ventured. 'I have a suggestion. One you might not like, but which I'd ask you to consider.'

'Try me,' Fraser replied. 'You're both up shit creek already, so why not keep paddling?'

'You're dead right, Sir,' McTurk continued. 'Charlie does have a clear conflict of interest here and he has no business being anywhere near this case.'

Reynolds shifted restlessly in his seat, then glowered at his partner. McTurk sailed on.

'In fact, Sir, there are too many conflicts of interest here.'

'Spit it out, then,' said Fraser.

'Sir,' McTurk went on, choosing his words very carefully. 'Charlie has a major issue here because, as you say, he is in a personal relationship with Janice Anderson who is the victim of a serious assault, which we believe was ordered by Frank Rafferty. And not only with Janice, but with her son Ricky too, who is now a major suspect in Rafferty's murder and on the run from the law.

But that's not all.'

'I'm listening,' Fraser nodded, the tension in his body language still getting the better of him. 'Get on with it, man. I don't have all bloody day.'

'Sir, you have a conflict of interest here as well, if you don't mind me saying so. And a massive one at that.'

Fraser stared at McTurk. McTurk stared back and didn't flinch. A few more moments of pregnant silence passed. Finally, the Chief Super raised both hands and sighed.

'I know, Andy, I know. Frank was flesh and blood. All in all, this whole thing is one big sorry f-----g mess, isn't it?'

McTurk nodded sympathetically.

'So, you want me to go and take confession with the blessed Pat O'Halloran, our esteemed Chief Constable?' said Fraser. 'Is that what you're suggesting, Andy?'

McTurk shook his head.

'No, not at all, Sir. There's another way.'

'Pray tell, Inspector, because as sure as hell I can't think of one.'

'Keep me in charge of the case and I'll nail Rafferty's killer. That's a promise, Sir.'

'And what about Charlie?'

'Whether we like it or not, Charlie is already involved and can't be expected to do nothing. It's too much to ask. He's in love with the boy's mother, for God's sake, and she's sick with worry about her son, as well as recuperating from a serious assault that half-killed her.'

'So, what are you suggesting, Andy? That I keep Charlie on the case too? With a conflict of interest like that? And just so that you two can continue your cosy little double-act?'

'No, Sir. In fact, I'm suggesting the very opposite. Keep Charlie off the case. And there's only one sure way to achieve that in the circumstances.'

'You're not suggesting …?'

'I am indeed, Sir. Send him home for a couple of weeks, in fact make it three. A wee holiday. Paid leave, gardening leave … whatever you want to call it. But send him home.'

Reynolds's face was a study, a strange amalgam of shock and anger. His words fell out like a child's sweets from a burst paper poke.

'Did you … did you just say what … what I think you said,

Andy?'

'Afraid so, buddy. It makes sense.'

Reynolds just sat eyeballing his partner in astonishment. What the hell was he up to? Fraser forced a strangled laugh.

'Go on, Andy. This is fascinating. Tweedle Dee finally sticks the knife into Tweedle Dum, after all those years of being joined at the hip like Siamese twins.'

'Send Charlie home, Sir, and leave young Sandy Sutherland and me to nail Rafferty's killer. God knows, he could do with spending some time with Janice. Help her in her rehabilitation, moral support and all that.'

'You about finished?' Fraser interjected.

'Not quite, Sir,' McTurk went on. 'There's still the small matter of what you do. About your own role, I mean.'

'And what exactly do I do, then? After all, you seem to have it all worked out. Do you want to swap bloody seats?'

'You go straight to O'Halloran ... sorry, to the Chief Constable. Tell him about your connection with the deceased and about Charlie's relationship with the fugitive suspect's mother. Then tell him about your decision to send him home. That way, you're squeaky clean because you'll have acted decisively to deal with both conflicts of interest. And then Sandy and I can get on with the small matter of bringing your cousin's murderer to justice and prove the Anderson boy's innocence.'

'And what do I do meantime?' Reynolds piped up, still recoiling from the shock. 'Apart from hoovering the carpet and washing the dishes, that is?'

'You reel Ricky in, Charlie,' McTurk replied. 'Sandy and I will keep you fully up to speed, and you bring the boy home before Rafferty's goons get to him.'

'And just how do I do that, Andy? Put a bloody advert in the local newspapers?'

'No, you use your charm, Charlie. And the wee lassie's charm too, his girlfriend, Iona. My guess is that Ricky will try to contact her. And the journalist too, Gerry McGhee. We'll keep you in the loop, you wait for developments then bring him in before the heavies find him. We'll make sure they know that you're out of the picture. They've got plenty of muscles, but only about six brain cells between them.'

Reynolds stared at McTurk, who just smiled and shrugged his

shoulders. It was Fraser who interrupted the fascinating non-verbal exchange.

'Okay, but on one condition, Andy. You need to keep up the momentum in the search for young Anderson. He is a murder suspect after all, and while none of us really want to believe that he killed Frank, the evidence suggests otherwise. If we get him before you do, Charlie, we throw him in the cells and almost certainly charge him with murder, then let the courts establish the truth. If you get him first and persuade him to turn himself in, then it will look a whole lot better for the boy.'

'But if Rafferty's lads get him first,' added Reynolds, 'then it's game over for Ricky. So, you had better deliver, Andy.'

Smokin' Joe had the last word as usual.

'Which is why we're not going to let that happen. Right, Andy, you're still in charge. Charlie, you're on three weeks' paid leave and I don't want to see you or hear from you until ... let me see ... Monday the tenth of October. Now, if you'll both excuse me, I have to make an important call to the Chief Constable.'

After graciously accepting some sage advice from a subordinate officer, albeit one for whom Fraser had the utmost respect, he had hastily re-established his seniority. Reynolds and McTurk recognised their cue and stood up, both mightily relieved that the impromptu meeting was over. It could have been a hell of a lot worse and they knew it.

More importantly, both had now been given the green light to go get the bad guy. And, of course, to save the good guy.

48

Molly Harper didn't even bother to look up when the pot-bellied stranger in the tight-fitting policeman's uniform walked into the shop.

It was a Saturday morning after all, and in Glentrool General Stores Saturday was the busiest day of the week. That was the day when the mums of the locale would come in to choose 'something nice' to put on the dinner table. It was also the day that the dads would purchase their copies of *The Sporting Life* to guide them through the afternoon's televised horseracing card and their six-packs of beer to anaesthetise them while they were being force-fed *The Generation Game* and *It's a Knockout*, the formulaic weekend

TV offerings. So, for young Molly, Saturday morning in her parents' convenience store was going like the proverbial fair. At least, by rural Galloway standards anyway.

Sergeant George Renfrew's complexion was so ruddy that it would have done justice to the well-worn Ayrshire expression, 'a face like a skelped arse'. When he marched towards the counter, the queue of four customers immediately parted like Moses commanding the Dead Sea, his unruly mop of wavy hair and ill-matching moustache suitably augmented by the smell of stale nicotine. He looked so much like the archetypal 1970s copper that he could have been picked out of the crowd by a bat suffering from myopia. However, despite his rather odd appearance, he nevertheless exuded an air of authority.

Old Mister Campbell, the village's long-retired veterinary surgeon, picked up his bag of treacle scones and gave a little cough, one designed to attract Molly's attention. It worked a treat. She immediately looked up and saw that her queue of eager customers had obediently stepped aside to allow the tubby officer to take centre-stage at the counter.

'Oh,' Molly remarked. 'Can I help you?'

'I hope so,' the officer replied. 'I'm Sergeant Renfrew of Southwest Scotland Police. I wonder if we could have a little chat?'

'Oh ... oh ... certainly,' Molly stammered, alternating her gaze between her regulars and the visitor. 'Can I ask what about?'

The sergeant's response was short and to the point.

'In private, please.'

Molly turned around to face the back-shop.

'Dad,' she shouted. 'Can you come through?'

'Aye ... in a wee minute,' came the impatient reply. 'I'm busy doing the books.'

'No, Dad,' she shouted again, 'Right now, please.'

A few seconds later, Tommy Harper, the shop's third generation owner, Grand Master of the local Masonic Lodge and long-time community stalwart appeared, looking somewhat irritated at his daughter's insistence, before clocking that an officer of the law had arrived on the scene.

'Dad, this man is Sergeant Renfrew,' she announced, 'And he wants to speak to me in private. Can you mind the shop for a few minutes?'

'Of course, dear,' her father replied, changing his tune in an

185

instant. 'That'll be no problem at all.'

He extended his arm in friendship and the two men exchanged handshakes. The sergeant then followed Molly through to her father's office-cum-store.

'Have you seen this young man recently?' he asked, handing her a black-and-white photograph and studying her reaction very closely.

Molly recognised the face immediately. How could she possibly have forgotten a gorgeous face like that? And the eyes, those eyes.

'Yes,' she replied, without hesitation. 'He was in the shop a couple of days ago. Standing through there at the counter where you were standing.'

'You sure it was him?'

'Positive. It was him, definitely him. Has he done something bad?'

The sergeant blanked the question.

'Can you remember what he bought?'

'I'll try. He asked for sausages, and ham, and eggs, and a loaf ... you know, stuff for a fry-up.'

'Anything else?'

'Yes, I remember that it was a kind of odd mixture of stuff.'

'Go on.'

'Well, he bought scissors ... yes, a pair of scissors. Oh yes, and a golf cap too.'

'A golf cap? What colour?'

'It was beige.'

'Beige?'

'Yes, kind of cream coloured, you know?'

'Now, this is very important. Did he happen to mention where he was heading?'

'No, he didn't say very much. Quite a quiet boy, really.'

'Nothing at all?'

'No ... nothing.'

'Okay, thanks for your help. I'm sorry to have dragged you away from your customers. It looks like a busy wee shop.'

'It is, especially Saturdays. They're always mobbed like this.'

George Renfrew turned on his heels and smiled an invisible smile. So, four customers in this God-forsaken place means busy? Hardly Woolworth's on Ayr High Street, is it?

'Oh,' young Molly said, as another recollection returned. 'I've

186

just remembered. When he was leaving the shop, he asked me where the local campsite was.'

'And where is it?'

'Turn right at the door, then about half-a-mile up the road there's a wee track that leads past a couple of houses and into a field. You can't miss it.'

Renfrew mumbled a polite apology for his intrusion to both father and daughter, thanked the latter for her assistance, turned right at the shop door and began marching briskly up the road to a waiting police car, in the driver's seat of which sat his youthful partner, Constable Danny Sanderson.

'Danny,' he said, 'get on the blower and find out how many uniformed officers we've got in and around the village. In total, I mean. Meanwhile, I'll get on my own radio and try to get instructions from DI McTurk on how to play this.'

Ricky Anderson might not have known it, but the boys-in-blue were closing in fast.

49

'Glentrool?' asked Zander McGinn, his huge square-shaped face a picture of perplexity under his self-fashioned skinhead haircut. 'Where the hell's Glentrool?'

'Search me,' Robert McDade replied, taking one last lung-bursting draw on his latest Benson & Hedges fag before chucking the stub into the coal fire. 'Somewhere near Girvan, I think. Country bumpkin land.'

Dan Rafferty's expression was a study of disgust.

'Would you two please remember what I pay you to do?' he asked, shaking his head. 'And I don't think it's for your navigational skills, do you? Ralph Baxter's your driver today. And Ralph knows exactly where Glentrool is, because that's what I pay him to do.'

'Baxter's just a wean, boss,' McGinn replied. 'Can hardly wipe his own arse.'

McDade waded in, in support of his kindred spirit.

'Aye, a wee boy, Dan. Probably not even started shaving yet. You need to get somebody with a bit of experience, not straight out of high school. One of these days, we might need a real driver to get us out of a jam, and in a hurry.'

'Yes,' replied Rafferty, 'And young Ralph's the very man for the job. Not only did he pass his driving test first time, but he then also sailed through his advanced test the following year. And of course, he got seven O-Grades at school as well, including Geography, so he knows where bloody Glentrool is. Which is more than I can say for you pair of clowns, who couldn't even spell it.'

McGinn and McDaid just looked at each other and smiled. If Dan Rafferty wasn't their paymaster, he'd be pushing up the daisies just like his big brother Frank, who now was. Which, of course, was exactly why they were being despatched today to Glentrool, wherever the hell Glentrool was, to administer severe retribution to Frank's killer, another young punk called Ricky Anderson.

A car horn peeped. Rafferty walked over and peered out of the lounge window. A young blond-haired lad got out of the driver's side and took a seat on the bonnet of his black Ford Corsair, chewing on his gum and lighting up a cigarette. The overlord and his latest protégé exchanged waves from either side of the glass pane.

As Rafferty showed his two right-hand men the door, it was McDade who asked the final question.

'What exactly do you want us to do with the Anderson boy, Dan?'

'Use your imagination,' Rafferty replied to the one they called Mad Rab. 'You've got carte blanche and I'm sure you can think of something appropriate. Something that Frank would have approved of.'

McDaid and McGinn exchanged leering smiles. They had never even heard of the term 'carte blanche' before, but they had just been handed it on a silver platter.

50

'Maria's café, Andy,' mumbled Charlie Reynolds, as the two Detective Inspectors walked towards their respective cars, sensing the laser-like stare of their boss burning onto the back of their heads all the way from his office window. 'I'll buy you a bacon roll and a cup of tea.'

'Done,' McTurk replied, trying his best not to move his lips for fear of Smokin' Joe clocking that they were up to something. 'It's about time you put your hand in your pocket.'

By the time the tea mugs and filled rolls had arrived, the two colleagues had already begun mapping out their strategy.

'Right, then,' said McTurk through a mouthful of semi-chewed food, a trickle of HP sauce dribbling down his chin. 'I've worked out my next moves, but I'm not so sure about yours, Charlie. Maybe you should just spend a couple of days at home with Janice and buy yourself a wee bit of thinking time before diving in.'

Reynolds laughed and handed him a paper napkin.

'Did your mammy never teach you any table manners?'

'None that I can remember. Something about not eating off your knife?'

'I'm itching to get on with this, Andy, but you're right. There's really not a lot I can do until Ricky tries to make contact. I can't see him getting in touch with his mum, because he'd need to phone my place and I'm not sure he trusts me enough yet. My guess is that he'll phone Iona.'

'Mines too. So, you might want to prime her in advance. Tell her what to say, get her to suggest that he turns himself in. What do you think?'

'Nah, I don't think Iona's the type who would appreciate a "to do" list when she eventually gets to speak to her boyfriend for the first time since he went AWOL. She's a smart girl, and she'll know how to play it when he calls. However, I agree with you about lying low for a bit. Make Dan Rafferty and his pack of hounds think I've had my wings clipped and grounded by Smokin' Joe.'

'You have, Charlie. Remember?'

'Aye, thanks for reminding me. My point is that Ricky will blow his cover soon enough, but only when he feels that the time is right.'

'Let's hope when he does, he only blows it to Iona. I'd much prefer you getting to him first before our boys catch up with him. And they will, Charlie, because he can't run forever, especially with winter just around the corner.'

'It's not our boys I'm worried about. McDade, McGinn and Baxter will now be operating under Dan Rafferty's orders. And Dan won't be a happy man. Sure, with big brother Frank out of the picture, he would have inherited the business, but young Ricky has just seen to it that the business is totally discredited, and prospective clients will now run for cover, so Dan will be absolutely furious. My guess is that he'll already have been tipped off by some bent copper that Ricky's fingerprints were all over the murder weapon, and he'll be desperate to get to him before we do. I think Ricky's in serious bother, Andy. I'm worried about him, and worried about

189

how his mother would cope if anything happened to him. She's been through an awful lot.'

McTurk washed down what was left of his bacon butty with a big slug of tea, before responding.

'I'm worried about him too, Charlie. Why aren't you eating, by the way?'

'Lost my appetite.'

'What's on your mind, buddy? Come on, if you're not going to eat your beans, then spill them.'

Reynolds took a packet of cigarettes out of his jacket pocket, stuck one in his mouth and handed another to McTurk who did likewise. He then lit both with the silver lighter that Donna had once bought him for Christmas, the one he had so often promised himself to launch in hard-won triumph from the Brig o' Doon into the depths of the River Doon. One of these days, he would have to let go of that damned lighter, and he knew that it meant finally letting go of Donna. However, that task might be a lot less difficult now that Janice had burst onto the scene.

'They'll try to take Ricky out, I'm sure of it.'

'You don't know that for sure, though, Charlie. Ricky's on the run from the law, so he's hot, very hot. So, why would Dan Rafferty want to take the risk of running straight into the arms of the cops?'

'To do a hit on him before we lock him up.'

'But why?'

'Because Dan wants revenge for his big brother's murder. And because he's bloody mad at Ricky for putting the knife into Rafferty Construction, the business that he stood to inherit but which is now down the plughole. Or ...'

'Or what?'

'Or because he already knows that Ricky didn't kill Frank Rafferty, but he knows who did.'

'I don't believe that Ricky killed him either, Charlie, but any number of people had motive. Rafferty had more enemies than Adolph Hitler, and it's my job to find out who did it.'

'These guys are nutcases, Andy. Taking Ricky out might convince the cops that he murdered Rafferty, especially with his prints all over the place. Throw them off the track of the real villain, you know?'

'What? Throw me off track? You must be joking. Once I get started, I'm like a bloody ferret. And don't you forget it.'

'I know. Why do you think I just bought you a roll and sausage?'

'I should have known that there's no such thing as a free breakfast.'

'Precisely.'

'Right, eat up your bacon sandwich like a good wee boy, then go home and see to that wee lassie of yours. Either that or I'll do it for you.'

51

Sergeant George Renfrew looked at his wristwatch. The time was already 10.40 a.m.

He cursed under his breath. It had taken a full twenty minutes for his boss, DI McTurk, to get back to him and he feared that the Anderson lad might already have flown the nest. He immediately gave the order, and the six uniformed police officers converged on the ridge tent that those vertically mismatched campers, Mick and Maureen, had described to him when he cornered them outside the village shop.

The cops didn't hang about. The first two on the scene grabbed the main tent supports and ripped them out of their grassy fixings, leaving a waterproof groundsheet exposed to the elements. On top of the sheet lay Ricky Anderson's modest array of essential accoutrements, including his sleeping bag and pillow, a small foldaway stove and gas canister, a couple of empty beer cans and a few crumpled paper bags where some foodstuffs once resided. However, no rucksack. And more to the point, no Ricky.

'Damn it,' Renfrew spat in disgust. 'He's gone. Something must have spooked him.'

'Not necessarily, Sir,' came the upbeat response from his hastily appointed second-in-command, Constable Danny Sanderson. 'He might just have gone to stretch his legs in which case he'll be back. Probably worth putting the tent back up, then just wait and see what happens, don't you think?'

'Aye, maybe you're right,' the sergeant nodded. 'But my guess is that he'll have heard that we're out in force around the village and scarpered.'

'So, what are you thinking, Sir?' Sanderson enquired, his eagerness to please bordering on downright sycophancy. 'How do you want to play this?'

Renfrew scratched his head and kept nodding as if in full accord with some invisible telepathic power that was communicating to him from the heavens, a trademark behavioural characteristic that his minions often mimicked in his absence. He turned to face the ambitious young constable.

'Danny, take two men and get yourselves hidden behind the bushes over there. Wait for a couple of hours … no, make that three … say, until 3.30 p.m. And if by then there's still a no-show, stand down, because we'll just be wasting good police time. However, be ready to nab young Anderson if he does return, and be very careful because I hear he can look after himself.'

'Yes, Sir,' Sanderson beamed.

Renfrew then turned to address the whole group.

'You have all seen his mugshot, but he bought a pair of scissors from the village shop, so he'll probably have lost the long hair by now. He might also be wearing a beige golf cap, but the only thing that matters is that you apprehend whoever returns to the tent.'

Then, facing the tent itself as it lay in a crumpled heap on the grass, he began jabbing his finger towards it like an angry parent chastising a truculent child.

'Whoever comes to this tent right here!' he emphasised. 'Even if it's a bloody Clydesdale horse wearing a Santa Claus outfit. Any questions?'

None were forthcoming, so he pressed on.

'The rest of you get back to your previous locus and carry on with the search. In the meantime, I'm going back into the village to ask around. I want to find out how anybody who wanted to escape from this God-forsaken place could do it without being noticed.'

As instructed, Sanderson selected a pair of uniformed officers and briefed them enthusiastically on their task. He then established three strategic vantage points with good cover and quick ease of access to the tent, in the event that the young fugitive might eventually choose to return. If he did, they would immediately close in and arrest him. If he didn't, then they would all have wasted the best part of a nice afternoon sitting on their backsides in the damp undergrowth and getting eaten alive by midges. The other three uniforms dutifully trudged back from whence they had come to resume their exasperating game of hide-and-seek.

Meanwhile, about fifty yards up the forestry track, Ricky Anderson knelt huddled behind the trunk of a massive larch tree observing the dynamics and listening to Sergeant Renfrew's commendable masterplan. However, the moment the cops finally disappeared from view to secrete themselves under cover of autumnal foliage, Ricky's detached amusement gave way to a stark sense of urgency.

He had to get out of there. And fast.

52

Cumnock Pharmacy's latest recruit was handing over a repeat prescription to old Mrs Gibson when the phone rang for the umpteenth time that morning. The young woman was so immersed in her duties that she hardly even noticed.

'Thank you, my dear,' the 94-year-old former primary schoolteacher said. 'If Doctor Blackie prescribes me any more pills, I swear I'll start rattling.'

'Can I help you out to your car, Mrs Gibson?' Iona McNish smiled. 'You won't manage to carry that bag with a walking stick in each hand.'

'That would be wonderful, my dear,' she replied. 'You are a very caring young lady. And you have such lovely, warm eyes. When I was your age, I used to be a real looker too, you know? The boys were tripping over themselves to ask me out.'

'I'm sure they were, Mrs Gibson,' Iona laughed heartily as she made her way around to the customers' side of the counter, before picking up a large paper bag and opening the door.

'I bet they're falling over themselves for you too,' the old lady continued, as she shuffled out the door on both sticks. 'Is there a special young man in your life yet, dear?'

Iona's heart suddenly felt as if it had been thumped by a sledgehammer. Her eyes began glazing over as the terrible reality of a truly desperate situation came flooding back to drown out the morning's frenetic activity.

'Where's your car parked?' she asked with a dry swallow. 'It's great that you can still drive at your age.'

An authoritative voice rang out from the back shop. It belonged to Mister Cochrane, the town's long-serving pharmacist and Iona's austere employer.

'Iona, the phone. It's for you. I'll see to Mrs Gibson myself. And please don't be long, we're very busy.'

Iona's heart skipped a beat as pharmacist and assistant swapped roles, the former ushering his elderly customer out into the cool breeze and the latter making a beeline for the back office. Please God, let it be Ricky, she pleaded inwardly while taking a sharp intake of breath. She closed the office door behind her and lifted the receiver from where Mr Cochrane had left it lying on his desk.

'Hello.'

Silence on the other end of the line. A long, lingering silence.

'Hello,' she said again. 'Who's there?'

Nothing. Not even the heavy breathing of a hopeful pervert trying his luck.

'Hello,' she repeated, only a bit more firmly this time. 'Who is this, please?'

'I just wanted to hear your voice again,' came the whispered reply.

'Ricky!' Iona gasped. 'Ricky … where … where are you?'

Then the tears came, a few to start with followed by a torrent. Right at that moment, Ricky Anderson would have walked on red-hot coals just to wrap his arms around her and wipe the tears away.

'I can't say, Iona,' he said. 'All I can tell you is that I'm safe and I'm well.'

'Please come home, Ricky,' Iona sobbed. 'Please.'

'I can't, Iona. I'm taking a huge chance just calling you on your work phone, but I had to hear your voice. I'm missing you like crazy.'

'Oh Ricky,' she blubbered, 'I really need to see you … to touch you … please …'

Ricky cut her off instantly. His voice quickly changed to exude a coolness that belied the emotions running riot in his head.

'Iona, I want you to listen to me. I need you to be calm and listen very carefully. Do you understand?'

'Okay, Ricky … okay. I'm listening.'

'I need you to do a few things for me. Don't write them down, because that could be dangerous. Just make sure you remember them, okay?'

'Yes, okay … okay … I'm listening.'

'Right, here goes. You ready?'

'Yes … yes.'

'First of all, tell my mum that I love her, that I'm absolutely fine and that I'll see her as soon as this Rafferty business is sorted. How is she, Iona?'

'She's better, Ricky, a lot better. She's staying with Charlie in Prestwick just now. Ricky, please just come home to us. Please.'

'Iona, I can't. And I need you to concentrate. You still okay?'

'Yes ... of course.'

'Right then, second thing. Tell Charlie I didn't do it. Tell him I was there in the caravan, and I found Frank Rafferty sitting on the couch with his throat cut. The cops will know that, but I know something that they don't. Will you remember to tell him that, Iona? I know something that the cops don't know.'

'Of course, I will.'

'Good, Iona, good. Number three. Contact a newspaper reporter called Gerry McGhee. He works for the *Glasgow Herald*. Tell him the same, that I didn't do it, and ask him if he's willing to help me find out who did. If he won't, he'll shop you to the cops, which is okay because you don't know where I am either.'

'Right, Ricky ... I think.'

'Nearly there, Iona. The final thing. Go to the phone box on the corner of Glaisnock Street and Townhead Street at exactly eight o'clock tomorrow night and I'll call you there. If there's someone else using it, just wait until they're finished. I'll know it's engaged and I'll call the moment it's free, so don't worry. You know the phone box I'm talking about?'

'Yes, the one at "McCubbin's Corner"?'

'Yes, that's it. I have to go now, Iona. I love you and I miss you. And I'll sort this mess once and for all, then we'll be together again. And together forever. Remember that.'

'I love you too, Ricky. So much that it hurts me.'

'Bye, Iona, take care.'

'Don't go, Ricky. Please just stay for another ...'

The line went dead, and with it went Iona's self-pity. She wiped the residual tears from her eyes and took several big deep breaths to compose herself, the way her dad had taught her to do during school exams or any time she got a bit anxious. She then picked the phone back up from its cradle and dialled a number that was becoming increasingly familiar.

'Hello, Janice,' she said. 'It's me ... it's Iona.'

Just at that, the inimitable James Cochrane, MPharm, strode back into the office and gave her a disapproving stare. Iona could scarcely believe the timing of his return. As she turned to face the back wall, her voice became a whisper.

'Can't talk right now, Janice,' she continued. 'Please just listen carefully, it's very important. Contact Charlie right away and get him to pick me up at the pharmacy when my lunch break starts at half-past twelve. I need to speak to him right away.'

A forced cough from the pharmacist served as a sharp reminder that Iona was now pushing her luck. On the other end of the line Janice was protesting in confusion.

'Janice,' Iona continued in a whisper. 'I really can't speak. But I do need to meet Charlie urgently. I'll explain everything later, I promise. Twelve-thirty, and tell him to come alone. Bye.'

Iona replaced the receiver, stood up straight and stuck out her chin, then marched back through to the front shop wearing her best stiff upper lip.

53

Ricky Anderson's journey along the A714 had taken only an hour and five minutes, much quicker than he had expected from a clapped-out old bus battling the cavernous hills and hairpin bends of rural south Ayrshire.

Thankfully, nobody had even given him a second glance, far less recognised him from the mugshots that had now almost certainly hit the local weeklies. The ruthless haircut which he had self-administered in a spartan campsite toilet block probably had something to do with that, the golf cap too. Momentarily, he wondered whether the boys-in-blue would still be playing hide-and-seek in the Glentrool woods waiting for him to return to his dad's old ridge tent, or whether the penny had finally dropped that he had flown the nest.

It was 4.15 p.m. when he arrived at the harbour port of Girvan. Plenty of time to get his bearings, grab a sandwich and hopefully locate a place to crash out before darkness fell. Perhaps even long enough to help him find a casual job to keep the wolf from the door. Nothing fancy, anything would do. And let's face it, he reflected, nothing could be worse than barrowing garbage around a dilapidated brickworks in the middle of a desolate moorland.

The main summer season had finally wound down in this quintessential seaside holiday town, which Ricky remembered with fond affection from daytrips as a wide-eyed little nipper with his mum and dad. Sure, the 1970s-style shops, cafes and clothes boutiques were still open, but now gone into hibernation were the colourful vendors flogging their pink candyfloss, giant red lollipops and windmills-on-a-stick. Well gone too were the sunburnt tourists clad in their straw hats and oversized sunglasses, sipping contentedly from their fruit-laden cocktails adorned with tiny plastic umbrellas. Even the gloriously confused aroma of fish suppers and hot dogs mingling with Chinese chop sueys and Indian curries had finally dissipated into the salty air.

Ricky decided to head for the harbourside, more for nostalgic reasons than anything of a practical consideration. There, his suspicions were confirmed. The city holidaymakers had all but disappeared, along with the vibrancy they always brought with them during the long sultry days of summer. Still, though, the town's old clock tower and the harbour itself stood resplendent and unperturbed by the lack of 'biz' about the place. So too did the boating pond and the putting greens, even if they themselves looked in desperate need of the company which had now all but deserted them.

Gone completely was Girvan's famous outdoor fair, save for its landmark Helter-Skelter, but no longer boasting its death-defying rides like the Rib-Tickler, the Waltzer and the Dodgems, all once circumscribed by a huge assortment of side-stalls which until very recently had succeeded in magnetising the eagle-eyed tourists to part with their hard-earned cash for the purpose of catching a plastic fish with a hook on a wooden cane and rolling table-tennis balls into the garishly painted gobs of giant clowns' heads. And, of course, all in search of the ultimate prize, a seriously undernourished goldfish incarcerated in a polythene bag, the poor creature having a fifty-fifty chance at best of living long enough to see its new home.

Staring in despondency at the big space where the fair once rocked-and-rolled to Mungo Jerry's 'In the Summertime' and the other contemporary top-ten hits, Ricky headed towards Girvan's indoor amusement arcade. To his great delight it was still open, so he pushed the door and walked in, temporarily forgetful of the fact that he was now a wanted man on the run from the law and about to introduce himself to another tranche of would-be eye witnesses to his presence in the harbour town.

Looking around, it was as if time had stood still. The long row of one-armed bandits that used to occupy countless hours of his adolescent days were still lined up against the wall to his left, beckoning him to part with pocketsful of coins, only five-pence pieces now that decimalisation had kicked in to render the old copper pennies sadly obsolete. Straight in front, stood the 'Laughing Sailor', a garish plastic effigy of a drunken old seafarer in a glass box who would suddenly spring into fits of uncontrollable laughter whenever a coin was shoved into the slot. However, it was the contraption on the far wall that really relit the flames of much happier days, this containing a colourful assortment of small cuddly toys, the successful seizure of which depended on the player's manual dexterity and skilful navigation of a big metal claw suspended on a wire. How vividly Ricky remembered the day when he finally captured the little red doll that his mum had yearned for, then ran over to hand it to her in gleeful triumph. The mum who had only recently been beaten half to death on the orders of a man whom Ricky had last seen sitting in a caravan with his throat cut open like a pig in a slaughterhouse.

In a heartbeat, the nostalgia was gone like dirty dishwater down a kitchen plughole. He stepped back outside and took a gulp of sea air. It tasted like nectar. The sentimentality had gone, shoved aside by the pragmatism that defined the perilousness of his ongoing predicament. He now had to do three things, and fast. First of all, get some food into his belly. Secondly, find a place to stay for the foreseeable future. And finally, get himself a job to pay for the first two. Okay, he still had over fifty pounds in his wallet, courtesy of his travails at Braddoch Brickworks, but with a bargain basement bedsit likely to set him back around ten quid-a-week, and a fish supper and a pint now as much as 25p apiece, his tidy little stash sure wouldn't last for very long.

Resisting the temptation to hit Girvan's famous old Fish Bar, the sustenance he chose instead was an egg mayonnaise sandwich and an 'empire' biscuit from a family-run café on Dalrymple Street, which along with his bottle of chilled Pepsi Cola he carried back down to the town's bustling port. There, Ricky sat on the harbour wall watching a succession of fishing boats come and go. As he munched on his takeaway food, he marvelled at the quaint simplicity of life in the seaside town, whilst reminding himself of the perils of the choppy waters that those brave and hardy fishermen had to tackle every single day in life just to earn their corn, and to supply the local markets with their daily catches.

A brazen seagull swooped down onto the concrete roadway and trotted over to within a couple of feet from where Ricky was sitting. Observing that the well-fed creature was about as big as a Golden Retriever, he surmised that it must be considerably more interested in his sandwich than his charming personality and greeted it accordingly.

'Piss off, seagull,' he shouted, stamping his foot on the ground, before necking the last morsel of his late lunch.

The seabird immediately took flight, but not before squawking at him in irritation and dropping a hefty airborne excretion which missed him by inches.

'Get your aiming straight, bird,' Ricky laughed, before downing his last mouthful of Pepsi.

A gravelly voice piped up from behind.

'I don't like them either, son. They're greedy bastards, and aggressive with it. I once saw a gull grabbing an ice cream cone straight out of a toddler's hand. The poor wee lassie nearly shit herself.'

Ricky turned around to see a bearded, fifty-something guy hauling a big thick rope towards him, his biceps bulging with every pull. He was wearing a pair of muddy wellington boots, washed-out jeans, a big chunky olive-green jumper and a black woolly hat with the words 'Ayr United' inscribed in a slightly lighter shade which might have started out life as brilliant white.

'Hi,' Ricky said, as he rose to his feet to chuck his rubbish into a nearby dustbin. 'I see you're an Ayr supporter.'

'Not me, son,' came the droll reply. 'Can't stand football, never had the time or the notion. Bunch of big long-haired jessies with more money than sense, if you ask me. My boy got me the hat for my Christmas, just to annoy me. I must have had it for ten years now. What are you doing here, anyway? Apart from chatting up the seagulls, that is?'

Ricky thought quickly.

'Just dumped my girlfriend,' he replied. 'Found out that she was doing the business with my best mate. Just fancied a wee break from everything.'

'And how's your best mate?' the fisherman enquired.

'Still counting the spaces where his teeth used to be,' Ricky retorted.

'My Sunday name is John Alexander Ferguson,' the guy said,

199

extending his hand in friendship. 'But everybody just calls me Sandy.'

'And I'm Jim ... Jim Morrison,' Ricky replied, accepting a vice-like handshake. 'But they just call me Jim.'

Ferguson smiled a big friendly smile. He approved of rustic wit.

'I don't suppose you're looking for a wee job, by any chance? I could do with a strong young man like you to help me out.'

'What kind of job? I don't like boats.'

'What kind of lad doesn't like boats? Don't tell me you're a pansy. You're not, are you son? Tell me that's not why your girlfriend dumped you?'

'No, you're safe enough. I just don't fancy spending my days puking my guts up on the high seas, that's all. I could manage a sail around the lake in one of those wee rowing boats over there, though.'

'Well, now I know for sure that you're a pansy. No boats, Jim, just a wee bit of hard labour. I'm the Harbour Master here. Stacking the fish boxes, mending the nets, that kind of thing. Interested?'

'Might be. How much?'

'I'll pay you a fiver a day. Cash. How does that sound?'

'Sounds like slave labour. Seven quid a day, cash up front and I want Sundays off.'

'Six. Take it or leave it.'

'Deal. You'll get your money's worth.'

'I'd better. Can you start tomorrow morning at seven?'

'No problem. When do I finish?'

'Say, about five.'

'That's fine with me, Sandy. One other thing. You wouldn't happen to know where I could get a bed in this joint, would you?'

'Aye, you might be in luck. The wife and I have a place in Henrietta Street. It's a small house, but we've got a wooden chalet out the back which we rent out to holidaymakers in the summer for a bit of extra money. It's fairly basic, but it's dry and weatherproof. I'm sure Martha would give it a good spring-clean for you.'

'How much?'

'Let's call it six quid a week, including your electricity.'

'Done.'

It was an arrangement that promised to work out well for employer and employee alike. Sandy had finally bagged his man for the equivalent of a fiver a day. As for Ricky, he had sorted his trio of necessities - a decent job, a safe place to stay and food on the table – and all in one fell swoop.

At least until the bloodhounds got wind of the fleeing fox and went straight in for the kill.

54

The atmosphere inside the black Ford Corsair was four parts nicotine to one part air, as dense as a North Sea haar. 'Mad Rab' McDade's gruff growl bellowed through the mirk.

'You know where you're going, Ralphie-boy?'

'Aye, Rab, fine I know where I'm going,' young Baxter replied. 'The problem is that I can't see anything for cigarette smoke. Wind down the back windows, for God's sake.'

'We seem to have been on this bloody road for ever, and all we've seen is sheep,' McDade continued. 'I've noticed the way you've been looking at them. You're not a sheep-shagger by any chance, Ralphie-Boy?'

A burst of laughter from the back seat, as Zander McGinn joined in the mischief.

'Aye, Rab, I've noticed too. Maybe he's not getting his nuts from that wee burd he's been going out with. You know, the one with the dyed blonde hair and the big hooters. What's her name again, Ralphie?'

'She's called Maureen,' Baxter replied, clearly miffed. 'And it's not like that, Zander. She's a really nice lassie. Not that you would know anything about nice lassies, because you'd have sex with a drainpipe.'

'Oh, did you hear that, Rab?' McGinn roared with laughter. 'She's a really nice lassie. Ralphie's in love. Wedding bells and all that. And he probably hasn't even had his hand up her jumper yet.'

'Aye, Zander,' McDade chipped in. 'That'll be why he's ogling at the sheep.'

Communal laughter this time. Even Baxter himself couldn't help joining in.

'Hold on a minute,' the young driver said, bringing a note of seriousness back to the conversation. 'There's a signpost coming up on the left ... see what it says, Rab.'

'Glentrool ... 4 miles,' McDade announced as the Corsair zipped past. 'Then Newton ... something or other ... 14 miles. I couldn't make out the last bit.'

'Newton Stewart,' Baxter answered with smug satisfaction. 'And Girvan 26 miles. With a navigator like you, Rab, who needs signposts?'

'You just do the driving, Ralphie,' McDade snapped back, blowing a long continuous cloud of nicotine-rich vapour straight into his young chauffeur's eyes. 'Frank pays me to crunch bones, not to sit on my arse all day behind a steering wheel.'

'Frank's history, Rab, remember?' McGinn interjected. 'He'll be pushing up the daisies this time next week.'

'Dan, then,' McDade conceded. 'What's the difference anyway? Two of a kind. Pinky and Perky. Only, Pinky's now gone to meet his maker.'

And thus the swapping of insults continued, its infantile content in sharp contrast to the giant adult frames and bulging muscles of the two main protagonists, as their car sped its way past a seemingly infinite number of Scandinavian pine trees which were doing their best to decorate the desolate peat bogs of the vast Galloway Forest. A few minutes later, the three hoods found themselves slipping into Glentrool, a peaceful little village whose indigenous inhabitants and visiting outdoor enthusiasts were blissfully unaware of the malevolent presence now right on their doorstep. Baxter pulled the Corsair onto a piece of waste ground, the sole occupant of which was a trailer abandoned by some distant cab which had long departed the scene.

As always, the task of rehearsing the masterplan fell to Rab McDade, the Rafferty brothers' recognised executioner-in-chief.

'Right,' he barked. 'Listen up, here's what we do. Zander, you make your way up to the campsite, because that young nurse you nabbed outside Ballochmyle Hospital told you that Anderson had a rucksack with him, so he might have gone camping up there. I'll have a wee word with the folk in that grocery store over there, to find out what the local gossip is. Ralphie, you just sit here in the car and fantasise about your sheep. Keep your eyes open, mind you, and let me know if you see or hear anything that might help us. And watch your backs, boys, because the polis will still be sniffing around. Got it?'

Two nodding heads. McDade continued, his words of menace caressed by staccato puffs of smoke.

'And Zander, no rough stuff for now. If you find Anderson,

you come back here to the car and tell me. If I find him, I do the same. This is going to be a hit, boys, and Dan wants there to be no witnesses, none at all. You both understand?'

McGinn nodded. Baxter rubbed his chin, clearly perturbed.

'What do you mean a hit, Rab?'

'God love him, Zander,' McDade laughed, before turning to eyeball Baxter. 'A hit, Ralphie-boy. An assassination. Dan wants Anderson out of the picture, and pronto. And we can't just walk up to him and whack him in front of a crowd of nosey old campers, now, can we?'

Baxter looked transfixed with shock.

'I've never ... I've never ... like ... actually killed anybody before.'

'And you'll not be killing anybody today either, son,' McDade replied. 'Just remember that Dan pays you to do one thing, and one thing only. Drive the bloody car. So, drive it, Ralphie-boy, and leave the rough stuff to Zander and me. Okay?'

Baxter just nodded, unable to find words. It was McGinn who asked the next question.

'When we find the boy, where do we do it, Rab?'

'When we find him, we bundle him into the car and take him for a nice wee picnic up in the hills. We take the toolbag with us, then you and I get to work on him.'

McGinn nodded his approval and McDade issued his final instruction to the dumbstruck young driver.

'There might be a bit of yelling and squealing, son, because that's what Dan thinks Frank would have wanted. So, you can watch if you want, or you can just bugger off for a bit and chat up the sheep. It's up to you.'

McDade opened the front door and McGinn the back before going their separate ways, leaving Baxter to contemplate the wisdom of his career choice.

55

Janice Anderson shot to her feet the moment she heard the doorbell ring. This time, the sharp pain in her ribs hardly even registered.

'Oh Iona,' she gasped as she opened the door, before grabbing her prospective daughter-in-law and giving her a mighty squeeze. 'Come in and tell me everything.'

The two women high-tailed it into Charlie Reynolds's kitchen, where Janice put the kettle on and listened with forensic attentiveness to Iona's account of the morning's events. Basically, her story was this.

She had been serving an elderly customer in the pharmacy when the telephone rang. The call was for her, and it was Ricky on the other end of the line. He said he was fine but refused to divulge his whereabouts, because he feared that walls had ears, and by doing so he might give the game away. Ricky asked how Janice was feeling and told Iona to tell her that he loved her, that he was safe and well and that he would see her soon. He then asked Iona to tell Charlie that he 'didn't do it', in the hope that Charlie might be inclined to help prove Ricky's innocence. Next, he asked her to contact a *Glasgow Herald* journalist called Gerry McGhee to ask if he would help him too. Finally, he told her to go to the phone box at McCubbin's corner in Cumnock town centre tomorrow night at eight o'clock, when he would talk to her again in a bit more detail.

As Janice stood beside the boiling kettle, she looked as if the sudden onslaught of information had been too much for her. Iona got up from her seat at the kitchen table and swapped places with her. She then made two cups of tea and sat back down and held Janice's hands.

'Janice, thanks for contacting Charlie this morning,' she said with a warm smile. 'He came and picked me up at lunchtime, and we had a really good chat. He said that we should call him the moment I got here, and that he would come over and bring us up to date with things, but I wanted to tell you about my conversation with Ricky first. Will you call Charlie, or will I?'

'Sorry?' Janice asked, her mind elsewhere. 'What was that?'

'Will you call Charlie, or do you want me to do it, Janice?' Iona asked again.

'Eh ... you do it, Iona,' Janice muttered, still clearly overwhelmed by the sheer pace of events.

Iona picked up the phone and began dialling. Janice sat sipping at her tea and staring out of the window, oblivious to the brief conversation that began only a few feet away. Iona then returned to Janice's side and started re-running the essence of her earlier discussion with Ricky, as much to kill time until Charlie arrived as to amplify the main messages.

Less than ten minutes later, the front door clicked open and Charlie Reynolds walked in to be greeted by simultaneous big hugs from Janice and Iona.

'Wow,' he laughed. 'How times have changed in this place. A few months ago, my wife runs off and leaves me here on my tod, and now I'm being smothered by two beautiful women. I think I've died and gone to heaven.'

Janice stood up on her tiptoes and pecked him on the cheek, and Iona dutifully loosened her grasp. Reynolds beckoned to them to join him at the table, then took out his notepad. The tea on offer would wait. He wasted no time and set about running through a series of numbered points in a situation which he said was developing very rapidly.

One. The Chief Superintendent had decided that Reynolds had a major conflict of interest in the case and ordered him to take three weeks' leave, starting today. Andy McTurk would remain in charge, but while Reynolds was now officially out of bounds, he would be doing everything in his power to 'reel Ricky in', and in that regard he would need all the help that both Janice and Iona could give him. However, he omitted to tell them that the whole thing was McTurk's suggestion in the first place, because he feared that they might not have fully understood the nuances.

Two. Iona had done really well by arranging to meet Reynolds earlier in the day to tell him about Ricky's phone call. Reynolds himself had managed to glean several things from that call. Most importantly, Ricky was alive and well, and while obviously still on the run, there was no reason to fear that he was in any imminent danger. McTurk had checked with the Clydesdale Bank and learned that Ricky had emptied his account of fifty-three pounds and a few pence, which would be sufficient to feed and shelter him for at least a week or two, if need be.

Three. Reynolds, rather than Iona herself, had since tracked down Gerry McGhee of the Glasgow Herald, who had met Ricky face-to-face on several prior occasions, and the journalist was also convinced that Ricky could never have committed an act of such violence. McGhee had already been running the rule over the dodgy Rafferty empire and the disgraced ex-councillor, Edwin Monk, in preparation for a major scoop in his newspaper column. However, Frank Rafferty's murder had since rendered the whole matter 'sub judice', and while there would therefore be no such article appearing in the Glasgow Herald until the case had eventually gone through the appropriate court proceedings, McGhee had already succeeded in unearthing some very interesting background information on the seedy goings-on between Monk and the Rafferty empire.

Four. Iona would go, as planned, to the phone box at McCubbin's corner at eight o'clock tomorrow night, to take Ricky's call. Reynolds would take her there, but stay in his car, parked discreetly out of sight but close enough to be on hand should she need his help in any way. No doubt, Ricky would have thought things through very thoroughly, and after quizzing Iona on the outcome of the actions he asked her to take in their previous phone call, he would probably have another 'to do' list for her. Iona would also tell Ricky that Reynolds had now been taken off the case, but that he would help him as much as possible 'on the QT'. Reynolds's hope was that Ricky would realise the risk that he is taking, and might then be prepared to speak to him on the phone or even meet him privately.

Reynolds then closed his notebook and stuffed it back into his inside jacket pocket. It was Janice who next spoke.

'If he agrees to meet you, Charlie, I'm going with you.'

'Me too,' Iona chipped in.

Reynolds's eyes met Janice's, then darted towards Iona's and back again.

'Nope,' he said, with a slow but firm shake of his head. 'That won't be happening. It's far too dangerous. Ricky is red-hot.'

'He's my son, Charlie,' Janice replied with a steely glare.

'He's also my fiancée,' added Iona.

'And he's my responsibility,' Reynolds said.

Both ladies' vehement protests gradually built to a shrill crescendo, at which point Reynolds could take it no more. He rose sharply from his chair and glared at them.

'Understand this,' he snapped. 'Ricky is my responsibility now. Not yours, Janice, and not yours, Iona. And I'm risking my whole career to take that responsibility on my own shoulders. So, we do it my way. End of discussion.'

And at that, he marched out of the kitchen and along the hall, leaving Janice and Iona open-mouthed in amazement. For the first time, each of them had seen a completely different side of Charlie Reynolds.

The side that scared the bad guys witless.

56

Dan Rafferty stood staring out of his lounge window, incandescent with rage. He grabbed his left wrist with his right hand and glared at his Rolex watch for the umpteenth time. A quarter-to-nine, it informed him. Be here by half-eight, he had told them. And still they were nowhere to be seen.

'Sit down, Dan,' the tall blonde lady said, as she walked into the room carrying the morning newspaper. 'They'll have got stuck in the traffic. The Holmston roundabout is dreadful at this time of the morning. Do you want another coffee?'

Rafferty glowered at his wife with an expression which conveyed a sentiment on the darker side of contempt. It was one that Maureen Rafferty had seen more and more often of late and she didn't like it, not one little bit. That expression worried her, and if truth be told, kind of scared her too. She hoped she didn't understand why Dan looked at her that way these days, because if she was right, she was in trouble. Big trouble.

'No, I don't want another bloody coffee, Maureen,' he snapped. 'And I don't want the bloody newspaper either. It'll be full of all this nonsense about Frank ... and Monk ... and that smart-arsed student. I just want those imbeciles to get here on time for once, so that I can find out what's going on and then send them on their way. I've got Frank's burial to organise, for God's sake, and I'm supposed to be at the funeral parlour by half-ten.'

Just at that, a black Ford Corsair pulled up outside. Dan Rafferty filled his lungs and stormed along the hallway. When he opened the front door, young Ralph Baxter was the only one who had even bothered to get out of the car, his blond locks blowing in the wind like a clump of pampas grass in a raging storm. Robert McDade sat stalk-still in the front passenger's seat, with Zander McGinn bending his ear about something from the back.

'Ralph,' shouted Rafferty from the top step, 'Tell those two chancers to get their arses in here, and pronto.'

'No problem, Mister Rafferty,' came the sycophantic reply, and a couple of minutes later the threesome found themselves seated around the dining room table facing their new boss, whose facial expression could have shattered toughened glass.

'Right,' spat Rafferty. 'Tell me everything. And make it snappy, because you're bloody late and I've got to be at the undertaker's in just over an hour.'

McGinn looked at McDade, who immediately assumed rank as always and leaned his hefty shoulders forward, causing the legs of his chair to creak for mercy.

'Right, Dan,' McDade's gruff voice proclaimed. 'I'll give you the short version and you can ask me to fill in the blanks. Okay?'

He looked at Rafferty for approval, who just returned his gaze and didn't move a muscle. McDade nodded, then continued.

'We went to Glentrool yesterday, like you asked. Strange wee place. More dogs on the street than folk. And visitors ... hillwalkers with their rucksacks and walking sticks ... and weirdos like that. And cops, Dan, obviously looking for Anderson as well, so we had to watch ourselves and look ... well ... look normal ... like we were just tourists ourselves, you know?'

Rafferty cast his eye over McDade's giant sumo-wrestler-like frame, then at McGinn's similarly oversized carcass, before making another suitably cutting remark.

'I bet that came naturally to you.'

McDade shrugged off the snide comment and continued.

'I went into the village shop and chatted up the wee lassie behind the counter. Told me nothing, hadn't seen anybody of Anderson's description. I didn't believe her, but when I started getting a bit more serious, her old man appeared from the back shop going on about how they had already told the cops everything they knew, so I figured I'd better butt out. Zander went up to the campsite, because the wee fat nurse I got hold of at the hospital told me that Anderson was carrying a backpack when she saw him on the bus. He spoke to a few of the campers, who knew sweet FA, then to a young couple who claimed at first that they had never seen the boy, but then decided to change their minds and described him to a tee.'

'Why?' asked Rafferty. 'Why their sudden change of heart?'

'It's amazing how some guys begin to talk when you're squeezing their nuts, Dan,' McGinn interjected with a menacing sneer. 'After the big lanky lad had coughed his guts up, I told him that if he ever spoke to the polis about this, I'd come back and cut them off, then make sweet love to his girlfriend. And I would have cut them off, boss, but I would never even have touched the lassie with a barge pole. Wee fat burd with a face like a bucket of frogs.'

'Never stopped you before, Zander,' quipped young Baxter, sending McDade into a fit of the giggles.

All three immediately saw the irritation etched on Rafferty's face. McDade took the cue and pressed on.

'The big boy with the swollen nuts told Zander that the cops had been hanging around all day waiting for Anderson to come back to his tent, but he never showed again, just left all his stuff lying there. He reckoned that Anderson had shot the craw and left the village. Probably hitched a lift or jumped on the bus.'

'And that's it?' Rafferty asked, arms outstretched in frustration. 'You come back here empty-handed and all you can tell me is that Anderson probably caught a bloody bus? Well, whoopy-doo, that sure helps a lot.'

'Dan,' said McDade, attempting to demonstrate that he was still on top of his brief. 'Think about it. There are only three places the bus can go from Glentrool. To Newton Stewart, to Girvan or back up to Ayr. And he'd never come back to Ayr. Anderson's too smart, boss. That's where Frank was murdered, so he'd want to be as far away from here as possible. And I don't know much about Newton Stewart, but it sounds like the back of beyond to me. My guess is that he's holing out in Girvan. Went there once as a wee nipper with my granny and papa. Busy wee place on the seashore, easy to get lost in the crowd. Anderson's in Girvan, Dan.'

'I suppose you could be right, Rab,' said Rafferty, his blood-pressure slowly falling from the danger-level mark. 'Maureen and I spent our honeymoon in Girvan, believe it or not. Nice wee place, quite touristy, got a bit of action to it. Unlike Newton Stewart which is ... well ... sleepy hollow. Girvan has loads of shops and pubs and cafes. Lovely wee boating lake, long sandy beach, big outdoor fair, busy wee harbour, that kind of thing. So, I think you could be right about it being a place where you could get lost in the crowd.'

Rafferty thought in silence for a moment, then turned to face McGinn.

'You ever been to Girvan, Zander?'

'No, never,' came the sombre reply. 'Heard of it, though. Is that not where they make the tatties?'

'I don't think they make tatties, Zander,' Rafferty smirked. 'They grow them in fields. But anyway, you can all find out for yourselves tomorrow, because that's where you'll be going.'

McDade, McGinn and Baxter all nodded and exchanged bemused smiles. Frank Rafferty had hardly ever let them out of his sight, but now that he was out of the picture, wee brother Dan sure was encouraging them do a bit more sightseeing.

Baxter was delighted at being given another opportunity to catch a change of scenery. He was the driver, after all, and it was much more fun driving along strange roads to strange places, rather than getting stuck in infuriating traffic jams along the Sandgate. Not so, McDade and McGinn, though. They much preferred the urban chaos that was Ayr, Kilmarnock and Irvine, and the line of employment that went with it, under the tutelage of the late, great Frank Rafferty. Namely, the administration of harsh retribution on those poor souls who had not been able to repay their loans and the two-hundred percent interest every month that went with it. As far as they were concerned, Baxter could keep his fancy Ford Corsair and his poncey advanced driver's licence, and they would keep their knuckle-dusters and the impressive selection of tools which they kept locked away in their favourite toolbox.

And Ricky Anderson was next on the hit list.

57

Harbour Master Sandy Ferguson's description of Ricky Anderson's new job was spot-on. Hard labour, he had said, and he wasn't kidding.

Sure, Ricky had got well-used to the muscle-jarring chores required of him in the wilderness that was Braddoch Brickworks, but only one day in this new job had transpired to ask even more serious questions of a quite different set of muscles. Hauling in the huge ropes to tie up the constant fleet of fishing boats made his biceps and shoulders ache. Stacking, to head height and above, the boxes of haddock, hake, dab, whiting and umpteen other species of white fish put an enormous strain on his back and neck. And worst of all, lifting the assorted pieces of heavy seagoing machinery and related accoutrements on and off the vessels made him feel like every muscle in his body was being stretched on a medieval torture rack. Yes indeed, Sandy would be getting his money's worth. And then some.

When five o'clock arrived, Ricky immediately downed tools and began trudging his way back to his Henrietta Street digs, where he had already spent a restless night of broken sleep and vivid dreams in a comfortable bed in a rather spartan wooden chalet at the rear of his new gaffer's own abode. He now needed a long bath and a good lie down. The black pudding supper from Girvan's celebrated Fish Bar would wait, as would the couple of pints of lager that would wash it down. Ricky's sincere hope was that he would then be so bushed afterwards that he would surely sleep like a log, even if he would hurt like hell the next morning. However, he was safe, at least for now. Safe until either the cops or Clan Rafferty's brain-dead heavies got hold of him. If either of those things happened, the game would be well and truly up.

Ricky's evening itinerary would therefore be a simple one. A long soak, a rest, a bite to eat and a welcome drink before the main event, which was the phone call to Iona. How he wished his new fiancée could help scrub his back in the bath, then lie down beside him on his new single bed. However, she couldn't, and a bittersweet conversation between two distant telephones would have to suffice for now.

By quarter-to-eight, the early evening plan had worked like clockwork. Suitably cleaned-up, relaxed, fed and watered, Ricky made a beeline for the phone box on the corner of Henrietta Street and Ballybroke Street. He looked at his wristwatch. It was now 7.53 p.m., time enough to run over his handwritten checklist before converting it to confetti and scattering it to the wind. Pacing up and down the pavement, he counted down the minutes until the witching hour of eight o'clock finally arrived, by which time he was glad to dive into the box and shelter from the light drizzle that had now become a decent shower. He cursed under his breath at the very thought of someone else being on the phone on McCubbin's corner in Cumnock, something which would only prolong the agony for both Iona and himself.

Ricky lifted the receiver, shoved a couple of five-pence pieces into the slot, took a deep breath and dialled. A brief moment of silence, then a double ring followed by a click.

'Hello?'

It was Iona's voice on the other end of the line, but to Ricky it sounded like the whisper of an angel. A lump formed in his throat as the cataclysmic saga of recent events began roaring back to overwhelm his normally cool and calm psyche. Words simply would not come out.

'Hello?' the voice said again, only slightly more anxiously this time. 'Is that you, Ricky?'

Ricky bit on the inside of his bottom lip to snap him out of it. As he spoke, he could already taste the blood.

'Hi Iona,' he said, his throat as dry as if he'd just swallowed a whole packet of Jacob's cream crackers. 'How are you, darlin'?'

Iona immediately dissolved in tears. Ricky had never called her darling before, and to her it sounded simply wonderful.

'I'm fine,' she sobbed down the line. 'I'm missing you ... it's ... it's driving me crazy, Ricky.'

'Me too, Iona,' he replied, as his composure slowly returned. 'We'll be back together soon, I promise.'

Iona knew that she had very limited time available and that the conversation simply had to turn from the emotional to the practical. She amazed herself at how easily she was able to dive straight in.

'Where are you sleeping Ricky? Are you sleeping rough? Like in a doorway or something like that? The thought of it is driving me mad.'

'No, Iona, I'm not sleeping rough. And you know I can't tell you where I am until this whole mess gets sorted. All I can tell you is that I'm safe, I'm getting fed, I've got a place to stay and a wee casual job to pay for my keep. It probably won't last long with the cops on my trail, because I'll have to keep moving. How's my mum?'

'She's doing fine, Ricky, and I told her you were fine too, but like me she's going round the bend worrying about you.'

'I know, I know. It must be terrible for both of you. But if I came back home now, I'd be in handcuffs before my arse hit the chair. I'm determined to keep on going until I can prove my innocence.'

A beep-beep-beep sounded in Ricky's ear. He quickly shoved another couple of coins into the slot.

'Iona, I can't speak for long, so we need to cut to the chase. Okay?'

'Okay ... I know.'

'Did you speak to Charlie and Gerry McGhee?'

'Well, yes ... and no. I met Charlie during my lunch break yesterday, and he drove me up to Dalblair Bridge for a wee chat. His boss, that guy you mentioned ... Fraser I think ...'

'Yes, Fraser, the Chief Superintendent, Frank Rafferty's cousin. What about him?'

'He's put Charlie on leave for three weeks. Too big a conflict of interest, with Janice and him now an item and you on the run. Andy McTurk's in charge of the case.'

'What? You must be bloody joking?'

'No, Ricky, it's alright, it's fine. Charlie seems okay about it. I think they all believe you. I mean ... that you didn't do it. Well, Charlie and Andy anyway. Not sure about the big boss, Fraser. Ricky, your fingerprints were all over the caravan and the murder weapon. You know that, don't you?'

'Aye, I know. I wasn't thinking straight when I found Rafferty sitting there and ... well ... I just panicked, I suppose.'

'What were you even doing there in the first place, Ricky?'

'Iona, can we leave that for another day? I need to know what's happening, and quickly.'

'Okay, sorry. Charlie and Andy met with Fraser yesterday afternoon, and they all agreed that Andy would concentrate on finding Rafferty's killer, if Charlie agreed to ... if he agreed to ...'

'Agreed to what, Iona?'

'Agreed to bring you back, Ricky. Back home.'

'No chance.'

'Well, the phrase they used was "reel you in".'

'What do they think I am? A bloody salmon? No chance.'

'Ricky, Charlie just wants to talk to you. Meet you if possible. Anytime and anywhere you say. He said, "tell Ricky, no handcuffs". What do you ...?'

'What about Gerry McGhee? You talk to him?'

'No, Ricky, but Charlie's going up to see him in Glasgow tomorrow. He doesn't think you did it either, and he's now got a lot of stuff on Rafferty's activities and on that other councillor guy.'

'Monk?'

'Yes, Monk, that's his name.'

'They're all trying to help you, Ricky.'

'I'm not coming in, Iona. There's no way I'm getting locked up for something I didn't do. I'm glad that bastard Rafferty is dead, but it wasn't me who killed him and I'm not taking the rap for whoever did.'

'I know that, Ricky. I know you could never have done something like that. And so do they.'

'They've got a funny way of showing it, then. Bloody cops everywhere, looking for me.'

'Ricky, it's not only the police who are looking for you.'

'What? What do you mean?'

'Charlie thinks that Rafferty's thugs are after you too. You know, to shut you up.'

'Bring them on, then. Bring them on. I'll take care of them. They might have duffed up my mum, but I'd like to see them trying it with me.'

'Those people are very dangerous, Ricky, and Charlie's worried about them. Please think carefully about this. I can't stand the thought of losing you.'

'You won't, Iona. I promise. I can look after myself. I've done it all my life.'

'Will you speak to Charlie?'

Silence. A long, lingering silence.

'I'm begging you, Ricky. Please.'

'I'll think about it.'

'Good. That's all I ask.'

'Did you get a private contact number for McGhee?'

'Yes. His home number is 041-353-5592. He'll be there until eight each morning and after seven most nights. Will I read it back to you?'

'No, I'm supposed to be a nuclear physicist, Iona. If I can't remember a ten-digit phone number, what chance have I got of blowing up Russia?'

'Charlie says there's no need for you to contact McGhee directly, though ... that you should just leave it all to him.'

'Aye, he's probably right, but it's good to have his number just in case. Iona, do one other thing for me, will you? Phone Professor Bernstein and tell him I'll be back at my desk as soon as this whole thing blows over. And tell him I didn't do what I'm being accused of doing.'

'Your mum already did,' she replied. 'He knows you didn't do it. His thoughts are with you and the family.'

Beep-beep-beep.

'I have to go now, Iona,' Ricky whispered. 'Can you do this tomorrow again? Same time, same place? I'll give Charlie his answer then.'

'Of course, I can,' came Iona's warm reply.

'I love you, darlin'.'

'I love you too ... darlin'.'

Then the line went dead.

When Iona stepped out of the phone box, she could just about recognise the flashing headlights of Charlie Reynolds's blue Ford Cortina through the tears which were doing their best to distort her vision. Meanwhile, 34 miles away in the harbour port of Girvan, Ricky Anderson gulped the biggest, saddest gulp of his life as he trudged back out into the pouring rain.

58

The atmosphere in The Lighthouse was considerably different this time around.

In the absence of Dennis Grant, that new whiz-kid editor of the *Glasgow Herald* broadsheet who was off to London to make one of his pretentious keynote speeches to an audience of budding journalists, Gerry McGhee had commandeered the head honcho's pad for the morning. McGhee's thinking was that chocolate-brown leather recliners caressed by emerald-green Yucca Filamentosa plants might generate a slightly more conducive ambience for such an important meeting than creaky wooden seats and bulging filing cabinets squashed up against the nicotine-stained grey walls of his own primitive office.

'Just tell me what you want to know, DI Reynolds,' said McGhee.

'Call me Charlie,' the big detective said. 'I'm off duty and everything's off the record. In fact, this meeting isn't even happening. You alright with that?'

'What meeting, Charlie?'

Reynolds smiled, nodded and pressed on.

'We both know the background to this whole saga, so let me just cut to the chase. I'm going to tell you what I know about Ricky's present predicament, then you can fill me in with what you know about the Rafferty-Monk business. Okay?'

'Okay, fine with me.'

'Right then, here goes. You'll know that Frank Rafferty was murdered in his brother's caravan last Wednesday. In fact, everybody and their granny now know, because it's been all over the papers, including your own. His throat was cut with a kitchen knife and he bled to death, but we suspect he had been drugged first, because when we found him, he was still sitting bolt upright like a well-behaved schoolboy at his classroom desk.'

'I heard that too. I have ... I have ... sources.'

'Well then, Gerry, here's something that your sources might not have divulged. Ricky was in that caravan.'

McGhee leaned back and blew an almighty sigh skywards.

He fumbled nervously in his jacket pocket, took out a packet of cigarettes and lit one.

'You don't mind, do you?' he asked Reynolds.

'No, I don't mind at all,' came the reply. 'In fact, I'll take one myself if that's okay.'

The ice had already been broken, but the cigarette-sharing routine succeeded in melting what was left of it. Reynolds pressed on.

'Yes, he was there all right. His fingerprints were all over the bloody place. On the murder weapon as well. And he was seen earlier in the vicinity by a couple of credible eyewitnesses, a bus conductress who gave him a ticket to Earl's Way and a local resident who passed him in her Mercedes when he was walking down the same street.'

'But, come on Charlie, you're not telling me that Ricky ...'

'Ricky didn't do it, Gerry.'

'Of course, he didn't. That lad has got class ... he's got ... well, a bit of gravitas. He could never have done anything like that, never in a million years. I'd put my bloody mortgage on his innocence.'

'So would I.'

'Where exactly is he now then?'

'As I said on the phone, all we know is that he's on the run. We think somewhere in the Galloway Forest. We've still got uniformed officers combing the area, but it's like trying to find a needle in a haystack. I don't think they'll nab him, Gerry, I really don't. Ricky's too smart. Anybody with an honours degree in nuclear physics isn't stupid enough to get caught with his trousers at his ankles in some god-forsaken wee backwater.'

'Level with me, Charlie, and I'll level with you.'

'What do you mean?'

'I'm not stupid either. I think you know something that your colleagues don't know. You don't want them to find Ricky, do you? Otherwise, why would you be talking to me when you're off duty, and when you've already been taken off the case?'

Reynolds just stared at McGhee with an expression on the surprised side of admiration.

'How do you know that, Gerry?'

'As I already told you, I have my sources.'

'Well, they must be pretty good, because you're right. I am off the case. Well, officially, if you know what I mean? And I don't know exactly where Ricky is, but I'll admit that I'm working on making contact with him. However, in the meantime, my colleague Andy McTurk … the good cop last time we met! … is in charge of the investigation. We need to nail the real killer, and fast. And that's where I'm hoping you can help.'

'If I can, I will. You have my word on that. I like Ricky, and I don't want to see him going down for a crime he didn't commit.'

'It's worse than that, Gerry.'

'How do you mean? What can be worse than getting locked up for fifteen years in the Bar-L, and for something you didn't even do?'

'Getting taken out by a bunch of crazies. That's what.'

McGhee closed his eyes and sighed.

'Rafferty's goons?'

'The very same.'

'Oh, shit. Now I am worried. I hear those guys don't mess about.'

'No, they don't. I've seen the fruits of their labours myself and they're good at what they do. And there's only one thing worse than a bunch of vicious nutters, Gerry. And that's a bunch of vicious nutters who enjoy their work.'

The journalist drew heavily on his cigarette and fidgeted with his fingernails. Reynolds pressed on.

'Right Gerry, your turn now. Tell me what you've found out about the big romance between Rafferty and Monk.'

'Okay, here goes,' said McGhee, as he began leafing through the crumpled pages of his well-worn reporters' notepad. 'I'll tell you everything I know, but as we agreed, it's all off the record for now. This will go out as a major exclusive once all the legal shite is out of the way. Okay?'

Reynolds nodded, stared and waited impatiently. McGhee took his cue and started painting his developing picture of the sleazy business relationship between the now deceased property developer and the disgraced former councillor. He began by detailing a list of existing and proposed building projects in Rafferty's ownership, which also had the fingerprints of Monk's political interference all over them. The level of blatant nepotism involved didn't really surprise Reynolds, but the sheer number of dodgy deals did.

McGhee had uncovered nine of them to date, and he wasn't even finished yet. Apart from the well documented major housing development on the seafront site of the former Sandbank Maternity Hospital, the three building conversions at Ayr Harbour and Monk's own exclusive new-build home down on the Ballantrae coast, all of which Reynolds already knew about, there were others that were breaking news to him. Those included the development of a fifteen-acre site on the edge of one of Ayr's most scenic golf courses which had received outline planning consent for the construction of twenty luxury villas; the conversion of an old red sandstone building, formerly a large hotel on the shorefront in Troon, into a nursing home for the elderly; the demolition of a two-hundred-year-old mansion house near the coastal village of Maidens and its replacement with another elderly care home; and the acquisition of a sprawling piece of real estate on the perimeter of Prestwick International Airport, no doubt to be utilised in the near future for the construction of yet another tranche of fancy big houses fit only for the landed gentry and upwardly mobile of the locale.

All nine projects had two essential features in common. Firstly, Frank Rafferty had acquired the properties and the land, and was in pole position as usual to secure the contracts. Secondly, Edwin Monk's committee had approved the planning permissions. The evidence and the audit trail were there for all to see, so rocket science this was not. Yet nobody, the police included, had so far managed to join the dots.

By the time McGhee was finished, Reynolds was completely lost for words. If the brash arrogance of Rafferty had been breath-taking, then the inconsequential gall of Monk was simply astonishing.

'Good God almighty,' the detective said. 'What a pair of conniving bastards those two are. All of this will come out in the wash when Monk's embezzlement trial hits the courts.'

'I heard that Monk has done a deal with the cops?' the journalist replied, pushing his luck. 'Shopped Rafferty in exchange for a reduced sentence further down the line, I'm hearing.'

'Wouldn't surprise me in the slightest,' Reynolds replied, taking care to avoid giving him a direct answer. 'It happens all the time. Sometimes it's the only way to get the villains to spill their guts.'

'I'd lock Monk up and heave the bloody key into the Clyde,' muttered McGhee.

'So would I,' Reynolds replied, as he rose to his feet. 'Thanks for all your help, Gerry. I'll keep in touch.'

'Charlie, you might want to sit back down for a wee minute,' McGhee said, with a wry smile. 'There's something else. And you might find it interesting.'

The detective's backside re-hit the seat instantly. Wry smiles always fascinated him. They invariably preceded revelations, minor and major. This one was about to fall into the latter category.

'You've got my full attention,' he said.

'You'll be aware that Frank Rafferty was a serial philanderer?' came McGhee's rhetorical question. 'In fact, my information is that he had more bits on the side than you and I have had pints of lager.'

'So they tell me,' Reynolds replied, with an expression which carried a judicious mix of intrigue and impatience. 'Come on Gerry, spill the beans.'

McGhee leaned over and handed Reynolds a brown A4-sized envelope. The big cop opened it and took out four black-and-white photographs, which he quickly recognised must have been taken with a telescopic lens from a good distance away. The photographs were of Frank Rafferty standing on the steps of a caravan. He was kissing a blonde middle-aged woman.

'Rafferty's latest floosie, then?' Reynolds remarked, looking singularly unimpressed. 'What's new?'

'Ah ...' McGhee teased. 'But she isn't just any old floosie, Charlie.'

'You've now got me hanging on your every word,' Reynolds replied. 'Spit it out, man.'

'She's Frank Rafferty's sister-in-law,' McGhee said. 'Wee brother Dan's wife.'

59

Ricky Anderson's steadily expanding biceps had more or less become acclimatised to the strain of two days' hard labour on the dockside, yet his hamstrings still hurt like hell. Six-quid-a-day wasn't a bad little number these days, but he sure was having to earn every penny of it.

As he stacked his last crate of mackerel for the morning, he noticed a dark-blue car pulling up at the entrance to the harbour. Closer inspection revealed that it was a brand-new Rover 2000 with the word 'POLICE' emblazoned in big white letters on its bonnet. As Ricky began sweeping away the wet fish scales and other assorted marine debris scattered across the concrete, he held his breath as he watched two uniformed officers emerging from the front seats and a third from the back.

When they started marching authoritatively down the path towards the small dilapidated brick building marked 'Harbour Master', Sandy Ferguson couldn't help noticing Ricky zipping up his jacket and pulling the hood over his head. Their eyes met.

Ferguson moved stealthily behind the cover of three stacks of wooden pallets and began walking in the direction of 'The Jolly Swagman', an old fishing boat owned by an ex-pat Aussie mariner that was moored at the south side of the harbour. With a deft curl of his forefinger, he beckoned Ricky to follow him. In the absence of any better ideas, Ricky took his cue and trotted after him like an obedient toddler.

'Get your arse into that boat, Jim, and keep your head down,' the Harbour Master instructed him in no uncertain terms. 'We'll talk about it later.'

Ricky shuffled his frame over the harbour wall and dropped down onto the deck of the old trawler which was bobbing up and down in the choppy swell of a Girvan high tide. Looking all around for somewhere to conceal himself from prying eyes, he noticed a sheet of off-yellow tarpaulin lying draped over a pile of fishing nets. It was a long time since Ricky had last played a game of hide-and-seek, but his options were now few and far between, so he immediately dived under the tarpaulin. The stink was appalling, but this was no time to crave aesthetic perfection.

Five minutes went past, then ten, then twenty. At least, that was Ricky's estimation, because he had left his wristwatch in his Henrietta Street digs and his only other means of telling the time was by looking at the big antique clock that hung on the wall of Ferguson's office, which doubtless was where the three coppers would presently be grilling his boss about whether or not he had seen anyone fitting Ricky's own description. And, of course, if they were, there was only one question that mattered. Would Sandy cough up and shop Ricky, or would he throw them off his fish-infested scent? Time alone would tell.

After what Ricky reckoned was a good half-hour, he started considering his options. They were in short supply. He could extricate himself right now from his temporary bolthole, walk into the Harbour Master's office and give himself up to the cops, hoping that they would either set him free because of the stink or arrest him on the spot and end his nightmare as a fugitive. Alternatively, he could just make a run for it back to his digs, get a quick wash and change of clothes, then hitch a lift to pastures new, somewhere like Stranraer to the south or Newton Stewart to the east. The final option was the one with the highest risk by far, but potentially the greatest reward. He could simply put his trust in an ancient mariner whom he had met less than three days ago and stay put under the tarpaulin until summoned.

Ricky decided to lie and wait. Nothing ventured, nothing gained. He had always been a pretty good judge of character. At least, until now.

A few more minutes passed before he heard the sound of footsteps and voices emerging from some muffled interior into the open air. Footsteps getting closer, voices becoming clearer. Had Ferguson sold him out, Ricky wondered for one horrific moment? If he was going to make a run for it, he would have to do it now. Where to, he had no idea, but would need to go like the wind in the hope that his young muscular legs could outrun those of his would-be pursuers.

As quietly as possible, he shoved back the tarpaulin and wriggled himself onto his knees. Getting himself up off the vessel's deck onto the higher terra firma would be the time-consuming part, a good five or six seconds at least, but the cops might not notice him until he started running. If they caught him, then it was game over, but if he got to his feet before they clocked him and really flared it, then at least he had a chance of reaching the main street before they did, where he could possibly get himself lost in the 'biz' of shoppers, tradespeople and visitors.

Ricky took a couple of deep breaths, pushed himself up to his full height and grabbed the edge of the harbour wall, as the fishing boat rocked like a rollercoaster beneath his feet. It would be a mighty scramble, but he could do it. After all, his liberty was at stake.

Strangely, though, the footsteps were now beginning to recede again, the voices too. Ricky stood stalk still, listening, keeping his head below the harbour wall. A car's engine sprang into life. Nothing unusual about that in a busy fishing port, he figured, but could it be the Rover 2000 about to whisk the boys-in-blue off his trail in despondency? If so, there could only be one plausible explanation. Big Sandy had delivered the goods.

He wouldn't have to wait long to find out. A pair of hefty footsteps clumped their way towards him. They smacked of impatience. So too did the gruff voice that accompanied them.

221

'Right boy, on your feet and into my office. And right now.'

Ricky complied without hesitation. He clambered out of the boat onto the harbour and began shuffling after his boss, whose shovel-like fist he could see in the distance hauling open the wooden door. Looking around in all directions, Ricky quickened his stride. Having discarded his only other options, his liberty was now fully in the hands of a hardened old sea dog whom, a mere few days back, he didn't even know existed. Ricky slinked into the office like a naughty schoolboy who had just been caught copying his best pal's homework.

'Shut the door behind you, Jim, and sit down,' Ferguson commanded. 'We need to have a serious talk. And it's not Jim anyway, is it?'

Ricky bowed his head, then shook it.

'No, it's not Jim.'

'Tell me, then, what is it? After talking to the police, I'm fairly sure I know, but I want to hear it from you.'

'My name's Richard Anderson, but most people call me Ricky. And I'm on the run from the cops.'

'Why, Ricky ... what did you do?'

'Nothing. Nothing at all. I went to pay a woman-beater a wee visit, but somebody else got there before me.'

'The story that's been all over the papers?'

'The very same.'

Ferguson picked up his copy of the *Ayrshire Herald* and pointed a stubby finger at the mugshot on the front page, the one adorned in dark shoulder-length hair.

'Is that you?'

'Yip.'

'What happened to the long hair, then?'

'Lobbed it off.'

'Good move. You look like a big Nancy-boy in that photo.'

Ricky couldn't prevent a nervous snigger from escaping. Ferguson maintained his steely stare.

'Tell me the full story, Ricky,' he said, eyeballing his casual labourer with avid concentration. 'And no bullshit. All I know is what I've read in the papers. So, if I'm harbouring a wanted man from the cops, I think I have a right to know why I'm doing it.'

'The long or short version?'

'The short one will do for now.'

'I'm a student. Glasgow University. At least I was until all this happened. My mum lives in Glenside. You know it?'

'Yes, I know it. I once went out with a lassie from Glenside. She dumped me for a student, so you're not exactly helping your case.'

'Sorry about that, Sandy,' Ricky smiled. 'Anyway, my mum got into a bit of trouble.'

'What kind of trouble?'

'Money ... or lack of it. My dad died a few years back and she never got over him. Motorbike accident. Lost her job, got into debt, that kind of thing. Ended up taking money from a guy called Frank Rafferty. Former schoolmate, now a property developer. Money lender too, protected by a bunch of thugs who knock the shit out of anybody who can't repay their debts and interest. Well, Rafferty made one big mistake. He had my mum hospitalised, nearly killed her. So, I went looking for him. Pay him a wee visit ... you know?'

'Was he the stiff in the caravan? The guy who got his throat cut?'

'Yes.'

'Did you do it, Ricky?'

'No, I didn't. I went to the caravan, though. Saw him sitting there on the settee, blood everywhere. I'm glad the bastard's dead, but I didn't do it.'

'But the cops think you did. According to the newspaper reports, your fingerprints were on the knife and all over the caravan. What am I supposed to think?'

'Think what you like, Sandy, but I didn't do it. And I'm not about to get locked up for a crime I didn't commit.'

'So, what's your plan, then?'

'Lie low until I can find out who *did* do it.'

'And just how the hell are you going to solve a murder that was committed up there in Doonfoot when you're mending fishing nets down here in Girvan? Come on, Ricky, get real.'

'I don't know, but I'm working on it. I've got a couple of people helping me.'

'Who are they.'

'Can't say.'

'Well, what are they?'

'A cop and a newspaper hack.'

'You're playing with fire, Ricky.'

'I know I am. But what choice have I got? Turn myself in and do time for somebody else's crime. No bloody way. I'll take my chances

223

on the run.'

'You won't need to run, Ricky. At least, not for now. You can stay in the chalet for a few days, but you need to keep your head down. You've still got your digs, but you can't work in the harbour anymore. You're too hot. I'll speak to Martha. We'll make sure you're fed and watered.'

'Why are you doing this for me, Sandy.'

The big harbour master took a deep breath and rubbed his chin.

'Martha and I had a son of our own. He got killed in a car crash ten years ago. He would have been about your age now. I'd like to think that someone would have done this for our Callum.'

Up until that moment, Ricky Anderson had known that his hopes of proving his innocence lay entirely in the hands of two potential allies, Detective Inspector Charlie Reynolds and investigative journalist, Gerry McGhee. Now he had a third.

Ricky's chances of evading the long arm of the law and proving his innocence were still very slim. In fact, long odds against. However, they had just become ever so slightly shorter.

60

The pot-bellied sergeant that was George Renfrew knocked gently a couple of times on the office door. He waited for a response, but when none was forthcoming, he just turned the handle anyway. The DI could be a bit tetchy some afternoons at the end of his shift, so Renfrew entered with caution.

'Can I come in, Sir?' he asked.

DI Andy McTurk, fag hanging out of his mouth as usual, glanced sideways and nodded. It was a nod that smacked of 'if you must' rather than 'what do you take in your tea?'

Renfrew stood and waited for McTurk to ask him why he was there. He could have waited all day.

'We still haven't found any real leads on the Anderson lad yet, Sir,' the sergeant ventured. 'As you instructed, we've been combing the coastal area all day, from Girvan through Lendalfoot and all the way down to Ballantrae. Nothing, Sir. It's as if he's vanished off the face of the earth.'

Finally, McTurk spoke, although it was more of a bark. A bark that radiated frustration, but one which cleverly concealed something else entirely. A sense of relief. Relief that young Ricky remained out there on the loose, meaning that Charlie Reynolds might still get to him before either the cops or the Rafferty brothers' goons did. Never before in his whole career had McTurk found himself in such an invidious position. On the one hand, his infamous ferret-like determination and impeccable professionalism were as attuned to hunting down his prey as a ravenous sparrow hawk on the trail of a petrified field mouse. On the other, every emotional instinct in his psyche was convinced that the prey was a completely innocent young lad who deserved to take his chances on the run and remain incognito until the real truth could be established. And, of course, it was McTurk's job to establish the real truth.

'Nothing, George?' he enquired, without even looking up. 'Absolutely nothing? As in hee-haw, you mean? Good God, man, I gave you three squad cars, eleven officers and two German Shepherds. Were you all wearing bloody blindfolds? Have the dogs got sinusitis?'

'It's been a very difficult day, Sir,' came Renfrew's weary reply. 'Anderson has totally changed his appearance and he's obviously covered his tracks very well. The only photographs we can show the local residents have got him with his long hair and all clean shaven, so even the photofit images haven't been ringing any bells.'

'I doubt if even a kirk campanologist would ring any bells with that lot of yours,' McTurk retorted, feigning exasperation but still managing to maintain the subterfuge. 'Keep looking, George. Suggest you split into two teams tomorrow. Keep one team in Girvan and send the second one to cover the country bumpkin areas around Dailly, Barr and Pinwherry. You never know, you might get lucky. Good God, a bell might even ring.'

'Will do, Sir,' Renfrew replied, before beating a hasty retreat. The DI could be the life and soul of the party at times, but he sure as hell wasn't in party mood today. As the office door closed, McTurk's telephone rang. He picked it up and instantly recognised the voice on the other end.

'How you doing, buddy?' it enquired. 'As crabbit as usual, I'm guessing?'

'Aye,' said McTurk. 'Just had George Renfrew in to tell me that eleven coppers spent the whole bloody day in Girvan looking for Ricky Anderson and came back empty-handed. That lot couldn't find a scarecrow in a window box.'

'Good,' Charlie Reynolds replied, much more quickly than he

had intended. 'It'll be far better for Ricky if I track him down myself and bring him in. Suspect hands himself into the cops, the papers love that kind of thing. So will the jurors, if it ever comes to that.'

'And if eleven trained coppers can't manage to bring the lad in, just how the hell do you propose to do it, Charlie?' asked McTurk, the weariness in his voice betraying a mood of rank discouragement. 'He's gone to ground. It'll be like trying to find a needle in a bloody haystack down there in the Galloway Forest.'

'His girlfriend, Andy. She'll help me. Iona spoke to Ricky last night on the phone. She told him I wanted to talk to him. He hesitated at first, then said he'd think about it. He's going to speak to her again tonight.'

McTurk perked up like a junkie after a much-needed fix.

'When? And more to the point, where?'

'Back off, Andy. We've got a deal, remember? You nail Rafferty's killer and I reel Ricky in. And Smokin' Joe's in on it as well, so you don't need to worry about your pension. I'll let you know as soon as I know, and hopefully you can then take the Keystone Cops off his trail.'

'Okay, but the longer this goes on, the longer it takes for my boys to track Ricky down and the more of a complete dick I look. Smokin' Joe will expect me to put my foot on the gas and step up the manhunt.'

'You leave the manhunt to me, Andy, and I'll deliver Ricky straight to your front door. In the meantime, I've got a very interesting new lead for you to follow up. I met up with Gerry McGhee yesterday.'

'And?'

'Not on the phone, Andy. Drop by at my place whenever you get a minute, and I'll show you some naughty photographs.'

'Photographs?'

'Of Frank Rafferty snogging a blonde on the steps of his brother Dan's caravan?'

'And who's the blonde?'

'Maureen Rafferty. His sister-in-law. Beloved brother Dan's wife.'

'Jesus Christ!'

'No, Andy, you can still call me Charlie. See you in a few minutes, old boy.'

61

As the dark-blue Rover 2000 police car pulled away from Girvan harbour and sped into the distance, three sets of prying eyes watched from behind the windows of a black Ford Corsair camouflaged from view by the assorted vehicles surrounding it in the small public car park.

'You see that, boys?' growled Robert McDaid, the twenty-stone, self-styled *caporegime* of Rafferty Construction's money-lending protection racket. 'The filth at their useless best. They went in hoping to nab the Anderson boy, and came back out with their tails between their legs.'

'So, where is he, then?' enquired his sidekick from the rear seat. 'The Anderson boy?'

'How the hell should I know, Zander?' McDade snapped back. 'But we need to find out what the guy in the Harbour Master's office said to them.'

'The guy in the Harbour Master's office?' young Ralph Baxter sniggered from behind the steering wheel. 'You mean the Harbour Master, Rab?'

'You're too smart-arsed for your own good, Ralphie-Boy,' McDade replied with a threatening glare. 'Just cut the wisecracks and concentrate on improving your driving. Got it?'

'What are you thinking, Rab?' asked McGinn. 'Should we go and have a wee word in his ear?'

'Aye, Zander, let's do it,' he replied. 'Ralphie, you just sit here and keep the engine running. This could get messy, son. When you see Zander and me coming out, get down there pronto and pick us up, then boot it. Okay?'

The young getaway driver just nodded silently. The sharp repartee had disappeared like snow off a drystane dyke. Ralph Baxter loved the pretentious status that went with being in the enforcement business, but he hated the rough stuff. It was at times like this that he found himself wondering whether he had chosen the right vocation.

The two heavyweights exhibited no such self-doubt as they extricated themselves from the Corsair with much more determination than grace. McDade wriggled his 46-inch waistband out of the front passenger's seat and spat his chewing gum onto the tarmac, while McGinn did likewise with his similarly elephant-sized backside and flicked the remnants of his cigarette into an airborne trajectory. Back in the day, when the late lamented Frank Rafferty had first employed his two favourite security men, social etiquette had not featured as an essential criterion in the job description. Neither had it blossomed with time, because the two goons still possessed all the collective charm of a pair of rabid Pit Bulls in a rabbit hutch.

Baxter remained in the car chomping at his fingernails while his two colleagues took a good look around. Pulling the collars of their leather jerkins up over the garish tattoos which adorned their respective necks like vandals' graffiti on the walls of a condemned factory, they began striding towards their chosen location. As a gentle sea breeze caressed the salty air and wafted over the handful of fishing boats bobbing contentedly in the harbour, they continued their pernicious march towards the tiny office, thereby contriving to lace the late-morning ambience with a most unwelcome contradiction. Seaside tranquillity was about to liaise with urban menace.

McDade thumped the office door twice with his massive fist. There was no answer, so he thumped twice again and turned the handle. Taking their first inquisitive steps inside, they saw a rather rustic-looking, heavily-bearded big man rising from behind his desk, the greying hair on both his head and chin dancing in the breeze. If ever there was a walking caricature of an ancient mariner, he was it.

'Don't look now,' McDade whispered under his breath to McGinn, as Sandy Ferguson made his way towards them, 'but it's Captain Pugwash himself.'

McGinn stifled a laugh and waited for his sidekick's next move.

'I wonder if you can help us,' McDade said to the old seadog. 'We're looking for my wee nephew. Goes by the name of Richard Anderson. He's done a runner, and his ma' has asked us to find him and bring him back home. She's worried sick.'

'Is that right, lads?' Ferguson continued, immediately clocking that whatever the two brutes before him might claim to be, they certainly didn't look like a pair of distraught uncles. 'The poor woman must be beside herself.'

'Can we come in for a minute?' McDade ventured, drawing on one of the principal lessons he had learned in the enforcement business. When you're about to give some poor bugger a right good kicking, close the door first and block his escape route.

Realising the potential risk, Ferguson hesitated at first before ushering them in with a wave of his hand.

'A couple of minutes, lads,' he said. 'That's all I've got. *The Drunken Sailor's* due to berth any minute and I have to go and meet the skipper.'

'Who's the Drunken ...? McGinn began with a puzzled expression, before McDade cut him off.

'It's a boat, Zander. A boat ... not an actual ... sailor, man. If brains were shite, you'd be constipated.'

McDade waited for Ferguson to smile, but his gaze met a facial expression of pure granite. He pressed on and gestured at McGinn to stay quiet.

'You didn't say what your name was?'

'No, I didn't. But you can address me as Harbour Master.'

'You're not being very friendly, Harbour Master.'

'No, I'm too busy to be friendly. What do you want? And I'm in a hurry, so be quick about it.'

Mc Dade's trademark scowl began to ripple across his big square face.

'You hear that, Zander? The Harbour Master's not being very nice to us. Tell you what I'll do, Captain Pugwash. If you tell us what you just told the cops a few minutes ago, we'll leave you with the use of your legs.'

'Get out of my office,' Ferguson said. 'And right now.'

McDade reached into the side pocket of his leather jacket and pulled out a metal knuckle-duster. McGinn recognised his cue and did likewise. Ferguson took two steps back and grabbed a crowbar up off the concrete floor, the one that he used for lifting the lids off the harbour drains. As the three protagonists waited to see who would make the first move, they heard the sound of footsteps approaching from outside. The office door creaked open.

'You all right in there, Sandy?'

The voice belonged to Alastair McGregor, the skipper of the *Jolly Swagman*. Behind him were Adam Lynch, his first mate, and Bertie Stevenson, the ship's engineer and general handyman. At six-foot-two and fifteen stones, Stevenson was the frailest of the three. A local saying went that if you ever wanted to move house, the crew of the *Jolly Swagman* would relocate it wherever you wanted.

'Aye, fine Alastair,' Ferguson replied, still brandishing the crowbar with unmistakeable purpose. 'These lads are just leaving. They're a bit lost. They've ended up in a nice wee place like Girvan when they should be back crawling under their rocks in the big city.'

The tension was as thick as chilled treacle, as Ferguson faced off his pair of would-be attackers, while his three hefty seafaring chums waited at the door, fists clenched and raring to get a piece of the action. It was McDade who climbed down first, deciding to slip his knuckle-duster back into his pocket and nodding to McGinn to do the same. As they slunk from the office in simmering retreat, McGregor made a point of bumping shoulders with each of them.

'And don't hurry back, boys,' he grinned through gritted teeth. 'The Harbour Master's got a lot of good pals. And they breed us hardy down here in Girvan.'

The screech of tyres from Ralph Baxter's Corsair was laughably superfluous. McDade and McGinn calmly opened the doors and slipped into their seats as if they were off to do their weekly shopping. As soon as the car roared away from the harbour, the air inside turned a very deep shade of blue, with expletives flying around like a barnful of bats set free at dusk. That was until Zander McGinn pulled a crumpled piece of paper from his hip pocket.

'What the hell is that, Zander,' McDade enquired, still seething.

'An envelope,' he replied with a grin. 'An envelope with an address on it. The Harbour Master's home address.'

McDade's face cracked open under the weight of a wide, pernicious grin.

'Well done, Zander my man,' he said. 'Did anybody ever tell you that you're not as stupid as you look? What do you think, Ralphie-boy?'

McGinn smiled back at McDade, then leaned over the front seat to face the young driver.

'And if I were you,' he said. 'I'd think very carefully before I answered that question.'

Baxter thought for a moment about making one of his cutting wisecracks, then decided that discretion was the better part of valour and kept his face shut. Probably, wisely.

62

Sergeant Sandy Sutherland could hardly believe his eyes.

'Where the hell did you get these from, boss?' he asked, as he stared in astonishment at the four black-and-white photographs that lay spread out before him on the office desk. The morning had started well.

'From a friend of a friend,' Detective Inspector Andy McTurk replied, a look of smug satisfaction having replaced the mask of doom and despair that he had been wearing the previous day. 'Watch and learn, young man. Watch and learn.'

Sutherland leaned back in his chair, rubbed his chin and smiled.

'So, what do you make of it, then?' he asked?

'No, Sandy, you tell me,' McTurk teased. 'What do you make of it?'

'Well ...' his young protegee replied. 'Let's see. Frank Rafferty is the main man ... sorry, was the main man ... and young brother Dan very much the wee boy, always in Frank's shadow. In awe of him, really. Maybe even scared of him. Frank goes on the run after this Edwin Monk business goes tits-up and wee brother Dan lets him hide out in his caravan. Then, to show his appreciation, Frank starts servicing Dan's wife for him. How does that sound, boss?'

'Sounds about right to me. But what does it tell us, Sandy? Come on, man, earn your corn.'

'It tells us that Dan Rafferty is now a murder suspect. And if we can establish that he knew big brother Frank was doing the business with his wife, then he's got to be a prime suspect.'

'And how do we find out if he knew?'

'We pull Dan and his wife in for questioning, boss.'

'Better still, Sandy, we pull Dan in for questioning and let him sweat for a bit, while we pay his wife a wee visit at home. She'll either collapse in a heap and confess to her affair with Frank, or she won't. And she'll either be able to provide Dan with an alibi for his whereabouts at the time of Frank's murder, or she won't. Either way, we then interview Dan.'

'Agreed, boss. So, how do you want to play this, then?'

'Take that young lad with you, the one who has just swapped his police uniform for a nice new suit. He needs to get out of the office and get it dirty. What's his name again?'

'Detective Constable Murray. Ian, I think his first name is.'

'Aye, well, take young Murray with you and track Dan Rafferty down, then bring him in. He'll probably be in his office at this time of day, or out on one of his building sites. When you nab him, stick him in an interview room with a uniform for company, and let him stew in his own juice for a couple of hours. Meanwhile, we'll drop in on the fun-loving Maureen, and see how she handles the pressure.'

'Should be an interesting morning.'

'Should be. We'll know by early afternoon whether or not we've got a watertight case against Dan. And if we have, young Anderson will then be able to come home and get back to his nice wee science experiments. But if we haven't, we've got a problem. A big problem, because the killer will still be out there on the loose.'

'You think there's any doubt about it, boss?'

'Sandy, one thing I've learned in this business is that nothing is ever certain. Even when you think your main suspect is absolutely stuffed, something can appear out of nowhere to bite you on the bum. What looks like irrefutable evidence can be turned upside down, or a key witness can suddenly change his story. No, the only sure way to nail the villain is to get him to confess. So, off you go and let's see if we can get our confession. You pick Dan up and leave him to sweat it out, then we'll meet back here at about eleven-ish.'

'Where are you going meantime, boss?'

'I'm off to Charlie Reynolds's pad. Ricky Anderson's girlfriend is meeting us there at half-nine. He was supposed to be phoning her last night and I want to hear the full story. We're hoping he's agreed to speak to Charlie either on the phone or in the flesh. Or better still, turn himself in.'

'Can I suggest something, Sir?'

'Sure.'

'Tell DI Reynolds to let young Anderson know that Rafferty's men will be out looking for him. One sure way to make the boy turn himself in is to scare the shit out of him.'

McTurk laughed out loud. Sutherland's quizzical stare begged for an explanation.

'Scare that young fella, Sandy? The bloody Kray twins couldn't scare Ricky Anderson.'

63

It wasn't often that a senior police officer and his second-in-command struck gold in two different places at the same time. However, unbeknown to each other, DI Andy McTurk and DS

Sandy Sutherland both hit the jackpot at precisely half-past-ten on the crisp autumnal morning that was Friday 21 September.

Flanked on either side of the kitchen table by Charlie Reynolds and Janice Anderson, Andy McTurk hung onto every word which slipped from the youthful lips of Iona McNish as she sat opposite recalling each last detail of the previous evening's telephone discussion with her runaway fiancé. To Janice's indescribable relief, Ricky was still safe and well, or at least so he had insisted under heavy cross-examination from Iona. He had lifted his summer's earnings before he went on the run, then picked up a casual job, which meant he now had food in his stomach and a place to stay, although God knows where.

'Think, Iona,' Reynolds beseeched her. 'Think carefully. Did he say anything at all that would give us a clue about where he was calling from? Anything that would point to a busy city centre, or a remote rural setting like a farm or that kind of thing? Any distinctive sounds, like heavy city traffic, or seagulls squawking, or background machinery? Anything at all?'

Iona's warm smile gave way to a disapproving scowl.

'I thought you wanted to speak to him in person, Charlie,' she remarked. 'Not send the dogs after him.'

Reynolds immediately raised both hands in apology. His embarrassment was palpable.

'Sorry, Iona,' he grovelled. 'I just can't seem to stop being a copper.'

'Well, in this instance, you're no longer a copper, Charlie,' McTurk piped up. 'This is my case and you're on leave, remember?'

'Anyway, the dogs won't be required,' Iona went on, the gentle smile slowly returning to her face to let Reynolds off his self-imposed hook. 'Ricky has agreed to speak to you, Charlie.'

The big detective took a long, deep breath.

'Where?' he asked. 'And when?'

'On the phone,' replied Iona. 'Not face-to-face, at least not for now. Same arrangement, same telephone box. McCubbin's corner just off Cumnock Square. Same time tonight, eight o'clock sharp. And if you try to trace the call and put the cops on his trail, he says he'll never trust you again. And he also said ... no, never mind ... forget it.'

'He also said what, Iona?'

'He also said he'd tell his mum never to trust you again.'

233

Reynolds turned and looked at Janice, who looked straight back at him with a stoical expression that required no further elaboration.

'I won't, Iona,' he said. 'And that's a promise.'

'Good,' she nodded, before continuing. 'And he said something else too. Something which he said would be of great interest to the police officer who is taking over the investigation from you. That'll be you, Mister McTurk.'

'It sure will,' McTurk replied. 'Go on, dear.'

'He admitted that he was in the caravan that night in Doonfoot, and when he went in Frank Rafferty was sitting on the couch with his throat cut, stone dead. Ricky promised me that he didn't do it. He did pick up the kitchen knife, though.'

'We already know that, Iona,' said McTurk. 'His fingerprints, remember?'

'Well, here's something you don't know,' she said, steely-eyed. 'Before Ricky entered the caravan that night, he saw a man leaving it in a hurry.'

McTurk stared at her, seriously wrong-footed.

'You sure about that, Iona?'

'That's what Ricky said. And my Ricky doesn't lie.'

'No, he doesn't,' Janice piped up. 'He's got his wee quirks and faults like the rest of us, but lying has never been one of them.'

'Was he able to give you a description, Iona?' McTurk asked, more in hope than expectation.

'Ricky said it was dark. He was on the other side of the road from the caravan and the only light was from the orange streetlight. He said the man looked about average height, stocky built, probably in his late-forties or early-fifties, but he couldn't be sure.'

Reynolds turned and stared at McTurk.

'Dan Rafferty?'

McTurk's eyes lit up like super-troopers at a rock concert. He nodded, then stood up and excused himself.

'I'm off to pay Mister Rafferty a wee visit. Thanks for your help, Iona.'

'You don't need to thank me. I'm not doing it for you, I'm doing it for Ricky.'

Reynolds accompanied McTurk to the door.

'I'll give you a bell tonight about half-eight, or whenever I've finished talking to Ricky,' he said. 'And no funny stuff, Andy. I know you've got to be seen to keep your boys on the chase, but

I'm determined to get to him first and bring him in. If you get that bloody phone tapped or set me up in any way, I'll have completely betrayed my trust with Iona and Janice. They would never forgive me, and I'd never forgive you.'

McTurk looked straight at Reynolds and shook his head in disgust.

'If I wasn't such a tough-skinned old bastard, I could maybe feel a wee bit insulted that the thought of me double-crossing my best buddy would ever cross your mind.'

'It didn't,' he replied, stony-faced. 'I just want absolutely nothing to get in the way of me bringing Ricky back home. That wee lassie can't stand the thought of losing him.'

'And you can't stand the thought of losing his mother,' McTurk said. 'Am I right?'

Reynolds nodded, and an uncharacteristically vulnerable look washed over his face for the second time that morning. Thankfully, his ordeal was quickly relieved by McTurk's radio springing into action.

'The eagle has landed, Sir,' DS Sandy Sutherland was heard to say on the other end, the excitement in his voice still clearly distinguishable above the metallic crackle. 'Dan Rafferty's in Interview Room 3. We nabbed him just as he was getting into his car outside his portacabin on the Sandbank building site. He did his best to look angry and indignant, but I think he's worried, boss.'

'Good job, Sandy,' McTurk replied, turning to give Reynolds the thumbs-up. 'I'll meet you in fifteen minutes at the Golden Eagle Hotel for a coffee and a bacon roll. Then we'll pay Maureen Rafferty a wee social visit. First, though, get the station boys to fingerprint Rafferty, then ask forensics to check his prints against the second set we found on the murder weapon and on the handle of the caravan door. See you in a bit. I'm buying'

'You're buying, old boy? Reynolds asked, feigning a look of astonishment. 'You really must be in a good mood this morning.'

'Never been better, Charlie,' McTurk smiled, slapping his sidekick on the shoulder as he walked out the door. 'You're going to bring young Anderson in, I've got my suspect in custody and I'm about to have a nice breakfast. Watch and learn, Charlie, son. Watch and learn.'

Reynolds laughed heartily, before deciding to ask a couple of questions which he knew would wipe the smug grin from his colleague's face.

'But what if it turns out that the second set of prints don't belong to Dan Rafferty? Or what if Maureen Rafferty provides her beloved husband with the perfect alibi? What then, Inspector Clouseau?'

'Then, we're back to the first set of prints and Dan Rafferty's off the hook,' McTurk replied. 'Which means that Ricky Anderson is still our number one suspect.'

'But he didn't do it, Andy. I know it, and you know it. If it turns out to be Dan Rafferty, then good and well. If it wasn't Dan who killed his big brother, then go and find out who did, because it sure as hell wasn't Ricky.'

'So, you do your job, Charlie, and bring him in. And get off my back and let me do mine.'

'I knew your good mood wouldn't last for long.'

'You know, Charlie, you've got this habit of bringing out the worst in people at times, did I ever tell you that? You, and your ... your ... persistence. You're like a bloody ferret at times.'

'Aye, I know, it's a rare talent I've been nurturing along life's way. Just phone me when you've interviewed the Raffertys and give me good news, Andy. Something positive to tell Ricky when I call him tonight, something that will give him a reason to come back home. I would really like to bring him in before the crazy gang catch up with him.'

'As I said, Charlie, I'll do my job and you do yours.'

'So, order a full Scottish breakfast, then go and get Rafferty charged for his brother's murder and give me the ammunition I need to convince Ricky.'

McTurk's nostrils were still dilated in annoyance as he walked down the garden path towards his car. Then he thought of the 'full Scottish' which awaited him and allowed his gastric juices to take over the controls.

On the other side of the door, Reynolds strolled casually back into his kitchen. Two sets of eyes stared at him with solemn intensity. He felt as if he had just walked into a promotion interview.

'How can two such lovely faces look so scary at times?' came the rhetorical question.

It was Janice who spoke first, not even cracking the faintest smile.

'Iona's got something to tell you, Charlie,' she said. 'And she didn't want to say it in front of Andy.'

'I'd trust Andy McTurk with my life,' he replied.

'That's fine, Charlie,' she said. 'Because we're about to trust you with Ricky's life.'

Silence. A deep, intense silence which lasted no more than a few seconds but felt like a particularly drawn-out winter's evening in the middle of a power cut. Iona drew it to a welcome close.

'He wants to meet you, Charlie.'

'When?' Reynolds asked, far too quickly.

'Tomorrow. One o'clock sharp. And if you're not there by five-past, he'll be gone.'

'Where?'

'Girvan. At the Stumpy Tower on Knockcushan Street. You'll recognise it by the big clock at the top of the tower.'

'Girvan? What the hell is Ricky doing in Girvan, Iona?'

'Trying to prevent you and your cop pals from finding him.'

'And now he wants to walk straight into my arms. Why me? Why do I deserve such an honour?'

'Because Ricky trusts me, I trust Janice and Janice trusts you. There's a lot riding on this, Charlie. Everything, in fact.'

'No pressure, then, ladies?' the big detective smiled, trying to bring some light relief to the tension of the moment.

Janice eyeballed him with that self-same stare that he had witnessed a few days back to his own gross discomfort.

'Ricky is my only child, Charlie, and he means the world to me.'

'And to me too,' Iona added.

'So, we're both putting our trust in you, Charlie,' Janice continued. 'Do you realise what that means?'

Charlie Reynolds leaned back in his seat, rubbed his chin and gave a little nervous laugh.

'Yes, I think so,' he sighed. 'You're both telling me that if I blow this, Ricky will be in big bother, but not as much bother as I'll be in. Is that about it, ladies?'

'Yip,' said Iona, turning to Janice for approval.

'Yip,' said Janice, turning back to Reynolds. 'I would say that about sums it up.'

'Well, I'd better be on my A-game, then,' he replied. 'Hadn't I?'

Neither even bothered to reply. Reynolds knew for sure that tomorrow would be one of the most important days of his life. All he needed now was for Andy McTurk to confirm Dan Rafferty's involvement in his brother's murder. Then, if he played things right, he would be bringing Ricky Anderson straight home for tea. However, if he really screwed things up, both Iona and Janice would be left heartbroken.

And without a shadow of a doubt, so too would Reynolds himself.

64

What was striking about Dan Rafferty's pad was its relative modesty. Relative, that was, to the opulence of the one that until very recently had been lorded and mastered by his dearly departed older brother Frank, whose near-decapitated corpse now lay prostrate on a cold slab in Ayr mortuary.

Most of the important possessions held by the two brothers seemed to underline that same relativity. Frank had boasted a magnificent eight-bedroomed mansion on a sprawling seafront site in up-market Troon, while Dan had to content himself with a mid-market, detached Wimpey house in the middle of a modest estate in a suburb of Ayr, one crammed on all sides by other buildings of such near-identical design that they looked as if they could have fallen out of a giant plastic mould. Frank had driven a brand-new, flashy white Jaguar XC-J sports coupe, complete with detachable roof in the event of a rare sunny day down on the Ayrshire coast, while Dan made do with a four-year-old olive-green Morris Marina estate, adorned by a horrid red scrape along the driver's door where it had been clattered one icy morning by the Post Office van. When Frank had shopped in Ralph Slater's on Ayr High Street, he always had his suits made-to-measure in the exclusive Ralph's Room, while Dan bought his straight off-the-peg. And, of course, Frank had wallowed in his superb Baroque-style holiday home on the Normandy coast where he could entertain his hordes of dubious friends and business associates, while Dan's feeble attempt at sibling emulation resided in a bog-standard static caravan languishing behind a row of trees in Doonfoot like a lonely child looking for someone to play with.

However, when it came to their most prized possession of all, it was the younger brother who had always enjoyed the upper hand, because Dan was married to the drop-dead-gorgeous Maureen, while Frank had been lumbered with the plain-and-frumpy Irene. Or Betty Boop and Olive Oil, as the two sisters-in-law were often referred to in local circles, in deference, respectively, to the silver screen's very first shapely cartoon sex symbol and Popeye the Sailor's less than aesthetically pleasing beanpole of a girlfriend.

So yes, it was certainly true that Dan had always lived very much in the shadow of his older brother with the latter's big swanky houses and fast cars and top-of-the-range wardrobe and over-the-top lifestyle. However, it was Dan who had married the real head-turner, whereas Frank was shackled to the veritable plain-Jane of a girl he had wed in a fit of pique after his final rejection from the real love of his life, the delectable Janice Robertson. As far as Dan was concerned, Frank could keep his fancy properties and flash cars and hand-tailored suits and indulgent house parties, because he had the real jewel in the crown. Dan had Maureen, and Maureen simply worshipped the ground Dan walked upon.

At least, she had done until recently. Until she had suddenly started rejecting his amorous advances rather than encouraging them. Until she had started looking at brother-in-law Frank differently. Looking at him that way.

Dan Rafferty would quite happily have put up with his big brother Frank's infinitely superior material possessions, because Frank had earned it. After all, it was Frank who had started the family business in the first place. And it was Frank who had won the lion's share of the building contracts. And it was Frank who had cultivated the political generosity of Councillor Edwin Monk, which had served Rafferty Construction so very well over the years. It was even Frank who had established the 'financial assistance' arm of the business, as it was rather respectfully called at the time, and which had now blossomed into very lucrative money-lending racket policed by those two fearsome enforcers-in-chief, McDade and McGinn, aka the Nutter Squad. So, in all fairness, it was right and proper that Frank should command the higher earnings, the more salubrious property holdings, the flashier cars and the more exquisite social circles.

However, it was Dan who took Maureen to bed every night, not Frank, and Dan knew that Frank hated the very thought. Not that he had ever said anything to him about it, not even once, but he just knew it. And he also knew that Maureen had never given Frank a second glance, at least not until recently. The problem was that he would have had to be Stevie Wonder not to have noticed the sudden change in dynamics, and he wasn't Stevie Wonder. He was Daniel Rafferty, blessed from birth with twenty-twenty vision. The same

Daniel Rafferty who as a young lad had been beaten senseless by Frank on more occasions than he even dared to remember, and who once even had his developing forearm shoved through a mechanical mangle by the same loving big brother.

Dan had put up with a great deal of grief from Frank over the years and had never once fought back, because he would never have dared. However, if Frank ever put his filthy hands anywhere near Maureen, not even a mechanical mangle would be sufficient to assuage Dan's need for retribution.

He would cut his f-----g head off.

65

In keeping with the relative modesty of Dan Rafferty's home in the sprawling urban development known locally as 'Spam Valley', his front door bore scant resemblance to that adorning his brother's opulent holiday pad in far-flung Normandy.

For a hand-designed, cut-glass exhibit garishly emblazoned with the words, 'Chez Rafferty', substitute instead a plain rectangular wooden slab of a door, the only notable characteristics of which were a matching aluminium handle and letterbox, and a tiny plastic doorbell which looked as if it might part company with its precarious fixing if the next visitor had the misfortune to sneeze. DI Andy McTurk pressed it anyway and counted to twenty. He then repeated the process another twice. The embattled detective inspector had done well, because a whole minute was at the very extremity of his tolerance level.

'Right Sandy,' he instructed his young sergeant. 'Go round the back, knock the door and keep knocking. I'll just stand here with my finger on the buzzer till she eventually answers. If she thinks we're just going to shuffle away quietly, she's onto plums.'

No sooner had DS Sutherland disappeared around the side of the house than Maureen Rafferty prised the front door slightly ajar and peeked out. She was wearing a white bathrobe and her long blonde hair was still soaking wet, no doubt from the leisurely shower she had been taking until she was so rudely interrupted. A fine-looking woman for her mid-forties, McTurk clocked right away, as she stood there in bare feet, towelling her hair rather self-consciously.

'Can I help you?' she said, radiating slightly more concern than irritation.

'Mrs Rafferty?' McTurk enquired as Sutherland, having heard the voices, reappeared by his side. 'Mrs Maureen Rafferty?'

'Who wants to know?' she asked, pulling her bathrobe taught around her torso as if to emphasise her feeling of vulnerability.

McTurk took his wallet from his inside jacket pocket and flashed his police ID card towards her. His younger colleague followed suit.

'I'm Detective Inspector McTurk of Southwest Scotland Police,' the former announced, 'and this is Detective Sergeant Sutherland. We would like to ask you a few questions. Can we come in?'

She hesitated for a moment, before nodding in resignation.

'Yes, I suppose ... if you must.'

'Thank you, Mrs Rafferty,' McTurk said, as his reluctant hostess pulled the door fully open to usher the two detectives in. 'This shouldn't take too long.'

'I'll need to get dressed first,' she replied. 'Just take a seat in the lounge. I won't be long. You can make yourselves a cup of tea, if you like. The kitchen's through there.'

'No, that's okay,' said McTurk. 'Thanks anyway. You just take your time, and we'll wait here until you're ready.'

Sutherland sank his tall, athletic frame into the big recliner by the window, while McTurk stood surveying the scene.

'Nice house,' he remarked to his junior partner. 'But not as posh as I had imagined for a successful businessman like Dan Rafferty. I hear his brother's patch is like bloody Windsor Palace. There's no doubt who the head honcho was in that relationship.'

He wandered over to the stone-built fireplace and began looking at three framed photographs that hung on the wall above. The one on the left was of Dan and Maureen's wedding day and the one on the right was a family portrait of the couple sitting beside Frank Rafferty and his wife Irene in some quaint rural setting on the bank of a fast-flowing river. However, it was the big photograph in the middle which commanded regal pride of place, an impressive portrait of the two brothers standing side-by-side in an oak-panelled room, wearing dark suits and sporting their solemn 'business' faces.

'Mutt and bloody Jeff,' McTurk exclaimed, much too loudly.

Sutherland expelled a little contrived cough, just sufficient to attract his boss's attention as Maureen Rafferty walked back into the lounge. The two policemen tried their best not to gawk open-mouthed at the elegant woman before them. She stood much taller in her white stiletto shoes than she had in her bare feet, and she had

241

somehow poured herself into an expensive-looking, figure-hugging, peach-coloured trouser suit. However, it was her stunningly attractive face which captivated her unannounced guests, replete with high cheekbones, deep-blue eyes and shimmering pink lips, perched on a slender neck which was semi-concealed by that same long blonde hair. She had looked good in the black-and-white photograph a few hours back, but not half as good as she did now in the flesh. Dan Rafferty had very good taste, the two detectives' telepathic exchanges confirmed. So too, it would appear, had the recently deceased Frank.

She beckoned McTurk to take a seat on the recliner at the other side of the window from his colleague and lowered herself gracefully into the three-seater settee opposite.

'How can I help you?' she asked anxiously, knowing full well that her visitors' impromptu presence and her brother-in-law's now-permanent absence were bound to be inextricably linked.

Andy McTurk was never one to beat about the bush. His powers of diplomacy knew no beginning.

'How long has your affair with Frank Rafferty been going on?'

Maureen Rafferty visibly recoiled. Tears welled up in her eyes. McTurk and Sutherland sat silently as the mascara began running down her cheeks, any lingering compassion suitably disguised by the cruel inscrutability that comes from years of bitter experience on the force.

'How ... how did you ...?' she began weeping, burying her face in her hands, her manicured red fingernails pulling at her long silky hair.

'We have photographs, Mrs Rafferty,' McTurk continued, presenting as always with robotic dispassion. 'Photographs of Frank Rafferty and you kissing on the steps of your husband's caravan. And not just a peck on the cheek either.'

'Oh my God,' she wept, her respiration accelerating by the second. 'Oh ... my ... God.'

Sutherland stood up, walked calmly into the kitchen and returned with a glass of water. She grabbed it with trembling hands and began sipping. Sipping and sobbing. Silence reigned for a few minutes, as the detectives allowed the enormity of her predicament to sink in. Sutherland picked up on McTurk's subtle nod and turned on the charm as usual. The good cop, bad cop routine still had its uses at times.

'Mrs Rafferty ... can I call you Maureen?'

'Yes ... yes, I'd like that.'

'Maureen, we know you were having an affair with your brother-in-law, Frank Rafferty. We just need you to confirm it, then we can move on. Having an affair isn't a police matter. It's not a crime, Maureen. However, Frank's murder is.'

'Yes ... yes ... okay, I'll admit it,' she blubbered, brushing the tears from her cheeks. 'I have been seeing Frank, but surely you don't think it was me who ... who killed him?'

'No, we don't, Maureen,' Sutherland replied. 'We don't think you killed him, but we believe you might be able to help us find out who did.'

'Do you know who did it?' McTurk interjected.

'No,' she snapped, lifting her head in defiance as her composure did its best to return and confront the bad cop. 'No, I don't. Is that not supposed to be your job, officer?'

Finally recognising that his continued hostile style of questioning was unlikely to prove productive, McTurk changed tack and lessened the aggression in his tone.

'I know this is very awkward for you, but did your husband know? Did Dan know you were having an affair with his brother ... with Frank?'

'No, of course he didn't,' she replied, before a puzzled expression began to waft over her puffy eyes. 'At least, I don't think so.'

'You don't think so? You mean, you're not quite sure?'

'Well, yes, but ...'

'But what, Mrs Rafferty?'

'I couldn't be absolutely certain. There were ... well ... signs.'

'Signs? What signs?'

'Just ... signs. You know? We hadn't been as close recently.'

'Close? In what way, Mrs Rafferty?'

'Oh, come on, officer, do I need to spell it out for you?'

Sutherland gave another little cough, this one designed to spare both his boss's and their hostess's embarrassment. The penny dropping at last, McTurk attempted to cover his tracks.

'Oh, right, I understand. My apologies, Mrs Rafferty. But I do need to ask you one other question. Do you think the fact that you hadn't been as ... as close ... might have raised your husband's suspicions that something wasn't quite right?'

'Maybe, I really can't be sure.'

'Well, let me ask you this, then. If his suspicions had in fact been raised, would he have had any reason to link this with Frank?'

'I don't think so. But again, I really can't be sure. Frank always had a way with women. And if he liked a woman, he wasn't all that good at hiding it.'

'Did he make it obvious that he liked you, Mrs Rafferty?'

'Oh yes, he always did, ever since I started going out with Dan. But it was just a bit of silly nonsense, and there was never anything in it. Any time Frank made a suggestive remark to me, Dan would laugh it off and say, "oh, don't worry about it, that's just Frank being Frank".'

'So, when did things change? You know, from Frank being Frank, to Frank having sex with his brother's wife?'

Sutherland glared at McTurk. The bad cop had stumbled back in again wearing his industrial boots, and the timing of his return was very ill-judged.

'Boss,' he said, shaking his head. 'This is already difficult enough for Maureen.'

Suitably rebuked by his junior, McTurk apologised again, but still couldn't stop himself having another go.

'Mrs Rafferty, I'm only trying to establish if Dan might have had a motive for killing Frank.'

'Dan has done some not very nice things, officer, but never to me and never to Frank. Dan worshipped the ground that Frank walked upon. He thought the sun shone out of his backside. If you must know, Frank and I have only been ... you know, together ... for the past couple of months.'

'Can I ask where?'

Maureen Rafferty inhaled deeply, closed her eyes and shook her head, as if trying to convince herself that her dalliance with her deceased brother-in-law had only been a very bad dream.

'Twice in the Caledonian Hotel in Ayr town centre, and four or five times in Dan's caravan in Doonfoot. I had never been unfaithful to Dan in six years together, and right now I'm feeling like a bloody tramp.'

McTurk blanked her emotive comment and swiftly resisted any temptation to play marriage guidance counsellor.

'So, what if Dan really did find out about you and Frank? That might have tipped him over the edge, surely?'

'Dan would never have done anything like that. Not in a million years. And certainly not to Frank.'

'You sure about that, Mrs Rafferty?'

'Absolutely certain. And anyway, he couldn't possibly have killed Frank.'

'Why?'

'Because on the night Frank died, Dan and I were staying with our friends, Alison and George Turnbull, in their house in Aberfoyle. I'll give you their contact details and you can ask them if you like.'

The two detectives hadn't seen that one coming. Simultaneously, they whispered inaudible expletives. Maureen Rafferty scribbled down the Turnbulls' address and telephone number on a sheet of fancy notepaper and handed it over, leaving the good cop and the bad cop to thank their hostess for her assistance in such trying circumstances, and trudge out the front door with their tails wedged firmly between their legs.

For Andy McTurk in particular, what had started out as a very good morning had just turned into an unmitigated disaster. If the killer wasn't Dan Rafferty, then just who the hell was it? And worse still, they could now kiss goodbye to any hope that they might once have had of persuading Ricky Anderson to turn himself in.

McTurk's 'full Sottish' began to do cartwheels in the pit of his stomach.

66

The moment McTurk and Sutherland walked through the door of Interview Room 3, the musty atmosphere hit them.

Nodding to the uniformed duty officer who stood guard over the detainee sitting on a hard plastic chair at the small table, McTurk muttered a matter-of-fact, 'you can go now, constable'. Turning to Sutherland, his next words carried with them an expression of disgust.

'This place smells like the Ayr United dressing room in a summer heatwave. Doesn't it, Sergeant?'

'It sure does, Sir,' Sutherland nodded, turning his nose up and wafting both hands in front of his face. 'It stinks in here.'

'Do you know something, Sergeant?' the DI continued, clearly enjoying Dan Rafferty's discomfort. 'Other than eleven sweaty men sitting in their dirty shirts and socks, there's only one other thing I can think of that smells like it does in here.'

'And what's that, Sir?' asked Sutherland, playing along.

'Fear,' McTurk went on. 'Fear, Sergeant, that's what it smells like to me.'

'You mean, like a worried man, Sir?' the sergeant said. 'A really worried man?'

'Exactly, Sergeant,' McTurk beamed. 'You're learning fast, my boy. You'll go far in this job.'

Rafferty could stand the mind games no longer.

'I want to know why I'm here,' he snapped. 'And why I've been left sitting here for three-and-a-half hours. Three-and-a-half bloody hours.'

McTurk was a master at creating tension, at turning the screw, at getting a suspect to shoot his own mouth off. He ploughed on with the pretence.

'Mister Rafferty, before we begin our interview ... which for your information is being recorded ... can I offer you one little piece of advice? From bitter experience?'

'And what might that be?'

'Never wear a dark blue shirt if you think you're going to sweat. I mean, look at the state of your oxters, Mister Rafferty. Anybody would think you'd been scooting them with a garden hose. And let's face it, it's not all that warm in here today, is it? So, my guess is that DS Sutherland is spot-on. You're worried about something. What are you worried about, Mister Rafferty?'

'Nothing. I sweat easily. It's a medical condition.'

'Ah ... a medical condition? Well, that's funny, because I've got a medical condition myself. It's something to do with my sense of smell. You see, Mister Rafferty, I can smell when somebody's telling the truth and when they're talking bullshit. And right now, my nose is telling me that you're talking bullshit. You've been sitting here sweating like a pig, not because of some fabricated medical condition, but because you're worried about something. And I think I know what it is that you're worried about.'

'Nonsense.'

'Mister Rafferty, how long have you been married?'

'Six years. Why?'

'Happily married, would you say?'

'And just what the hell has that got to do with you?'

'So, will I put that down as a "no", then?'

'No ... I mean, yes.'

'Yes, put it down as a "no"?'

'No, don't put it down as a "no", put it down as a "yes". Because yes, my wife and I are happily married. Not that it's any of your bloody business.'

McTurk lit a cigarette and turned to face Sutherland.

'Show him the photographs, Sergeant.'

Sutherland tossed four black-and-white photographs onto the desk.

'Do you happen to recognise the two people in those family snaps?' the young sergeant enquired.

Rafferty didn't even bother to pick them up. He cast his eyes over them for a second or two then looked away and shook his head. His face turned pink at first, then red and finally halted its transformation when it reached beetroot. He looked as if he was fit to blow a gasket.

'Well, Mister Rafferty?' Sutherland asked again. 'Do you recognise them or not?'

'F-----g slut!' he shouted, bringing his clenched fist down onto the desk with a hefty thump.

McTurk gestured to Sutherland to stay silent. They allowed the silence to hang in the air for a good couple of minutes, by which time Rafferty was visibly trembling with rage. Sutherland then took his boss's next non-verbal cue and continued.

'Who are the two people in the photographs, Mister Rafferty?'

'Fine you know who they are,' he replied through gritted teeth. 'It's my wife ... and my brother.'

'Your wife Maureen and your brother Frank?'

'Yes.'

'Or to put it another way, your wife Maureen and your now-deceased brother Frank?'

Rafferty just glared at Sutherland. McTurk picked up the questioning again.

'I can understand why you look so angry, Mister Rafferty. But if you don't mind me saying so, you don't seem all that surprised.'

No reaction from Rafferty, only quiet simmering fury.

'Am I correct?' McTurk continued, running his forefinger over one of the photographs. 'I mean, look at this, it's as plain as day. That's your wife Maureen there, right? And that's your brother Frank beside her, isn't it? And they're kissing each other, aren't they? Believe me, Mister Rafferty, if that was my wife kissing my brother,

I'd be more than a little surprised. Mind you, I have to admit I'd be angry too, bloody raging just like you are right now. In fact, I'd probably feel like cutting his throat.'

'I didn't kill Frank!' Rafferty shouted. 'I'm glad the bastard's dead, but I didn't do it.'

'I never said you did, Mister Rafferty. Did you know your wife was having an affair with your brother?'

'I had my suspicions.'

'Suspicions? Based on what?'

'The way she's been behaving towards me recently. She's been a bit ... well ... distant.'

'Distant? In what way?'

'Do I need to bloody spell it out?'

'No, you don't. However, I would have thought that a man of your means ... a man with your connections, shall we say ... would have been able to find out if his suspicions were correct.'

'I could have, if I wanted to. But I just didn't want to know. I actually love my wife, if you can bring yourself to believe that.'

'And your brother? Do you ... did you ... love him too?'

'I don't want to talk about that. About him.'

'Mister Rafferty, where were you on the evening of Thursday the thirteenth of September between late-morning and early evening?'

'I can't remember.'

'I suggest you try.'

'That would be a week past on Thursday, right? The day that Frank ...?'

'Yes, the day Frank was killed.'

'That's easy. Maureen and I were staying with friends in Aberfoyle. We were there from the Wednesday till the Friday.'

'What are your friends' names?'

'George and Alison. George and I were playing golf on the Friday afternoon, because that's when I got the message that Frank was dead.'

'Their surname, please?'

'Turnbull. George and Alison Turnbull. She's Alison Goldie to her own name. You can check with Aberfoyle Golf Club, because George had to sign me in as a visitor.'

McTurk's expressionless face totally belied the sheer exasperation he felt in his gut. The knowing glance from Sutherland didn't help either. However, the knock on the door did. It gave him the excuse he needed to wander nonchalantly out of the interview room and storm along the corridor cursing like a trooper with a serious dose of Tourette's syndrome.

The welcome intruder went by the name of Nigel Cooper, the chief forensic scientist for Southwest Scotland Police, and he was carrying a light-blue folder under his arm. Cooper wouldn't have needed to be all that good at his job to conclude forensically that McTurk was not in a particularly playful mood, but he just so happened to be the best in the business. He followed the DI into his office without saying a word. Sutherland joined them, leaving Rafferty again in the interview room with the duty officer.

'Give me good news, Nigel,' the DI sighed. 'God knows, I could do with some.'

'The deceased, one Mister Francis Rafferty, was drugged before he was killed, Andy,' Cooper announced. 'We found significant levels of Rohypnol in his blood. It's a relatively new drug, recently developed as a safer alternative to Barbiturates. Biochemical name, Flunitrazepam, which is a Benzodiazopine, not dissimilar to Valium.'

'Can you give me that in English, Nigel?' McTurk grunted. 'My head's bursting.'

'Basically, it's a very modern drug,' said Cooper. 'And a very effective one at that. It can be administered either intravenously or orally. Rafferty had been drinking. Gin and tonic, we believe. The killer probably slipped it into his drink.'

'What would the drug do to him?' McTurk asked.

'Render him catatonic. He would be fully conscious, but his limbs would be temporarily paralysed and he'd be totally unable to move. The tabloids are already branding Rohypnol as the "date rape" drug. Slip a pill into the poor lassie's fizzy wine and she's all yours until she wakes up again with her knickers at her ankles.'

'Jesus Christ, what's the world coming to? Nigel, tell me something. As you know, we found Rafferty's body sitting up straight as a poker on his settee, with his throat cut. Could the killer have slipped him the mickey, then talked to him for a bit?'

'Absolutely. He could have sat there beside the poor guy, reciting *War and Peace* and taken as long as he liked to describe what was about to happen to him before he did it.'

'Now, that's what I call someone with a grudge. He pays his big brother a visit in the caravan, pops a pill into his glass when he's away taking a leak, sits there calling him all the bastards of the day for screwing his wife and describes what he's going to do to him, then cuts his throat. Yes or no, Nigel?'

'Eminently possible.'

'Any joy with the second set of fingerprints on the knife? Other than the boy Anderson's, I mean?'

'Very smudged, no positive ID. But there's one thing I can tell you for sure.'

'And what's that?'

'They don't belong to Dan Rafferty.'

The morning that had started so well had now completely fallen off a cliff.

67

As the black Ford Corsair sped through the sleepy little village of Maidens, Robert McDade rolled down the front passenger-side window and flicked what remained of his latest fag onto the grass verge.

'I could get used to this, boys,' he announced, expelling a thick stream of nicotine-infested exhaust fumes from his lungs before replacing them with a mighty gulp of salty air. 'Two trips to the seashore in as many days. Better than a sharp stick up your arse.'

Ralph Baxter nodded in accord from behind the steering wheel, his long blond locks blowing in the breeze like celebratory bunting from the flagpole at a summer fete. Zander McGinn just grunted, as he lay sprawled across the full length of the rear seat with his arms folded across his impressive beer-belly. McGinn's grunts often conveyed much more information than his rare, expletive-rich sentences. This was a particularly sophisticated grunt, though, one which implored McDade to button it so that he could doze in peace until they reached their destination.

McDade completely blanked his kindred spirit's wordless plea for tranquillity.

'Say Zander, Dan the Man was decidedly pissed off with us, am I right? I mean, what were we supposed to do down here in Girvan yesterday? Hang about all bloody day and night till the Anderson boy eventually showed up? No chance. I wasn't missing my Friday night darts match, not for Dan Rafferty and not for anybody. He can go and screw himself.'

Snoring reverberated from the back seat. A deep, rhythmic snoring, not unlike a clapped-out motorbike engine gasping for its very last breath.

'For f—k's sake, Zander, you listening to me, or what? Wake up, we're nearly there and we need to get our act together. This is a hit today, man. An assassination. Not grabbing some skinny smack-heid who owes us money and giving him a wee slap.'

'Right, Rab,' came the mumbled reply, as McGinn hauled his great hulk up into a sitting position. 'I'm listening.'

'You all remember the drill, then, boys?' McDade continued. 'Listen up and let's go through it again. Anderson will be at his work down at the harbour, and we know what he looks like, so we case the joint first then move in whenever he appears. And no really heavy stuff, Zander, because the cops will be all over the place and that dick of a Harbour Master is well protected. We just wait till Anderson shows up, then we clatter the wee bastard, feed him with the chloroform and bundle him into the car. After that, it's straight out of town and up into the hills where the only witnesses will be the sheep. And you can chat them up, Ralphie-boy, while we get to work on the boy. Dan wants us to take as many photographs as possible while we're doing the business, so that he can send them to the boy's mother. You got the Polaroid camera ready, Zander?'

'Aye, Rab,' McGinn replied, his latest grunt radiating full approval. 'All loaded up.'

'You got all that, Ralphie-boy?' McDade enquired of his youthful chauffeur, whose facial hue had now completed the journey from rosy to ashen.

'Okay, Rab,' Baxter replied, gulping deeply as he drove past the salubrious Turnberry Hotel. 'If that's what Dan wants.'

'That's exactly what Dan wants,' McDade confirmed. 'And what Dan wants, Dan gets, because Frank is history. Dan's our new boss now, like it or bloody lump it.'

Silence descended once more. The bluebottle buzzing around the car windows might have been forgiven for thinking that the three hoods were experiencing a rare moment of compassion for the deceased Frank Rafferty. McGinn soon put paid to that thought when he smacked the unsuspecting beast with the back of his hand.

'Aye, you're right, Rab,' McGinn opined. 'Frank's history, and Dan's now the godfather. And we're all just going to have to get used to it.'

Completely oblivious to the fact that the same Dan Rafferty was now sitting sweating in a police interview room undergoing intense interrogation, McGinn began pulling the wings off the deceased bluebottle while McDade lit up his umpteenth fag of the morning.

The only residual buzzing that remained in the toxic air was that of eager anticipation as the car zipped ever closer to the quaint little harbour town of Girvan.

68

Charlie Reynolds arrived at his destination at precisely 12.40 p.m., a full twenty minutes before his ETA. This was one meeting for which he was determined not to be late, young Iona McNish's words still ringing in his ears.

'Ricky will meet you at one o'clock. And if you're not there by five-past, he'll be gone.'

Reynolds parked his Ford Cortina half-way down Girvan's Dalrymple Street. He had time to kill, so he decided to take a stroll down memory lane and attempt to resurrect a bit of welcome childhood nostalgia.

First up was the harbour town's ever-popular artificial lake, where an armada of little motorised boats lay tethered to their housings, awaiting the latest influx of tourists who, given that this was now late-September, would be a long time coming. How vividly Reynolds remembered the excitement of sitting at the wheel beside his mum and dad, both now long gone, and his elder sister Christine, marvelling at the putt-putt-putt of the engine as the boat zipped around the contours of the lake, the reek of petrol tickling his nostrils and making him feel strangely grown-up. And, of course, the heart-crushing disappointment when the traditional 'come in number seven, your time's up' call got bellowed out by the officious little guy sitting in the wooden hut puffing on his pipe.

Next, Reynolds took a stroll along the length of the harbour and watched a succession of fishing boats pull in and push out as they offloaded their catches and set sail in search of piscatorial replenishment. Making his way back up from the harbour in the direction of Knockcushan Street, Reynolds could never have known that he had just retraced his young fugitive friend Ricky Anderson's very recent steps.

Yes, Girvan certainly held some striking recollections for Charlie

Reynolds, most of which had been very happy indeed. Sadly, though, not all. Filed away in his more contemporary memory banks, as a then wide-eyed and bushy-tailed detective sergeant, was a particularly gruesome multiple murder in the town several years back, one which had seen an escaped convict run amok in the town centre with a loaded shotgun, resulting in the violent deaths of two innocent men and one heavily-pregnant young woman from the womb of whom doctors had then attempted but failed to save her unborn baby daughter. He prayed silently that his imminent meeting with Ricky would transpire to be one with a considerably happier ending.

Reynolds reached his rendezvous location at 12.58 p.m. precisely, the big clock on the face of the tower confirming a rare moment of punctuality. He certainly didn't want to be late, but he didn't want to be too early either, because that might signal to Ricky that he was overly keen to pin him down and hence inadvertently scare him off. An ancient court and jail from as far back as the thirteenth century, the Stumpy Tower had always been a central landmark in Girvan town centre. Better known locally as 'Auld Stumpy', its name was derived from the Gaelic, *Oliadh Stiom Paidh*, meaning 'Great Circle of Justice', and even King Robert the Bruce himself was said to have held court in the tower. The irony of the meeting place wasn't lost on the big detective. Ricky was hell-bent on clearing his name and he had now entrusted his liberty in Reynolds, whose job it was to see to it that justice would be done.

The tower clock struck one, signalling that it was now showtime. Trying to look like a tourist taking in the architectural splendours of the ancient courthouse, Reynolds surveyed the scene. Knockcushan Street was a veritable hive of activity, Saturday afternoons invariably attracting shoppers in their droves, so Reynolds quickly surmised that his chances of spotting Ricky among the crowds were considerably less than Ricky's of spotting him.

By the time one o'clock had become five-past, Reynolds was beginning to feel a bit irritated. If punctuality was good for the goose, then it was good for the gosling too. By ten-past-one, the big cop's patience had all but run out, and by quarter-past it had completely expired. He muttered a few oaths under his breath and left without looking around any further. If Ricky wanted the meeting to take place, then it was entirely up to him. Furthermore, he knew what Reynolds looked like, but Reynolds no longer knew exactly how Ricky might present with whatever change of image he had fashioned since they last met. Ricky would have to find Reynolds, not the other way around.

Passing one of Girvan's many ice-cream parlours, Reynolds stopped to look at the range of confectionery adorning the window. It readily reminded him of his younger days when the sun shone from dawn till dusk and his eyes were considerably larger than his stomach. Huge red lollipops on tiny sticks, countless stalks of 'Girvan rock' of all shapes and sizes, ice-cream receptacles galore from cornets to wafers to 'oysters' and even plastic tubs. You name them, and the assorted sweeties were cluttering the big bay window. Nostalgia had frozen Reynolds to the spot.

'Don't turn around, just keep walking.'

Hearing the familiar voice, Reynolds fought the temptation to do the polar opposite. He wasn't accustomed to taking orders from suspected criminals, but this was no time for misplaced dignity. So, he did what he was told and headed on down Dalrymple Street, deeply conscious that other footsteps were now following his own so closely behind that the pair of them could have danced the Gay Gordons.

'My car's parked just along ...' Reynolds began.

Ricky cut him off in mid-sentence.

'I know where it is. Don't say anything, just keep walking till you get to it, then open the door and get in.'

Reynolds didn't know whether to be annoyed or amused by the young man's brash cockiness. He chose the latter and grinned in resignation. On reaching the Cortina, he took the key out of his trouser pocket, unlocked the driver's door and climbed in. Pulling it closed it behind him, he leaned across and threw open the front passenger's door. Ricky had a quick look around, slipped into the seat and slammed the door shut.

Reynolds turned and gave him a quick once-over.

'Hello, Ricky,' he said. 'Long time, no see. What happened to the gorgeous hairdo, then?'

'Just drive.'

Reynolds turned on the ignition and looked at him again, eyebrows rising in synch with his amusement.

'Where are we going, Ricky? Give me a clue.'

'Head south out of town, towards Ballantrae.'

Reynolds again did as he was told. Ricky had agreed of his

own accord to come out of hiding and meet him, so the least he could do was play along. The Cortina quickly gathered speed as it zipped past the 'Girvan Thanks You for Driving Carefully' sign. He immediately got down to business.

'Your mum and your fiancée are both missing you. They're worried sick.'

'They'll see me soon enough. But only once this mess has been cleared up. In the meantime, you can tell them you've met me and I'm fine.'

'Aye, you're probably right. I wouldn't go home either with a haircut like that. Did your barber lose his bifocals?'

'Very funny, Charlie. Is my mum okay? Is she recovering? Still staying with you?'

'Yes, yes and yes. She's doing really well, Ricky. Still a bit sore, and the dentist is spending more time with her than I am, but she'll get there.'

'And how's Iona?'

'She's fine, Ricky, absolutely fine. She's a very strong young lady, but she's missing you badly. They both are.'

'Same answer, Charlie. They'll see me when we get this mess all cleared up. Who killed Rafferty?'

'Well, the official line is that you did. After all, you were definitely at the crime scene, because you very helpfully left your fingerprints all over the bloody place. On the knife, on the back of the settee, on the handle of the caravan door. It's a wonder you didn't pour yourself a beer while you were there. And, of course, to convince any remaining sceptics of your guilt, you immediately went on the run, and you're still on the run.'

'And the unofficial line?'

'Dan Rafferty, Frank's brother.'

'Rafferty's own brother? Good God. I thought they were joined at the hip?'

'They were. At least until Frank started screwing Dan's wife, that is. And in the same caravan that he let his beloved brother use to lie low from the cops.'

'You're kidding, man?'

'Nope.'

'Nice family, eh? Was she the blonde woman in the photographs that Gerry McGhee took?"

'Yes, that was Maureen Rafferty.'

'So, what happens next then, detective?'

'Several things. There was another set of prints on the murder weapon and we really need them to match Dan Rafferty's own. We also need him to fail to provide an alibi for his whereabouts around the time of Frank's murder. Then, ideally, we need him to cough his guts up and confess.'

'And when will we know?'

'Any time now, Ricky. Andy McTurk and Sandy Sutherland will be interviewing both Dan and Maureen Rafferty as we speak. Sutherland is a young detective sergeant and he's as sharp as a tack. Well taught by Andy, who is an old fox. The forensics will be looking at Dan's prints right now. Andy is going to radio in when he knows the score. In fact, I was hoping he would already have called me by this time.'

'That would be a good result.'

'It certainly would. Then it would just be a matter of me driving you straight home to the two women in your life. Right, Ricky?'

'We'll see. Pull in over there, beside that old tractor.'

By this time, Ricky's dogmatic behaviour was beginning to grate on Reynolds, but he decided to keep biting his lip. After all, he now had Ricky in the car, and one radio message was all he needed to extricate the young fugitive from the long arm of the law. And, of course, from the unthinkable retributions of the Nutter Squad.

Reynolds drew his Cortina to a halt behind the stationary tractor and switched the engine off.

'You want to tell me where you've been for the past week, then?'

'A magical mystery tour of Ayrshire and Galloway,' Ricky replied, clearly intent on keeping the details to himself. 'Ended up here in Girvan.'

'Girvan? Why Girvan, of all places?'

'Why not? It's got a lovely beach.'

'Have you got a place to stay? Money for food, that kind of thing?'

'Met a guy. He gave me a wee job, good money. He also gave me a bed.'

'So, he's no idea who you are, then?'

'Yes, he knows. Full story, all the gory details. The lot.'

'Why has he not shopped you to the cops, then?'

'Because he likes me, and he's got other reasons. He also knows I didn't do it. And you know that as well, Charlie.'

'I do know that, Ricky, and Andy does too. But he's got a job to do. Track you down and bring you in for questioning, establish your innocence, then nail whoever did it. But trust me, he knows I'm trying to reel you in. He's not looking too hard.'

'That all sounds fine, but it's the reeling-in bit I don't like. If I let you do it and then for some reason your mate doesn't manage to pin the murder on Dan Rafferty, it'll be my arse on the line, not yours, Charlie. So, if it's all the same to you, I'll take my chances on the run.'

'And what if I don't let you? I could just thump you right now and handcuff you to the door handle.'

'You could try.'

Reynolds laughed and shook his head. Ricky laughed too. It was the first time he had laughed in over a week. A garish crackle disturbed the unlikely mirth. It was coming from Reynolds's police radio handset.

'DI Reynolds?' he said.

'Bad news, Charlie,' came the reply. 'And times two. First, Dan Rafferty claims he was in Aberfoyle at the time of his brother's murder, and so too does his wife, Maureen. Two other reliable witnesses, everything checks out. He's got the perfect alibi.'

'And second?'

'The other set of prints on the murder weapon weren't his.'

'For f--k's sake,' Reynolds cursed, grabbing the steering wheel in disgust. 'I don't believe it.'

'Me, neither,' McTurk replied. 'How did you get on in your phone call with young Anderson last night? Do you think he'll let you bring him in?'

'No chance, Andy,' Reynolds replied, turning to face Ricky. 'Especially now, after what you've just told me. I've got no bargaining chips left. If we could have pinned the murder on Dan Rafferty, then I think I could have talked him into meeting me, and maybe letting me bring him home. But not now, no chance.'

'Aye, I know, Charlie, it's a real bastard. But if Rafferty didn't do it then he didn't do it, which means that someone else did. Have you made any arrangements to speak to Ricky again on the phone?'

'Well, kind of.'

'How do you mean.'

'He told me to go to the same telephone box at the same time tomorrow night. He said he might call, but if he decided not to, then our cosy little chats were history. He's pissing me off, Andy, but I've got no alternative other than to keep dancing to his tune. There's far too much at stake here.'

'Well, you're not going to like this, but I now have to step up the search. Anderson has just reverted again to being number-one suspect.'

'I know, Andy, I had managed to work that all out by myself.'

Ricky made a grab for the door handle, but Reynolds held up his left hand, beseeching him to stay put. Ricky decided to give him the benefit of the doubt. At least, for now.

'Charlie,' McTurk continued over the radio waves, 'I know it's a difficult one for you, but did the lad happen to let anything slip that might give us a clue to his whereabouts? Anything at all? And remember, it's not just us who are after him. The Nutter Squad could get to him before we do. Your own words, pal.'

'Aye, Andy, I know.'

'Well?'

'Of course, he didn't tell me where he was.'

'Nothing? Come on, man, you're the best in the business at picking up the scraps and turning them into gold dust. We've got to get young Anderson off the streets. It's for his own good, Charlie.'

Reynolds looked Ricky straight in the eye and put his forefinger over his lips.

'There was one thing that I did pick up on.'

'And what was that? Come on, Charlie, you need to trust me to handle this.'

'He might not be down by the seaside anymore. Just before he hung up on me, I heard something from what sounded like a fairly distant tannoy system. I couldn't really make out what it said, but I thought I heard the word "thirteen".'

'You mean, like a railway station?'

'Could have been, but I can't be certain.'

'Well, if it was, there's only one station in the whole country with thirteen platforms. Glasgow Central.'

'That's what I was thinking too, Andy.'

'So, even assuming that he had actually been in the Girvan area in the first place, it would have been fairly easy for him to get back to the big smoke, wouldn't it? Train from Girvan to Ayr, then Ayr to Glasgow Central. Very risky though, with our uniforms out in force looking for him. You don't think he'd have been daft enough to go back home to his flat in Highburgh Road, do you?'

'I very much doubt it, but it's the obvious place to start. I gather he's made a lot of friends in Glasgow. You could try looking a few of them up.'

'Okay, I'll go back to Smokin' Joe and ask him if he'll approve me switching the main focus of the search to the city centre.'

'Probably wise, Andy. I'll let you know if Ricky changes his mind about meeting me in the flesh. Speak soon, over.'

'Oh Charlie, and one more thing. Our new best pal, Gerry McGhee, just phoned me because he couldn't get hold of you at home. The hotshot investigative journalist, remember?'

'Of course, I remember. What did he want?'

'He's still working on his big exclusive, and he wanted to tell me where the Nutter Squad have been hanging around over the past couple of days.'

'Where?'

'Girvan. It seems that everybody and their granny are heading to Girvan these days. It's more popular than Benidorm.'

Reynolds took a sharp intake of breath before responding. He hoped that the brief pause had gone unnoticed, but he knew McTurk could detect even the slightest wobble in a speech pattern from outer space.

'Well,' he hit back, demonstrating commendable contrived confidence. 'It's just as well Ricky's back in Glasgow, then, isn't it? Over.'

'Aye, it is,' McTurk replied. 'It certainly is. Over and out.'

Ricky just stared at Reynolds. Only one word came out.

'Why?'

'Because I know you didn't do it, Ricky,' Reynolds replied. 'And because Iona and your mum love you ... and because I love your mum.'

'Well,' said Ricky, 'you'd better bloody look after her, or you'll have me to answer to.'

'I will, Ricky,' Reynolds replied. 'And that's a promise. But a couple of real bad guys are now hot on your heels, so I need to look after you first. Either that, or I'll have two very scary women to answer to.'

69

Edwin Monk was in one of his self-proclaimed 'reflective moods'. Only this time his reflections were on a somewhat less bumptious scale.

Certainly different from those he used to boast about to his assorted minions, in a valiant attempt to convey the impression that he was one of the world's great thinkers. Perhaps less of a Plato or a Socrates to his own mind, Monk often fantasised that he had been descended from the great man himself, Karl Marx, upon whose all-embracing leftie philosophies his own superb political career had been founded.

'Is Councillor Monk available?' David McPherson, his Director of Planning would traditionally enquire at the door of his office in the corridors of power.

'I'm afraid not, Mr McPherson,' Carol McCreadie, the Chairman's personal secretary would reply, privately desperate to wink at him and split her sides laughing, but terrified to do so. 'He's having a morning of reflection.'

However, that was then, and this was now. Today, the self-same Edwin Monk, now stripped of his 'councillor' title, retained no more delusions of grandeur. To say that his standing in the public eye had received a blow would be akin to describing Jack the Ripper as a bit of a rascal.

As he looked all around his study, the first thought that hit him was its pretentiousness. The oak table and matching chairs at which he had never once done a minute's proper work. The ornate fireplace that hadn't seen a lump of coal since dinosaurs walked the earth. The grand antique bookcase with its eight shelves of leather-bound reference books, not one of which he had ever lifted out of position, far less attempted to read. The high-backed swivel chair upon which his hefty backside and steadily widening middle-age spread now slumped uncomfortably, as he reflected that all those physical pretentions and many more were simply a microcosm of what had now become of his own pathetic life. A music hall act, nothing more and nothing less, and one which would have done Ayr's Gaiety Theatre proud.

As he sat there drawing anxiously on his fifth consecutive cigarette since the loyal Kathleen had brought him in a cafetiere of his favourite Columbian coffee just over an hour ago, Monk's dominating thought was of his recent spectacular fall from grace, one that had been delivered so cruelly and so publicly. Without doubt one of the most influential elected members in the vast Southwest Scotland Council until only a few weeks ago, he had seen his chairmanship of the council's Planning Committee being ripped from his grasp, his hitherto lifelong membership of the Labour Party withdrawn amid a blaze of toxic publicity, and Southwest Scotland Police press a raft of criminal charges against him, the consequence of which was almost certain to see him being locked up in Barlinnie or some other high security prison for three years at least. There in the infamous Bar-L, he reflected, Columbian coffee would probably not be on the menu. And that was just the part that the general public would see. What they could never have known, though, was the sheer extent of the influence of Rafferty Construction in the car crash that was his own downwardly spiralling life. Okay, Frank Rafferty was now dead and out of the picture, but he still cast a giant shadow. Three of them, in fact, and in completely different guises.

First, there was his younger brother Dan, who at last had seen his dream of being crowned the business empire's head honcho come true, and who although seemingly not as heartless or vicious as his elder sibling, was certainly no shrinking violet either. Nor was he averse to a bit of the heavy stuff when required, as Monk's recent rendezvous with him in some dark and dingy garage had demonstrated only too terrifyingly.

Next, there was the Nutter Squad, and in particular those two brutal brain-dead thugs, McDade and McGinn, who just lived for any excuse to torture, maim or even assassinate whichever poor misguided soul was next on the Rafferty hitlist, and whose very existence simply terrified Monk to the extent of inducing recurring nightmares of particularly gruesome proportions.

Finally, there was the big stitch-up. The litany of barefaced lies that Monk had agreed, under extreme pressure, to tell the police for fear of his own sad little life, to frame Richard Anderson for murder. Sure, young Anderson had been the prime mover-and-shaker in exposing Monk and Frank Rafferty for what they really were, a pair of manipulative cheats at best and heartless extortionists at worst, but Anderson was only a mere boy, an innocent lad who would have done anything to protect his vulnerable mother. And, of course, the poor woman herself had earlier been seriously wronged by Monk, when on Rafferty's instructions, his Appeals Panel had thrown out her entirely laudable claim for financial assistance, after which she had been beaten half to death by that callous lunatic, Mad Rab McDade.

Worse still, Monk had then fitted Anderson up for a murder he didn't commit, and now he couldn't even enjoy the luxury of the slightest shadow of doubt that the boy actually could have done it. No, Monk knew with one-hundred-percent certainty that young Anderson had absolutely nothing to do with Frank Rafferty's murder. And he knew it because the memory of that ill-fated Thursday would never, ever leave him. As he sat in his study agonising over his desperate predicament, the sequence of that terrible evening's events came flooding back once more in three-dimensional technicolour to haunt him like some faceless ghostly demon.

So vividly clear were his recollections, that he began reliving the evening all over again ...

The phone call from Frank Rafferty demanding that Monk meet him in his brother Dan's caravan. 'Be there at half-seven,' Rafferty had barked down the line. 'And bring the letters with you,' he had demanded, the ones from the four competing building contractors who had submitted to the chairman - under highly confidential cover, of course – their separate competitive tenders for the new housing development in the Ayrshire village of Monkton. The car journey down to Doonfoot, when in an anxiety-induced lapse of concentration, Monk had very nearly mown down an elderly lady as she stepped off the pavement onto a zebra-crossing. His frantic efforts to find the location of Dan Rafferty's caravan in time for the witching hour of seven-thirty and thence to avoid incurring big brother Frank's wrath for being late. The heart-stopping moment when he walked up the steps of the caravan, chest pounding like the mighty engine of a Ferrari 312B racing car, to be greeted by that cold, menacing grin. The unbearably tense discussion that followed – if it could even have been called a discussion – as Rafferty sat sipping his latest gin-and-tonic and smoking a Cuban cigar, thumbing his way through the four competing contractors' costings in order to establish the minimum capital sum that would secure the building contract for Rafferty Construction.

However, those had only been the necessary preliminaries to the main event of the evening, the curtain-raiser for the opportunity which then presented itself when Rafferty decided to go and take a leak. That was the moment Monk got his big chance. His chance to drop the little white pill into the crystal glass of G & T that sat fizzing like his nemesis's infamous wrath on the coffee table. Rohypnol it was called, a relatively new drug imported from the United States, one single pill of which Monk's pharmacist cousin Ben Findlay had reluctantly given him under the pretext of sexual experimentation with the allegedly willing Kathleen. Monk shuddered at his vivid recollection of hearing the toilet flush, and since the pill had still not quite dissolved, swirling the glass to help it on its way and managing to spill a few drops on the table, whereupon Rafferty on his return had then casually mopped them up with a paper tissue before resuming his fascination with the forbidden documents.

The first time Monk realised the enormity of the events which he had set in motion was when Rafferty took his next big slug from the glass. Over the hatch it went with no visible reaction from its consumer. Another mouthful was soon followed by another, by which time Rafferty had started slurring his words like a seasoned wino. It wasn't so much the drug's dramatic effect which surprised Monk, more its swiftness of action. Less than ten minutes later, Rafferty was sitting like a veritable zombie, eyes staring without focus and pupils fully dilated. The glass slipped from his fingers and landed on his lap, what was left of its contents pouring over his trousers. Monk picked it up and sat it back down on the coffee table.

Inhaling deeply, he found his voice again. It was trembling.

'Frank?' he asked. 'Frank ... are you ... are you all right?'

Nothing, not a word. Rafferty sat there on the settee like a lifeless mannequin, hearing everything, saying nothing. It was precisely the effect that Ben had said it would induce in the luckless Kathleen when she was supposed to have been ravished like never before, fully aware of everything that was happening to her but totally defenceless to do anything about it. Catatonia, Ben had called the condition, temporary of course, but utterly overpowering.

'Frank ... Frank, can you hear me?'

Silence. Total silence, except for deep breathing from a diaphragm that rose and fell so rhythmically that it could have been on life support. Slowly but surely, Monk's initial dread of his masterplan going wrong began to give way to a sense of wicked excitement. He rose to his feet, lifted the gin glass from the table, took it over to the sink and washed it out thoroughly, drying it with

263

a tea-towel. He then walked back over to where Rafferty still sat corpse-like and pulled his chair around to face him head-on. This was the moment he had been waiting for and he was going to enjoy it. The old familiar feeling of all-embracing power had suddenly returned from its enforced hibernation to reignite Monk's legendary megalomania.

'Frank, I know you can hear me. And for once you are going to listen to *me*. Now, won't that be something?'

He paused and watched. No response.

'I've given you a drug called Rohypnol. I put it into your drink when you were at the toilet. It's a really interesting drug, Frank. It induces a medical condition called Catatonia. As you will already be aware, it leaves you completely awake and fully aware. You are still able to see, hear, feel, smell and taste, but ... and this is the interesting bit ... you are now completely paralysed. Totally unable to move, Frank.'

Another pause. Still no response.

'Let me give you an example, Frank. If I wanted, I could open that drawer over there, take out a kitchen knife and stick it straight in your eye, and there is nothing you could do about it, absolutely nothing. Sure, you would feel it ... oh, yes ... you would feel the pain, the excruciating agony of me gouging out your eyeball ... but there is nothing you could do, not a thing. Until you eventually came out of your catatonic state, that is. But that won't be for another hour or so. Maybe even longer.'

Yet another pause. Monk stared into Rafferty's eyes and started sniggering. Soon, the sniggering had progressed to hysterical laughter. He rebuked himself, stood back up and wandered over to the kitchen area of the caravan and opened the top drawer. Grinning like a feral cat with a petrified fieldmouse in its claws, he took out a long-bladed kitchen knife and returned again to his chair. For the merest instant, he thought he detected fear in Rafferty's eyes. This sure was turning out to be a great evening down by the seaside.

'We're going to have a little chat, Frank,' he smiled. 'Just you and me. Well, when I say "chat", I'll be the one doing the chatting. And since you can't speak, you'll be the one doing the listening. Is that okay? Just shake your head or say no if you don't want me to continue, and I promise I'll stop right away.'

Monk leaned forward and gave Rafferty a quizzical stare. He picked the kitchen knife up from the table and began waving it around like an orchestral maestro's baton.

'Well, Frank, since you didn't shake your head or say no, I guess I'll have to assume you're happy to proceed.'

With Rafferty still sitting there on the settee bolt upright and motionless, Monk found himself likening the scene to his visit to the Madame Tussaud's wax museum in London a few years back, when to Kathleen's and his own amusement he had squared up to a very lifelike model of former British prime minister, Harold Macmillan, and told him in no uncertain terms what he thought of his Tory policies, safe in the knowledge that there would be no demeaning response. Now, for the first time in his illicit ten-year relationship with Rafferty, Monk felt safe. Safe from verbal humiliation, safe from public ridicule, safe from physical and emotional harm.

'You and I go back a long way, Frank,' Monk continued. 'In the time we've known each other, we've done a lot of business. It all started out well, didn't it? Do you remember our first deal, Frank?'

Another pause. The captor grinned at his dumbstruck captive.

'Well, let me refresh your memory. It was the old burnt-out hotel on the outskirts of Stevenston, wasn't it? The Mill Inn, it was called. You bought the hotel and the land, and after you approached me, I managed to get my committee to approve the demolition of the hotel and to grant planning permission for your six detached houses, despite all the hostile local opposition. But that was when I made my first mistake, Frank, because when we were leaving the committee room you stuffed a brown envelope into my suit jacket pocket, remember? I didn't even look at it until I got home that night. When I opened it, there was money inside. A lot of money, for me anyway. Two-hundred pounds, in fact. I knew there and then that I shouldn't have taken it, but I did. I should have reported the matter to the council's Chief Executive. He would then have reported it to the police and that would have been the end of it. But I didn't, I took the money instead. And I took it because Kathleen had just lost her job and we needed it. I promised myself that it would be the first and last time I would accept any of your gifts. And I meant it, Frank ... I really, honestly meant it.'

Monk suddenly shot to his feet. Grasping the handle of the knife in his fist, he pressed the blade against Rafferty's stomach. He tried to summon the strength to ram it home, right up to the hilt, but no strength came. His boyish grin had deserted him and his face had become as expressionless as the one sitting opposite. Finally, the tears came. His voice began shaking, and coherent diction got overtaken by increasingly furious words tumbling from bone-dry lips.

'But you wouldn't leave it, Frank,' Monk sobbed. 'You just wouldn't let me go, would you? You threatened to tell my colleagues and grass me into the cops if I didn't keep going with … with the cheating … and the lies … and the corruption. And when the stakes got higher, when six houses became twenty, then fifty and then a hundred … when harbours and golf courses and even hospitals became real estate for you, Frank … the envelopes in my pocket got bigger and fatter. And by the time I realised what was really happening, I was trapped … trapped in this web of lies and deceit and violence … it was too late, just too late.'

Still the knife wouldn't budge. It was as if some invisible force was holding onto Monk's arm. He was falling at the last hurdle and he knew it. By then, the tears were almost blinding him.

'Keep going, you told me, Frank, and the payoffs will follow. And so too will the flash cars and the foreign junkets and even the fancy new houses. But stop, and you're a dead man walking. That's what you said, Frank … dead man walking. I knew I only had two choices. One … do what you said and the money would keep pouring in. Two … say "no more, Frank" and the big pantomime would be over. But so too would my political career … and you would then set those two thugs on me … that Mad Rab and the other brute, McGinn. Hobson's choice, Frank, Hobson's choice. That's what you gave me.'

Monk gripped the knife handle with every ounce of strength he could muster. However, try as he might, he just couldn't bring himself to skewer Rafferty's vital organs. As anguish turned to anger, the tears began to dry and the diction hardened.

'It all … it all had to come out sometime … and it did. My life is now in ruins, and all because of you, Frank. You and your … your shady deals … and your bribes … and your hooligans. All in ruins.'

By then trembling with rage, Monk pulled the knife away and shuffled his way around to the back of the settee. He grabbed a handful of Rafferty's long greasy hair and yanked his head back so that his lifeless eyes faced the ceiling. He then placed the blade underneath the left side of his victim's chin, and with one mighty pull, drew it all the way to the right.

It was the horrifically graphic memory of the huge spray of

bright-red blood that finally snapped Monk out of his daydream. Suddenly, he was back in the real world. As he now sat in his study saturated in sweat and paralysed by dread, the tragic sequence of events on that fateful Thursday evening had just come flooding back to haunt him like some ghoulish gothic nightmare, and now those awful images had to be thrust back into their cage like a petrified stray mongrel ensnared by an over-zealous dog warden.

However, for Monk there was one huge consolation amid all the carnage that now defined his life, and that was this. The police might well have enough evidence to lock him away for a couple of years on charges of misappropriation of public funds, but they would never suspect him of being anywhere near that caravan on the night of Frank Rafferty's murder, and for one very good reason. The cops now knew who the real killer was.

And as far as they were concerned, the real killer was Ricky Anderson.

70

'Hey Zander, see that blue Cortina over there? Is that not big Reynolds's car? Remember you dropped me off in the police station car park to stick Frank's message on his windscreen the night I duffed up the Anderson lassie?'

Zander McGinn peered at the car from the rear passenger's seat, before responding.

'Aye, Rab,' he replied, his expression more of perplexity than certainty. 'It could be, but there's a lot of blue Ford Cortinas on the roads these days.'

'There's only one with that number plate, though,' McDade muttered in response. 'That's the one Frank gave me that night.'

'You sure?'

'Positive. That car belongs to Reynolds.'

'So, what's he doing down here in Girvan, then?'

'How the hell should I know, Zander? Unless ... unless he knows where the Anderson boy is as well. Maybe he's come to take him home to his wee mammy.'

'That would not please Dan. Not one little bit.'

'Nor me. I'm looking forward to meeting him myself.'

'Me too, Rab. Then, that must be Reynolds sitting there in the driver's seat?'

'I don't know, impossible to tell from this side. If it's an unmarked police car, it could either be him or some other cop driving it, I suppose.'

'You want me to go and take a look?'

'Aye, that would be really clever, Zander. He'd clock your big ugly mug the minute he saw you. I mean, look at you. You don't exactly mingle with the crowd, do you?'

'Well, you go yourself, then.'

'What, you don't think he'd recognise me as well? I didn't exactly fall out of Burton's shop window either, did I? He's locked us both up more times than we've had pints of heavy. If he clocks us, he'll have us hauled in again just for the hell of it.'

McDade tapped Ralph Baxter on the shoulder as the young lad sat quietly behind the security of his steering wheel.

'What about you getting out and having a week look, Ralphie-boy? Does Reynolds know what you look like?'

'I've no idea, but that's not the problem.'

'So, what is the problem, then?'

'I don't know what he looks like, Rab.'

'Jesus Christ. We're like the Three Stooges, just sitting here scratching our arses. Well, one of us is going to have to try and get a positive ID on the driver, because if that is Reynolds, then we need to follow him and see what he's up to. It's far too much of a coincidence for him to be down here at the same time as we are. He's got to be looking for Anderson. This could be our big chance.'

As the blue Ford Cortina sat parked outside the food takeaway shop on Dalrymple Street, the black Ford Corsair did likewise a few yards back and diagonally opposite, the sole occupant of the former seemingly oblivious to the multiple occupancy of the latter. McDade was determined to keep it that way. He had a very healthy respect for DI Charlie Reynolds. A total of five criminal charges, two missing teeth and a nose at an angle of sixty degrees to his face would testify to that.

'Right, I'll go myself, then,' McDade muttered as he leaned over to open the car door. 'I just need to get a better look at him, even from the back. I'd recognise that smug bastard from outer space.'

'Wait, Rab,' McGinn said, grabbing McDade's shoulder. 'Who's that kid coming out of the shop? The one carrying the plastic bags and the bottles of coke? And look, he's getting into the car.'

'That's Anderson,' McDade replied, grabbing his copy of the

Ayrshire Herald and doing a double-take of the mugshot on the front page. 'He's lost the hair, but it's him all right.'

'You sure?'

'One million percent. Right, Ralphie, start the engine. Wherever they go, you follow. And don't bloody lose them.'

Young Baxter jumped to McDade's command like a willing puppy giving a paw for its next training biscuit, and the Corsair's two-litre engine rumbled into action. It needn't have bothered, because the Cortina didn't budge an inch. After a few minutes, McDade commanded Baxter to cut the engine, leaving the three fully-signed-up members of the Nutter Squad to sit and gawk in silent frustration as they watched both men delving ravenously into the contents of their plastic pokes.

Eventually, Mc Ginn spoke. He could stand the temptation no longer.

'I could murder a fish supper. How about it, Rab?'

'Me too,' Baxter piped up. 'Or maybe even a haggis supper. And two pickled onions. No, three.'

'Are you guys for real?' spat McDade. 'Can you imagine Dan's face when he asks us whether we've bumped the boy off yet, and I tell him that we were just about to finish the job but then got nabbed by the polis coming out of a shop carrying haggis suppers and pickled onions? Just sit there and button it, the pair of you.'

Eventually, the driver of the Cortina opened his car door and got out to dump a pile of food wrappings in a nearby wastepaper bin. McDade and McGinn exchanged leering grins. It was Reynolds all right, and as sure as Frank Rafferty was now pushing up the daisies, it was Ricky Anderson in the passenger's seat.

'Right boys, we're on,' McDade said. 'Keep your distance, Ralphie, but lose them and you're history. You got that?'

'Got it, Rab,' Baxter replied, trying his best to look cool.

A puff of smoke blew from the Cortina's exhaust pipe. The car nosed carefully out of its tight parking space, and an elderly lady driving a white Mini flashed her lights and waved the driver on his way. Baxter drove off in pursuit, keeping a good few yards behind the old dear in the Mini. From a distance, she reminded him of his granny. How he would have loved to be sitting right now in her cosy little kitchen in Mossblown, stuffing his face with homemade pancakes, rather than driving a pair of brain-dead, muscle-bound numpties around this God-forsaken joint in pursuit of their next unfortunate victim.

It took Reynolds a mere couple of minutes to reach Ricky's temporary digs on Henrietta Street. Ricky went to open the door, but Reynolds was quick to tell him to stay put.

'Now remember,' he counselled the youngster, handing over a small white envelope. 'Keep your head down until I tell you it's safe. Then, and only then, I'll come back for you and take you home. I know you'll probably hate accepting charity, but for now there's no alternative. Your new pal Sandy has really delivered the goods by letting you stay here for free, and there's enough money in this envelope to keep the wolf from the door for the foreseeable future. This is no time for self-righteous vanity. You can pay Sandy and me back later.'

'That's not the way I was brought up, Charlie. My mum and dad always told me to pay my way through life.'

'Aye, well, you can take your mum and me on a Caribbean cruise when you win the Nobel Prize for Nuclear Physics, but until then the fish suppers are on me. Phone me tomorrow night. My place, seven o'clock. Your mum will be there, and she'll be desperate to hear your voice. Iona too, so you can whisper sweet nothings in her ear as well. Hopefully, Andy McTurk will have made a breakthrough and I'll be able to give you some good news. You could use it.'

'Thanks for doing this for me, Charlie. I realise you're putting your reputation on the line, and I don't know how I can ever repay you.'

'I've told you, the Caribbean cruise. But for now, your blessing for my relationship with your mum will do fine.'

'You've got it. Tell her I love her.'

'She knows, but I will. Do you still remember my phone number? Don't write it down.'

'Yip, I'm shit-hot with numbers, remember? I could recite nuclear equations three-feet-long from memory. Speak to you tomorrow.'

'Keep your head down, Ricky. I've now got the uniforms heading north to Glasgow, so the coast should be relatively clear down here, although the Chief Superintendent will have my guts for garters if he ever finds out that I've sent them on a wild goose chase. I'm still a bit worried about the Nutter Squad, though. I wouldn't be surprised in the slightest if Dan Rafferty has put McDade and McGinn hot on your trail. You've upset the apple cart for Rafferty Construction, Ricky, and big time. Dan might have been mad at his brother for doing the business with his wife, but that's nothing to how furious he'll be at you for exposing the family empire's dodgy secrets.'

'Don't worry, I can take care of myself.'

'Not against those guys, Ricky. Trust me, they're complete nutters, hence their handle. If you even sniff that something's wrong, phone me immediately. Do you hear me?'

Ricky opened the door, got out and gave Reynolds one of his mock military-style salutes.

'Loud and clear, sir.'

Reynolds returned the salute with a beaming smile, then fired the Cortina into action and sped off into the distance.

Ricky made to walk up the garden path that led around Sandy Ferguson's house towards the wooden chalet, but stopped in his tracks after only a couple of steps. He chortled quietly at Reynolds's dubious words of wisdom, but looked all around in a 360-degree sweep anyway. As he expected, nothing seemed in the least bit untoward.

Not even the black Ford Corsair parked under the trees at the far end of the street.

71

It was DS Sandy Sutherland's turn to press the bell that commanded pride of place on the glass-fronted door of the Monk residence.

Bracing himself for another clanky rendition of 'I Did It My Way', DI Andy McTurk grimaced. This time, however, no such dubious choral splendour could be heard above the faint rumble of urban traffic trundling its way along the adjacent Alloway Road, in fact nothing that would even suggest that the bell was working at all. Sutherland waited a few moments and went to ring it again, but McTurk beat him to the punch. Displaying his legendary impatience, he rattled the door four times with his well-weathered knuckles.

Surprisingly, it was Edwin Monk himself who answered. McTurk watched his initial weary expression nosedive into one of pleading desperation.

'Hello again,' said the DI, with an air of wicked anticipation. 'Are Sinatra and you not speaking anymore?'

Monk just stared, first at McTurk and then at Sutherland, a pair of anxious eyes finally returning to meet those of the detective inspector.

'Eh, no,' he stammered. 'The bell ... the bell ... it isn't working. It blew a fuse.'

'Ah,' said McTurk, shaking his head in badly contrived empathy. 'That isn't good. Nasty things can happen when you blow a fuse. Can we come in, Mister Monk?'

'Is this ... is this really necessary, inspector?' he asked.

'Not really,' McTurk replied. 'We could do it down at the station instead, if you would prefer. We'll be happy to give you a couple of minutes to get ready.'

A look of resignation enveloped a weary face that appeared to be looking more lived-in by the day.

'Come in, inspector. You too, sergeant.'

'Thank you,' McTurk nodded. 'We appreciate your time. We know you're a very busy man.'

Monk managed a little sarcastic laugh.

'Busy man? Well, I certainly used to be, inspector, but alas no longer. Not since all this nonsense blew up in my face. My whole life has been turned upside down since then.'

Andy McTurk had three pet hates. HP Sauce, lumpy custard and self-pity. Especially the latter. He followed Monk into his study, muttering silent expletives. Sutherland brought up the rear and closed the door behind him.

'Well, I'm afraid it's this nonsense, as you call it, that we want to talk to you about,' McTurk said.

'Can you please call me Edwin?' Monk pleaded, alternating his gaze from one officer to the other. 'It would make me feel less stressed.'

'That would not be appropriate, Mister Monk,' McTurk replied. 'This is a formal police investigation, as you well know.'

If the disgraced former politician's bottom jaw had fallen any further, it would have crash-landed on the laminated floor. McTurk pressed on.

'So, Mister Monk, let's go over your story again, shall we?'

'Inspector, please. I've already told you everything I know. I swear on my mother's grave.'

'Well, let's see, shall we? I'd like you to tell us again about the evening of Thursday the thirteenth of September. The whole story please. And in your own words.'

'Thursday the thirteenth? Sorry, inspector, but I'm struggling with the date. My head's all over the place just now.'

'Well, let me help you there. You'll remember we visited you on the morning of Friday the fourteenth, Mister Monk. And you told us about what had happened to you the previous evening when you were out walking. Walking alone, with no witnesses. We just want to tie up a few loose ends, because your story has some gaps and inconsistencies in it. A few things that don't quite add up.'

'Oh ... oh, I see ...'

'So, go over it again, please.'

Monk slumped down on his leather-backed swivel chair behind the big oak desk, searching for security but failing miserably in the search. McTurk and Sutherland took their seats opposite, clearly hanging on his every word. Sutherland spoke for the first time.

'So, tell us, sir. And in your own time. We've got all morning.'

Monk rubbed his left eye, then his chin, and took a long deep breath. He realised that his story had better add up or he was in for the high-jump, and from a great altitude.

'Okay then, I'll try my best. But please remember that it was well over a week ago.'

'We're waiting,' said McTurk. 'DS Sutherland might have all morning, but I don't.'

The good-cop/bad-cop routine had already reared its manipulative head again, as the senior officer directed a mock glare in his subordinate's direction. Monk subconsciously decided to focus on the good cop because the bad one scared the shit out of him. He felt he had a slight chance of hoodwinking Sutherland, but knew with innate certainty that McTurk could see right through him with all the clinical precision of one of those super-duper new X-ray machines that had just hit the nation's health service.

'Okay, sergeant, let me see. I was out walking. It was about nine-thirty, I think. It was raining, and I ...'

Sutherland held up his hand and stopped him in mid-sentence as he leafed through his notes.

'9.45 p.m., you told us last Friday, sir. Not 9.30 p.m. It's a small detail, but it might turn out to be important.'

'Oh, I see,' Monk continued, his respiration gathering steam. 'Well, I know I got home just after 10.00 p.m., because News at Ten had just started on ITV. I remember Sandy Gall reading out the headlines. I had only been walking for about a quarter-of-an-hour before the lad Anderson attacked me, so I guess that must have been about 9.4 5p.m., as you say. Sorry, sergeant, my memory has been like a sieve since all this happened to me.'

McTurk again clocked the self-pity, and again it sickened him to the stomach. To him, it smelled like diarrhoea in a heatwave. He went straight for the jugular.

'Mister Monk, Richard Anderson was seen sitting on a bus during the late afternoon of Thursday the thirteenth. We have a reliable witness. He was travelling from New Cumnock to Dalmellington and carrying a rucksack complete with camping gear. He was also seen walking through Craigengillan estate later that same evening. Another reliable witness, Mister Monk. We therefore believe that your story is simply not credible. For Mister Anderson to have been in your own backyard at the time you say is well-nigh impossible. Not only does he neither have a car nor a driving licence, but he would have needed a helicopter to get there by a quarter-to-ten, and to the best of our knowledge he doesn't have a pilot's licence either.'

Sutherland stifled a chortle. Monk's mouth fell open again. He quickly snapped it shut and tried to engage his best stiff upper lip.

'Are you accusing me of lying, inspector? Do you realise that I'm a Justice of the Peace, a man with a very long and distinguished career in public service? My reputation precedes me.'

'Your reputation is totally shot, Mister Monk,' McTurk hit back. 'It's in shreds and you know it. You are a liar and a cheat. You have fabricated a story to stitch up Richard Anderson in order to save your own skin, and if it's the last thing I do, I'll prove it. What I want to know is why you seem so intent on framing an innocent young man with a great future ahead of him?'

'I can't believe you think I've made all this up,' Monk gasped, clearly determined to sustain his latest theatrical performance. 'I'm horrified that you would even think that for one moment.'

'Who gave you the black eye, Mister Monk?' McTurk asked, changing tack and hitting him from leftfield with a completely different question. 'I mean, who *really* gave it to you? And before you answer, it certainly wasn't Ricky Anderson, because he wasn't even there that night, and you know it. So, I ask you again. Who gave you the black eye?'

Monk opened his mouth to speak, but no words came, only a pathetic little squeak. He stared out the window of his study, his eyes glazing over like a piece of wet pottery overwhelmed by the searing heat of a clay oven. The self-pity was gone, now replaced by a look of despair. Complete and utter despair. He was beat and McTurk knew it. He was now another one of the many would-be defiant interviewees to join the DI's ever-expanding list of conquests. His hall of infamy, as he preferred to call it. He winked at Sutherland. The bad cop's job was done. The time was now ripe for the good cop to enter the fray.

'Mister Monk,' Sutherland said, his voice as soft and reassuring as he could muster in the circumstances. 'We know you've had a very difficult time recently, but it doesn't have to be this way. Would it not just be easier for you to tell us what really happened that Thursday night and get everything off your chest?'

The two detectives glanced at each other, waiting for a reaction. Monk continued staring out of the window, as if hypnotised by the leafy branches of the cherry trees swaying in his front garden. Their blossom had long gone and so too had anything that was left of Monk's scant resilience. Sutherland saw his opportunity.

'Mister Monk, I'm going to tell you a wee story. And it's a true story. It's about my father. He's called Tom and he's just turned 68.'

Monk turned and faced Sutherland. His face was expressionless, but he was listening, so the young detective continued.

'My dad had been having trouble at the toilet. Blood, you know? This had been going on for weeks, months in fact, and he hadn't told anyone. Not my mother, not my sister, not me, nobody. But we all kind of knew something was wrong, because he just hadn't been his usual self. He was more distant, a wee bit uptight and the big laughs just weren't there anymore. Anyway, we eventually managed to get him to go to his doctor, and to cut a long story short, he was diagnosed with bowel cancer.'

Finally, Monk spoke.

'I'm sorry to hear that, son,' he said. 'But what's that got to do with me?'

'Well,' Sutherland replied. 'Let me explain. You see, my dad had been worrying all the time about his health, not eating well, not sleeping, things like that. I suspect that you're a bit like that just now, Mister Monk. Anyway, a funny thing happened after he was diagnosed. The news was a huge blow to him, a real sickener. But the thing was that it was no longer his own little secret. It was finally out in the open, and he could talk about it, share his fears with family and friends. He was no longer having to wonder about what was wrong with him, because he now knew the full story, everything. Suddenly, instead of having to deal alone with all the uncertainty, he was able to face up to his predicament, knowing that things were out in the open. And the strange thing was that he felt much more relaxed about life, even although he now knew he faced a huge battle ahead.'

Monk pondered where all this was leading.

'I still don't know why you're telling me all this.'

'I'm just thinking that you could make things a lot easier on yourself,' Sutherland replied. 'I mean, if you just came out and told the truth. You never know, it might make you feel a lot better about yourself. Sure, like my dad, you'd still have to face up to the harsh reality of what lies ahead, but at least there would be no more secrets eating away at you.'

Silence descended again like a bank of low cloud coming down to spoil a sunny day at the seaside. McTurk and Sutherland let it hang there. Finally, Monk spoke. Six short words came out in a pitiful monotone. They sounded like a naughty schoolboy confessing to his latest episode of truancy.

'It was me. I did it.'

McTurk and Sutherland stared at each other. They held their breath and studied Monk's face. Had they heard him correctly? Sutherland picked up where he had left off. This was now his gig and his boss knew it.

'You did what, Mister Monk?'

Silence again, a deep and resounding silence that battered off the four walls like a bass drum in a phone box.

'What was it you did, Mister Monk?' Sutherland nudged with delicate caution. 'Did you lie to us about Richard Anderson assaulting you? Did someone put you up to framing him? Tell us, Mister Monk. You'll feel better about yourself if you do.'

'I told you, sergeant,' he said, turning to face Sutherland head-on. 'I did it.'

'You did what, Mister Monk?'

'I killed Frank Rafferty.'

72

Driving back north from Girvan towards Prestwick, Charlie Reynolds found himself in a bit of a quandary.

On the one hand, he was desperate to get straight back home to speak with Janice and Iona, both of whom would be waiting with bated breath for any news on Ricky. However, on the other, he knew he had to contact Andy McTurk immediately, to get the lowdown on whether his investigation into Frank Rafferty's murder had thrown up any further morsels of hope that might persuade Ricky to return to the fold.

Reynolds decided to track McTurk down first. He wasn't particularly looking forward to that conversation, because he would have to continue with the deception that had led to McTurk taking the hounds off Ricky's trail down Girvan way and sending them up to Glasgow on another wild goose chase. Reynolds and McTurk had been bosom buddies ever since they had first met nearly twenty years before, and neither would ever have dreamed of deceiving the other, never at any time. However, a young lad's liberty was at stake here, possibly his life too, and Reynolds simply had to do what he had to do. He would explain his actions later, and it would be up to McTurk to judge them in the circumstances. For now, though, he urgently needed to know the bottom line. Only then could he decide whether or not he had sufficient new information to persuade Ricky to give himself up and take his chances with the law. After meeting with McTurk, he would then drive straight home and inform Janice and Iona accordingly. They could certainly do with some good news for a change, but only time would tell if he could deliver it.

Just as Reynolds was about to make a left turn at Holmston roundabout on the outskirts of Ayr and head towards the town's police headquarters, his radio crackled into action. He picked it up and turned left anyway. It was the control room. DI McTurk needed to speak to him urgently. Taking liberties with police protocol as usual, Reynolds ask the operator to let McTurk know that he'd be in Maria's café in ten minutes' time.

The ten minutes felt like an hour.

'Give me good news, old boy,' Reynolds said as McTurk joined him at his table. 'Christ knows, I could do with it.'

'For heaven's sake, can I sit down first?' McTurk protested, before stopping the young waitress who was walking past. 'A coffee and a fruit scone, love. You want another one, Charlie?'

'No, I'm fine, can you just get on with it?'

'Good God, you're in a hurry today. Okay, listen up. We've got our killer. Full confession, the lot. And you're not going to believe who did it.'

Reynolds's heart skipped a beat, then a couple more.

'Easy. It has to be Dan Rafferty, because neither McDade nor McGinn would confess to taking a piss, even if they were caught in the lavvie with their zips down.'

'That's what I thought too, Charlie, but we were both a long way off the mark. The killer is none other than our esteemed representative of the people.'

'What? You don't mean ...?'

'Yes, I certainly do. Councillor Edwin Monk himself. Or as we now refer to him, plain old Mister Monk. He's just coughed his guts up to Sandy and me, and sitting in his own house too. I didn't want to tell you until we had hauled him into the station and got a signed confession. It's now in triplicate, all duly witnessed by his lawyer who begged him not to sign it but was powerless to stop him.'

'Edwin Monk? I wouldn't have thought he could burst his own way out of a wet paper poke, let alone slash someone's throat with a kitchen knife. My money would have been on Dan Rafferty all day long. Means, motive and opportunity. A stick-on.'

'Mines too, Charlie. But he had a wee helping hand. A drug called Rohypnol. Monk told us that he slipped a pill into Rafferty's G & T in his wee brother's caravan, and then sat chatting to him as he fell into a trance. Told him what he thought of him and what he was going to do to him, then did it. Now, that's what I call getting even.'

'Good God almighty. Well, there's a real turn-up for the books. I can guess why Monk might have wanted to do it, because he was as deep down in Frank Rafferty's pocket as an old snotty hanky, but I would never have thought he had the guts to go through with it.'

'Me, neither.'

'Any idea why he decided to confess?'

'Aye, I think he just suddenly had a moment of dawning realisation. One minute he was churning out a pack of bloody lies as if they were going out of fashion, and the next he just stopped the charade and spilt his guts. It was young Sandy who got him to do it, he was brilliant. Told him some cock-and-bull story about his own father getting diagnosed with cancer, and suddenly it was as if a light had been switched on in Monk's head.'

'It's no cock-and-bull story, Andy. Sandy's father is Tom Sutherland. He's a friend of a friend, and he's only got three months left to live. You really should learn to take a bit more interest in your subordinates.'

'Oh dear. Sorry.'

'Right, I'm now going to head back home and speak to Janice and Iona. It's about time they got some good news for a change.'

'Good decision, if you don't mind me saying so. Do you think that should be enough to convince the boy to come in now? Surely?'

'We'll see, Andy, we'll see. Hopefully, he'll phone again tonight, then I'll let you know. Will you be at home?'

'I'll make a point of it.'

Reynolds pulled his chair back from the table and stood up.

'Okay, speak later. Enjoy your scone, old boy. You should've brought your knitting with you.'

73

'Are we just going to sit here all day, Rab?' Ralph Baxter pleaded. 'My legs have gone to sleep and I'm bursting for a piss.'

'You'll sit there until I tell you different,' Robert McDade snapped at the young driver. 'Dan Rafferty pays you to do two things. To drive and to do whatever else I tell you. That means if I tell you to batter your napper on the windscreen, then you batter your napper on the windscreen. Either that, or I do it for you. Got it?'

Baxter just nodded. It was a nod of the wise.

'Ralphie's got a point, though, Rab,' Zander McGinn butted in. 'We've been sitting here for over an hour now, and there's absolutely no sign of the boy. Is it not about time we were making a move?'

'Aye, maybe you're right, Zander,' McDade sighed. 'I was sure he'd have to come out at some stage, even just to grab something to eat.'

'But he's just wolfed some stuff from the bakers' shop, so maybe he's in for the night. It's possible, Rab.'

'Aye, I suppose it is. And I'm not spending another minute more than I need to in this dump. Okay boys, listen up. Here's what we do. Young Anderson didn't go in the front door of the house, he went around the side. He's maybe using the back door, either that or there could be a shed or something back there that he's sleeping in. Ralphie, when we go out, you switch the engine on and keep it running. We'll be throwing the boy into the back seat with Zander, so you'll need to be ready to flare it when we do. Okay?'

'Okay, Rab,' Baxter replied, the butterflies in the pit of his stomach slowly transmuting to albatrosses.

'Zander,' McDade continued. 'You and me, we go in together, right? We go round the side of the house, check the lie of the land and take things from there. If there's a shed, we walk straight up and hit it. Kick the door right in. If there isn't, he's in the house, so we try the back door first, but if it's locked, we batter it in. You got your cosh, Zander?'

'Aye,' McGinn said, smacking the heavy wooden weapon against the palm of his hand and grinning.

'Me too. What about the other stuff?'

'Sorted,' McGinn nodded. 'Chloroform and hankie right here in my jacket pocket.'

'Any final questions, boys,' asked McDade.

'Aye,' Baxter replied. 'What about the woman?'

'What ... what woman?' McDade muttered, looking puzzled.

'There's a woman in the front living room,' said Baxter. 'I've seen her wandering about near the window. I thought you had too.'

'No, ... no, I didn't,' said McDade. 'You might have bloody told me.'

'I just did,' Baxter replied, pushing his luck again.

'So, what's Plan B, Rab?' McGinn enquired. 'Just in case things go tits-up?'

'We don't have a Plan B, Zander,' McDade replied. 'In fact, when I come to think about it, we don't even have a Plan A. It's just a plain old-fashioned door-off-the-hinges job. We grab Anderson, batter him with the cosh, and hard, because I hear he's a tough young bugger. Then the chloroform hankie over the nose and we drag him straight out and into the car.'

'And the woman?' Baxter enquired, clearly agitated about the clinical violence that was about to unfold before his eyes.

'You leave her to Zander and me, Ralphie-boy,' McDade replied. 'If she gets in the way, a hard crack on the skull with the cosh and she'll be out the game until about Tuesday.'

McGinn chortled at Baxter's obvious discomfort.

'You sure you're cut out for this, Ralphie-boy?' he teased. 'Maybe a wee job with Station Taxis would suit you better. That way, you'd be helping old ladies take their suitcases onto the big choo-choo-train, instead of dragging cheeky wee students up into the hills to answer for their sins. I could write you a reference, Ralphie.'

'Write a reference, Zander?' McDade laughed. 'The only thing you ever learned to write was a bookies' line.'

Just at that, an elderly couple came into view walking their West Highland Terrier on an extended lead. The three fully signed-up members of the Nutter Squad just sat and stared in silence, daring the little white dog to come anywhere near their getaway vehicle as it strolled past. If it did, there would be three serious casualties, two of a geriatric nature and one canine. Thankfully, it didn't, and stillness again descended on Henrietta Street.

'Hit the engine, Ralphie-boy,' McDade commanded. 'And keep it running.'

Both front and rear passengers' doors sprang open and Rafferty Construction's two principal enforcers-in-chief began striding up the garden path before disappearing from view around the side of the house.

The timber-framed chalet came into view immediately. It was built on red-brick foundations and sat semi-sheltered from the elements under a row of trees which separated the Fergusons' property from their next-door neighbours. A brown tomcat lay snoozing at the foot of the chalet's wooden steps. As soon as it heard the two strangers' footsteps, it rose to its feet, arched its back and hissed. McDade swung a hefty boot in the cat's direction, failing to connect but sending it scurrying into the unkempt foliage at the back of the lawn.

'Listen, Zander,' he whispered. 'Do you hear that?'

'Aye,' McGinn replied. 'It's music. He must have the wireless on. Either that or he's got the Rolling Stones in there with him.'

'Right, Zander, hit the door.'

When McGinn's size-twelves reached the top step, his right boot belted the chalet door full-pelt. It burst open on impact and he was in, swiftly followed by McDade. Sitting stretched out on the settee, Ricky Anderson spun around to find out what all the commotion was about, but it was already too late. With one mighty swing of his arm, McGinn brought his cosh down on the back of Ricky's skull. The young student's head shot forwards and his feet began twitching on the old grey rug that covered the wooden floor. A copious river of blood began pouring down his neck.

'Jesus Christ, Zander!' McDade yelled. 'You were only supposed to knock him out. His head's like a burst melon.'

'Well, you said he was a hard man, Rab,' McGinn hit back. 'I wasn't for taking any chances. Will I give him the chloroform now?'

'Chloroform?' McDade scowled. 'The way you hit him with that cosh, he won't be needing chloroform until next summer. Just help me get the boy into the car. This place is like a bloody butcher's shop.'

He opened the chalet door as wide as it would go, had a quick look around to check that the coast was clear and grabbed Ricky under the armpits.

'Get the legs, Zander. And you go first.'

'How come it's always me that gets the legs? And how come it's always me that has to walk backwards?'

'Just shut up and get out of here, Zander. We need to get the boy in the car before the whole bloody street sees us. Christ, man, it looks as if you hit him with a machete.'

It took a good couple of minutes for the two strong-arm men to haul the dead-weight of Ricky's comatose body down the steps, then around the side of the house and back up the front garden path to the waiting Corsair, where its driver sat welded to his seat in horror at the sight coming into view in his rear-view mirror.

'Get your arse out of there, Ralphie,' said McDade. 'And open the back door.'

Baxter stumbled out, hands shaking and words tumbling incoherently from parched lips.

'You can't … you can't put him in there. Look … look at the blood. Oh shit, just look at it.'

'Open the bloody door, Ralph,' McDade yelled. 'And hurry up.'

The yell was just enough to attract the attention of the mysterious lady whom Baxter had seen earlier pacing around at her living room window. This time, though, he was so transfixed at the nauseating sight of his two sidekicks ramming the blood-soaked body into the back seat of his car that he didn't even notice.

Meanwhile, Martha Ferguson stood dumbstruck in disbelief at her window, witnessing the terrifying scene which was unfolding before her very eyes right outside her own front gate. Peering from behind the security of her curtains, she could just make out Ricky's prostrate body lying slumped across the full length of the car's back seat, his legs resting on top of one huge brute of a guy while another squeezed himself into the front passenger's seat beside the ashen-faced young driver. The Nutter Squad now had themselves a guest, and he was going for a little ride.

Wobbling erratically towards the front door, Martha just managed to turn the handle. She tried to scream but nothing came out, her voice paralysed by fear. Thankfully, though, her ears were in perfect working order.

'Byne Hill!'

Those were the last two words that she heard the fearsome-looking man in the front seat bellow to the driver on his right before the black Corsair began screeching down Henrietta Street.

And before the latest in a long, long line of Hypoglycemia-induced fits sent Martha crashing to the floor like a felled oak.

74

It was almost five in the afternoon before Charlie Reynolds eventually managed to tear himself away from the clutches of Janice and Iona, and slip out the front door.

Reynolds turned the key in the ignition and glowered in frustration at the fuel gauge. Between a quarter-full and empty, he cursed, just sufficient to get him to Girvan but certainly not enough to take him back to Prestwick, with or without Ricky Anderson. To hell with it, he decided, just get there as fast as you can, Charlie, and fill up when you arrive, because making contact with Ricky is easily your most pressing consideration. The news of Edwin Monk's confession would now surely be enough to persuade the young fugitive to return home. Wouldn't it?

It took Reynolds a mere thirteen minutes to reach the south side of Doonfoot. He shuddered at the thought of Dan Rafferty's blood-soaked caravan still sitting at the foot of the tree-lined Earl's Way down towards the beach, the very caravan in which the butchered body of Dan's elder brother had been discovered only nine days earlier. The irony of a gruesome murder scene lying amidst the cosy opulence of this peaceful little suburb wasn't lost on him.

Turning off to the right just before the Burns Monument Hotel, Reynolds booted his Cortina into more serious action the moment he hit the end of the 30-mph speed restriction, whereupon a few spots of rain began peppering his windscreen like random punctuation marks on a badly-written police report. A twenty-minute drive along the A719 then took him into the village of Maybole, by which time the wet stuff was positively lashing down, and where to his consternation the 'low road' was blocked off due to major roadworks, a big garish sign directing him on the slightly longer detour up the 'high road' and sending him on his way towards the picturesque little seaside village of Maidens.

Several minutes later, when he was passing between the salubrious Turnberry Hotel on his left and the world-famous golf course of the same name on his right, Reynolds checked his watch and the Cortina's fuel gauge. The first said five-thirty, and the second empty. Reynolds cursed again before reminding himself that the tank would still have about half-a-gallon left in reserve, probably just enough to get him to Girvan's Henrietta Street where he would attempt to deploy his considerable charms to persuade Ricky that he should now come back in from the cold. His main objective then achieved, he would deal with fuel replenishment later. At least, that was the theory. However, the practice wasn't listening.

As soon as Reynolds passed the 'Girvan Welcomes Careful Drivers' sign, just before the town's railway station, his engine had all but given up the ghost. An uncomfortable splutter became a desperate groan and finally an asphyxiated gasp, as the Cortina freewheeled into the Esso garage on his right, finally collapsing in exhaustion about twenty yards short of the nearest petrol pump. As he made to get out, a cheery male voice piped up, displaying all the hallmarks of the rustic good humour that defines this delightful part of the country.

'Do you think it's a fireman's hose I've got here, pal? I'll shove, and you steer.'

With the attendant having pushed the car all the way to the pump and about to start the considerably less demanding task of filling the tank, Reynolds, still sitting in the driver's seat, checked his wristwatch. It now read 5.53 p.m. He'd be at Ricky's chalet well before six, and with a fair wind, back in Prestwick by seven at the latest to herald the young student's emotional return to the two women in his life. However, as he sat there twiddling his thumbs and listening to the gregarious attendant babbling on about every topical subject under the sun, Reynolds contemplated one very possible scenario. The Nutter Squad might already have beat him to it.

And if so, they had a good hour's start.

75

Andy McTurk poured himself a stiff measure of Grouse whisky and downed half of it in one big gulp.

It was an act borne of smug self-satisfaction, but also one designed to give him a much-needed injection of Dutch courage. McTurk simply hated phoning Chief Superintendent Fraser at home, particularly on a Saturday evening. Smokin' Joe's boorish soliloquy on the day of McTurk's elevation to the heady ranks of detective inspector wasn't so much still ringing in his ears, as blaring.

'Inspector,' he had announced to McTurk, staring at him with those piercing blue eyes of his. 'Always remember one thing. I am a man who insists on being fully informed at all times. And while I prefer good news to bad news, I can handle bad news. However, what I really can't stand are surprises. So, Inspector, if you ever have something to tell me, even if it's about some disastrous cock-up you've made, then tell me. If you don't, and I end up getting caught with my trousers at my ankles, you'll be a man with a great career behind you. Understand?'

'Yes, Sir,' McTurk had responded with an appropriate degree of sycophancy. 'Loud and clear.'

He necked the rest of his whisky, then picked up the phone and dialled his boss's home number. Smokin' Joe still made him nervous, even after all those years.

'Chief Superintendent Fraser here.'

'Hello, Sir, it's Andy McTurk. Sorry to disturb you on a Saturday evening, but it's important.'

'Good news or bad, Andy?'

'Good for a change, Sir.'

'Tell me.'

'We've nicked Frank Rafferty's murderer. Full confession, matching fingerprints, signed written statement, the works. I thought you'd like to know right away.'

'Our Dan then, I assume? I'll need to get myself all geared up for the press having a bloody field day at my expense. Police chief's young cousin murders his own big brother, and all that crap.'

'Well, you can relax, Sir, because it wasn't Dan who killed Frank. It was the great people's champion himself, Edwin Monk.'

'Jesus Christ almighty, Andy. Edwin Monk? You sure about that?'

'As sure as the pope's a catholic, Sir. Dan has a rock-solid alibi and Monk's in the cells contemplating a ten-stretch in the Bar-L.'

'Well, that's a result for sure. I suppose you can now go and tell that bosom buddy of yours to bring the Anderson lad in from the wilderness. His mum will be missing him.'

'Charlie's hoping Ricky will phone him tonight. We've been rummaging through the streets of Glasgow looking for him. He's a resourceful wee bugger.'

'The sooner he's home, the better. What about the pair of goons that Frank hired to do his dirty work? Have you got a tail on them?'

'McDade and McGinn? No, not a tail as such, Sir. We've had both of them in for questioning. Nothing to go on, I'm afraid, so they're back on the streets.'

'They're dangerous people, Andy. And my guess is that they'll be looking to get even for Frank's murder, which puts the Anderson boy right in the firing line.'

'If we can't find Ricky, neither will they, Sir.'

'Put a tail on them right away. And Andy, that's an order.'

'Okay, Sir. I'll also make sure they get the word that it was Monk who did it, not Ricky, and that Monk's in the cells.'

'Good man, Andy. That's certainly brightened up my Saturday night. Sarah was making me sit through yet another episode of *The Generation Game* when you rang, and I can't stand that bloody Bruce Forsyth. He's about as overrated as Kevin Keegan.'

'Have a good evening, Sir. A wee dram might take the edge off *The Generation Game*. It works for me.'

'Aye, it just might. Have one on me too, Andy. I always told you I preferred good news to bad news.'

'Yes, you did, Sir. But you also told me something else that I never forgot.'

'And what was that?'

'That you hated surprises. And I've just landed you with one.'

'That kind of surprise I can cope with anytime. Good night, Inspector.'

'Good night, Chief Superintendent.'

76

For Jock Simpson, the role of pump attendant didn't just involve pouring petrol down the parched throats of assorted fuel tanks. It incorporated the combined functions of private investigator and tourist officer as well.

'So, what brings you to Girvan, then?' the 75-year-old ex-postman enquired, giving Charlie Reynolds the once-over as he dispensed his latest ten-gallon concoction of Saudi Arabian petrochemicals. 'You're not from around here, son, are you?'

'No,' replied Reynolds, looking at his watch and hoping that his respectful indifference would register. 'I'm from up north.'

'Ah,' said Jock. 'I knew it. From your accent, I mean. I'm pretty good at accents, you know. It's something I learned from my father. Like him before me, I'm really into in amateur dramatics. I've even performed in The Gaiety theatre in Ayr, would you believe? And I've done all the different dialects, son. Cockney, Geordie, Scouser, Irish, Aussie, you name them. Even Czechoslovakian, because my granny was from Prague.'

'Is that right?' Reynolds muttered, trying valiantly to avoid the eye contact which could have prolonged the dialogue until darkness fell. 'Are we about done here?'

'Where up north, then?' the persistent thespian continued. 'I'm guessing more Inverness than Aberdeen.'

'More Prestwick than Ayr, I'm afraid,' Reynolds replied, biting on his lip. 'Is the tank nearly full? Sorry, mate, but I'm in a hurry.'

'Oh well,' his new-found buddy soldiered on, unabashed. 'I'm a bit off the mark there, I suppose. Still, I imagine you'll be wanting a wee bit of local knowledge while you're here? Good pubs, decent walks ... that sort of thing? The eating places down here are pretty good, but you've got to watch a couple of them. A bit dodgy, like. Gastroenteritis on a plate, if you know what I mean.'

'No thanks,' said Reynolds, trying to demonstrate a tasteful mix of good grace and impatience at the pointlessness of a conversation that was on the verge of driving him insane. 'If you could just stop pumping now and I'll settle up with you? I really need to get going.'

This time, the message did register. As old Jock pulled the nozzle from the tank and trudged his way back towards his kiosk, the disappointment on his face was about as clear as the setting sun in a cloudless night-time sky. Reynolds looked at his watch again and decided that he didn't have time to feel sorry for him. It now read 5.58 p.m.

He settled his bill, bade the old man farewell, and hit the accelerator once more. It was precisely 6.04 p.m. when he reached the Ferguson property on Henrietta Street, where he hoped that Ricky would be nestling in his wooden chalet round the back. However, the moment he drew up at the gate, he could tell that something was badly wrong. The front door of the main house was wide-open and there were pronounced skid-marks on the road. His intuition suggested that a wide-open front door on a wet and breezy evening didn't quite compute, while his experience as a battle-weary copper told him that a vehicle had just pulled out from the kerbside in far too much of a hurry. The combination of the two observations immediately put his antennae on full alert.

Reynolds got out of his car and began striding towards the wrought-iron gate which separated a pair of tall hedgerows that partly concealed the Fergusons' house. He saw the blood immediately. It was everywhere. Smeared on the pavement, dripping down the gate-handle and trailing all the way along the garden path. It looked as if some inebriated painter-and-decorator had just staggered its full length spilling a tin of post-box-red gloss in his wake.

The other bizarre apparition which confronted him was that of the prostrate body of an elderly woman stretched out at the front door, her head lying on the top step and her torso jammed between the far wall and the door itself. Still attempting to internalise the possible relationship between both scenes, he bolted towards the woman and knelt down by her side. A quick visual examination revealed no obvious contusions or bruises, but a trickle of blood was oozing from her left ear. A fall rather than an attack, Reynolds suspected, and immediately radioed for an ambulance. Rolling her gently to the right into the coma position, he spoke clearly into her left ear.

'Madam, can you hear me?'

Nothing. Not a thing.

'Madam, can you hear me? I'm a police officer and you've just had a very nasty fall. An ambulance is on its way. Can you hear me?'

As Reynolds tried to elicit a response from the poor woman, he suddenly felt conflicted. He knew that he had to stay with her until the ambulance arrived, but he also had to get round the back of the house to check that Ricky was okay. The problem was the voice in his head which kept telling him that Ricky was far from okay. It was a voice that had seldom been wrong in a long career. A pair of heavy footsteps clumped up the concrete slabs of the front garden path.

'Martha!' a gruff voice roared.

Reynolds turned around to see a well-built, sixty-something

giant of a man running towards him, his meaty fist ready to deliver what he instinctively knew would be a thunderous blow. He leapt to his feet just in time to grab his would-be assailant's arm and force him to the ground before he reached the steps.

'Sir, I'm a police officer,' he yelled, as he wrestled with him on the garden path. 'Just calm yourself down.'

Sandy Ferguson's eyes were ablaze with fury.

'What have you done to Martha?' he roared, as he fought to break free from the big detective's grip. 'What have you done to her, you bastard?'

Reynolds managed to spin Ferguson over on his front and shove his arm up his back.

'Sir, listen to me,' he shouted again. 'I'm a police officer and I'm trying to help the lady, not harm her. She's badly injured and I've sent for an ambulance. Now, either calm yourself down, or I'll have to knock you out. I don't want to do it, but it's your choice.'

Reynolds felt Ferguson's muscles begin to relax, but he kept a vice-like grip on his arm anyway.

'Okay,' Ferguson spluttered. 'Okay. Let me up.'

Reynolds slowly released his grasp but held a clenched fist ready to lash out if need be. Breathing heavily, Ferguson turned around to face Reynolds, who helped him back to his feet and up the steps towards his unconscious wife.

'Martha,' he spluttered. 'Martha darlin' ... you're going to be all right, I promise.'

Martha Ferguson lay motionless on the floor, save for the rhythmic rise and fall of her diaphragm. Still, the blood trickled from her ear.

'I'm Detective Inspector Reynolds from the Ayr branch of Southwest Scotland Police,' he said to the big guy. 'What's your name? Do you live here?'

'I'm Sandy Ferguson,' came the reply from the stunned harbour master. 'And yes, this is our house.'

'Right, Sandy. It looks to me as if your wife has had a very bad fall, but the ambulance should be here shortly. I can't see any obvious cuts or bruises, so I don't think she's been attacked or anything like that.'

'She's probably had another fainting attack. She suffers from Hypoglycemia, and it happens all the time. It's just that when I saw you standing over her, I thought ...'

'I would have thought the same, Sandy. Forget it.'

'Sorry.'

'No need to apologise. However, there's something I have to do. I understand you've got a young man living in your chalet round the back. Ricky Anderson? He's a friend of mine. Would you mind if I just checked to see that he's okay? You can stay here with your wife till the ambulance arrives.'

'Sure.'

'In the meantime, I suggest you slip a cushion or something under her head and cover her up with a blanket? I'll be back in a couple of minutes. Okay?'

'Okay, no problem.'

The sound of a siren could just be heard in the distance, its unmistakeable din drawing closer by the second. Reynolds shot to his feet and leapt down the concrete steps, then began running down the path, a few pools of semi-congealed blood sucking at the soles of his shoes like a burst tube of superglue on a DIY geek's fingers. Please God, not Ricky's blood, he beseeched the heavens.

As soon as he reached the rear of the Fergusons' house, he knew his worst fears were about to be confirmed. The trail of blood continued from the slabbed path right up to the top of the wooden chalet's three steps, where the door swung precariously at an angle, its top hinge burst from the facing. An old garden rake lay adjacent to a big pile of wet leaves. It had seen better days, but it would still double as a tidy weapon. Reynolds picked it up and climbed the steps, then used it to shove the ailing door fully open, at which point the bottom hinge gave up the ghost and the door crashed to the floor.

Holding the rake like a hostile highlander wielding his claymore in pitched battle, he stepped inside. There were no real signs of any significant struggle. A pile of assorted belongings lay scattered around, including a beige golf cap on top of a black V-necked sweater draped over a plastic chair, and a pair of damp walking boots drying next to the three-bar electric fire, one bar of which was still glowing red-hot.

Two things struck Reynolds immediately. The first was the golf cap which he recognised as the one Ricky had been wearing when they had met earlier in the day. The second was the place of origin of the blood trail. It was the fawn-coloured settee that sat in front of the fire. There, the blood had sprayed copiously all over the settee's left arm and matching cushion before resting motionless in a sickeningly graphic pool of red-black gloop on the seat.

Reynolds established the scenario in no time. Ricky had been sitting right there, no doubt about it, his backside on the left-hand-side of the settee, his head propped up on the cushion and his feet resting on the grey rug. Someone had then kicked the chalet door in and walloped Ricky on the head before the poor kid had a chance to move, and he had walloped him hard. So hard, in fact, that as he was dragged out his blood now trailed from the locus of the attack down the steps of the chalet, all around the garden path to the front gate, onto the pavement and into a waiting getaway vehicle, almost certainly the same one which had left its skid-marks on the road as it screamed away into the distance.

Ricky Anderson was in trouble, deep trouble. If he wasn't dead already from his head wound, then unless he got medical attention very soon, it would only be a matter of time. And there was just one reason that his assailants could possibly have had to make them go to the enormous effort of dragging him all the way around the house and into their car.

They had unfinished business with Ricky.

77

Falling, falling …

Deeper and deeper. Deeper down into the bowels of the earth. Down to where pain stops and peace awaits. Down to be reunited again. Reunited with the most important person in the world, the one who was ripped away from those who loved him so much. Reunited with the one they called Big Davie. Reunited with dad.

Falling deeper and deeper. Soon, the pain will stop. Soon, I will be at peace. At peace with my dad.

Look … I can see his face now. His strong jawline, his dark wavy hair, his kind blue eyes. He is smiling. Deeper and deeper. Closer and closer. His face is becoming clearer, and he is smiling.

Listen … he is speaking to me now. My dad is speaking to me. Soon, I will be able to touch him. To hug him and tell him how much I have missed him.

Falling and falling. The pain is beginning to leave me. Soon, I will be at peace. My dad is getting closer. I can almost touch him now. He is speaking to me. He is telling me something. His voice is calm, so very calm. What is he saying?

Deeper and deeper. His face is becoming clearer and clearer. His words too. 'Ricky,' he is saying, 'Ricky.' It sounds wonderful. Soon, I will be with him. Then the pain will be gone, and I will be at peace. At peace with my dad, at last.

Deeper still. So deep, I must be nearly there. I can see his face very clearly now. And hear his words too. But wait ... he is no longer smiling. He is looking sternly at me. And his voice has changed. His voice sounds stern too.

No longer falling. Just floating. Floating on air.

My dad is telling me something, and he wants me to listen. 'Ricky,' he is saying. 'Ricky, go back.'

I try to speak, to protest, but no words come. My dad tells me again. 'Ricky, go back. This is not your time. Your mum needs you. Tell her I love her. And I love you too, Ricky. Someday we will all meet together again, but this is not the time. I am at peace now, but you have your whole life ahead of you, and you must go back.'

Drifting upwards. Higher and higher. My dad is getting further away, and the pain is returning. I try to shout to him, but again no words come out.

Drifting and drifting. Higher and higher. My dad is sliding away from me, but I can still hear his voice. It is calm, so calm. He is sending me one final message from his place of peace.

'Go back, Ricky.'

Drifting up and up. I am almost at the surface now and I can see the light. It is so bright, much too bright. As I open my eyes, the light pierces them like red-hot daggers. My dad is gone, and my head is aching.

I am now back on the surface. I can taste blood. And I can smell that awful smell. I have smelled it before. What is it?

I remember now. Playing football. Playing for Glenside against New Cumnock when I was only twelve. A clash of heads and I fall into a deep, deep sleep. Falling and falling. Deeper and deeper. Until that awful smell stops me from falling and brings me back to the surface.

I remember it now. They called it ... smelling salts.

78

By the time the two ambulancemen had checked out Martha

Ferguson's vital signs and lifted her onto their stretcher, the tiny handful of inquisitive neighbours at her front gate had grown to a small crowd, genuine concern etched across their faces. Concern for Martha's health, concern for the drama now unfolding in this normally sleepy part of town, but mainly concern about the blood decorating the pavement.

'Keep talking to her, Sir,' the older crew member pleaded with Martha's husband as they carried her down the path towards the waiting ambulance. Sandy Ferguson's distraught gait was at serious odds with the usual upright posture of a mean physique that would have done justice to a man ten years younger.

'If she hears your voice she might come around,' the ambulanceman urged. 'So, just keep talking to her.'

DI Charlie Reynolds felt conflicted as he stood on the front lawn, police radio set in hand. In different circumstances, he would have stood shoulder-to-shoulder with Ferguson until his wife had been safely tucked up in the ambulance. However, she was now in good hands and much more urgent matters demanded his attention.

'DI Reynolds here,' he said into the mouthpiece, facing away from the anxious onlookers. 'I know I'm supposed to be off-duty, but I'm down here in Girvan. We've got a problem, a big problem. They've got the Anderson lad, the one that's on the run, and he's in bother. Blood everywhere, but no sign of him. Contact DI McTurk right away and tell him it's got to be the Nutter Squad, no other explanation. Can I leave it to you guys to send the cavalry?'

'No problem,' the controller replied. 'But Girvan, DI Reynolds? Why Girvan, of all places? Richard Anderson was supposed to be lying low in Glasgow? The uniforms are combing the streets up there looking for him.'

'I'll explain later,' Reynolds said, rolling his eyes in recognition that he had just been rumbled on his failed masterplan to keep Ricky free from police capture. 'It's a long story.'

'Any idea where they've taken him, Sir? I need to know where to send the squad cars?'

'Not a clue where he is. He's been crashing out in a wooden chalet down here for the past few days. The address is 178 Henrietta Street. The main house belongs to a Mr and Mrs Alexander Ferguson. He's the local harbour master and she's on her way to hospital. Fainted, we think, and probably clattered her head when she hit the deck. She's got an underlying medical condition, but I wouldn't be surprised if it was the sight of the lad being dragged out covered in blood that made her pass out.'

'Back-up is already on its way to the Henrietta Street locus, Sir. Did you manage to speak to the injured lady? Ask her if she has any idea where they're taking the boy?'

'No, she was out stone-cold. Blood pouring out of her ear. Concussion, I'm thinking, but it could be more serious.'

'Okay, but she might recover and give you a clue. We've already got two local officers winging their way to the address right now. They should be there any minute. The rest of the cavalry will be there within the hour. Sir, please let us know immediately if you find out where they've taken the boy and we'll divert the cars.'

'Thanks, you're a star. I need to go now. The patient's husband is waving at me to come over. Don't know what he wants, but I'll keep you guys fully informed. Over.'

'Over and out.'

Sandy Ferguson was standing at the rear door of the ambulance when Reynolds pushed his way through the sizeable gathering of inquisitive neighbours.

'Byne Hill,' the harbour master said.

'What?' asked Reynolds, looking perplexed.

'Byne Hill!' Ferguson repeated, only this time with considerably more emphasis. 'That's where they've taken Ricky. Martha has regained consciousness, but she saw what happened before she fainted. Two big bruisers with short-cropped hair, one with a purple scar on his face, both wearing jeans and black leather jackets. She also heard one of the big guys shout at the driver to head for Byne Hill. It's a local beauty spot. The driver had blond hair, by the way, and looked very young.'

Reynolds just stood staring at him.

'If you don't mind me saying, Sandy, that's a hell of a lot of detail from a woman who was out stone cold and has just regained consciousness.'

'She used to be a police officer,' came Ferguson's curt reply. 'She was walking the beat when you were still in short trousers. So, come on man, get your arse in gear. They've got Ricky, and they must have a good head start on you.'

'Where is it?' asked Reynolds. 'This Byne Hill, or whatever it's called?'

'Head south out of town along the A714 and you'll see the

294

signpost at the end of the seafront. You can't miss it. A waymarked walk, popular with tourists, but it'll be quiet at this time of year. And get a bloody move on. He's a fine young lad, is Ricky Anderson, and he's your responsibility now.'

Reynolds bolted towards his car, key in one hand to open the door and radio in the other to update the control room and get them to divert the troops to the Byne Hill locus. As he fired his Cortina into action and began accelerating along Henrietta Street, he glanced in his rear-view mirror and watched the ambulance pull out to follow in his wake. However, something else caught his attention as well. It was the imposing figure of Sandy Ferguson standing behind on the pavement, and it left Reynolds with one big question.

Why had he not gone to hospital with Martha?

79

Janice and Iona sat slumped at Charlie Reynolds's kitchen table, sipping nervously at their mugs of tea, their fourth in as many hours. They stared wordlessly at the wall-mounted telephone, begging it to spring into action.

It wasn't the phone that rang, it was the doorbell. Janice jumped and sent hot tea cascading all over the table. Iona got up and dashed towards the sink for a dishcloth while Janice made straight for the front door. It had to be Andy McTurk with some good news at last, hadn't it?

It was neither Andy McTurk nor good news. When she pulled the door open, a sturdily-built middle-aged man stood on the other side, his solemn face a kaleidoscope of agitation, anxiety and pent-up rage. He looked vaguely familiar. Only vaguely, though.

'Can I help you?' Janice enquired, clocking the stranger's unnerving body language and quickly contemplating a hurried defence strategy. 'Do you want to speak to my husband?'

'You haven't got a husband,' he replied through gritted teeth, his puffy eyes narrowed in defiance. 'Your husband got killed in a motorbike accident. Or have you forgotten now that you're screwing your new boyfriend, you bitch?'

Janice immediately put her shoulder to the door and shoved, but her uninvited guest beat her to it by jamming his foot against the wooden facing.

'Get out!' she screamed. 'Get out of my house!'

By the time Iona had managed to stumble her way along the hall, the stranger was inside the house, glaring menacingly at Janice and brandishing a long-bladed knife in his right fist. Iona froze to the spot like a hypnotist's volunteer under a receptive spell. It was Janice who tried to speak, but the words wouldn't quite come out.

'What ... what ... what do you ...?'

'Shut your face!' the intruder barked, his eyes ablaze with what Janice hoped was fear but knew with innate certainty was fury. 'Don't say a word, not a bloody word!'

Iona screamed and burst into tears.

'And you too, you little trollop,' the stranger spat, his eyes darting from the middle-aged lady standing terrified in front of him to the young girl leaning unsteadily against the wall, now sobbing like a baby.

'Who ... who are you?' Janice stammered, backing gingerly along the hallway, her hands shaking like autumn leaves in a howling storm. 'What ... what do you want with us?'

The stranger didn't reply. Instead, he just stood there staring, as if in a bewildered stupor, the knife glistening in the beam of the ceiling light. Still, Iona cried. Janice addressed her directly.

'It's all right, Iona, just do as the man says. Take a few deep breaths and try to stop crying. Then go ... go and put the kettle on.'

She couldn't believe she had just said that. Here she was talking to a menacing stranger who was holding a knife, and she had just told Iona to go and put the bloody kettle on. There was no turning back now, so turning to her assailant she decided to continue the pantomime.

'Can we just go through to the kitchen and sit down? I think we could all do with a wee cup of tea. Don't you?'

To her amazement, the stranger's demeanour began to metamorphose before her eyes. He nodded. It was a sheepish nod that smacked of resignation and humiliation. Janice could see a look of defeat slowly enveloping his face. However, he still held the knife in his hand, so although the rage had gone into temporary hibernation, the peril level was still at red alert.

Janice moved slowly towards the kitchen. The exterior of her ribcage ached from the impact of the front door having been slammed against it, and the interior from her rapidly accelerated breathing. Closing her eyes momentarily in silent prayer, she turned again to face her sinister visitor.

'Well, are you coming or not?' she ventured, displaying remarkable boldness.

He followed her like a well-trained gundog. As Iona stood trembling in shock beside the kettle, Janice ushered her impromptu guest to sit down at the table. He complied without demur, and she lowered herself slowly into the chair opposite.

'Iona, can you make the tea please, while I have a wee chat with Mister … sorry, I didn't catch your name?'

He muttered something, but it was virtually inaudible.

'Sorry …'

'Rafferty,' the man said, staring mindlessly at the psychedelic pattern on the waxcloth table cover. 'Dan Rafferty.'

For Janice, the penny dropped immediately. Frank Rafferty's younger brother. He had been in third year at secondary school when she and Frank were in fifth year, that's why she had recognised him. She had to think very quickly. She had to keep his attention and win his confidence. And most importantly of all, she had to get him to drop that knife.

'Not Frank's brother?' she enquired, displaying an air of real surprise. 'I went to school with Frank, you know. It was a terrible thing that happened to him. Have they got the person who did it yet?'

Rafferty's eyes shifted their focus from the table-top and homed in on Janice's own. All of a sudden, they were on fire again. Janice bit her lip and kept biting it until it bled. Every sinew in her body screamed at her to leap towards him and gouge his eyes out of their sockets with her fingernails. Instead, she sat stalk-still, tasting the blood and beseeching her nostrils not to dilate and give the game away.

'Do you want to talk about it?' she said, her outer voice considerably calmer than the one in her head. 'Get everything off your chest, I mean?'

Rafferty's body language seemed to continue oscillating from the one extreme to the other. The fire receded and the look of defeat once more returned to his pallid face. Janice Anderson was no psychiatrist, but many years' experience of life as a district nurse had taught her to recognise when someone had finally lost their marbles, and this guy was a basket case. A basket case holding a knife.

'Mister Rafferty?' she continued. 'Do you want to talk about it? Tell me what's wrong?'

Rafferty's head dropped like an anchor, his eyeballs concealed from view by eyelids of solid lead. Janice stared at him with all the fake sympathy she would need to muster if he suddenly looked back up at her again. She thought about grabbing the rolling pin that lay on the adjacent worktop and smashing it over his head. However, he still held the knife in his right hand and might be able to beat her to the punch, so she decided to continue playing amateur agony aunt.

'Mister Rafferty?' she ventured. 'Or can I call you Dan?'

Rafferty took a sharp intake of breath and opened his eyes. By now they were tearful and puffy against a rapidly reddening complexion, and formed the centrepiece of what instantly reminded Janice of the painted face of a circus clown. He looked utterly ridiculous. An involuntary giggle welled up inside her frame and came out as an undignified snort, which she immediately managed to disguise by fabricating a little cough.

Finally, Rafferty spoke. It was the voice of a vanquished man. Self-revulsion had finally prevailed over self-pity.

'My life is a mess, a total mess.'

Iona held her breath as she briefly contemplated flinging the kettle of boiling water straight in the odious intruder's face, before concluding that Janice would probably suffer severe collateral damage if she did. Janice looked at Rafferty but received no eye contact. She then looked again at the knife he still held vice-like in his fist.

'So? Do you want to talk about it?' she asked in a tone so soft and gentle that it could have seduced a poised cobra into submission.

'What is there to talk about?' Rafferty retorted with a pathetic sneer. 'It's all finished. I'm finished. The great Dan Rafferty has been found out at last. A bully, a cheat, an extortionist ... and now about to become a murderer.'

His eyes finally met those of Janice. They now looked cold and lifeless, like glass marbles stuck in a stuffed dead dog's head by an enterprising taxidermist. He stared at the knife, saw his own repulsive reflection and smiled a smile of terrible resignation. Rafferty's life may well have been finished, but his blade was far from it.

'Mister Rafferty ... Dan,' Janice whispered, her throat so dry that every word nipped like a bee-sting. 'Can you please put the knife down? It's frightening young Iona over there … and it's frightening me too.'

'Your son,' Rafferty said, completely oblivious to her pleas, a pair of inhuman eyes radiating heartless indifference. 'That bastard son of yours. He caused all this, you know. You and him. None of this would have happened if you had just agreed to be Frank's wife. He loved you, you know. And now you have to pay. You and your bastard son have to pay.'

Janice Anderson's fear for her own safety lingered momentarily, then disappeared into thin air. All she could think about now was her precious son.

'Dan, do you know where Ricky is? If you do, please tell me. He's my only child and he's all I've got left.'

Rafferty stared at her without the slightest hint of compassion.

'You and your son caused all this. Everything. You rejected Frank. You ruined his life and turned him into a monster. Your son set Monk up and he set Frank up. And he set Frank against me. And now you both have to pay.'

'Do you know where Ricky is?' Janice asked again, a distinct edge in her voice this time. 'If you do, please tell me.'

'Of course, I know where he is,' he said with a mocking grin, a trickle of sweat dribbling from his lips down over his chin. 'But the last person on earth I would tell is you, you bitch. All I'm going to say is that the cops had better catch up with him fast, because I've sent the hounds after him. Don't worry, though. When they get him, they'll send him straight back to you. One piece at a time.'

Janice inhaled sharply, the horror of her son's predicament now becoming tortuously graphic.

'Just answer this one question, please. Will you tell me where my son is? I'm begging you.'

'For the last time, no!' Monk yelled. 'He can rot in hell beside his father!'

The rage welled up like an erupting volcano. Sucking in a huge gulp of air, Janice made a lunge for the rolling pin. Rafferty went to raise his knife, but it was Iona who reacted first. She grabbed the earthenware casserole dish that was lying on the kitchen worktop and brought it down over the back of Rafferty's head with all the fury she could muster. As the dish shattered into smithereens, his skull split open and his face hit the kitchen table with an almighty thump, sending a set of splintering dentures skiting across the table and slithering onto Janice's lap.

As the clatter and tinkle of pulverised pottery slowly faded away to silence, the two women stared at each other.

Iona's voice was trembling.

'Janice ... Janice ... I think I've killed him.'

Janice swotted Rafferty's fractured false teeth off her lap, stood up and calmly placed her fingers on his neck to feel for a pulse.

'No, Iona,' she said. 'You haven't killed him. But he won't be eating any sweeties for a while.'

Not really sure whether to laugh or cry, the two women hugged each other and did both in turns.

'Maybe we should let Andy McTurk know?' Iona said, her voice still very shaky.

'Yes, you're probably right, Iona,' Janice replied, and picked up the telephone. 'But only after we've called for an ambulance. Mister Rafferty is in a lot more bother than we are.'

80

Charlie Reynolds was a fast driver at the best of times, but on that autumnal Saturday evening Mario Andretti himself would have been left languishing in his slipstream.

He reached the tiny car park on Girvan's southern seafront at precisely 6.45 p.m., where a big sign proudly heralded the waymarked Byne Hill walk, the very location that Sandy Ferguson had told him about a few minutes earlier. Just one other vehicle sat in the car park, a black Ford Corsair that had only recently been washed and polished up like a gleaming new shilling, save for more scrape marks than a rugby prop forward's battle-hardened face. And then there was the blood. It caked the rear door handle and the door itself, and it peppered the potholed track that ran parallel to the seashore.

Reynolds recognised the car right away. He contacted the station to tell them that he had arrived at the Byne Hill car park, only to receive a predictable lecture about the need to wait for police reinforcements before he set off in pursuit of Ricky and his infamous captors. He listened politely, then grunted a brusque 'over and out' to his well-meaning colleagues and chucked his radio handset onto the back seat. The very last thing he needed now was a police radio crackling into action while he was scurrying incognito through the undergrowth that lay on the hills to his left.

He got out of his car, started looking for footprints and immediately found himself spoilt for choice. Scores of recreational walkers had trampled over the ground. However, in the midst of the jigsaw of prints of all shapes and sizes, he noticed something else as well. A trail of fresh-looking scrape marks, which as he hurried along seemed to manifest themselves every few yards or so. The intrepid ramblers had been striding out with their customary gusto, but one of them had been dragged along, half-walking at best. At that moment, the normally optimistic Charlie Reynolds could only see one outcome from his pursuit of whichever poor beggar's toes were currently bursting out of his shoes, and it wasn't a particularly pleasant one. Not only that, but the poor beggar in question simply had to be Ricky Anderson.

Following the route along Woodland Bay past the confused geology that constitutes Horse Rock, his hurried march increased to a canter until he noticed that the drag-marks had ended where the well-formed track gave way to a grassy path. Reynolds stopped for a breather and quickly surveyed the panorama. A few miles offshore to his right sat the impossibly symmetrical little isle of Ailsa Craig, or 'Paddy's Milestone' as the mariners preferred to call it in deference to its half-way position between Glasgow and the port of Belfast, while further away in the distance lay the sprawling expanse of the island of Arran. However, it wasn't the splendour of the westerly view that had now consumed his attention, it was the graphic mental image of what he might find as he turned to tackle the hill track to his east.

Following the waymarked signs, Reynolds ignored the narrow road leading to Shalloch Mill and the bridge over the Bynehill Burn, and turned left up the next farm track. He quickened his pace and soon reached a further track that led uphill to a wooden gate, on the top slat of which a small smear of blood was enough to confirm that he was still heading in the right direction.

A chill ocean breeze began whipping up the dry hillside foliage, increasing in intensity the higher he climbed, playing tricks on his ears like a ghostly cry in a long-abandoned country mansion. He stopped, listened for a moment and heard the sinister sound again. This wasn't merely an innocent sea breeze, nor indeed some other-worldly wailing. It was a voice, a human voice. One voice definitely, maybe even two.

Looking straight ahead, he could just make out the top of what appeared to be some kind of giant man-made structure, almost like a drystane dyke that had been built vertically towards the heavens rather than horizontally to the horizon. He heard the voices again. Plural this time, no doubt about it.

Reynolds marched on, deeply conscious of the fact that the sea breeze on his back would serve to carry the sound of his footsteps and heavy breathing in the direction of the voices that were becoming louder and more distinguishable by the minute. Approaching the brow of the hill-track, he slowed his brisk march down to a more measured walk and lowered his head in anticipation of the source of the voices coming into view, in recognition that if he suddenly caught sight of them there was every chance that they would clock him too.

As the highest point of the track drew closer, all Reynolds could see was the cloud-lined skyline and the topmost part of the giant stone structure which seemed to be expanding before his eyes. He shuffled his stooped frame sideways from the path and into the adjacent heather-clad peat bog, sank down onto his knees and began crawling towards the locus of the vocal activity. By this time, his Ralph Slater suit had seen much better days, but he couldn't have cared less.

As soon as he had scrambled his way to the brow of the hill, the whole scenario came into sharp focus. The tall stone structure that he had first seen from just above the car park sat on a solid square foundation and towered in decreasing width in a triangular formation some fifteen-feet high towards the heavens. Reynolds was not to know that this strange monument was in fact the obelisk erected away back in the late nineteenth century in memory of the father of Lord Ardmillan, one of the locale's most prominent Court of Session judges, whose elegant castle building still stood proudly in the background. Nor indeed would he have cared. The only thing that mattered to him was the gut-wrenching sight of an ashen-faced young man sitting propped against the north-facing elevation of the monument, his face covered in blood, and his hands and feet tied behind him with rope. That, and the spectre of two huge brutes standing over him and barking insults into his face, one holding a camera and the other what looked like a black toolbag.

The Nutter Squad had come to Byne Hill, and not just for the

302

fresh air either. They had come to administer Ricky Anderson's agonising demise.

81

While four police cars and an ambulance were busily racing each other southwards through the streets of Girvan, one of each description had already arrived at the Reynolds's abode in Prestwick, some 24 miles further up the Ayrshire coast.

Janice Anderson led DS Sandy Sutherland through to the living room, while in the kitchen one paramedic tended to the minor scratches on Iona McNish's right hand as another attempted to revive the semi-conscious Dan Rafferty, both medical conditions the result of the former's thunderous blow with the earthenware casserole dish to the latter's skull.

Iona then walked rather sheepishly into the living room to join her prospective mother-in-law and the young policeman who had been appointed temporary officer-in-charge while his boss, DI Andy McTurk, was winging his way at speed towards the fun and games down Girvan way.

'Hello again, Iona,' Sandy Sutherland smiled. 'I wouldn't want to bring a broken pay packet home to you, lass, that's for sure. God help Ricky if he ever tries.'

Janice giggled and Sutherland followed suit. Not Iona, though. The very mention of Ricky's name was enough to set the tears pool up in her soft brown eyes. Sutherland took his cue and shuffled through to the kitchen to pour her a glass of water, by which time a bewildered Dan Rafferty was being strapped onto a stretcher, restrained by police handcuffs and head covered in surgical dressings.

'How is he?' Sutherland enquired.

'He'll live,' came the paramedic's blunt reply.

'Pity,' the young sergeant muttered, as he glared at Rafferty while heading back out the door in the direction of the living room. 'Let's hope it's nothing trivial.'

Sutherland had the preliminary formalities tied up within minutes. It all appeared fairly straightforward. The knock on the front door. Dan Rafferty barging in, brandishing a knife which the forensic lads would soon be dusting for prints. Iona initially freaking out, while Janice did her best to keep everyone calm and defuse a very dangerous situation. Janice reaching for the rolling pin in synch with Rafferty raising his knife, but Iona winning the race and clattering Rafferty with the casserole dish. Then a communal moment of euphoric hysteria before Janice called the cops and the medics.

'Is that about it?' Sutherland asked.

'Yes, that's it,' Janice replied, glancing over at Iona for corroboration.

Iona nodded. 'I thought about flinging the kettle at him, but I was afraid the boiling water might hit Janice too.'

Sutherland couldn't prevent himself laughing. 'When Ricky gets home, I must remember to tell him never to get on the wrong side of you, Iona.'

'If he ever gets home,' Iona said.

'He will, Iona,' the detective sergeant replied. 'Charlie and Andy and the rest of the lads will be working on that right now. Trust me, he'll be home before the night's out.'

Iona stared at Janice, who stared back. Neither of them was convinced. And if they had known about the desperate situation in which Ricky had now found himself, neither would have given him a snowball's chance in hell.

'You'll both need to give us a formal statement down at the police station later,' Sutherland added. 'Okay?'

'Okay,' Janice nodded, Iona following suit. 'So, what happens now?'

'Well,' said Sutherland. 'It's all pretty much wrapped up, as far as I'm concerned. Frank Rafferty is dead and Edwin Monk has admitted to killing him, and has even signed a statement to that effect. Dan Rafferty had a watertight alibi because he was elsewhere at the time of his brother's murder, but he doesn't need that now since Monk has spilled his guts. Dan probably thought he was off the hook, and he was until the whole situation eventually became too much for him. He then completely lost the plot and came after both of you, with the clear intention of harming or even killing you. And in the course of his folly, he admitted in front of two witnesses that he's the one who has sent the Nutter Squad after Ricky. So, make no mistake about it, Dan's going down as well.'

'Who exactly are the Nutter Squad?' Janice asked, cringing. 'Is the big man who assaulted me one of them?'

'Yes, he is,' Sutherland replied. 'Robert McDade was the one who put you in hospital, Janice. His sidekick is another big bruiser called Zander McGinn, and there's a third one called Ralph Baxter, but Baxter's a pussycat compared to those two. Frank Rafferty called the shots, and McDade and McGinn carried out his instructions, which normally meant duffing up some poor guy for failing to pay the interest on their loan.'

Janice visibly shuddered.

'And now Dan Rafferty calls the shots?'

'Well, he did ... for a few days there. But he won't be calling any more shots from behind bars, you can be sure of that.'

'And what about McDade and McGinn? They've gone after my Ricky, haven't they?'

'Well Janice, the honest answer to that is ... yes, almost certainly. Dan Rafferty said as much to you, didn't he?'

Another shudder.

'Yes, he did. Do you have any idea where Ricky is?'

Sutherland steeled himself in preparation for giving her half a story, because he certainly couldn't read her the full chapter. At least, not until everything had played out for better or for worse. And right at that moment, Sutherland's money would have been on worse. Much worse.

'We think he's down in Girvan, Janice,' he said. 'And half of Southwest Scotland Police force are out looking for him.'

'But so are the Nutter Squad,' Iona interjected.

'And so is Charlie Reynolds, Iona,' Sutherland hit back. 'And if my own life was ever at stake, I'd want Charlie to be the one right by my side.'

82

Charlie Reynolds continued scrambling through the undergrowth on his elbows and knees until he had reached to within about twenty yards of the drama that was playing out at the giant stone monument. He was now close enough to recognise the gravelly voice.

'Smile for the camera, son. We're going to send some nice photos to your wee mammy for the family album.'

It belonged to the brute who rejoiced in the name of Mad Rab McDade, and what it lacked in cultural charm it certainly made up for in pure menace. Ricky didn't answer, he just stared at McDade in semi-conscious defiance. Meanwhile, his sidekick dropped his toolbag on the wet grass and snapped it open.

'Hacksaw first as usual, Rab?' Zander McGinn enquired, his eyes bulging in manic anticipation from underneath a square brow that overhung his bloated face like a thatched roof protecting rotting windows. 'Then the blowtorch to finish the job?'

Ricky visibly squirmed, struggling vainly to free himself from the ropes that cut into his hands and feet. Reynolds inhaled deeply from the partial camouflage of the Ayrshire heather, but remained silent.

'Etiquette, Zander,' McDade replied, sniggering. 'Etiquette, man. How many times have I had to tell you? The hacksaw's the main course and the blowtorch is the dessert. But first, there's the starter.'

'And what's that, Rab?' McGinn asked. 'Remind me.'

'The hammer, Zander,' McDade responded. 'We always start with the hammer. Break a few bones first, just to warm things up. Remember that big lanky guy from Tarbolton? The one who refused point blank to pay Frank his dues and told you to go and f—k yourself?'

'Oh aye, Rab, that's right,' McGinn chortled, as the gloriously gruesome recollection came flooding back. 'He was rolling about like a puppet with its strings cut off before we got really started on him with the rest of the gear.'

'So, get your hammer, Zander,' said McDade. 'And start cracking some limbs, man. Is it a written invitation you're waiting for?'

McGinn nodded gleefully, fumbled around in his toolbox for a few seconds and took out an old rusty claw hammer. He then knelt down beside Ricky and started waving it backwards and forwards in front of his face. Ricky spat a bloodied spittle straight into his captor's eyes.

'You'll pay for this, you big ugly bastard,' he cursed. 'And that's a promise.'

McGinn grimaced, wiped the gunge from his face and raised the hammer to shoulder height.

'Camera ready, Rab?' he sneered, nostrils fully dilated.

'Aye,' said McDade, grinning like the cat who got the cream. 'Smile for your wee mammy.'

'Touch him and you're both history!'

McDade and McGinn both spun around like a pair of synchronised sumo wrestlers, two sets of double chins dropping in astonishment. They had a bagful of lethal weapons at their disposal and Charlie Reynolds was as vulnerable as a new-born baby in its first shawl, but he was now on autopilot. He marched towards them, arms pumping furiously.

'Drop the gear, lads, and I'll take your good behaviour into consideration when I bang you up. I've taken both of you out before, and you've still got the bruises to show for it.'

'Aye, maybe so,' McDade grinned. 'But not both of us at the same time, you haven't. And not when we're carrying chibs and all you've got in your pocket is a nice clean hankie. You're dead meat, Reynolds.'

Just at that, the sound of police sirens could be heard approaching along the seafront. They sounded to Reynolds like his favourite Beach Boys' chorus, drawing closer by the second.

'You hear that, McDade?' he smirked, as he strode forward. 'The cavalry has arrived. Late as usual, but it's here at last. And you and your big dumb clone are going down. So, tell McGinn to drop the hammer like a nice wee boy and I might put in a good word for you. They do a lovely ice-cream in the Bar-L, if you just happen to know who to ask.'

McDade thought about it for a moment, then bent down and grabbed a screwdriver from the toolbag and shot back up to his full height. Clocking the sudden change of mood, Reynolds stopped dead in his tracks. McGinn stood stalk-still holding the hammer, looking at his sidekick for inspiration. In the distance, a blond-haired youngster could be seen scurrying away in the opposite direction. Ralph Baxter had come out of hiding with a long overdue change of mind about his chosen career path.

'I see your driver has just handed in his notice,' Reynolds said. 'Not that you'll be needing him anymore, McDade, because you'll be leaving this place in either a cop car or an ambulance. Your choice, pal.'

'No copper ever called me 'pal',' McDade roared, and began propelling his oversized frame straight towards Reynolds, his screwdriver poised in the stabbing position.

McGinn hesitated at first, then hared off in McDade's substantial wake towards Reynolds, grasping his hammer. This would be a fight to the death, two giant lumbering thugs armed to the teeth against one completely unarmed police officer whose only defence would be his own fitness and guile. Meanwhile, young Ricky Anderson could only wriggle and squirm in exasperation, knowing full well that he could do absolutely nothing to shift the odds in Reynolds's favour and settle the score with the animal who had maimed his mother.

If Reynolds had one advantage, then it was the fact that he was in a slightly elevated position when his adversaries closed in on him. He had met McDade's dubious acquaintance on numerous occasions, and given him a right good pasting on one of them, but he had never before seen such incandescent rage written all over the big man's face as he lashed out at Reynolds from head height with the screwdriver. However, before the blow could land, Reynolds swung his foot with every ounce of strength he could muster and booted him in the groin. McDade let out a howl of agony and sank onto his knees in the heather, at which point Reynolds drew back his fist to hit him again, only to feel the full force of McGinn's hammer brushing narrowly past his head and shattering his collar bone as a second prize.

The pain was excruciating. Reynolds yelled and fell backwards, grabbing his left shoulder with his right hand. When he looked up, all he could see was the imposing frame of McGinn standing over him, his huge fist and its resident claw hammer silhouetted against the pale blue sky. As the second mighty blow descended, Reynolds somehow managed to spin his body sideways and the hammer buried itself a good four inches deep into the soft peaty ground. Clenching his right fist, he watched as McGinn's momentum brought his head down in tandem with the hammer and lashed out, catching him flush on the nose and sending a huge spurt of blood spraying across the foliage.

With a face like a burst ripe tomato, McGinn lunged at Reynolds and managed to pin him to the ground with his colossal weight, by which time the big detective's left arm was practically paralysed from the trauma to the nerves attending his collar bone area. McGinn recognised his plight immediately and grabbed his right wrist with both arms, disabling him completely. Still holding his nether regions, McDade hauled himself up onto his feet and stumbled over to where his kindred spirit's immense frame still lay on top of his incapacitated prey. He knelt down and held the blade of his screwdriver to Reynolds's heavily contorted face.

'You ready, Reynolds? This is where you die, you piece of shit. One eye at a time.'

McDade didn't even know what had hit him as his lights went

out. Not so McGinn, who at least had the dubious fortune of seeing a hefty, full-bearded guy bring his crowbar down onto his crown with tremendous force before joining his partner-in-crime in the land of nod.

Sandy Ferguson grabbed McGinn's prostrate bulk by the shoulders and hauled him off the injured detective.

'How the hell did you get here?' Reynolds gasped through laboured breath, pulling his torso up off the wet ground.

'A wee bit of local knowledge,' Ferguson grinned. 'There's more than one way to climb Byne Hill. And I bet you're glad I did.'

'Bloody right,' Reynolds said, grimacing from the pain in his shoulder. 'Help me up, Sandy, will you? I've had better days.'

'Aye, I can see that,' replied the old harbour master. 'And your suit might need a wee visit to the dry-cleaners when you get home.'

Reynolds looked at the felled bodies of McDade and McGinn, as they lay flat on their backs on the turf, bloated bellies protruding skywards, foreheads bloodied and lifeless eyes confirming that they were sleeping either the sleep of the comatose or the sleep of the dead. Whichever it turned out to be would be fine with Reynolds. This was the life they had chosen, and it was their funeral. Perhaps, literally.

'I hate to disturb you, guys,' came a strained voice from behind. 'Just when you're ready, of course.'

Ricky Anderson might have lost a bucketful of blood, but he still hadn't lost his sense of occasion.

'Allow me, Ricky,' Ferguson said with a smile, and hurried over to the obelisk to administer his young employee's freedom. Still nursing his sagging shoulder, Reynolds offered to help, but Ferguson brusquely declined.

'I've been tying knots in ropes since you were in nappies, so I don't think I'll be needing any help to untie them, do you? And anyway, where's your police radio? We need to get this young man to hospital immediately, and those two big brutes as well. If they're still breathing, that is.'

'I left it in my car,' Reynolds replied. 'I didn't want to give the game away when I was playing hide and seek in the heather.'

'Bugger it,' muttered Ferguson, unravelling the last turn of rope from Ricky's wrists to reveal friction marks that resembled raw meat. 'Then you'll need to take him back down the hill to your car, and pronto. I'll stay here with those two lunatics till the cops arrive.

Do you think you'll be able to walk, Ricky.'

By now wobbling unsteadily on his feet, Ricky just nodded.

'No, Sandy,' said Reynolds. 'We need to do it the other way around. You take Ricky back down to the car park, and hopefully before you get there the ambulance guys will be on their way to intercept you. Meanwhile, I'll hang on here with our two friends. And Sandy, leave your crowbar with me.'

'Fine,' Ferguson replied. 'We'll do it your way. You're the copper.'

Reynolds, his left arm swinging back and forth like a pendulum on an antique grandfather clock, wrapped his right around Ricky's shoulders while Ferguson did his best to wipe the blood away from his eyes and face, and steeled himself for the harrowing trek back downhill. Suddenly, Ricky's eyes exploded like searchlights from fatigued sockets.

'Watch yourselves!' he yelled, shoving Reynolds violently away in one direction and Ferguson in the other, as the huge frame of McDade came staggering towards them with McGinn's claw hammer flailing in his grasp.

Instinctively, Ricky drew back his fist and caught McDade flush on the chin with a thunderous uppercut, sending him reeling backwards. He took two strides forward, kicked the hammer out of his hand and grabbed hold of his ear. Still holding it, he then thumped him four times on the face with such force that the dislodgement of teeth and the crunching of bone found themselves competing for maximum sound effect. Ricky then let go and McDade collapsed on the ground like a sack of Girvan's famous potatoes.

Reynolds and Ferguson squared themselves up and rushed over to where the victor stood over the vanquished.

Ricky glared at McDade's bloodied and distorted face. His voice was clear and calm.

'And if you ever come near my mum again, I'll kill you.'

Reynolds knelt down and checked McDade's pulse, then wandered over to do likewise with McGinn, while Ferguson stood shoulder-to-shoulder with Ricky.

'They'll both live,' the big detective announced, the tone of his voice registering considerably more surprise than relief. 'Are you okay, Ricky?'

'I'm fine,' he replied, head drooping in exhaustion. 'But can I go home now?'

'I think that's a very good idea, Ricky,' replied Reynolds, as he set about tending to the angry-looking gash on the back of the youngster's head. 'And when you do, I think you can expect a decent welcome.'

With the detective's cloth hankerchief draped over Ricky's gaping head wound and held in place by the hood of his jacket, he set off downhill, Ferguson's muscular arm wrapped around his shoulders for support. Less than ten minutes into their laboured descent towards the sanctity of the seaside, they found themselves able to sink to the ground in relief at the glorious sight of four dark-blue uniforms and the same number of green tunics approaching. The cavalry had finally arrived in the shape of Southwest Scotland Police force and the St Andrew's and Red Cross Scottish Ambulance Service, the former trudging on ahead to come to the aid of the beleaguered DI Reynolds and clap handcuffs on the two comatose founder members of the Nutter Squad, while the latter lifted a seriously-injured Ricky Anderson onto their stretcher before administering the emergency first-aid that would see him through the remainder of the downhill trek to a waiting ambulance.

Girvan's celebrated Byne Hill had witnessed many a daring adventure over the years, but never one quite like this. How it now longed for the peace and tranquillity that would surely follow once the assorted players in this searing drama had left the stage.

83

Ricky Anderson took a sharp intake of breath as he stared at the big wooden door.

On the other side lay his future, the one that only a few days ago he had thought he'd never live to see. A chilly late-September breeze gnawed at the eleven stitches on a partially shaved skull decorated with a patchwork of badly-cropped hair and surgical dressings. He pulled the door open and stepped inside.

He squeezed Iona McNish's hand and she squeezed back. So, this was where her fiancé had been plying his trade for the past four-and-a-bit years? The university building wasn't at all like what she had imagined. Very old and traditional, antiquated even, and certainly not the ultra-modern all-singing, all-dancing, state-of-the-art centre of excellence that she had conjured up in her mind.

A rat-a-tat of footsteps came tumbling down the stairwell,

revealing four youthful-looking female students all clad in flared denims and adorned with the large frizzy hairdos which were now very much in vogue. They glanced sideways as they passed Ricky and Iona on the stairs. However, one of them did a quick double-take and stopped dead in her tracks. Ricky squirmed when he recognised the dreaded Miranda Fletcher-Greene, she of the fluttering eyelids and titanic bosom.

'Ricky!' she exclaimed, as if she had just been reunited with her long-lost lover. 'You're back at last! I've been reading all about ... well, you know ... about everything. What happened to your hair?'

Iona squeezed Ricky's hand again and looked at him quizzically.

'Hello, Miranda,' he mumbled, climbing the stairs two at a time to escape his admirer's unwelcome attention, with Iona doing likewise in his wake. She could feel the girl's evil glower burning into the back of her head.

'Had an argument with a tiger in Calder Park Zoo yesterday,' Ricky quipped. 'Sorry, Miranda, but I'm in a bit of a hurry this morning.'

'So, who was that, then?' Iona asked when they had climbed the first flight of stairs, a naughty smile betraying deep insecurity.

'That was Miranda,' Ricky replied. 'Miranda Fletcher-Greene, one of my undergraduate students. Posh accent, biggest mouth on the campus.'

'And biggest boobs I've ever seen,' Iona added, studying his face forensically.

'I couldn't give a damn,' he said, pulling her towards him. 'Because I've got you, and you are an angel. And this time next year, you'll be my wife.'

Their kiss on the half-landing was quickly interrupted by another clatter of hurried footsteps descending the concrete steps. A couple of minutes later they were in Professor Bernstein's outer office, being plied with tea and biscuits by the loyal Moira whose over-the-top enthusiasm at welcoming Ricky back to the fold couldn't have been disguised if she had been wearing a NASA spacesuit. The door creaked open and in walked the great man himself, replete with his trademark three-piece suit, white shirt and bright-blue bowtie.

'Ah ... Richard, my boy!' he exclaimed, his warm eyes radiating genuine pleasure at being repatriated with his star protégé. 'You're back at last, thank the good Lord.'

'Yes, Prof, I'm back at last,' Ricky laughed. 'If you'll still have me after all this time.'

'Of course, I'll still have you,' the old academic laughed. 'But you've got a bit of catching up to do on our recent Magnox research. You'll need to get your sleeves rolled up, because we have to win the big race and not let those terrible people from St Andrews University beat us to it.'

Turning to face Iona, he smiled a big friendly smile.

'And who might this beautiful young lady be, then, Richard my boy?'

'Prof, this is Iona. Iona McNish. And this time next year she'll be Iona Anderson. I hope you approve.'

Iona rose to her feet and accepted Professor Bernstein's willing handshake.

'Lovely to meet you, Iona,' he said. 'He's been on his adventures recently, you know?'

'Oh, believe me, I know he has,' she laughed. 'It's a pleasure to meet you too, Professor. Ricky never stops talking about you ... and all the important work you do here.'

Switching his attention back to Ricky, his face took on a more a puzzled expression.

'And what do you mean you hope I approve? You don't need my approval for being in love with this charming young lady, although if you did you would most certainly have it.'

'I know I don't need your approval, Prof, but you've been as much a father figure to me as anyone over the past few years.'

The Professor was visibly moved by Ricky's uncharacteristically revealing remark, but quickly regained his composure to put an end to the uneasy silence that followed.

'Well, that is very kind of you to say so, Ricky, but if I get my way, our relationship is about to change again.'

'What do you mean, Prof?'

'The thing is, Ricky, I've been thinking. Thinking while you were ... well, while you were away on your wild adventures ... and wondering whether we would ever see each other again. And thinking about your role here if we did. Here in the university, I mean.'

'I'm not following you, Prof.'

'Richard, I'm offering you a job. Every other academic institution in the land is coveting you, and I don't want them to get their greasy paws on you. So, I want you to work for me as my senior research

313

assistant. My right-hand man, if you like. All contingent on you getting your PhD, of course, and you're now miles behind in your work, but I'm sure you'll get back up to speed very quickly.

More silence.

'So, Richard? What do you say?'

Ricky turned to face Iona, who just smiled and nodded.

'Well, I suppose I'll have to pay the rent somehow,' he quipped. 'And Iona here is pretty high maintenance.'

She glared at Ricky and nudged him in the ribs. The professor laughed heartily.

'Just ignore him, dear,' he said. 'I've heard him with the other students, and he's a terrible tease at times. Well, Ricky, I'm waiting.'

'You're on,' Ricky replied. 'A hundred grand a year and a brand-new Jaguar XJ-C, okay?'

'I was thinking of something a bit more modest to start with,' Professor Bernstein smiled. 'A five-year-old Morris Mini, perhaps?'

'It would be an honour and a privilege to work for you, Prof,' Ricky said. 'In fact, I'd do it for nothing.'

'Excellent,' the great master beamed. 'And you certainly won't be doing it for nothing. We can work out the details later.'

'Would it be alright if I took tomorrow off and started back on Wednesday?' Ricky asked. 'I've got a hospital appointment and a few other things that need to be done.'

The professor nodded, and a firm handshake then gave way to a raft of warm goodbyes. A few minutes later, Ricky and Iona found themselves walking hand-in-hand down University Avenue in the direction of the sprawling expanse of Kelvingrove Park. Words were superfluous. Relief and contentment ruled the airwaves. Relief that they were back together once more and contentment that their future was beginning to shape up very nicely.

As they approached their waiting lift, the same metallic-blue Ford Cortina that had played such a central role in this whole blistering saga, Iona nudged Ricky with her elbow.

'Look,' was all she said.

And there in the driver's seat sat Charlie Reynolds, with Janice Anderson's head resting on his shoulder, the pair of them holding hands as if they would never let each other go.

Ricky battered the roof of the car with his fist and the two lovebirds jumped with a start.

'Ricky!' Janice barked, as her son opened the back door for his fiancée, beaming from ear to ear. 'You're not too old to go over my knee, you know.'

'Who do you think I am, mum?' he teased. 'Charlie?'

Communal laughter. Reynolds turned the key in the ignition and the Cortina sprang into life.

'Where to, boss?' the big detective asked.

'Harry Lauder's bar in Sauchiehall Street. We're treating an old friend to lunch.'

'A newspaper hack, by any chance?' enquired Reynolds. 'Gerry McGhee?'

'The very same,' Ricky replied. 'I owe him. And for a lot more than just the two lunches he has already bought me.'

'That's good,' said Janice, straightening herself up and fastening her seatbelt. 'I'd really like to meet this man.'

'So would I,' added Iona. 'He sounded very nice on the phone.'

'He's actually a crabbit old git,' Ricky remarked.' But I still owe him big time.'

'You sure do,' Reynolds said as he pulled his car out of its parking space and onto the road. 'He helped us put three very nasty people away, and probably saved your life too. So, now's your chance to show your appreciation.'

'I fully intend to,' replied Ricky. 'But one other thing, Charlie.'

'And what's that?'

'You're buying. I'm skint.'